New York
Theater Review 2009

Also in this Series

New York Theater Review
ISBN 13: 978-1-4116-6483-8
ISBN 10: 1-4116-6483-3

New York Theater Review 2007
ISBN: 978-0-6151-4307-1

New York Theater Review 2008
ISBN: 978-0-6152-0056-9

Black Wave Press
www.nytr.org

New York
Theater Review 2009

Brook Stowe, Editor

Black Wave Press
New York

BLACK WAVE PRESS
790 Washington Avenue #303
Brooklyn, NY 11238
www.nytr.org

Cover Photography by Erica Parise
Cover Design by Sheila Callaghan

ISBN: 978-0-578-02284-0

First published in April, 2009

Body Text set in Garamond 11pt.
Auxiliary Text set in Palatino Linotype
Printed in the United States of America

<u>On the Cover</u>: Our profound apologies to the Cherry Lane Theatre, 38 Commerce Street, West Village

This edition is dedicated
to the memory of

Arthur Sainer
playwright critic teacher

1924 - 2007

Contents

Contents

The Plays, cont'd

Illustrations

Acknowledgments

Acknowledgments are always among the final notes I write up each year as we stagger towards publication, and I find myself once again in a place of being both indebted to and humbled by the extraordinary contributions of so many people working for the meager table scraps (if that) I am able to offer by way of compensation (as for me being humbled, don't worry – it's only a temporary condition). As yet another edition (our fourth!) races towards its date with the printer, I feel both the desire to thank *everyone* who helped inspire and realize it and the resignation that such an undertaking would require a complete volume in itself. With that in mind, there are a few essential extra-spesh thanks I want to set down here – to **Maryjane Treloar** for the photographs of Arthur and for her general graciousness in making his life available to Justin and me; to **Lane Pianta** and **Ben Spatz** for the essential extra help in editing down their interview manuscript; to **Libby Emmons** and **David Marcus** of Blue Box Productions for stepping up and filling the gaping holes created by my ever-increasing obligations to the academy; to **Mame Hunt** for stepping up and taking a swing at it; to **Ingrid Wang** for the photo scanning and for the many nights spent sitting on the couch in my office nodding sympathetically to my strangled cries of, "I'll never make it ... I'll never *make it* ..."; and to the affable gents at the **Green Apple Café**, from a back table at which most of this manuscript was edited.

New York
Theater Review 2009

Shelter from the Storm
Introduction to the 2009 Edition by Brook Stowe

On a crisp Sunday afternoon early last autumn, I made my way up from the 79th Street subway station to one of those grand old apartment buildings that still grace West End Avenue. The occasion was a memorial celebration for Arthur Sainer, the playwright, teacher, critic and midwife to the birth of NYC's alternative theater whom I had discovered, become immersed in, invited to contribute to the *Review* and lost, all in the span of about nine months.

Inside, the apartment was a good size for maybe two people and a small dog. As I squeezed through the front door, I ballparked the room, estimating I was about the sixty-third person packed in there. Inching along the wall to the improvised bar, I managed to pour a glass of some lavender-shaded fizzy water and find an unclaimed chair between a tall plant and a woman named Alicia before the sea of Arthur's friends closed around me. I would be anchored there for about the next two and a half hours.

That Alicia and I clutched identical glasses of the same mysterious purple water coupled with the rather Sartreian nature of our close proximity invited conversation. Not surprisingly, it wasn't long before the topic came around to Arthur and how we had each met him. My story was rather brief, as I didn't really have a relationship with Arthur. It was just by chance that I had discovered him at all. It was early 2007 and one of those this-book-lead-to-that-book-lead-to-this-book and then I was staring at Arthur's *New Radical Theatre Notebook* on amazon.com.

"We never met, actually," I said to Alicia as we traded sips of our special water. "You?"

"On a streetcorner," she answered, laughing at my reaction. "I got caught in the rain. Arthur offered to share his umbrella."

I thought what a common gesture this was – how many times I've seen it around town – two strangers, a sudden downpour, one umbrella, shared – and through this, two strangers become less strange; perhaps – as with Alicia and Arthur – friends, even. Sharing an umbrella, and common ground. I thought of my own "conversations" with Arthur – a few emails exchanged between Saratoga Springs and NYC – and how quickly our common ground had become the utter frivolity of mainstream theater. I thought particularly of Arthur's recounting of the night in October 1962 when he had watched JFK's televised speech on the Cuban missile crisis and then hurried uptown to catch a "happy Broadway revue" that left him suspecting that "while one is staring at the concocted events onstage, some more energetic and imaginative soul is busily ransacking one's house."[1]

Over the past eight years that mercifully ended January 20, some very "energetic and imaginative souls" were busy ransacking America's house while it sat dreamily staring at such concocted events as "American Idol" and "Dancing with the Stars." During the seemingly interminable George W. Bush administration bookended by the infamous "Mission Accomplished" flight suit strut on one end and a hurled pair of Baydan Model 271 shoes on the other, America was enticed, hoodwinked and fleeced before being hurled into an economic abyss deeper than any it has had to climb out of since the Great Depression. Through it all, through all of the Bernie Madoffs, the Countrywide Financials, the subprime mortgage bond sales and the credit default swap schemes, there was no bigger "concocted event" than Bush's alternate reality that lead America into Iraq.

I've been concerned – I can't say bothered, really ... well, maybe I can – but I've certainly been concerned that through three editions of the *Review*, the war in Iraq – as refracted through NYC alt-theater – has not been represented upon these pages. This is not because I haven't been interested. Or looking. It is because, before being dragged to David Ian Lee's *Sleeper* at a little shoebox of a theater in the West Village last summer,[2] the Iraq-war-and-related theater put up on NYC stages, had been largely confined to self-flagellating liberal agitprop (count how many times and in how many incarnations Lynndie England popped up around town) or well-meaning, stereotype-reinforcing agitprop (think *Masked*, think *Betrayed*, think...). As Mac Rogers points out in his introduction to *Sleeper*, playwright Lee simply "refuse(s) to allow" the convenient crutch of agitprop to prop up his play. Rather than espouse an agenda, *Sleeper* explores the causes and the consequences of a nation tossing fitfully in the long, national nightmare we are only now beginning to wake from. At last! The "Iraq play" I had long been looking for that wasn't even (directly) about Iraq.

* * *

Joining *Sleeper* as the other full-length selection in plays this year is Ellen McLaughlin's *Kissing the Floor*, her ninth play directly inspired by classic Greek texts and the first – I am somewhat embarrassed to disclose – I have read. Recommended to me by a mutual friend,[3] my initial response to the play was equal parts repulsion and attraction. In the introduction to her text, Ellen writes,

---

[1] *The Sleepwalker and the Assassin*, New York: Bridgehead Books, 1964, 22
[2] Thanks, Johnna Adams!
[3] Thanks, Katie Mac!

"With the Greeks, I'm always looking for the thing I can't understand or the thing that gives me bad dreams." While I can't say the play gave me nightmares, it had a distinctly disturbing quality that prevented me from shaking it off or easily categorizing it as "that kind" of play, as I too-often tend to do, especially when considering many texts for scant publication space. Like David Ian Lee's, Ellen's process as a playwright is a journey of discovery, of grabbing hold of an image or a poem or – in this case – Sophocles' *Antigone* and feeding it through her own subconscious loom of dead fathers and pedophilia and Depression-era America and creating, ultimately, a wrenching, compelling, fiercely original play on the bonds and perils of blood ties and the limits to kinship.

* * *

In nearly seven years here now, I have far too seldom seen theater about the Middle East and Middle Easterners unfiltered by Western apology and/or agenda. Where were the Middle Eastern voices in NYC theater and why wasn't I hearing them? To answer this question, I did what any reasonable editor would do – I went to writer, director and activist Cynthia Croot, whose theater work in Syria and Iran make her a particularly relevant choice to explore this topic. Under Cindy's gentle prodding and poking in, "This 'Tool We Dream Through': Theater in NYC and the Arab Middle East," six Arab and Arab-American theater artists, Maha Chehlaoui, Eyad Houssami, Mohammad Bani Hani, Rana Kazkaz, Ramez Alaswad and Leila Buck speak thoughtfully and candidly about being Arab theater artists bridging both disparate cultures and simply surviving in this most Darwinian of theater environments.

* * *

On a cold night in late 2002, I found myself at a deliciously dilapidated dive called ABC-No Rio on the Lower East Side. I can no longer remember why I was there; in my early days here, I often just wandered around, slowly learning the City's geography from its theaters and performance spaces. A downstairs gallery that had more rats than people in it featured a Bruce Weber exhibit; upstairs, a guy named Ben Spatz was doing a show called *neverland*, a cross-pollination of Peter Pan with an Angela Carter short story. It was an extraordinary exploration of the potential of theater, performed by an exuberant cast in a performance space the size of a moderately-sized coat closet. Impressed by this performance, I tried getting in touch with Ben for an interview on my old website, *theater2k* – but by the time I managed to track him down, he was in Poland, and the idea slipped away. Six years later, a very talented writer from Maryland, Lane Pianta, sent in a cold pitch for a piece on Ben Spatz and his Urban Research Theater and their "Changing the Space" interview is the result. As I had seen in *neverland* back in '02, Ben's work continues to expand the boundaries of what theater is and how it is defined/confined, until it isn't anymore, until it is performed without the boundaries of the stage, until it explodes out into the streets, becomes not just theater *in* the City, but something *of* the City itself.

* * *

"The playhouses need dynamiting," Arthur Sainer concluded in 1963. Since becoming familiar with his work, I've wondered not infrequently what he would have thought of Sticky, Manhattan's Blue Box Productions' ongoing series of short, original theater staged in various dive bars and other borderline establishments around lower Manhattan and Brooklyn. Sticky's is not the lower Manhattan of *The Sleepwalker*'s early 1960s or *The Radical Theatre Notebook*'s of 1975 or even the updated (*New*) *RTN*'s of 1997. It can't be. It's not the same NYC. Across Bowery from the Bowery Poetry Club, Sticky's current home base, a ground-up luxury high-rise recently opened; down the street, Patti Smith sang a final goodnight to CBGBs two and a half years ago (already!) Arthur may not have recognized the neighborhood, but I suspect he would have felt at home once he settled into a Sticky show at the BPC; like a latter-day Caffe Cino, perhaps, or Judson Poet's Theatre, a respite from the "stifling bourgeois palaces" of mainstream theater he so wanted to detonate. For this 2009 edition, Libby Emmons and David Marcus, the seemingly indefatigable engine that powers Blue Box, have pulled together a dazzling dozen from the more than two-hundred short plays Blue Box has produced in the Sticky series.

* * *

I haven't seen Alicia since that Sunday afternoon last October, but I think of her chance encounter with Arthur whenever I open my umbrella against the rain and I think of all the things I should have asked her then: what was the first thing he said to her? How did a friendship grow from that simple gesture of chance streetcorner kindness that brought her to this place sitting next to me years later? I was thinking of that last Christmas at my neighborhood supermarket as I trolled the aisles for my usual fare of caffeine-based products and anything microwaveable. Impeding my progress down the aisle holding the Keebler shortbread cookies was a large plastic trash can swathed in cheery Santa giftwrap paper and haphazardly stuffed with an eclectic offering of five-dollar umbrellas. Historically, I've always gone for the most compact, single-person unit, the ones good for about 0.3 NYC summer thunderstorms. This time, I chose the largest one in the bin, unfurling it with flair over the first fellow New Yorker who happened down the aisle – a woman clutching a bottle of salad dressing who veered quickly away, cringing. No matter. I tossed the big guy atop my Stouffer's and headed for the checkout line. It hangs in my closet now, large enough for two. Whenever it looks like rain, I take it with me.

– Brook Stowe
Brooklyn, NY
March, 2009

Essays

Arthur Sainer: A Radical Life

An Appreciation
by Justin Tracy

It was January 2004 and I was excited. The second semester of my junior year was about to begin at the State University of New York at Albany and I was enrolled in two classes with a mythical, enigmatic professor named Arthur Sainer. I had heard he was a former drama critic for the *Village Voice* and would be teaching what he lived: the Radical Theater movement of the 1960s and 70s. Radical Theater! An epic period, shrouded in mystery – didn't they run around naked and take their rebellious ways to the streets?

The first day of class I met a man in his late seventies. He was frail in body, but had a razor-sharp mind. He was weathered like a mountain tree, blasted by fierce winds into a totem of truth. Rooted by love, passion and a passion for love, he was legendary like the period he had outlived – yet similarly delicate, as a walk around the blustery UAlbany campus often illustrated; there were days he would grab my arm to keep from literally being blown over.

Who was this Arthur Sainer? Critic, author of over forty plays, professor, screenwriter, poet, novelist, husband, friend, Jew, and one of the most influential members of 20th century NYC popular culture and theater. He was also the most important unknown in the "downtown" NYC theater movement. He had taught at Bennington, Wesleyan, Hunter, Middlebury, the New School and Sarah Lawrence. Many of Arthur's plays had been produced Off-Off-Broadway at La MaMa, Theater for the New City, Playwrights Horizons, Theatre Genesis and a number of regional theaters around the country, including Firehouse in Minneapolis, the Odyssey in Los Angeles, the OM-Theatre Workshop in Boston, and the International Theatre Festival in Parma, Italy. A two-time grant winner with the National Foundation for Jewish Culture, recipient of awards from the Ford and Rockefeller Foundations, a charter member of the Open Theatre in the early 1960s, and even invited by Jerzy Grotowski – the developer of the Poor Theatre which called for a "holy" actor – to participate in a workshop with the Polish Laboratory in Wroclaw, Poland in the late 1970s.

Anne Bogart, co-founder of Saratoga International Theatre, has said that Arthur was "highly respected, listened to and heeded." For Bogart, Arthur's reviews had a deep and resounding personal impact. When she directed her first NYC production, "an adaptation of Shakespeare's *Macbeth* centering around the relationship between Macbeth and Banquo," it was Arthur who gave the first review. "Because it was so accurate and so direct, his review became the voice in my head, policing my weaknesses and unconscious proclivities," Bogart remembered. She was struck by one phrase in particular: "A visual intensity without the inner necessity." Bogart reflected, "That sentence did me in. He nailed both my strength and weakness as a director." This was Arthur's true gift, and one that would be brought up again and again at the memorial service at his cousin's home in October 2008: Arthur saw the truth behind the mask, the spirit and the purpose. He had the vision to know artists through their work straight through to their souls.

*   *   *

Born in 1924 to a Polish immigrant family in the Bronx, Arthur spent his childhood days playing baseball, reading, and playacting with friends. Always frail – stricken twice in his youth with rheumatic fever – Arthur was never much of a ball player, but he loved the Yankees with true Bronx Bomber "belovitivity."

Arthur wrote his first work of fiction when he was about eight. He began "writing" plays about the same time, first improvising the action with a cousin, then with boyhood friends. As an adolescent, he began writing texts and was first published in *PM*, which Arthur later described as an "odd, wonderfully progressive New York daily."

Throughout the 1950s Arthur wrote fiction, plays – he was selected in the second wave of playwrights to join New Dramatists – and occasional articles while attempting to break into the young but blossoming world of television drama. Two of his TV scripts were developed during this period, including "The Dark Side of the Moon," which performed live during primetime and was nominated by the Writers Guild for Best TV Drama of the Year.

In the 1960s, Arthur found a home at the *Village Voice*, beginning an eighteen-year tenure there as drama critic. He also contributed articles on literature and film and was briefly the *Voice*'s book editor as well. From this vantage point, Arthur was able to watch the 1960s and the Radical Theater movement unfold.

By 1962, Arthur was a potent force on the NYC theater scene. Not everyone always agreed with his reviews – as one would expect of a critic – but he was well-regarded for his love of the creative act and for his empathy towards artists. At Arthur's memorial gathering, George Bartenieff, actor in more of Arthur's plays than any other performer, reflected on his friend and colleague, "Arthur was such a supportive and inspiring voice at a time when it was needed the most. He knew what was happening. He knew what the moment was about and he gave everything to it ... I can't imagine it, actually, without him."

Arthur was, however, a hammer to the skull of Broadway indulgence. His first book, *The Sleepwalker and the Assassin*[4] – a time capsule of reviews from February, 1962 through October 1963 – is a boiling kettle about to scream. The world had seen Brecht, Beckett and Artaud; Vietnam was about to splash across front pages, and President Kennedy would soon be assassinated. Yet Broadway was steeped in frivolity. In the case of *Little Me*, for example, with book by Neil Simon, lyrics by Carolyn Leigh and directed by Cy Feuer & Bob Fosse at the Lunt-Fontanne Theatre, Arthur wrote that is was "supposedly a spoof on the pure-in-heart in the toils of our corrupt world, but in fact it is about NOTHING ... NOTHING ... NOTHING."[5] It was mainstream productions such as this that drove Arthur to declare in exasperation, "the playhouses need dynamiting."[6]

By this time even the great Tennessee Williams was falling from favor. Arthur wrote, "Against the tautness of Ionesco, he seems slack. Against the controlled horror of Beckett and Genet he seems undisciplined, too juicy."[7] Indeed, the tide had begun to turn. Theater companies unique in style and purpose pushed open previously unnoticed doors. Arthur himself was perhaps personally closest to the Living Theatre, led by Judith Malina and Julian Beck, and the Open Theatre, run by Joseph Chaikin (who was also a founding member of the Living), and the Bridge Collective, the company Arthur himself led.

It is to the Living Theatre that the entire Radical Theater movement's roots can be traced. Jack Gelber's *The Connection*, about a group of heroin addicts concerned only with their next fix, opened on July 15, 1959 and was, to many, almost unreachable, not because of its content but because, "it had to do not with character being made but with performers ceasing to make performances ... the Living Theatre production fluctuated, in the subtlest manner, between performers performing and performers not performing ... comfortably in the context of self until those moments when Gelber's script called for them to take themselves out of self and back in to the play ..."[8] *The Connection* was called by contemporary critic Kenneth Tynan, "beyond the reach

---

[4] New York: Bridgehead Books, 1964
[5] Ibid., 33
[6] Ibid., 25
[7] Ibid., 21
[8] *The New Radical Theatre Notebook*, Applause 1997, 9

of drama, as we commonly define the word."[9] For Arthur, this "beyondness" was the beginning of a "radical loosening of the fabric of drama … involving the attitude of the performer offering self rather than character."[10]

With this "loosening" came the real possibility of theater moving beyond mere entertainment. It became the center of many artists' collective dream to understand the audience/performer interaction. For Arthur this was true for the rest of his life. In an unpublished 1995 letter to members of the theater community regarding the resurrection of his theater group, the Bridge Collective, Arthur wrote that the purpose of theater was "to bring to our audiences a sense of why we're alive … how we function as spiritual beings both within ourselves and to one another … to understand how we reach out to an audience and how it reaches out to us." This might include physically, as with Boston's OM-Theatre Workshop's *OM, a sharing service* in which the performers, eyes closed, crawled toward audience members, hands outstretched. If they felt "positive signs – vibrations"[11] then the actors would touch the audience.

This was a new magic with the potential for deeper effect than traditional theater had ever enabled. Double-edged and honed sharp, this new blade of Radical Theater could simultaneously slice away social disease and mainstream verdure. But there were complications. In *The Sleepwalker,* Arthur wrote that at a performance of Kenneth Brown's *The Brig* at the Living Theatre in the Spring of 1963, "a woman left in a state of near hysteria. There have been similar moments during the run of the play and it indicates a flaw. Horror has been let loose."[12]

The Brig burst upon the Living's stage like an aberrant limb from the flaccid torso of status quo theater. Refusing story, shrugging off hero, with stage "empty of foreground," the "initial horror has told us everything and from that point, after the Marines have been put through their paces, nothing new is introduced … it is a still photograph, except that the audience cannot choose when it has had its fill."[13] Brown's play allowed for no release; rather, pressure continued to build unrelieved in a kind of torturous version of a Steve Martin joke, where anticipated punch lines are denied in a steady escalation of comic pressure, forcing the audience to laugh on its own, often in awkward and unexpected places.

---

[9] Ibid.
[10] Ibid.
[11] *The New Radical Theatre Notebook,* 36
[12] *The Sleepwalker and the Assassin,* 23-24
[13] Ibid., 24

Such is the "flaw" in *The Brig*. The play kept ratcheting up the pressure with no release valve of relief, to which Arthur offered this suggestion: "Somehow horror must flow from stage to audience but then back, it must always be on the move like a current and not lodge itself with any one being. It is almost as if horror were a third person, needing to maintain its uniqueness."[14]

Despite the downtown theater community's capacity for chaos or even simple stupidity, Arthur saw the writing on the wall in early 1964: "There are stirrings in America, in the theater," he wrote in the final chapter of *The Sleepwalker*, "we are about to make fresh mistakes, we are about to be unbearable, not unbearably dull as in the past few years, but insufferable. In short, we are about to become absurd."[15] This insufferable quality, Arthur warned, occurred when "we learn from theater instead of learning from life." Indeed, many theater practitioners, and for that matter artists of all genres, feed their art with the art of others, a practice as prevalent today as it was forty-five years ago. For Arthur, theater needed always to be fueled by the experiences of life.

This is not to say, however, that it is "the business of drama simply to report to us that people in life have problems or that society is malformed," rather "it is the theater's business to give life to the quality of despair or, as in Brecht, to ritualize the political and economic implications of society. To reach us, the theater must reach into us, it must dredge up the daemonic in us and the fantastic."[16]

* * *

Over the next eleven years, the fledgling movement of which Arthur was a primary force began to take wing and fly. This was the age of the ensemble – together, like-minded artists were able to forge their ideals into tangible expression. Stylistically and ethically opposed to the myth of success so close to the heart of Wall Street and Broadway alike, these new ensembles attempted to sustain one another while fighting against the exploitation of both their art and of each other. Unfortunately, ideals and reality didn't always mix well. The Living Theatre was a prime example of this. After facing mounting problems in the US with the Internal Revenue Service, members of the Living fled to Europe, where they toured constantly to keep food in their mouths.

---

[14] *The Sleepwalker and the Assassin*, 24
[15] Ibid., 123
[16] Ibid., 124

When Arthur met up with the Living in Geneva at the beginning of 1968, Julian Beck spoke pragmatically about sustaining a theater company committed to life on the fringes. "Sometimes people accuse us of not living up to our word. We attack the establishment, we attack the middle class, and yet we play in those theaters which are largely supported by the middle class … it's a dilemma. We've got forty-one mouths to feed [in their traveling company], we've got to play in what's available, what will keep us alive."[17] And yet, the Living remained optimistic, "We're going to make a new work," the Becks told Arthur in early 1968, "A work of joy … [t]o be called, *Paradise Now.*"[18]

* * *

In his 1995 letter hoping to resuscitate the Bridge Collective with his fellow 1960s theater revolutionaries, Arthur stressed that in order for an ensemble to learn to perform at the highest level, they must try to avoid deadlines, "that is, not opening if we're not ready." Only by working intensively with one another for an extended period of time could true commonality and non-verbal shorthand develop. Topping the list of damaging Off-Off-Broadway practices was the radically truncated rehearsal period. While often considered a necessity for the sake of budgeting, having a four or three or two week-long rehearsal period with "a new package of artists for each production militated against the possibility of serious work because much of the rehearsal time was used up learning to adjust to one another's work habits."[19]

Arthur was aware of the challenges; he was aware that the way of the communal ensemble home – where all members of the theatrical body helped with everything from cleaning toilets to cooking to stage managing – was a dream. "I keep hearing, it ain't the Sixties any more – so it ain't the Sixties," he wrote in the letter. "But we are alive at this moment and I think we have a responsibility to be serious artists, and somehow, *somehow*, find the money to keep ourselves alive. Easy enough to throw in the towel, any idiot can do as much."

But it was not to be.

* * *

Upon leaving NYC and moving upstate to Saratoga Springs, Arthur continued to write, teach and produce. *The People Impeach the Bushes*, a propaganda piece he wrote, directed by Tim O'Leary, performed at Café Lena

---

[17] *The New Radical Theatre Notebook*, 294
[18] Ibid., 295
[19] *The New Radical Theatre Notebook*, 13

in Saratoga to strong crowds in May 2005, as did *Jews and Christians in the End Zone*, directed by the author of this article, in April 2006.

Joan Shultz, a former student of Arthur's at Sarah Lawrence who now teaches courses on Radical Theater at the College of Staten Island said, "His was a mind that responded to theater and made it into something that the audience could handle. What they were doing at that time looked like a bunch of weird stuff, and he gave them context. He always took into consideration the artist that he was going to see, speaking to where the artist was coming from, not chopping them up and spitting them out."

For Arthur, in life as in theater – as he wrote in a 1998 letter to a friend, there is always a need for "joy, humor, a wonderful inventiveness."

Arthur passed on November 18th, 2007 and is survived by his wife, Maryjane Treloar.

Arthur Sainer

This "Tool We Dream Through":
Theater in NYC and the Arab Middle East
A Roundtable Discussion with
Six Arab and Arab-American Theater Artists
by Cynthia Croot

In the past few years of creating work domestically and abroad, I've had the privilege of working with many accomplished Arab and Arab-American theater artists. For this edition of NYTR, I asked them a few questions about living and making theater today in the US and the Middle East. – Cynthia Croot

CYNTHIA CROOT (CC): *Please briefly describe your personal and professional background – the sort of work you do, where you're from, etc.*

MAHA CHEHLAOUI (MC): I am of Syrian and Filipino heritage born and raised in New Jersey, then, Bahrain and London. I returned to the States for college and grad school (MFA, Columbia University) and have been in NYC ever since. In 2001, I co-founded Nibras, an Arab-American theater company, and was Artistic Director until 2006. I have also served as Artistic Director of the New York Arab American Comedy Festival. I am primarily an actor now – I most recently played Anitra in *Peer Gynt* at the Guthrie, and Fatima in *Toe to Toe*, a film premiering at Sundance this year.

EYAD HOUSSAMI (EH): I live in Beirut, Lebanon and work as a director, researcher, and performer. As a student at Yale, I directed seven major theater pieces and produced Masrah Arab, a year-long festival of staged readings from the Arab Middle East. Armed with a Fulbright fellowship, I then moved to the Levant and on the winter solstice of 2007 staged a performance art piece, *A Moment of Silence for the Shuhada' of Iraq*, in the Dead Cities of northern Syria. In 2008, I wrote and produced *Mama Butterfly* in Damascus. The project was shut down by the government five hours before curtain. These days, I organize and host Theatre of Desire, a monthly performance cabaret in Beirut, inspired by Deb Margolin.

MOHAMMAD BANI HANI (MBH): I am a theater director and actor living and working in Jordan. During four years of experimentation based on playwrights like Artaud, Kantor, Brook, Al Qasab ... etc., I have attempted to reach an act of creation, innovation and renewal rather than an act of copying, repetition and imitation. While managing the Philadelphia Festival (three consecutive seasons) I came into direct contact with the theater of Jordanian and Arab youth and began to understand the rupture between the sender and the recipient in theater. I am currently establishing my own company Jassad (Body) for Arts Performance in Amman.

RANA KAZKAZ (RK): I'm a Syrian-American filmmaker and theater artist living between the US and Syria. I've been acting, producing, writing and directing theater since the age of eight, and films for the past five years. My screenplay, "Gibran," about the life of Lebanese-American writer and author of *The Prophet*, Kahlil Gibran, was an official selection of the Tribeca Film Festival All Access Program, the first Middle East Screenwriter's Lab held in Jordan in Association with the Sundance Institute, and selected for Mediterranean Films Crossing Borders at the Cannes Film Festival. My short film, "Kemo Sabe" continues to enjoy screenings around the world.

RAMEZ ALASWAD (RA): I am Managing and Artistic Director of the Al-Khareef Theatre Troupe in Damascus, Syria. I earned my BA in Acting from the High Institute of Drama in Damascus in 1998, and have been working as a professional actor since then. I've appeared on television, in movies and in the theater, and established my own independent theater troupe, Al-Khareef Theatre, early in 2006. We have toured our original production, "The Solitary" in venues internationally.

LEILA BUCK (LB): I am a Lebanese-American actress, writer and teaching artist based in NYC. I'm a Usual Suspect with New York Theatre Workshop (NYTW) and a member of the Public Theater's 2008 Emerging Writers Group. Since 1998 I've toured internationally with my solo show, *ISite*, on Arab-American identity. I was also a founder of Nibras, Artistic Director of Nisaa Arab-American Women's Collective, and a writer and performer for the New York Arab-American Comedy Festival.

My latest works, *In the Crossing* and *Hkeelee* have received additional support from Theater J, Silk Road, Epic Theatre Center, the Lark Theater, and Golden Thread Productions. *In the Crossing* is both about my experience in Lebanon with my Jewish husband before, during and after the Israeli-Hezbollah war of 2006, and about the difficulty of telling that story here in the US when I returned. *Hkeelee* is becoming a play about the Arabic language, the controversy of teaching it here in the US, the loss of memory and history through language and immigration, and how all of this shapes who we are as a nation.

CC: What does it mean to you to be a Jordanian, Syrian, Egyptian, American, Arab-American, New Yorker, etc.? How is your identity reflected in your work (or not)?

MC: Post 9/11 I felt a sort of drive to work within the Arab-American community. There was a lot of discussion about Arabs and Muslims and it was important to make sure people from those communities represented themselves. Also it felt like Arab-America 101 was a course everyone needed to take. Now, I am less driven in that reactive way. I also burned out a little bit on trying to "represent" – I found the responsibility ultimately stifling – too many conversations among people ultimately tied together by ethnicity and not by much else in terms of aesthetic or experience for example.

As an actor my identity is reflected in my work in terms of what I am called in for by casting directors. I will go in for things one friend may be outraged by, another excited by. Most jobs I take where I am representing an Arab make me nervous. I always fear I am pissing someone somewhere off, no doubt. Though when I see my male counterparts playing ridiculous terrorists on TV, I have to admit I laugh and call them and thank them for taking one for the team. I remember some show where one guy actually ordered a pizza and then menacingly sliced it up with a box cutter. Oh, dear.

In a production of *Peer Gynt* at the Guthrie I played Anitra and the exoticism of the scene coupled with the buffoonery definitely touched on the exotic/thieving Arab stereotype. At the same time, the way the play was framed was through Gynt's imagination and it worked brilliantly. This was a man who would have had very little experience of the Middle East beyond what orientalism he had been exposed to. And it was very funny. Also, any time the veil comes up in any of my plays I know there will be a deep examination of if it was necessary, well-portrayed, and so on, for example with *Betrayed*. My first role on TV was as an extra. I "played" a dead pregnant Arab teen. At my audition I asked how I died and explained I felt a responsibility for representation. They told me my white boyfriend killed me. Great! I took the job! Interestingly in the show, the detectives were sure it was an honor killing. I did think it funny that nobody told the detectives they were being absurd. The number one cause of death in pregnant women is murder by the father of the child. Pretty bad detecting if you ask me!

RA: Theater is an art where you reflect your nature, society and background, different countries for me means different backgrounds, traditions ... etc. I'm Syrian so I belong to the Syrian society and its traditions, habits, ideas. I can't think but as a Syrian when I make theater because first of all this is me. And I believe work that truly succeeds locally does so because it succeeds on a universal level too.

EH: If one were to read my academic and artistic work for questions of identity, I would argue that my writing and theater reveal the instability of the constructions of cultural and national identity. For instance, the self-proclaimed, fundamental question of *Mama Butterfly* is "How do war and diaspora fragment the meaning of family and reshape the experience of loneliness?" It is a play about solitude, about the family and the city. It narrates the story of a woman, from French-occupied Damascus, who falls in love with a man from Beirut and adopts the city as her own. Globalization, war, and occupation dismember her city and launch her and her family into a state of migration. Bereaved of her husband, going blind, and left with two children in the Gulf and no family in Beirut, she withstands the pressure to leave and, instead, chooses a life of fixed solitude in Beirut, the city she calls home. In so doing, she and the city together become the axis of family. While national and cultural identity is a peripheral concern in this play, *Mama Butterfly* demonstrates how we worm ourselves in and out of communal identities, shedding skins and donning new hats with the tides of history.

LB: I have always lived between Arab and American culture, with my mother born and raised in Lebanon by a Muslim father and a Christian mother, and my father a WASP Arabic-speaking American diplomat whose work had us living in Kuwait, Oman, and Iraq for half of my childhood, the rest between Washington and Canada. Along the way I came to understand that cultures are both different and similar, and always connected. One of the problematic parts of being Arab-American is that because I am more easily accessible to many non-Arab Americans, I am often asked to speak as a representative of "Arabs" as if they were all the same. In my teaching, activism, artistic and personal life I feel my role is a bridge, a connector, someone who can translate one side to the other and help facilitate direct and nuanced connections between them. I'd like to also add that I identify very much as a New Yorker and I think that influences my work in my gravitation toward unexpected intersections, juxtapositions, different ideas, peoples and cultures coming into contact in ways that sometimes produce conflict, sometimes intimacy, and often a combination of the two.

MBH: The whole matter of identity is a thorny issue … especially when it is linked with cultural work and artistic work in specific. I ask myself almost every day, "Whom and what do I belong to?" And I always find myself outside of the frameworks established, for despite my love for my country and my respect for society, I do not introduce myself through this narrow angle. I am from Jordan, that's true, Arabic yes, but what is more important than all this is that I am a human being.

CC: What (if any) differences have you observed in the way that work is made in the US (NYC in particular) vs. other countries where you have worked?

EH: Whereas directors in Damascus work almost only in Arabic and are obliged to cooperate, for better or worse, with the Ministry of Culture, cultural production in Beirut often demands that directors navigate between Arabic, French, and English, and the role of the Ministry of Culture in Lebanon is meager at best. The vast majority of theater producers in Beirut rely on private, corporate, or international sponsorship while the Ministry of Culture in Damascus sometimes provides financial support and also monitors the production process far more effectively than its counterpart in Lebanon.

But this is not to say that the state, failed or totalitarian, governs the way theater is made in Beirut or Damascus. In fact, I would submit that the forces of American capitalism are as much, if not more, of a determining factor in the creative process in NYC. These economic circumstances have led to a commercialized theater, bound by the laws of profit. In the NYC rehearsal room, time is limited and costly, and ideals of economic efficiency determine how people collaborate. Whereas theater makers in the states are subject to the pressures of capitalism, artists in Beirut or Damascus are far less restrained by the burden of profit.

MC: Eyad raises an interesting point. I have already mentioned the economic burden of creativity being stifling in NYC. I am not sure I would equate it with censorship. We can say what we want but the ways in which we say it might be limited. We might say it wearing junkier costumes in a drafty loft in Brooklyn rather than gorgeous robes in a well-maintained auditorium. Well, we can say what we want, but expect a bit of a backlash if we are saying anything about Palestine.

LB: I don't know enough about how theater is made in Beirut or Damascus to compare, but certainly capitalism plays a huge factor in getting work done in the States, particularly NYC. However, just as in Beirut or Damascus I imagine there are creative ways around censorship, as long as you don't mind being somewhat underground, in NYC you can always make your work happen if you are, as Maha says, "scrappy," provided you are not insistent on performing in one of the more mainstream spaces.

MBH: I found during my visit to Washington D.C. and the Humana Festival that American theater (without generalization) often depends on theatrical text as a primary reference for the theatrical performance. There is no harm in this but what is unfortunate is that it does not give any space for experimentation or trial and navigation in the seas of creativity. I have also noted that the playwright has the most important authority in the performance and the director's task is limited to giving life to his characters and giving them their material dimensions. I also found that the sets besiege the viewer with excessive realism, despite perfect execution and intriguing magnitude, they present a literal implementation of the text.

As for the stage (Arabic), work ranges between innovative experiments and the superficial. The experiments I respect are performances that depend on research and reflect our existential issues, addressing pressing social, political and religious themes, wrapping them with creative philosophical thinking that inspires us to reflect, and engages the recipient as a second director for the theatrical performance. And of course it is a theater packed with fear and horror and war and concerns of living in peace and freedom, where the daily death chain in the region affects our artistic and cultural subjects. This simply reflects our collective urge to live and dream and continue.

RK: The first thing that comes to mind is the quantity of theater in New York versus these other cities. Whereas in New York, two hundred plays are running at any one time, in Damascus one might find one or two at any given moment. I lived in Moscow in the 1990s and learned so much about the creativity of the artists who had lived under government censorship and the work that came out of that was often remarkable. They were forced to be innovative in the way they communicated their story. Issues of artistic censorship always make me think of Arthur Miller's *The Crucible*. I think the Arab world can learn much from these examples.

As for my own experience with censorship in Damascus, I've just written a screenplay that we hope to shoot in Damascus soon. The government has to approve every page before we can shoot. The restrictions are strict, however I get the sense that the "censors" are eager to be more open but wary of exactly how to go about doing that. We'll see what happens.

RA: I can't talk much about the NYC kind of theater but what we know as a stereotype is Broadway, which produces huge shows. Making theater is a little bit different West and East, here in Syria we care more about psychological acting approaches – we're so infected by the Russian method, which suits our nature as artists. Compared with what I saw in the US, where performances are about dealing with society's stories from a very technical point of view, in Damascus we take a little bit more of a "go for the emotion" kind of approach.

LB: From what I see from friends making work there and reading Lebanon's *Daily Star* online, Beirut is a very intimate, smaller setting, so it seems like the work done is seen by a broader range of the city or at least of those in the city who pay attention to the arts. It seems like work is made more quickly in response to things like the 2006 Israeli-Hezbollah war, and that the devastation wreaked by that war on Lebanon politically and economically has made the artistic responses to it more widely appreciated than similar work might be in a place like NYC that is bigger and less visibly affected each day by the war in which its nation is still embroiled.

I feel that our work as Arab-American theater artists in NYC is often challenged by the scarcity of time and resources, particularly for actors who are responding to the work we get on that level, and simultaneously attempting to create more interesting work for ourselves as writers, producers, and more. Many of us have spent a great deal of energy and time in the sustaining of producing structures which can fuel but also take away from our ability to actually create new work, as so much time and energy is required to simply navigate NYC schedules and sustain a commitment to projects before they are fully funded or recognized on a larger scale. However in recent years I see our individual successes as actors, writers and more starting to fuel our ability to make our own work at levels that allow us more time and resources to do so on our own terms. The New York Theatre Workshop has been invaluable in offering space and time to many of us as emerging writers to create and explore new work with physical space and artistic guidance from NYTW artistic staff, as well as access to their network of Usual Suspects and the connections that come from that network.

CC: What images of Arabs have you seen on US stages, and/or what images of US citizens have you seen in theater productions in the Middle East? What did you make of those representations? Are things getting better or worse? What sort of trends have you observed, or experiences have you had?

MC: I have seen Arabs portrayed a ton in some very moving documentary theater and one person shows here in NYC. The disproportionate representation in docudrama does scream to me, "you can't discount this story because it is true!" There is a well-based fear that Arab voices will be stifled by people throwing "facts and figures" at the stage, making fictional representations oddly burdensome. I am a huge fan of Naomi Wallace, as she is grappling with a lot of Middle East-related questions while still playing artistically and poetically with her characters and their sense of language, space and time. I also really enjoy Yussef El-Guindi's work – his play *Back of the Throat* followed a fantasy that I and a lot of my friends have had.

I have played Arab women several times and there is a bit of an obsession with head gear. I kind of get it though – I think it is a very visual reference especially in terms of speaking about Iraq or Iran where you have secular women unhappily choosing to wear the veil out of fear for their lives, not because of familial or religious ideas. I do think it is one that should be handled with care, since there are many women who actively prefer to wear the hijab, and more power to them. I guess one school of thought is that you have to address the ignorance of the audience – to make it clear that some women choose to wear the hijab and they are happy but the woman in this play is secular and it is a huge personal political sacrifice. I don't believe in catering to the most ignorant person in the crowd. It irritates me no end.

I have also seen representations of Arabs where the accent was horribly off, even recognizably of a different origin and that makes me angry – angrier than missteps with trying to tell a story. A producer would never think of letting an actor do a Brian Friel play with a Welsh or Scottish accent – they would go Irish all the way, usually down to the right county. It just reeks of "brownwashing" to me. Now, I don't mind if a role is not played by an Arab, as long as attempts to meet and audition those actors were made. But once the part is cast, give that actor the tools they need!

MBH: I have not personally seen the depiction of Arabs in the US, except through what is being promoted through mass media and especially in American movies that promote negative (hostile) Arab characters. During dialogue with some American artists, I sensed a complete ignorance of the essential creative and scientific riches of Arab culture. Maybe some of them know a little about Harun Ar-Rashid and some of what is mentioned in *A Thousand and One Nights*.

As for the portrayal of American characters in the Middle East, they are often in the form of the usurper and occupier (Marine troops, etc.). And I believe that these are no more than superficial images or models that do not reflect the reality of both societies. Arabs are kind people and so are American people. What we need is human communication far from politics, and to adopt realistic and constructive criticism. We need to give ourselves the opportunity to speak far from all of the distortions created by policies of war and hatred. Bin Laden does not represent me (he does not even belong to humanity) and George Bush is the flip side of the same coin and therefore does not represent American society.

And this can only be achieved by research, cooperation and genuine partnership, and through contact with individuals who carry the most faithful picture of their communities. We are proud of independent American artists, innovators and intellectuals representing the truth of the American character such as Robert Wilson and Richard Foreman and Martha Graham and many others. I met the American director and writer Joe Martin who surprised me with his play (*Rumi's Son*) and whom I was pleased to meet for such a deep philosophical and amazing intellectual character. This is what we are in need of.

RK: Depictions of Americans in the Arab world tend to be via American plays in translation – Williams, O'Neill, etc. In terms of modern representations of Americans, I often see images of the American soldier or politicians related to the wars in Iraq, Afghanistan or against terrorism.

As for on the American stage – Arab characters seem to dealing with issues ultimately related to terrorism and fundamentalist Islam. Even if the characters have various occupations and goals, terrorism and religious fundamentalism somehow come into crucial play in their lives. Ultimately, I think things are getting much better.

RA: I saw some US theater pieces during my trips, but unfortunately since I live in Damascus, and with the bad political situation between the US and Syria, I haven't seen much US theater in Damascus, nor Syrian shows in the USA. I believe my troupe might be the only Syrian theater troupe ever to perform in an international festival in the US – the Midland International Theatre Festival 2006. And I believe things are getting worse since the politically-directed media is much more powerful than the individual's voice.

LB: Most of the images of Arabs I have seen on US stages portray either victims of violence or perpetrators of it. Sometimes both. Very rare are portrayals of Arabs just being people. I think this happens because non-Arabs writing about Arabs are drawn to write about them for the dramatic value of the "clash of civilizations" or the political/military conflicts in which their Arab characters are embedded (think *Guantánamo, Masked, Betrayed, Sixteen Wounded*). And many Arab-Americans, myself included, are writing the untold stories of Arabs also entangled in these conflicts from a perspective we usually do not hear in the US as regularly.

As it stands, most of the most widely-seen plays that portray Arabs are not written by Arabs or Arab-Americans. While this isn't necessarily problematic (one of my favorite pieces in recent years is *The Fever Chart*, by Naomi Wallace), some images of Arabs written by non-Arabs are more troubling. I'm thinking in particular of *Masked* and *Betrayed*. Both are steps in the right direction – plays that complicate the prevailing idea of a good American "us" and an evil Arab "them." However, each of these plays ends up feeding other stereotypes in more subtle, perhaps even unconscious ways. In an American context, given the prevailing image of Arab and particularly Palestinian men as violent by nature, what I saw in *Masked* was three brothers who, while talking eloquently about the struggles they face at the hands of Israeli occupation, were primarily ensnared and threatened by their own people. In the end, the greatest threat we feel viscerally on stage is the danger these brothers pose to each other and the violence they face from other Palestinians.

I spoke on several panels for *Masked*, and found my perception of the play's underlying message reinforced by the responses I would receive when I raised this point. At three different talkbacks, audience members blithely responded to me, "Well, the Arabs are just more violent than we are;" "It's because they teach their children to hate," and, "As Golda Meir said, if the Arabs only loved their children as much as they hated the Jews ..." What disturbed me about these comments was that when they were made, no one else in the audience so much as batted an eye. Not only can we be grossly misrepresented, as so many other groups have been and continue to be, but when we are, most people, even those who would be horrified at similar comments made about others, don't even notice.

I give the producers of *Masked* great credit for making sure that there was an opportunity to dialogue around these issues so consistently after the play, and for inviting me back several times even though I expressed views critical of the play itself. And I do realize that simply having a play about three Palestinian brothers which portrays their love for each other, struggle against occupation, and layers of nuance between and around them, is a huge thing to see on an American stage. And that is part of the problem. Seeing a play which portrays Palestinian men as human should not be something I have to gush about in 2008. Particularly when in the end one of them still has to kill his own brother, because otherwise, other Palestinians would kill him instead. The most challenging thing for me personally about these deeply disturbing representations is that they come from incredibly progressive, well-meaning artists, who I believe are simply not aware of or perhaps in some cases, interested in, their own unconsciously absorbed generalizations and stereotypes of the Arab and Muslim world.

We need more writers, both Arab-American and non-Arab American who are writing Arab characters not simply for their sensational dramatic connection to the Iraq war, or torture, or the Arab-Israeli conflict, but with the range of complexity we have started to see more and more in images of other groups traditionally underrepresented on US stages – Latinos, African-Americans, Asian-Americans, etc. As an Arab-American artist it feels like we are at the beginning of a movement that other groups began years ago.

CC: What Arab theater artists (playwrights, directors, actors, etc.) should US theatergoers get to know, and what US theater artists should audiences in the Arab world get to know? Why?

MC: Naomi Wallace would be interesting in the Middle East. I also think the work of Elevator Repair Service and companies like them creating their own text-inspired work might be of interest in terms of bringing over some of our more edgy work. I also think things like the New York Arab-American Comedy Festival would be a lot of fun for Arabs to see. This Arab-American identity thing causes some laughter and confusion in the Middle East as it sometimes does here. It was not a term I ever thought to use to describe myself until post-9/11.

EH: American theatergoers might be moved and riveted by the work of Saadalla Wannous, Jalila Baccar, Lenin el Ramli, Jawad al Assadi, Sulaiman al Bassam, Lina Saneh, and Rabih Mroué. My experiences as an audience member or a reader of these artists' projects have been enlightening, emotionally and intellectually. These artists, like all exceptional theater makers, unleash the full potential of the theater as a phenomenon in and of itself. I trust that theatergoers in the US or elsewhere would be similarly taken.

MBH: The Lebanese artist and creator Roger Assaf, who was recently awarded the Golden Lion award of the Venice Biennale. Roger is considered a teacher of directors who have influenced and still are influencing the Arabic theatrical movement and he is one of the pillars of theater in Lebanon and the Arab world. There is also the Iraqi creator Salah Al Qasab, the leader of image theater and Dr. Awni Karume, whom we lost in 2005, a creator, professor and theater theoretician. Tunisian Fadhel Alhaabi. And other young theater people who hold the future of the Arab theater reflecting their concerns, dreams and their creative and intellectual humanity.

RK: I think Al-Khareef Theater and Naila Al-Atrash in Syria are doing very interesting things artistically.

RA: In Syria we study many US writers such as Tennessee Williams and Eugene O'Neill, but we also have some very famous writers such as Saadalla Wannous, Farhan Bulbul and many others who I believe the reflect the strength of Syrian playwriting.

LB: Naila al Atrash – Damascus. She's a director, actress, collaborator, professor who has taught most of the actors and theater artists coming out of Damascus' national theater academy and is highly regarded in Syria and beyond.

Wajdi Mouawad – Lebanese Canadian actor-director-playwright, artistic director of the Canadian National Arts Centre's French theater since 2007. He crosses disciplines to tell stories that are both specific to Lebanon and also deeply universal.

Rabih Mroue in Lebanon – he is a center of the theatrical community in Beirut and from what I hear and read, he and his collaborators create work that interrogates the legacy of the civil war and beyond in satirical, visual and very unique, collaboratively-created ways.

For the Arab world: Heather Raffo. Her poetic melding of real people puts Packer's work to shame and shows how fiction can often be more representative than "truth." Her combination of the two is breathtaking, deeply moving, and moves past the models of heroes and victims to portray a range, depth and breadth of Arab women never before seen on US stages.

CC: *If you could create a US/Arab theater collaboration, what sort of project would you like to see happen, how would the work be created, and to what end?*

EH: I would like to see a project whose aims are higher than "intercultural understanding and exchange" – a collaboration that transcends the temptation to labor on cultural difference, a collaboration that acknowledges political currents but does not surrender to them, a collaboration that results in the highest quality performance. The project could be spearheaded by a duo or trio of transnational theater artists who are seriously embedded in the artistic networks of major American and Arab cities. The objective of such a theater collaboration should be institutional sustainability.

MBH: The institution that I am about to set up Jassad (body) for Arts Performance involves partnering with others. My company's belief is that dialogue and partnership are the basis of this human existence, and since our discourse is on humanity and the human being, we went through more than one experience within this framework. The latest was the performance (*Chained Dreams*) which I directed with the participation of a Spanish actress and another Dutch one; and in Arabic, English, Dutch and Spanish languages. I had started thinking of such a project while visiting Washington, it would be with actors, directors and American technicians who would come to Jordan and present joint work with Jordanian actors and directors.

RK: It would be a physical as well as artistic exchange. Artists from the Arab world would work in the US and vice versa. That way, the Arab world has more witnesses – something it desperately needs.

RA: Why don't we start with understanding each other and exchange productions, to make ourselves familiar then we can talk on many other future projects. Actually, my troupe is trying to do that – this year we traveled to the Frigid New York Festival (www.frigidnewyork.info) as the only international troupe participating among twenty-four US and four Canadian companies.

LB: I would love to see an exchange sponsored by a major theater in the US and one in the Arab world (my vote would be Cairo or Beirut), to allow American and Arab theater artists to spend time in each other's cities and countries, seeing theater, working with artists from the host culture, presenting their own work in translation to the host culture, and culminating in a collaboration with artists from the host institution. The purpose would simply be to increase understanding of what is "out there" beyond each country's own scene, to see the kinds of work the host country is producing, to experience how another country creates work, and to combine the best of both worlds wherever possible in a form to be shared with audiences in both countries. Seeing where work is easily translated and where it is not is also interesting to me as a writer and performer – where does it require cultural as well as linguistic translation for a piece to work from Beirut to NYC or vice versa, and where is a piece accessible across language and culture – what defines the language of theater in each place, and can each culture begin to incorporate elements of the other's vocabulary? What is lost and gained in that transaction?

When reading script submissions for a festival of Palestinian plays here in NYC for example, part of what I felt was a need to balance wanting to tell unheard stories let's say about Israeli occupation, with telling them in a way that an American audience could actually hear and absorb them. Some of the work we would get from the Arab world was so intensely heightened that I felt an American audience would feel "banged over the head," and so we would go with more metaphorical or nuanced pieces. Yet at the same time, there is something to be said for training an American audience to understand that work from the Arab world might have a different energy, in the same way we are trained to watch Chekhov or Shakespeare with an ear for their own unique language and worlds.

CC: What do you think is the biggest challenge facing Arab theater artists today? What about NYC artists?

MC: NYC theater artists are challenged by the fact that it is so expensive to live here and the time and space conducive to theater making are not readily available. Sometimes I wonder if the only theater artists who endure are the scrappy ones – so we have an overabundance of scrappy theater! As though there is some Darwinian force ...

EH: The increasingly mediated nature of daily life is the biggest challenge facing theater artists everywhere.

MBH: I think that what surrounds us are crises at all levels of economic, political, social and security. These have resulted in new concepts, data and frameworks which have negative effects on human beings. The world today is more closed than ever before, and even more extreme than it was, and more material. We live in a dire world still where the act of killing and confiscation is normal and natural, while shouting objections is prohibited by force. We have become chess pieces acting in accordance with the rules of this global system assassinating the human in us. And the theater before anything is a pure humanitarian act. Here is the dreaming lover, and here are his stolen laughs and tears, here is his choking scream. Theater is a tool we dream through. It is that mental pleasure, which calls for the other to share our dream by implicating him in sensory, mental and visual worlds that root a purely human experience which can be shared by both the sender (the performer) and recipient (the viewer) for the moment and post-theatrical performance.

RK: I think figuring out how to have longevity in one's career is crucial. So many people have temporary jolts of interest because they are all of a sudden the *crème du jour* until some other ethnic group replaces them. Arab artists need to hone their craft and be attentive to quality instead of just jump on a fashionable bandwagon. Then the other obstacle is funding. For any artist it is so hard to get funding, but the Arab community has been slow to patronize and support the arts financially. It's getting better, but there is still a ways to go.

RA: The world is undergoing a huge change now and everything is moving forward so fast, theater should be catching this movement. One of the big problems here is financial, which means artists leave for TV series more and more. I believe in such a bad financial and political situation there could be some good individual experiences but it's hard to build a foundation for sustainable theater.

LB: Both NYC and Arab world: the dominance of the web, satellite TV, and film. Making theater accessible and relevant in an increasingly media-driven world. In NYC, getting funding in the current economic climate, getting new work by less-known writers produced at a level to be widely seen, battling the dominance of anti-Arab stereotypes even amongst those who consider themselves progressive liberals. Writing outside of these perceptions is harder to do. But I think we are starting to do it.

CC: Finally, what hope do you place in art, and theater in particular?

MC: In these messy economic times my hope is not so much resting on the arts but in the people. I am hoping that people will remember the necessity of the arts and do everything in their power to bring the arts back into schools and bolster the arts up as a vibrant part of our society and even economy. There are thousands of people ready to work in theater, films, orchestras and the like but without support those people can't work. Where is our economic bailout plan? And I think we need one, because I believe the arts – and theater especially, allow people both onstage and off a moment suspended in time and place where pure empathy might exist. And for those who are able to practice the arts – at any level, there is the opportunity to work at something, to lose oneself in something, to attain some sort of communion – with an instrument, an audience, a dance partner, a paintbrush that is wonderful. And I think striving for that – whether attained or no, is of immense value.

EH: The hope that I place in the theater is to know, like Vladimir in *Waiting for Godot* that "at me too someone is looking, of me too someone is saying, He is sleeping, he knows nothing, let him sleep on" – to conjure the past and to share my deepest experiences – light and dark – with a group a people.

MBH: I exercise my existence through this act, I do not know exactly, but I do dream of achieving a level of absolute communication with the audience.

RK: For me personally, art is about achieving one primary goal – to change me. I do not want to be the same person I was prior to experiencing the art in question. It should make me think, feel or know something that I didn't prior to it being in my life. If I'm also inspired to change my behavior and act differently towards myself and the world, then even better.

RA: Art is the most beautiful thing on earth. Theater is one of the most powerful arts, reflecting reality in some creative way that lets you stand with yourself for a moment and think, whenever you think, you're living, and inside of that awareness is the potential for you to be a better human being.

LB: As a playwright, I believe theater can cross political, social, economic, religious and cultural divisions, and connect people to those they normally see as the "other" on the most intimate, human level. As an actor, I have always felt that connection to be something spiritual.

Performing the Soul:
Observations on the Practice of Ben Spatz
and Urban Research Theater
An Introduction by
Lane Pianta

In August of 2008 Ben Spatz and I sat down to record a conversation about his ongoing work under the moniker Urban Research Theater. Over the course of ninety-plus minutes we discussed his background, the ethics that guide his performance practice, the social context that motivates him and a number of other relevant topics. Urban Research Theater (URT) originated in Poland in 2004 and while its projects have incorporated the talents and energies of a number of participants over the last four years, those persons have orbited around a single nucleus: Ben Spatz of New York City. The centrality of the term "research" in the moniker he has chosen should be borne in mind to understand the methodology, purpose and even the aesthetic of Spatz' work. Owing much to the song/action research of Gardzienice Theatre and the Workcenter of Jerzy Grotowski and Thomas Richards, Spatz has nevertheless plotted a singular course for himself. Whether the fact that URT has struggled to maintain a fully committed company of performers has hindered or liberated Spatz, it has certainly not deterred him from pursuing a singular vision and the interview that follows represents an attempt on my part to understand the guideposts by which he navigates.

Exactly one year prior to interviewing Spatz, I had the pleasure of participating in one of Urban Research Theater's "Another City" projects. I already knew something of Spatz' work in practice, but I was wholly unprepared for the sheer delight of that experience as I and about seven other project participants joined him and his full-time partner Michele Farbman for a truly mind-bending tour of the Big Apple. The "Another City" project incorporated elements of movement improvisation, group singing and dramaturgical choreography into a twenty or twenty-five minute work of guerrilla theater that we performed in fifteen to twenty locations around the city over a three-day period. This work prioritized the experience of the performers (those of us engaged in the performance structure) over that of the spectators (the accidental assortment of strangers and passers-by whom we encountered on the streets), insofar as our performances did not seek to elicit a specific response from the observers.

Our performances functioned on many levels, but seemed perfectly designed to challenge a fundamental assumption of most theatrical performance: that empathic bonds between performer and spectator must function homogeneously. Personally, I have always doubted that assumption, as it encourages the actor to emote when they should be engaged in the performance of cold, hard action. In practice, however, I understood how as we opened our own minds to a changed perspective, the mere fact of our presence in public necessitated a change in perception for those around us as well. While we held no intention of eliciting a specific emotional response, our actions catalyzed individual responsiveness in all those we encountered that day. The experience seemed at once to re-affirm this basic principle of empathic response, while at the same time opening a door to another possibility for theater as an art, one charged with the potential to affect change on a city-wide scale. I found this to be a result almost unique in my experience as a practitioner or spectator.

URT's methodical and rigorous investigation into song as a vehicle for purposes beyond the demonstration of pure virtuosity seems to lie at a pole diametrically opposed to the typical use of song in theater. While Broadway and regional playhouses may produce box-office successes, they have failed miserably at sustaining a culture of meaningful artistic investigation. Add to this the fact that in colleges and theater departments across the country faculties choose to emulate the failing modalities of the theater industry in lieu of cultivating a new generation of theatrical innovators and it becomes easy to despair for American theater as an art-form. It is against these trends and against that very pessimism that the work of Ben Spatz and Urban Research Theater asserts itself. Theirs is a mission, not to transmit the known, but to embrace a set of known principles in search of the new; not to describe a form, but to fulfill authentic technique. Their exploration of song as psycho-physical action, incorporates traditional acting techniques and improvisatory movement, but elevates those tools into mechanisms that pierce the quotidian.

This very active and living investigation into performance practice leads URT to the verge of something quite new. Any attempt at categorizing the "Another City" project from 2007, at least according to established genres of non-traditional theater (street theater, devised theater, invisible theater, theater of place, ecological theater), however applicable, inevitably fail to capture the totality of the event. Likewise, the totality of Spatz the performer evades easy categorization. Part soloist, part ensemble member, part auteur, part autodidact, part teacher, part student; his role as leader of and co-participant in Urban Research Theater transitions fluidly to meet the demands of each discrete project, from moment to moment, always in service of understanding, embracing and celebrating the total human being, whether in himself or in others. As Spatz himself discusses, not every purpose can – nor should – be labeled in the name of process. The words in this interview that Spatz has chosen to represent himself and the nature of his work with careful accuracy, apply the nomenclature of performance craft to what I perceive as a fundamentally spiritual endeavor, the search for a meeting between individuals that is rare in art, of a performance that unfetters the spectator's perception, and reveals that which surpasses description.

While he might hesitate to name it thus, I would posit that the methodology he employs enables him to represent for a group of witnesses the performance of his own soul.

The work that URT brings to fruition now in a series of invited showings taking place from 2008 to 2009 may be understood as the culmination of several prior years of investigation, and at the same time as the beginning of a new phase of research, one in which the spectator's presence is, at last, essential. How many other artists are working in this way? If they are pursuing as ascetic a practice as URT in the frantic density of New York City, it may be impossible to ever know. Besides, Spatz goes on record here as feeling more kinship with yoga and the martial arts than with the vast majority of theaters. While I suppose that all forms of performance have the potential to embody the active spiritual search of the performer, I have encountered few individuals or companies whose work manifests this quality so palpably as that of Urban Research Theater.

Ben Spatz

Changing the Space
An Interview with Ben Spatz of Urban Research Theater
by Lane Pianta

Part One

LANE PIANTA (LP): *Ben, you lived in Poland from 2003 to 2005. Can you tell me about the projects you worked on in NYC before going to Poland?*

BEN SPATZ (SPATZ): When I first came to NYC, I worked on a number of shows in various technical and other capacities. With Ruth Wikler on *The Circus of Vices and Virtues* and with Yelena Gluzman on *I'm So Sorry for Everything!*, for example. I also worked for a couple months with Brad Krumholz and Tannis Kowalchuk of North American Cultural Laboratory. After that, I began to make pieces of my own. These were what I called "unscripted." Essentially they were structured improvisations. I was unwilling at that time to set a script, or to determine precisely what would take place. I was looking for a certain quality of realness – that it be alive every time. I could not accept the idea of setting the text or anything else. So it was invented every night, with very uneven results: sometimes fantastic, sometimes boring, sometimes fantastic when no one was there to see it. And sometimes with the actors floundering around not knowing what to do.

The first piece of this kind, called *neverland* (at ABC-No Rio in 2002), was based on combining the characters from *Peter Pan* with a short story about amateur terrorists – "Elegy for a Freelance" by Angela Carter. This piece managed to be successful despite its lack of structure, because of the quality of the performers and the sheer energy that we poured into it. The second piece, called *the desert* (at ABC-No Rio and HERE Arts Center in 2003) was also fully improvised but less successful. The actors struggled with the lack of structure, yet I still refused to set the text. I resisted the idea of using improvisation and then playwriting to devise a play and then perform that play. I simply could not accept that as a way to produce a more structured product, even though I knew that structure was crucially lacking in these works. Again, I wanted this quality of *realness* that seemed to me impossible to keep once a narrative text was set.

That's when I began to look for where, who to train with, how to get some more training and figure out what it was that could set. I was asking: is there a way to set text that would not kill the realness? Or can something other than text be set? I also did not want to set choreography and movement. I looked at some possibilities for training or apprenticeship in the United States, but they were not satisfying, or they didn't have an opening for the kind of apprenticeship I wanted. I ended up going to Poland to find these answers.

LP: *What was your experience in Poland? What did you do there?*

SPATZ: At first I went and apprenticed with the Gardzienice Theatre Company, near Lublin. I joined their academy of students, and I also joined the ensemble as a performer. I was with them for eight months. I toured with them and performed in the ensemble in two of their pieces. Then I received a Fulbright Fellowship to conduct my own research at the Grotowski Institute (then called the Grotowski Centre) in Wroclaw, Poland. There I was able to work with a number of amazing artists who came through that institution during the year, all of them connected in some way to Grotowski. I also led a six-month research project in Wroclaw, called Badawczy Teatr Miejski or "Urban Research Theater."

I did workshops with two of Grotowski's former actors during that year: Rena Mirecka and Zygmunt Molik. I also participated in Eugenio Barba's International School of Theatre Anthropology. Peter Brook came and I got to work with two of his actors. I did a two-week workshop with Song of the Goat Theater. I saw the performances of Theater Zar several times. Finally I went to Moscow for a three-week session with the Workcenter of Jerzy Grotowski and Thomas Richards. All of this was like a trajectory for me. Gardzienice was a very important eight-month-long starting point, and then I passed through these smaller workshops with other people, until finally that three-week encounter with the Workcenter at the end. When that finished, I came back to the United States. Everything had been turned on its head. I started from scratch.

LP: *Why the name "Urban Research Theater"?*

SPATZ: While I was with Gardzienice, I was always thinking about what I would do when I returned to NYC. I was very interested in Gardzienice's history of "expeditions": going to small villages in order to both research and present their theatrical performances, and to give them a life in a setting where communal song and communal festivity were still alive and not uncommon. "Urban animal" was a phrase that I was using at that time to think about human life in the built environment of a city. Almost all the theater work I had done in college was about the interface between the human being and technology. I used multimedia projections, television screens, and interactive video channels. But then I moved completely away from that. I began to care more and more singularly about the human organism and its possibilities, and its place in the city. I didn't feel a need to bring technology into the theater, since technology is all around us every day. Now I think of the relationship between the human organism and technology as analogous to the relationship between live performance work and the urban environment.

"Urban Research Theater." It means that there is a kind of research using theatrical techniques that can be conducted specifically in an urban context. It means that I am asking: what place can this kind of work find or make for itself in the city? What place does communal singing have in the city? How can these techniques be useful in the world I come from? The word "research" names a practice that is considered respectable in science and academia. However, the applicability of that concept to work in the performing arts is very significant. It's not just a question of throwing that word onto the performing arts because it's a respectable word. You can't just say that anything in the performing arts is automatically a kind of research. That's too easy. There is a specific angle on the performing arts, a specific approach to performance techniques, which can be called research in a rigorous sense. This kind of research bears the same relationship to the performing arts industry as scientific research does to technology industries.

LP: What is the role of song and singing in Urban Research Theater?

SPATZ: Almost all of the companies that I worked with in Europe have dedicated, long-term relationships with specific groups of songs, with song traditions. Most of these song traditions are still alive somewhere. Some of them are not. Gardzienice's current work is on reconstructed ancient Greek music, so that's not a living song tradition, but it is a very old song source. In an earlier period Gardzienice worked with Ukrainian and Polish folk songs, and on medieval chants. Teatr Zar works a lot with Georgian liturgical music, and Song of the Goat has worked with Bulgarian mourning songs and also with Mozart's Requiem. The Workcenter of Jerzy Grotowski and Thomas Richards works very extensively, and in a unique way, with African and Afro-Caribbean songs.

I was looking at those ways of working and asking a very American question: "Which songs could I work on?" Maybe the most obvious answer, especially for people familiar with Grotowski's work, would be that I should work on Jewish songs because I am Jewish. But I don't want to do that, at least not right now. One of the issues I wanted to investigate – maybe because I'm American, maybe because I'm secular, maybe because I'm Jewish – is the question of whether one can do a related work on songs that are not so old. In other words, can a research work be developed in relation to songs that don't have the weight of folk traditions? What would that work look like?

LP: Do you mean that a contemporary song, in theory, could function as well as any other kind of song?

SPATZ: In Poland, with that first six-month project, we worked on the beginning of the *Saint John's Passion* by Bach. We worked on a piece of electronica by a group called Emergency Broadcast Network. We worked on an ancient Aramaic song performed by a French woman on a CD. And we worked on a beautiful melodic track taken from a Puff Daddy song. We took these four pieces and it was an experiment, asking: "What works?" It was an interesting experiment, but none of the pieces really worked in the end. The Bach was too melodically complex. The electronica was too fun and too funky. The Aramaic song worked, but it could only be performed in solo.

I was very much resisting this feeling that one has to somehow "choose" between all the incredible existing song traditions that are out there. The idea of choosing – that didn't make sense to me. In order to go deeply towards a specific song tradition, you must have some clear inner directive telling you to do so. I've never felt that way. I've never wanted to be a "song collector" like Alan Lomax. The idea of "collecting" songs gives me a bad feeling. The clear directive for me was to find something more pure, more simple, something that could not be traced to any particular source or tradition.

LP: So you began to invent your own songs.

SPATZ: Yes. With this group in Poland, we began to invent sections of songs. For example, the melody that came from the Puff Daddy song – we started by singing that melody in a hip-hop rhythm, with beat-boxing, matching the track that it came from. But slowly it moved away from that. We took out the hip-hop beat and it became like a dirge – or even like some anonymous Jewish folk song, depending on how we sang it. Also, the Bach song was completely unrecognizable by the time we were done with it. It became a complex two-part harmony with made-up vocables. That was the first time we made up syllables to put into the melody. We sat in a circle, and everyone took a piece of paper and wrote out random syllables that they liked. Then we went around the circle, and any syllable that anyone didn't like was crossed off. We were left only with the syllables that everyone could agree on, and we put those into the song.

These were a beginning attempt to invent songs that could be used in a theatrical and fully performative context. When I came back from Poland, I ended up working alone for quite a while. I felt an incredibly strong need to sing in the studio, because I had been singing the whole time in Poland. I found myself singing the songs from my group, and also Gardzienice songs and Workcenter songs and other songs from the groups I mentioned. I felt: these songs are activating something in me that's important. I need it. But I can't build my own work on these songs because they're not my songs. Even if they were directly from the Afro-Caribbean sources by themselves, without the Workcenter as intermediary, still it would not be proper to build my work on them. But especially since other theater artists have been working on these songs for so long ... clearly I can't build my work on these songs.

So I started to look for ways of tapping into the same activations that were happening in those songs. I began to look for song fragments that could activate those same things in me, and it was surprisingly not too difficult to come up with these little song-fragments that worked in this way. They just seemed to be in the air with me, in the studio. I didn't feel that I was composing them. I never sat down and recorded them, and I never really wrote them down either. I was looking for the most organic process of song generation. This is how I imagine most folk traditions to have originated. You just have some people, and they're doing something, and someone starts to make up a song. And if it's a good song then everyone will pick it up, and it might even be returned to on another day.

LP: Can you elaborate on what is being "activated" by these songs?

SPATZ: The act of singing involves many aspects. I've never formally enumerated them, and I don't want to do so formally, but of course you can talk about the melody, the formal rhythm, the tempo, the overall pitch or key, the syllables and articulations. And then the many subtle kinds of dynamic and rhythmic shifts that produce the emphasis of the different parts, which is almost proto-verbal. These are some of the ways you can talk about singing in technical terms. And then you can also talk about the quality with which it's being sung, which is extremely important, and which, as Grotowski pointed out, can't be written down.

LP: By quality do you mean tonal quality?

SPATZ: The quality of the resonance, the type of vibrations and where they're coming from in the body. And something like the "depth of engagement" with the song, the actual depth from which the song originates within the body. What is it that's activated? It's a very good question. What is it that *can* be activated? Because to produce the sound, you have to activate the body. The making of the sound is the making of vibrations in and with the body. And then, the musicality of the song immediately begins to have some kind of meaning.

Let's say you start to sing a song, you make up a song, and it has a certain kind of rhythm. Immediately it has some kind of way of being. It does something to the space. Immediately you know that this song is fun and could be sung at a party, whereas another song is more personal and you wouldn't necessarily want to sing it at a party. Immediately you know that there are songs that can give you energy, that can energize you in a general way. And there are other songs that you probably shouldn't even try to sing unless you already have a lot of energy to work with, because they require a more subtle touch. So these kinds of meanings are immediately present in the song, in the technical details of the song.

What I've found is that, when you make up a fragment, those kinds of meanings, those things that are activated, they just come with it, they're right there for you. It's no problem. The difficulty is in keeping the song alive over time and in returning to it later. And then in figuring out how it can not only activate those same parts again but also, in time, go much deeper. So, the initial meanings that come up – like, "oh, this is a fun song for a party" – you can go much deeper than that over time. It's not that it stops being fun, but the fun becomes deeper and richer. It's deeper in you, it's a deeper way of producing the song that happens over time, so that what was initially, "oh, this song is fun" can become a song that's so powerful that you can – I want to say: you can bring that particular and precise moment or action of "fun" into any room with that song.

LP: *Which comes first? Is it the feeling of something that needs expression through song, or is it somehow being receptive to whatever song is available to you and then just listening to what that song represents, or what that song embodies, or what emotional resonance the song already carries?*

SPATZ: I don't think I have ever started from a specific meaning and intentionally tried to incarnate it in a song. The problem with that is, in my way of working, the technical rigor associated with the songs is very important. The meaning, the territory of meaning, is also very important to us, but we don't talk about it in technical terms. That's why I took the example of fun. Even the word "sad" I would shy away from. Because it's never that simple. I never approach it in that way. So, when a meaning arrives, it's not necessary that it's less specific, but it's less articulable. It may be less specific. It's the *song* that arrives in a way that can be captured, and then can lead back towards a meaning. We don't usually speak in a technical way about the meaning side of the equation. It's the technical side that we try to capture and repeat, at least in the beginning.

LP: *Do you consider yourself a songwriter?*

SPATZ: No. To be a songwriter or a composer means that you make songs. I don't really make songs in that sense. That's why I call them "song fragments." They're not really songs. Some of the songs that I'm singing are so simple – it would make no sense for someone else to say, "I'm going to sing that song." It's just a few notes. If you just take the melody – it disappears. It evaporates. One of my songs is just five notes, or even just four notes in repetition. The melody is so simple. There is nothing there, unless you are going to follow the more delicate aspects of the singing. So maybe each of the four notes has a specific vibratory quality, and a rhythmic quality that is inside the overall rhythm of the song. And maybe it's also linked to a very small line of actions. But then you are really talking about the act of singing and not what we usually call a "song." The word "song" doesn't usually include all of that. It could, but if it does – if "song" includes "action" – then it isn't something you can write or compose. It has to be developed or discovered or brought forth in a different way. Not what I would call composition.

LP: *The songs you create are not sung in English – they're not sung in any known language. I will not call them gibberish because that suggests that the words that are chosen have no meaning. I'll call it an invented language. Can you talk about that? What is the source of this invented language that you use?*

SPATZ: The groups that I mentioned in the beginning – they're all working on songs that are not in their language. And they don't make an effort to learn the meaning of the words. It's not like in opera, where you learn the meaning and the story behind the words even if they are in Italian or German. In the groups I'm describing, it seems that they purposefully avoid focusing on the linguistic meaning of the words. I find this very significant because what it does is point away from the discursive content towards the embodied or "non-lexical" content of the vocables.

Our songs have precision at the level of articulation and syllables. The way that this is arrived at is the same as with the rhythms and melodies. It's a process that at the shallow end is simply "making stuff up" and at the deep end is the arrival of a technical element linked to a territory of meaning. So the fact that there are no words is the same as the fact that we are inventing the melodies. I'm simply trying to avoid putting in any misleading discursive content that could lead the performers or the witnesses away from the immediacy of what is taking place. I don't want to be looking outside the room for the meaning of the event. So for that reason it should be nonsense – it should be just a tune that I made up – so that it's clear that whatever happens is not the result of any external or referential content. If anything is going to happen, it's just because of whatever is inside the room with us. It's just because a human being is present.

Part Two

LP: *Talk about how this work operates when it's occurring in tandem with another performer. And generally what that experience has been like, of bringing in another performer into this process that you yourself are discovering.*

SPATZ: I've been working with a woman named Michele Farbman, who did not have a performance background prior to working with me. We started working together less than two years ago, and for much of that time I have been giving her basically a very intensive introduction to what I know of movement, song, and acting techniques. The reason I'm working with someone who did not have a performance background, rather than someone who already was a singer or an actor, is that Michele happens to have a very unique background in a non-performative spiritual technique. This gives her a perspective from which it makes sense to work in an extremely long-term way. She has wanted to meet regularly, at least four times per week and throughout the whole year, but with no production frame. Simply meeting and developing our techniques towards the greatest possible depth. I haven't found anyone in the performing arts world who wants to work in this way. So Michele has been an extraordinary partner. I can't conceive of what would have happened or what I would be doing without her.

Early on, we passed through a period in which I introduced her to a number of movement techniques, to awareness of the body and my approach to movement. To embodied activity and play. And we were able, after months of work, almost a year of work maybe, to find a certain kind of contact in the physical work. It was a contact that could include our challenging each other in athletic ways, but it could also include more subtle interactions. Then we passed through another period in which we returned to the songs we had been singing together in the beginning and began to look for that same kind of contact in the singing. This is very different, partly because the songs in our work are set rigorously, whereas the movement is very open. But also, I think, because of the fundamental differences between singing and movement.

Acting techniques are yet another domain. In fact, this whole working process, I understand it as a question about the relationship between song techniques and movement techniques and acting techniques. When I talk about acting techniques, I mean "internal" acting techniques. That is: associations, imagery, relationship. I don't mean physical acting techniques such as clowning or commedia – anything where the emotions are indicated through a form. I am talking about acting techniques where real things are contacted somehow in the person, and it can't be predicted exactly how they will manifest in the body. So we can set what the person is thinking about, we can have them put their attention towards something that interests or is significant for them. That is what I would call an "internal" or "acting" technique. And then on the other hand, there are song and movement techniques, which are external. In other words, they can be very precisely regulated on an external visual or auditory level. So, investigating the relation between external techniques and internal techniques is where we're at now. And this means that when we work together, we're looking for something that is not only "singing well" together, and not only a playful contact as we've had in the physical work, but which can also involve acting techniques.

The question of how to work on that in a partnership is very open right now. In my experience, this kind of contact is usually monitored by an outsider, by an "outside eye." When we are doing individual work, one person is sometimes able to go quite deep into something because the outside eye is holding the space. The question now is how the two of us can go into something like that together, without an outside eye. That's a current question for me.

LP: You've talked a little bit about this work and its effect on the performer, and you're beginning to talk a little bit about the song and its effect on the space. These are ideas that connect to the Objective Drama and later work of Grotowski. Can you elaborate a little bit more on what you are looking for in terms of the song's impact on the space?

SPATZ: At this moment, I wouldn't distinguish between the person and the space, the performer and the space. When I say that the song affects the space or affects the person ... let me try to give an example. We all know how it is when you're having a conversation with someone on a relatively mundane topic, and then one person says, "Oh, and what about X?" – and suddenly the other person changes, and the whole moment and the whole space changes, because X is more serious. Or because X is so exciting that the person becomes enthusiastic and the air becomes electric. Something has been pointed to using words, and that something arrives and changes the people and the space. The moment suddenly becomes somber, or nervous, or enthusiastic, because of the meaning of the thing that has been pointed to. That thing is not physically in the room, but suddenly it is in the room, in a way, because it's part of the people who are in the room. And the rhythm changes, the rhythm of the people and – you could even say – the rhythm of the space. Of the moment.

That's what I mean by changing the space. It's not something compositional, like changing the arrangement of the furniture. The people in the room make the atmosphere, the human atmosphere. Its rhythm or its energy, so to speak. So, what I am talking about is a process in which you develop a structure that is made of songs, and each of the songs functions in the way I just described. Each song points toward a specific territory of meaning. So you have a line of songs, and each song – or each part of each song – directs the focus and the attention of the singers. The song says: "Focus on this aspect of your life for a moment. Work on this project. Work in relation to this thing, or to this part of yourself." Then, as you pass through the songs, you are passing through parts of yourself, different aspects of your consciousness. You are putting your attention on different aspects of your life. And the space manifestly changes – if you in fact pass through those territories of meaning.

LP: Describe the "Another City" project.

SPATZ: "Another City" is the name of a particular kind of work session. I originally envisioned a work-session of five days, or even seven days, that would be designed like an Outward Bound program for urban singing. The participants would spend all day with me from dawn until dusk, sunrise to sunset, and we would spend some of that time in the studio and some of it out in various parts of the city. In this way, the participants could experience a change in their relationship to the city. A kind of ecological change. Because they would be spending all their time during the day working on embodied contact, on singing, on listening to the human voice, on group perceptivity, and on the kind of searching-for-meaning that I've been describing. And we would live this process for about a week. It's a kind of para-theater.

I also related this idea to vegetable co-ops that bring organic food into the city, and to rooftop gardening, and to urban bicycling projects – and also to martial arts studios, yoga studios, and dance studios. All of these are places where people are asking: What kind of ecologies – food ecologies or body ecologies – or in my case perhaps ecologies of song – what kind of *human* ecologies can we have in the city? In a city which currently is so dominated by cars, by recorded music and video screens, printed imagery, and buildings. What kind of place can we find for these other things, which are also part of human experience – such as people singing together in a group, people walking, people not being inside buildings all the time ... I envisioned that the presence of our small group, in the "Another City" workshop, could somehow alter urban space – even just slightly – by having a different relationship to it. So we are looking for a different way to *be* in the city. Like a rooftop garden, but through embodied action rather than through actual landscaping.

In the city we are living on top of and inside a very recent crust of urban technology. This is not to say that urban technology is bad, or that there's something perfect underneath it at all, but simply to say: Let's not forget what is underneath this urban crust. Who are we? Are we still animals? Do we still have a use for communal song in this era?

LP: *In the literature for "Another City," it says: "to discover another city, another self."*

SPATZ: Yes. To discover – or rediscover – the city as it is ecologically. Because we don't live in that perception of the city. We live inside a lot of illusions and falsehoods about the city. By which I only mean that the city as it stands is completely unsustainable – in terms of the amount of garbage that it exports, for example. And we don't navigate the city, on a daily basis, in a way that acknowledges that profound unsustainability. We don't think about the city as a wild, irresponsible, kind of adolescent escapade. Just think: To build these ridiculously unsustainable cities, to produce thousands of tons of plastic, and just throw it out and put it in a big hole. It's this wild party that we're throwing, and we sort of know it is going to collapse and become impossible to maintain. But we can't admit it to ourselves. We don't act like: "This is so wild, oh my god! I have indoor plumbing on the fourth floor! That's certainly not going to last, so I'd better enjoy it for now!" We act as if the city is sustainable, and as if the whole system that built it is sustainable.

So the "other city," for me, is the city where you stop and you say: "Wait! From the perspective of the ecology of the planet, which is the ecosystem in which the human organism evolved – what is this thing that we're in? Who built this? Why did they build it like that? What is this material? Will this building still be here in 200 years? Will it be functional? Or will it be totally derelict, and everyone is gone? Or will it have been knocked down to make a new building, in which case where did all the trash go?" What could it mean to look from the place of the organism – to be in the city the way a dog or a cat, or a rat or a roach, is in the city. What is all this stuff? What is this Coke can? What is this piece of metal? What does it smell like? Who made it and where is it going?

LP: And what is so sublime about the "Another City" events, at the same time, is that while the stated purpose is to impact the participants, the doers – by the doers going forth and engaging in the performance structure, they are observed by hundreds of onlookers who had no expectation of witnessing a performance. While they're on their way to work, or while they're sitting at a restaurant, or while they're waiting for a cab. And yet, from the look on their faces it's very evident that they themselves are having a 'changed' moment. So while the emphasis is the effect on the doers, there is also an empathetic factor. There is the fact that it reaches out to these strangers and perhaps gives them pause about the assumptions they had, about what they were seeing, about the city that they occupy at that moment.

SPATZ: If it works that way, then that's exactly what I meant about changing a space by changing the people in it. Like when I say: "What about X?" – and it affects you in a certain way, and I didn't know it was going to affect you in that way, but suddenly the whole space is different and I feel that. If you become serious when I mention X, then I become serious too. I follow you. I think: "Oh, that was serious." And maybe also: "I didn't mean to bring up something so serious!" So the question is – it's an open question – how to bring people into the "other city," that is the actual city, the city as it is, as this bizarre and particular landscape that has been created by human beings over the past few hundred years. How to accomplish this shift?

In "Another City," we exercise a lot of restraint in the outdoor work. I don't want to create a street performance that tries to change the space in an aggressive or invasive way. I am very sensitive to this. I don't like the feeling that street performers are attempting to change the space without changing themselves. Trying to change others through volume and intensity. That isn't my way. It doesn't feel sustainable, and sustainability is the key for me. Not to do something crazy once, but to really discover and open a different possibility. Not to declare that there ought to be another relation to the city, but really to find that relation, in practice. Otherwise it is just a performance, not a real event. The space is not really changed. So from my perspective, there's no need to think about who you are performing for, who will see your work. It's rather: What is your way of being in the city?

That's why it is a research. Because you are not making noise about what you want but actually looking for the way to get what you need without disturbing others. It takes time. You have to try out different things and discover what meaning is brought along by each possible technique. So it isn't an indication of freedom, but an actual search for freedom.

Part Three

LP: *We've talked a little bit about how the effect on the doer doesn't have to be the same as the effect on the spectator. Is that accurate by your sights?*

SPATZ: I'm not sure what that means. In a certain sense, it couldn't possibly be the same. The song is not a machine that "does" something to you. It's more like, as I said before, a conversation in which the song reminds you to approach a certain meaning or a certain task. Clearly this meaning or task won't be the same for people in the audience, or even for your partner in the work. No one else will be having exactly the same task or the same association.

Could the audience understand something completely different from what the performer understands? I suppose they could. Of course the audience always invents their own stories and associations. But for me, that isn't really the point. Because, let's say there is a moment in a song that evokes in me – and I intentionally have it evoke in me – a specific memory. This is very important: That memory is *not* the content of the work. The content of the work is what *happens* in me as a result of the memory, of having that memory called up or referred to. Another time I might use a different memory. Or the same memory might have a different affect on me. The event in me is what alters the space and what can be shared – as a single event – with the witnesses. Not the image in my mind. Someone could guess what that image is, but it doesn't matter to me whether they get it right.

The song and the association work together to *activate* some part of the person. Now, what is that part of the person? It can't be named. The only way we could name it is by naming technically the elements of the song. We could also maybe name technically the elements of the association. But we can't really name the "territory of meaning" in the person – the thing that is being called through those technical elements. But *that* unnamable thing is the content of the work.

So, I'm not trying to communicate to anyone else the content of my association. That is irrelevant. That is private. It's rather that I'm using that association, in connection with the song, to bring forth or to work on, or to call up some part of myself – and that part of me is the content. So there is no intended "effect" on the audience, except that they are present to that part of me. It's neither more nor less than a witnessing of the person. Some part or fullness of the person is revealed that is not usually shown.

LP: Is the experience of sharing that song or that aspect of yourself with witnesses fundamentally different than practicing alone in the studio?

SPATZ: It is. It's hugely different. And so we have a real question: When do we show this, and to whom, and in what way? This is not a rhetorical question, it is a re-asking of the basic theatrical premise. Let's say you're doing this as an embodied practice, as a practice to contact those aspects – but there's another aspect, which is mysterious: You want to contact these parts of yourself, but not just for yourself. You also want to share them. It's a paradox. It's part of the mystery of being human. Because without other people we are nothing, and yet as soon as someone else is present, we are limited and not fully ourselves. Our possibilities are closed off. So we're always looking for privacy in order to rediscover the vastness of ourselves – but then, at a certain moment, that vastness becomes meaningless if it is not shared.

And so, to do alone is one thing. To do alone – it must be that you need to go through these places in yourself, and you simply use the tools right then to do it. And that would be a very full doing, I would think – if there were no thought to an audience at all, and you are just alone, doing it out of the need to do. And the paradox is that this is the doing everyone wants to see – the private doing – but they can't see it because you won't do it unless you are alone. For this reason we develop a sharing with a partner over a long term, where you develop intimacy and trust and so maybe you can approach that fullness of doing that you would have alone also when you are with this other person. And if you can do that, then maybe together you can find a kind of safety and support so that you could together go towards this fullness to a greater or lesser degree even when you invite some other people to come and sit and watch. I think this would be a very special kind of sharing. Not the same as what we usually call theater.

LP: For someone who may be reading this conversation and feels inspired by what you are describing – what quality is most important for them to possess? What quality should they work on first, before the other qualities can fully arrive?

SPATZ: I don't think I can answer that question. All I can do is put a piece of language out there, and I can't possibly know what language will activate another person who I haven't even met. Perhaps I could answer it just for myself. I could ask: "What is the quality that I am looking for most directly?" And for me the word *honesty* would have a lot of power here. Honesty in terms of: What are my actual desires? What do I want to do, why do I do anything at all? Why go into a studio space when nobody else cares and sing? Why organize a workshop? And also, honesty in terms of: What am I doing? What am I actually doing? I don't want to be saying that I'm doing more than I'm doing. But I also don't want to be saying that I'm doing less than I'm doing. I want to find a way to be *honest* about what I am doing.

In the singing work, it is also very often about honesty. Being honest about where you are as you are singing, and not trying to pretend that you are where you were last time. And also: knowing what the structure is and engaging with it honestly. So both in the larger picture and in the smaller picture, it's a search for honesty. Or you might say, integrity. It's a recognition and acceptance of reality – which means that you are both lesser and greater, in different ways, than you think you are. And to get through those illusions is just work. So there is a circle of language: How do you get to honesty? You work. What is work? It's when you engage in a process that makes you honest. So the words *work* and *honesty* orbit around each other. But I wouldn't prescribe these words for others. These words are in orbit around me. With another person I would ask a different question.

LP: *Is it fair to say that honesty is the quality you look for in yourself first and foremost?*

SPATZ: In this moment that seems fair. I wouldn't want to bind myself to a certain word, labeling it as the thing I look for in myself. But I would say that this move away from theatre towards something that employs theatrical techniques, where I'm using theatrical techniques but I'm not making any theater per se – that for me is about honesty. It's about what those techniques were for me, what I believe they're capable of, what they can do, what can be done with them, what I believe is valuable, what their place is going to be in my life. That's about honesty. It's about tracing a continuous line between the inner and the outer. Finding my place in the world.

LP: *What is on the horizon for Urban Research Theater at the end of 2008 and going into 2009?*

SPATZ: We are still developing our craft and our practice. We intend to have a series of showings in the coming year, perhaps just one showing each month for a year or longer. Each time inviting a small number of people. In order to find out, at the current level of what we do: Is this work visible? Is it useful to people? Is it interesting to watch? Does the work invite people and do people want to watch this? Usually people don't want to go and just watch a yoga class. And you certainly wouldn't invite ten people to watch a yoga class. Unless there was a visiting master, someone who had been doing yoga for many years. What we do is more theatrical than yoga, more theatrical than a meditation or even a martial art. At the same time, it is less theatrical than theatre. So it's a question of finding the proper framing for it and finding the right people who want to see it for what it is.

My sense is that there are many people in the performing arts who would like to have more time for research on craft – more time for exploration – more time for what's sometimes called workshopping or devising. A slower, more patient process. And they don't have to go and be fanatic about it, the way I am now. They don't have to exit the entire frame of production in order to find something useful or helpful in what we are doing. I suppose there is a kind of *permission* that I want to give. I want to say: "You people who are doing dance and theater – this already is your practice. You already can think of it as your long-term practice. You can give yourself permission to approach it in that way." You don't need permission to do slower, process-focused work. You don't need a production timeline in order to begin a research process. You don't have to do things so fast necessarily, or be so concerned with showing results within a predetermined time frame. Maybe you can let go of some of that, and find a more honest and more patient work.

I perceive a lot of rushing – especially in New York – a feeling that things must be done fast. If you are going to workshop something, you should do it as fast as possible – and you have to justify your research periods as soon as possible with a production to show the "results." I have the sense that a lot of people would like to slow it down. To slow down the process of working – and maybe also the process of living. And just to be able to think of one's work as a continuous work rather than a series of discrete, disposable productions. But at the same time, people seem very nervous about the prospect of slowing down. There is so much pressure from external sources – from the theatre industry and from the grant-makers. So it's like: "Well, if I make a slow project, how will I find people to work on it with me? Who is going to be willing to make that kind of commitment?" The dance community seems to be much further along than the theatre community in this regard.

I'd like my work to be a weight on one end of that scale. And this is what I have found in my amazing partner, Michele. She doesn't have that same sense of being in a hurry, because she doesn't come out of a performing arts background. She comes out of a background of serious yogic practice. Not a physical yoga, but an internal yoga – in which, she has said, it is understood that maybe you'll start to see some visible results from the practice after ten or fifteen years. And of course, in that context there is no such thing as "putting on a show." I want to take my own theatrical techniques all the way in that direction, because that's where I need them to function for myself. I've left the theatre in a certain sense, and I'm looking to reconnect with the origins of performance as embodied practice. And maybe that can be useful for other people, too. Maybe I can offer the possibility of a kind of relaxation. Not relaxation in terms of quality, but in the realization that quality does not have to depend on putting on a show. There are reasons to be disciplined and to push for higher and higher levels of ability that have nothing to do with putting together a performance for an audience.

I'm not saying that everyone should work more patiently or pay more attention to these "other reasons." I'm just following a hunger and a need in myself. Of course it's perfectly valid to make quick work. I'm really just proposing that it's *possible* to work more patiently. It's *possible* to have a slower process. It's *possible* to go more deeply into the techniques that you already have. It's not your obligation as a performer to learn more techniques, or to stack up more productions on your resume. Everything you have is already enough to begin the sustainable practice that you want your life to be.

LP: *Thank you.*

Michele Farbman

Plays

Grateful to the Greeks
An Introduction to *Kissing the Floor*
by Ellen McLaughlin

I've been looking over a couple of years' worth of notes on *Antigone*, trying to track the process that led to this odd response to it, and I ran across a Muriel Rukeyser poem called "Easter Eve 1945," a fragment of which I had copied into my notebook:

Whatever world I know shines ritual death,
wide under this moon they stand gathering fire,
fighting with flame, stand fighting in their graves.
All shining with life as the leaf, as the wing shines,
the stone deep in the mountain, the drop in the green wave.
Lit by their energies, secretly, all things shine.
Nothing can black that glow of life.

Perhaps I have misread this poem, but what it conjures whole for me is the mind of Antigone, her obsession with the death in life, the life in death. Late in the play I have my character Annie say to her sister,

"Just listen. Ah, God, it's here, they're all here, shining in the air like mist. Death is the element we live in, it's so obvious. Even the most commonplace things are speaking to us, always, and always about the dead, murmuring constantly, these walls are singing, the filaments in the lights are humming with it, you just have to listen. All, everything, tells us about the beauty of death, the beauty of the dead."

Which is precisely what has always been the problem with Antigone for me.

But then I suspect that from the start Antigone has made the rest of us feel uncomfortable. Such exemplars of radical idealism always do. (Come to think of it, I don't imagine St. Joan was all that much fun at a dinner party, either.) Antigone is, after all, the woman who chooses to give up her life for a gesture. She dies because she has defied the king, her uncle Creon, by ritually throwing sand on the corpse of her brother to whom the king has forbidden burial. She has much to live for – she is loved not only by her sister but by the young prince Haimon, Creon's son, who expects to marry her before she decides to sacrifice her life by committing what she knows will be a capital crime. She maintains that any alternative is unthinkable because not to bury her brother would be an offense to the gods and would relegate him to an eternal spiritual limbo. Her rigidity of principle is mostly admirable when she is faced with her uncle's secular political arguments, but it is unnerving when she is confronted by those who love her and are simply begging her to embrace life instead of death. Her sister Ismene in particular makes a singularly wrenching plea, which Antigone harshly mocks as cowardly.

However much one may respect such a character, she doesn't inspire affection. Probably because she doesn't seem quite human. Antigone's name, which can translate to something like "instead of" or "anti" generation, is apt. With her death she effectively brings her own family line to an end. She forgoes procreation and becomes a bride of Hades when she chooses to bestow her life and love on a dead brother rather than on a living husband. But she is very much her father's daughter, and his grotesque distortion of the generative process through parricide and incest is her blighted legacy.

And then there's her brother.

What seemed clear to me as I thought over the Sophocles play in translation was just how morally compromised Polynices is in that text. By anyone's standards, Polynices is an ethical nightmare – a traitor who would rather destroy his own city than allow his brother to continue ruling it. When Antigone treats that treason as irrelevant, and indeed goes so far as to die to protect her brother's spirit from what she believes it would suffer if his corpse lay unburied, she is pursuing a logic to its end in a way few mortals could manage. We never realize what moral relativists we are until we are faced with a person who is blind to context and deals only in abstract essences.

Kissing the Floor is the ninth play I've written that is directly inspired by a Greek text, and though it wanders farther from its source than any of my other work, it is still along the lines of a modern rendering of the Sophocles. I've always approached the adaptation of Greek plays aslant, privileging intuition over intellect and allowing the plays to disturb and disarm me before I make any moves to find my own way in.

I have found time and again that there is an emotional knot, a psychological conundrum, at the heart of each of these plays, some fundamental mystery. That knot is probably different for each reader, but until it's discovered, there's no point in putting pen to paper. With the Greeks, I'm always looking for the thing I can't understand or the thing that gives me bad dreams. That is the grain of sand the oyster makes into a pearl, the necessary problem it takes the writing of a play to resolve. In this case, it was my ambivalence toward the title character that kept me up at night, my suspicion about her motives and my discomfort with her ultimate decision. I began to have some insight into her character when my own father died and I realized how much of my life was now spent with my ear to the ground, metaphorically speaking, constantly in conversation with a man whose responses to my questions I could no longer hear. I felt a kind of panic as I realized that with every day he became more and more my own creation as the reality of him slid farther into the past. A growing certainty that I would never see him again, not only in life but after life, made the loss just that much harder to bear than it had been when I didn't have to think through what I really believed death must be. It was in this state of mind that I found myself beginning to understand Antigone at last. And when the image of a woman kneeling on the floor to tap in Morse code to her dead father came to me, I trusted it.

Then the problem was what to do about the dead brother. It seemed clear that Paul, as he became, should be alive because I wanted the siblings to be able to talk, but more importantly, I wanted to discover a way I could put the same kind of pressure on my Annie's devotion and sense of duty to her brother that Sophocles puts on his Antigone's. Was there any human action universally recognized as so contemptible that a sister's loyalty to a brother who committed such an act would be morally debatable? I decided there was.

I let Ismene become the person telling the story, framing the play for us, since it was her agonized impotence to prevent her sister's tragedy that always moved me most in the Sophocles. I dispensed almost completely with Creon, feeling that his argument had already been thoroughly explored in other adaptations—Jean Anouilh's in particular comes to mind. A trace of his secular and rational authority remains in the figure of Brennan, the man who runs the island prison where Paul is held. I wanted someone older than the siblings and outside the family to be able to see their actions objectively. He functions a bit like the chorus in the Sophocles; he is our way in, someone able to speak for us and articulate the issues clearly. I also liked the idea of having some figure tell the story of Oedipus and Jocasta, so I recruited (and resurrected) Eteocles (Eddie) simply to walk onstage and address us directly as Paul's identical twin. I find it theatrically satisfying to see the actor playing Paul transform into Eddie. Each of these stunted souls is the other's fraternal counterpart.

As these notions fell into place, the play began to take on an idiomatic life, and fragments of it started to show up in my dreams. Images of Depression era America kept occurring as I wrote, and then I happened upon James Thurber's 1934 piece from the *New Yorker* archive about the abandoned and dilapidated Pulitzer mansion, once so splendid, now the home of mice and pigeons, with its "grey and dismal" ghostly crystal chandeliers, and the world of this play bloomed whole for me.

I'm always grateful to the Greeks for their insistence on posing the hardest questions. They force us to consider the mystery of blood kinship and ask: what do we owe each other? How far must that obligation and loyalty extend? Past what is unforgivable? Past death? Or does it never quit, does the demand of blood beseech us without end, even as we peer blindly into that darkness which is the darkness that awaits us all? The character of Antigone still haunts me and disturbs me, but now she is all too familiar, the sister I never had, speaking to me just out of earshot. She's impossible to ignore because now I think I know what she's likely to be saying. But it seems she's with me for good and I will always be listening for her, even when I've successfully silenced her.

KISSING THE FLOOR
by Ellen McLaughlin

KISSING THE FLOOR

Ellen McLaughlin
c/o *New York Theater Review*
790 Washington Avenue #303
Brooklyn, NY 11238

Kissing the Floor received an initial reading at The Public Theater in New York City in June, 2007. Les Waters directed the following cast:

IZZIE...Elizabeth Marvel
ANNIE..Laura Heisler
PAUL/EDDIE...Bill Camp
BRENNAN..Jay O. Sanders

KISSING THE FLOOR
by Ellen McLaughlin

(We hear a tapping, rapid, assured, and quiet. Slowly, we begin to see. Dim light. ANNIE is crouched on the floor, she is engaged in a conversation conducted in Morse code, tapping, then listening, and tapping again. IZZY stands to the side. IZZY speaks to us. ANNIE speaks to herself, preoccupied and intermittently listening for responses to the questions she asks the floor.)

IZZY: The questions. She'd ask you these questions. It was a sort of game, I guess. But since she never told you the rules, it was a game she played *on* you rather than *with* you. You were helpless to protect yourself. You never knew precisely *how* you'd betrayed yourself, just that you had somehow. You could feel it, see it in her eyes. But all you were doing was answering these questions of hers. It was a sort of story you went on together. A journey you took. You always started in a forest.

ANNIE: It's the beginning of a journey. You're in the middle of a wood. Describe it to me. Describe it to me like I'm standing next to you and I'm blind.

IZZY: And you were off. There was a bear, there was a body of water, there was a house, there was something else, several other things, it took some time. There was lots you had to do, decisions to make, places to think up, until you got to the last question, which I knew was coming, but could never prepare for.

ANNIE: You've reached the end of the journey. Tell me what you see.

IZZY: But I never could. Because as soon as she said that, I saw nothing. Blank nothingness. You couldn't even call it darkness, it was just the end of sight. It terrified me.
It wasn't until I was all grown up that she told me what I was trying to look at. *(She watches ANNIE for a moment.)* Yes, that's her. Well, this is how I see her anyway. Along the lines of a memory. A story we go on together. Hers. Well, mine. Mine. The answers to the questions I keep asking. It's this particular night again. I keep coming back to this. The last night. And she's waiting. For him. I'll get to that. Him. I'll get to that.

ANNIE: Early morning. Yes? A ferry boat? Across what? Lake? River? Midpassage. Thin rain.

(She continues inaudibly.)

IZZY: What's she doing? She's talking to the dead. Well, specifically, my father. Our father. Who is also our brother. Long story. Bad story. You've probably heard it.

ANNIE: Something running? A horse? Horses running in the field above the shore. Beauty? Beautiful? Beauty.

IZZY: Yeah, it's Morse code. Tippity tap. She thinks the dead know it.

ANNIE: He did.

IZZY: Well, he did, in fact.

ANNIE: Learned it in the trenches.

IZZY: They came in handy, the things he learned in the trenches.

ANNIE: He was magnificently ... capable.

IZZY: But still he blinded himself when he found out. It was kind of an odd thing to do.

ANNIE: But it was the one thing he seemed to feel good about.

IZZY: It was like he was proud of that somehow.

ANNIE: 'Cause he did it himself. To himself.

IZZY: And then he lit out. Took her by the hand and never let go. She drove that '32 Buick down back roads day after day, month after month, years they drove.

ANNIE: Didn't talk much. Just played the radio.

IZZY: It was the way he liked to figure out where they were.

ANNIE: "Don't tell me, don't tell me. Just turn on the radio, Annie."

IZZY: Local polka shows, country music with yodeling, recipes, call-in advice for the lovelorn. There was always a giveaway, a sound that could only happen there.

ANNIE: And he would always, always guess right.

IZZY: They told the time by waiting for the moment when the neon motel signs came on with a jiggle of light, like an irritated eye fluttering. He liked to hear the names.

ANNIE: Stop-a-Mo Motel, Smokie's Bait and Bide, Auntie Cupcake's Hideaway, Rest-A-Wee Kountry Kabins.

IZZY: In the cool of the evening, they'd start to slow as they passed each one.

ANNIE
No Vacancy, No Vacancy, No Vacancy ...

IZZY
Until at last she'd be clapping her hand down on some forsaken tinny bell somewhere and waiting for the Missus or the Mister to come out and survey the strange couple the night had flung in. Grimy girl with finger-combed hair and no lipstick holding the hand –

ANNIE: ... always holding the hand

IZZY: – of the old gentleman at her side. No one could ever describe him well afterward because after one glimpse of those hollow, blackened eyes flayed with vivid scars, you weren't about to look his way again. It was too terrible. But you did take in something, some awful certainty about him, his height, a military stance, even then, in that ragged hank of a coat, and a kind of clarity of mortal taint that came off him like the steam rising from him on a wet cold night when they'd come into the overheated lobby from the sleet outside. He was remarkable and appalling.

ANNIE: Both at once. Even when they couldn't describe him later, they never forgot him.

IZZY: She'd sign for them both and then stoop for the one scuffed red suitcase, all they had, and lead him down the hall. Twin beds, I guess. That's how I picture it anyway. Pushed together so that he could reach her. See, long experience had taught her not to drop that hand in sleep or he'd wake up screaming and thrashing. So their clasped hands would ride together in the gap between the beds, hers prickling with the blood drained away, but she learned how to endure it. And at night sometimes she would wake to feel him tapping into her hand in her sleep.

ANNIE: Morse code.

IZZY: Wake to stare up at the darkness of the motel ceiling, trying to hear the message he was sending her in his dream.

ANNIE: Dit DA dit.

IZZY: He taught her. It's not like they had a whole lot else to do. Days and weeks, remember, travel as relentless as it was aimless. So I picture the two of them, listening to the radio, driving the blue highways all those years. Her left hand on the wheel, and into her right hand, which is cupped to receive it, like a nest lying on the cracked leather of the Buick's front seat, into that hand he is murmuring with his left until she catches him gently by the wrist and he turns his hand like a ear to take her tapping.

ANNIE: "Describe it to me, Annie."

IZZY: So she tells him about the towns they pass, churches and pool halls and gospel tents lit up with the shadows dancing and that moose who stood like a homely building in the middle of a shallow lake. It was so easy to teach her. She picked it up fast and soon could go like lightning. His face would crease with harsh pleasure as he nodded, listening to her in his hand. He said he was glad he taught her. Said it might be useful for her when he was finally gone.

ANNIE: And he was right.

IZZY: Because now, she thinks, that's how he talks to her. *(To us.)* Can you hear it? *(Silence, while we listen.)* Yeah, neither can I. Nobody can.

ANNIE *(listening)*: Yes? *(Smiles.)* Of course.

IZZY: She won't say how he died. Nor where. Won't tell anyone. We just know he's dead and that's the end of it.

ANNIE: I drove all the way home with his dust in the creases of my hands.

IZZY: We hadn't spoken, we hadn't laid eyes on each other in years, still the first thing she asks when I open the door:

> *(ANNIE is up from the floor, in a scene with IZZY.)*

ANNIE: Where's Paulie?

IZZY: He's in jail. Been there for a while now.

ANNIE: Was it a little girl?

IZZY: Well, no. Breaking and entering. But really, yes, a little girl. Pammie MacAfee.

ANNIE: What'd he do to her?

IZZY: Looked at her.

ANNIE: Just looked at her? That's all?

IZZY: Well, from the foot of her bed. *(ANNIE exits. IZZY continues, to us.)* She'd seen him before, Pammie had. He was the one, his fingers twined through the chain link, always looking at her in the playground when she was playing Duck Duck Goose.
And then this one night Pammie wakes up and there he is, that same man, but now he's standing at the foot of her bed, staring at her like that. Annie visits him in prison. She's the only one who does. He hasn't seen a soul else since they put him in there.

> *(Prison visiting room. ANNIE is having difficulty breathing and she can't stop shaking.)*

PAUL: What'd you do to your hair?

ANNIE: I don't know. Did I? Do something to it?

PAUL: It's different somehow.

ANNIE: More'n likely. It's been six years.

PAUL: Nah. Can't be.

ANNIE: Yes, Paulie. Long time gone.

PAUL: What you shaking for?

ANNIE: I got the closets in here.

PAUL: Oh, right, the closets. Poor old lynx cat. Afraid of closets. Right down to her little cat bones.

ANNIE: Yes.

PAUL: Iddy kitten lynx cat. Eddie locked you up in the attic closet. Said you were bad and that's what became of bad girls. People had to lock them in closets and just walk away. Remember that?

ANNIE: Not much. I remember screaming. No one heard me.

PAUL: 'Cept me. I heard you. About sunset, it was. Opened the door and there you were, shiny cat's eyes blinking in there. Teeth chattering like earthquake teacups in a china cabinet.

ANNIE: I can't remember.

PAUL: Splinters under your cat's claws from where you'd been going at the door.

ANNIE: I can't remember. It was too late by then.

PAUL: How old were you? Little biddy thing.

ANNIE: Five. I was five.

PAUL: My best girl after that. Yes you were. Thought the moon rose in my eyes.

ANNIE: The sun. *(He looks nonplussed.)* What rose in your eyes. I thought the sun rose in your eyes. Clichés, Paul, you gotta get them right.

PAUL: Jeez, we had some good times, Annie. You were my little lynx cat.

ANNIE: I was.

PAUL: I petted you and you would purr.

ANNIE: Paul?

PAUL: Lifted your little chin and I would scratch it. Kitty, kitty.

ANNIE: Tell me what you were going to do to her.

PAUL: Who?

ANNIE: Pammie McAfee.

PAUL: Is that what you're here for?

ANNIE: What?

PAUL: Same as the others? *(Does an officious voice.)* "Just a few questions, Paul, this won't take long ..."

ANNIE: I wanted to hear it from you. Describe it to me like I'm standing next to you and I'm blind.

PAUL: Just wanted to know which one.

ANNIE: Which one what?

PAUL: Which one of her stuffed animals she slept with. I heard her talking to this other girl, said she liked all of her animals but there was only one, *only one* she could ever sleep with, 'cause he was special. That's all. Just wanted to see that, for myself.

ANNIE: Which one was it?

PAUL: Lion. Sad old lion with matted hair, looked like it'd been cried on.

ANNIE: I'm sure it was.

PAUL: It was just that.

ANNIE: So why'd you leave the van running?

PAUL: Did I? Stupid fuck.

ANNIE: And you had the clothesline to tie her with looped over your shoulder, the length of cloth tape for the gag stuck to the front of your shirt.

PAUL: I had to come prepared.

ANNIE: In case what?

PAUL: In case she didn't want to come with me.

ANNIE: Come with you where?

PAUL: The tree house.

ANNIE: Our tree house?

PAUL: Thought she'd like it there.

ANNIE: I see.

PAUL: Same one.

ANNIE: But she didn't want to come?

PAUL: No. She woke up and saw me. She made a sound.

ANNIE: Started screaming?

PAUL: Her mouth got so wide. Big, I thought for a little girl. Never saw such a big mouth on a little girl.

ANNIE: You could have left. You still could have made it. The window was open. First floor, you wouldn't even have had to jump. Why didn't you leave?

PAUL: 'Cause I wanted to look at her. Touch her. I knew I'd never be able to touch her if I didn't right then. But she was all squirmed up in the corner of the bed. And I couldn't think straight because of the sound coming out of her. She couldn't hear me. I kept trying to talk to her. Trying to calm her down.

ANNIE: What were you saying?

PAUL: I don't know, just, you know, "Kitty be good. Kitty be quiet. Kitty come here," like that.

ANNIE (this is all too familiar): Yes, right.

PAUL: And then as soon as I get my hand to her face – I just want to pet her, you know--she bites. Fangs she's got. Right down into my finger there. Still got the mark of it. Look. And then I see her daddy in the doorway. Got a shotgun long as your arm catching the glow from her night light. And that was that. And all I wanted was to see, you know, to see which one it was she slept with.

(Pause.)

ANNIE: The lion's name was Lennie. I got him on a trip to Heywood Falls. Yes, his mane was matted. Lots of tears.

PAUL (vaguely): Oh, I remember that.

ANNIE: Lots of tears. *(Pause.)* I can't do this anymore. I got the closets too bad. I have to go.

(She gets up.)

PAUL *(he barely notices)*: Big difference, lynx cat. You never bit. *(She's gone. He smiles.)* Lennie the Lion.

IZZY: She sees him twice a week for months, even though every second she's in that cell with him, she's tasting her lunch at the back of her throat. Not to mention that she can't stop shaking.

ANNIE: There's nothing I can do, it's just the animal. She shakes.

IZZY: But that doesn't stop her seeing him. And she starts noticing things. Marks on him. A way he keeps shaking his head, like the way you shake a stopped watch. Trying to unconfuse himself, she thinks. She goes to see the warden. She asks to meet outside, looking out over the water from the island prison.

(Sound of wind. Buoys, tankers passing. PATRICK BRENNAN, older man, with an Irish accent.)

BRENNAN: Surprised you wanted to meet here on this hill.

ANNIE: It's where I always come after the visits. Clears my head. Only place I can breathe on this island.

BRENNAN: So you don't know what you're standing on I guess.

ANNIE: What do you mean?

BRENNAN: It's Potter's Field we're standing on. This. It's where the city's unclaimed dead go, stacked like tins of mackerel, hundred fifty to a grave. The prisoners bury them.

ANNIE: How many are here?

BRENNAN: Got it all down some place in a book. Call it the Doomsday Book, inherited it from the fellow before me. A few hundred thousand anyway. All on this hill here.

ANNIE: Pretty spot, really. The view across. The green hills on the other side.

BRENNAN: I've often thought so myself. A bit crowded, though I don't suppose they mind at this point.

ANNIE: This their headstone? *(He nods. She reads.)* "And He shall call His own by name."

BRENNAN: Nobody else will, that's for sure.

ANNIE: Who were they?

BRENNAN: Who knows? That's the thing. Poor sots found under bridges, in sewers, hit by trams, washed up in the river. Lot of babies, of course, left in the parcel room of the train station, back of a city bus, side of the road. Entire people thrown away like empty matchbooks. Keeps the boys busy, I tell you, burying them all. Boats come in twice a week, about six thousand bodies a year now.

ANNIE: So many. Can there be so many unloved people in the world?

BRENNAN *(laughs)*: You're asking the wrong fellow. That's my entire acquaintance, dead or living. The sons of bitches no one's ever loved. Excuse my language.

ANNIE: That's not true. Not always.

BRENNAN: Ah, yes. That's why you're here.

ANNIE: My name is –

BRENNAN: – know who you are. Of course.

ANNIE: And my brother –

BRENNAN: Him I know. Know your man quite well. As well as anyone could stand to know such a person.

ANNIE: What do you mean by that?

BRENNAN: What you think I mean? Got over two thousand of the scum of the earth in my care and he's the least popular of the lot. They've tried to kill him every day he's been here. Every blessed time I turn around, I have to break up some dogfight he's in the middle of, curled like a baby, getting the kicks with the billy boots.

ANNIE: Ah. That's about what I thought was going on. You can't protect him any better than that?

BRENNAN: If you'll pardon my saying so, Miss, it's not my job to keep your brother in a world that doesn't want him much. And my interest is flagging in the project. As it is, during the day I have to shift him out to the auld loons and cripples, the ones who've been in so long they don't remember who they are anymore. I let him make brooms with the droolers out in the shacks, just so I don't have to spend every waking minute looking after him. But they're getting wise to the situation and it's just a matter of time before he won't be safe there either. Those that still have teeth in their heads will bite the nose off him once they figure out who he is.

ANNIE: You know they couldn't make the charges stick, don't you? They only got him for breaking and entering?

BRENNAN: Well, the boys don't care too much about the legal fine points. That's not their area of expertise. They put things together in their own way, these fellas, and the verdict came down without the benefit of a single law degree. They just want him dead.

ANNIE: Is there anything I can give you? Something you need? Something that would –

BRENNAN: – Bribe me, like, to coddle your little prince 'till he can get out and do the same again? Is that it?

ANNIE: Yes.

BRENNAN: It's girls like you I can't figure out. Look at you. You might have a decent pitch at life if you put yourself together and looked the other way. You're not ugly. But you come out here, regular as my da's gold watch, to stare into the eyes of a waste of food like that brother of yours. What is the living point of that? You know what the monster's done.

ANNIE: Yes. Better than you.

BRENNAN: This is your life going by, Miss. For him. Such a man.

ANNIE: He's my brother.

BRENNAN: Ah, Miss. We're standing on a mountain of brothers. Nameless
(MORE)

BRENNAN (cont'd): bones and dust. All the glory of creation, to end up here. The waste of it, it's past thinking of. Little mite gets left like a bundle of snotrags in a bus station lost and found. He's just a stone chucked into a pond. Over before he's even started it up. He didn't have a chance at it, that mite. No one put the choice to him: Here's your life, do you want it or not? You think you have the right, Miss, in the face of that, to throw yours away for a man like your brother? It's an insult to every single soul whose body you're standing on. Weep for them. Visit them. It'll make as much difference. It'd make as much sense. Some of them must have been decent folks at least. Somewhere in this mountain of poor souls, there were bound to be a few worthy of your tears.

ANNIE: But he's my living brother.

BRENNAN: Yes, Miss, he's above ground for the nonce anyways.

ANNIE: I'm grateful to you.

BRENNAN: Don't be. Last couple of times I saved his neck was just luck on his part. I happened to come by. Why shouldn't he be dead? What's the use of the life of a shite like that? I hate your man at least as much as any of the rest of them do. Maybe more, now that I'm thinking. I got two little girls of my own. *(He looks at her. With contempt.)* Your brother.

> *(He leaves. ANNIE hears something. She kneels on the dirt, listening for the dead.)*

ANNIE: Yes? I can hear you. Yes. You're high up ... yes. You dropped a gold coin through the slats? Yes, it's shining down there in the mud, you can see it. And now you're scrambling down somewhere. Under a bridge? Yes. And the light on the river is like ... what? Metal? Hammered tin. Yes. Then what? The sound of a boot, someone there, standing...wait, wait. Oh, someone else ... you want to talk about the last moments? Yes? The wind of the train as its headlight comes out of the tunnel. The thunder of it, heat, it's a hot night, and, yes, you're holding something, a piece of paper, a letter? Something, something white, the wind of the subway flutters it like a what? A moth, a moth's wings, the paper you're holding, yes, and it's so simple, a step, just a step, the simplest thing ... I can't hear you anymore. Who is this now? Wait, wait, oh ... yes? You're wrapped, swaddled in, what, a blanket? A quilt. Brown and black diamonds on it, yes, wrapped too tight, your feet are — wait, I can't, a dog barking, yes, and then ...? No, yes ... you have to, I can't, it's too, there are too many voices now, I can't ... wait — *(suddenly she can hear one voice clearly)* — ah, hello, love, who are you? Something about stars? Yes? Turning like ... what? Doorknobs. Shining. Black, black night, and the stars are turning, bright, turning, yes. Opening the door to ... what? This. Where we are now. Yes. Yes.

(IZZY has entered and has been watching her. She speaks to us.)

IZZY: It's hard not to believe her, isn't it? It's like she's throwing a party. And she's a marvelous hostess, attentive, curious, she has a knack. So much better with the dead than with us, the living. For us, she only has the handful of questions. And we never answer them right.

(ANNIE is now in a scene with PAUL.)

ANNIE: You're starting a journey. You're in a wood. Describe it. Describe it to me like I'm standing next to you and I'm blind.

PAUL: Black trees, no, it's black stuff hanging from them. Bats. It's bats. They're hanging upside down. Sleeping.

ANNIE: So we won't wake them up.

PAUL: We just gotta be quiet.

ANNIE: Right. So we're past that. Past the bats. Now we come to a body of water. Describe it.

PAUL: Body of water? Lake, pond, river, what?

ANNIE: Sure, anything. Just water. Water of some kind. You choose.

PAUL: Well, maybe there's a hose. Someone left a hose on somewhere.

ANNIE: Uh-huh.

PAUL: So there's this stream, well, not a stream, hose-water, coming down this bank of mud. Looks like a snake.

ANNIE: Uh-huh. And now I'm supposed to ask you ... you cross it somehow —

PAUL: — what do you mean "supposed to ask me"? Is this a test?

ANNIE: Well, kind of.

PAUL: I hate tests. You know that, Annie. Why you giving me a test?

ANNIE: It's not a test like you mean. It's just for fun. Psychological, you know. You find out things about how you think.

PAUL: Why do you want to find out things about how I think?

ANNIE: Not, you know, specifically *you* so much –

PAUL: – why you giving me a test?

ANNIE: – like, there are these symbols in it. Like you get asked, there's a bear, what is the bear like, what do you do to the bear, you know? And the bear means ... it's a symbol, the bear ...

PAUL: Gotta kill it, right?

ANNIE: Not necessarily –

PAUL: 'Cause you got this *bear* standing in your way, you can't just *walk around it*, even if it's just like a story, you have to, right, kill it? No choice. *(Pause.)* So what's the bear, you know, what does it *mean?* *(Pause.)* You were going to say.

ANNIE: Your father. It's the symbol for your father.

PAUL: Well, fuck. You should have told me.

ANNIE: Well, see, that's kind of the point.

PAUL: 'Cause now I can't do it. I'm all self-conscious. I'd be thinking, "Ooh, can't give myself away. Ooh, did I just come off as some sick fuck? Was that the *right answer?*"

ANNIE: It's just for fun. It doesn't really mean anything.

PAUL: Well, sure it does. Sure it does. Surprised you didn't bring your notepad, jot this shit down. *(Imitates her.)* "Oh dear, bats? Did he just say, 'Bats'?" So, yeah, O.K., what was that first part?

ANNIE: The forest?

PAUL: Yeah, getting off on the right fucking foot *there*.

ANNIE: It's just, you know, where you feel you are at this point in your life right now. It's just the present tense.

PAUL: Uh huh. And the water? You had a question about it? The "body of water" from the hose?

ANNIE: Well, it's just, um, how you get across it, which is, in this case pretty ...

PAUL: Well, you got to turn it off, right? Go find out who left it running, find the spigot and turn that sucker off, right?

ANNIE: Right.

PAUL: So what's it mean?

ANNIE: Well, um, water is usually associated with, um ...

PAUL: With what?

ANNIE: Well, with *love*. So how you deal with it, you know, some people see, like a lake, and they dive into it or something ...

PAUL: And then there's me.

ANNIE: Yeah.

PAUL: Someone like me.

ANNIE: Yeah.

PAUL: Kinda different.

ANNIE: Yeah.

> *(They look at each other. PAUL begins laughing a bit. ANNIE joins him. They're not quite sure why this is so funny. But it is. End of scene. ANNIE exits.)*

IZZY: She's still going to the prison. She's never been a cook, but she spends the day before going through my mother's dusty cookbooks, the bindings coming off in her hands sometimes, looking for difficult recipes. Usually sweet. Then she brings it in for the warden. Never anything easy. Blackberry cheesecake one time, blackberries picked from our own rock slopes. She comes home one afternoon with a bucket full of them. She's got bruises and scratches up and down her legs and arms, blood and flattened mosquitoes dotting her

(MORE)

IZZY (cont'd): forehead. If he ever ate the stuff, which I sincerely doubt, I'm sure he could always taste it like ashes in his mouth, the joyless work she put into the things. But I suppose that was the point for her. Penance or something.

> *(ANNIE, wearing white gloves, a headscarf, a sundress and sunglasses, visits with PAUL. As usual, she's having difficulty breathing easily and she still shakes a bit.)*

PAUL: You look like a movie star.

ANNIE: Well, sure. That's me.

PAUL: What's with the sunglasses?

ANNIE: There's something in my eyes.

PAUL: What?

ANNIE: Poison ivy. Also my hands.

PAUL: How'd that happen?

ANNIE: Picking blackberries.

PAUL: Why were you picking blackberries, Lynx Cat?

ANNIE: Something I made for your warden, Mr. Brennan.

PAUL: What do you want to do a thing like that for?

ANNIE: He's been kind to you. *(Pause.)* Hasn't he? *(Pause.)* Hasn't he? *(Pause.)* Paul? Have they laid off at all?

PAUL: I wish you hadn't talked to him.

ANNIE: Well, I wanted to know. You wouldn't tell me.

PAUL: I'm all right.

ANNIE: Of course you aren't.

> *(Pause.)*

PAUL: You do, you look like a movie star. Ruth Champion, *Bicycle Built for Two*. Must have seen that twenty times.

ANNIE: Why that one? It's so hokey, that one. All that grinning. I couldn't stand it.

PAUL: They're having that party, they're dancing and singing, "Daisy, Daisy, give me your answer do," and this little girl comes down in her nightgown and everyone's saying, "What are you doing up?" and "Go back to bed, Kitty" but she's, you know, *determined*, she wants to stay up, she wants to *sing* and first it's this sort of racy song that she suggests, "Where Were You Last Night, Brother?" or something, and they all shout her down about that, but then she talks Ruth into doing a song and a dance with her, right there in her nightgown with everybody watching. And she's got dimples, and then she gets a little tired and someone picks her up and takes her up the stairs to bed, just carries her up the stairs because she's so sleepy and she's limp in his arms and she's smiling because she had such a good time down there in her nightgown. There's a kind of, it's a perfect thing. That little girl, I don't remember her name.

(Pause.)

ANNIE *(with difficulty)*: I'll tell you what I'm worried about, Paulie, when you get out ... ?

PAUL *(suddenly remembering)*: One of the times I saw it, you know? It was one afternoon, a matinee? There was this girl's birthday party there. Must have been seventeen little girls there and they've all put on their best dresses and they're squirming around on their seats and giggling a lot and whispering to each other. No parents or anything, just the little girls. And they smell like, you know, <u>cake</u> and I'm watching them watch it, you know, and when it gets to/the part –

ANNIE *(carefully, disturbed)*: How do you know what they smelled like?

PAUL: 'Cause I was sitting right with them. It was cake with chocolate icing, she had it on her fingers.

ANNIE: Who?

PAUL: Jeanette? Suzette? *(He's sure.)* Jeanette. She let me lick it off her fingers.

ANNIE: Where did you do that? Lick it off her fingers.

PAUL: I helped her. She had to go to the bathroom, so I helped her.

ANNIE: Oh yes?

PAUL: And then she helped me.

ANNIE: She helped you.

PAUL: She wanted to. Said she did it for her brother. Said she liked it. *(Off her look.)* She liked it.

ANNIE: And then what happened?

PAUL: What? Nothing. We went back to the movie. Saw the whole thing. I held her hand.

   (Long pause.)

ANNIE *(quiet, intense, internal)*: Will it never stop? Will it never stop? Will you *never stop?* Will there ever be a day when thinking about you and what you might have done, what you might do doesn't ...? When you don't ... worry me?

PAUL: I told you I'm all right. And I get out in a month. I'll be back home with you. You don't have to worry about me. Not me. We'll have us some fun times, Annie Lynx Cat.

ANNIE: Yeah, we'll have fun. High times in the old house.

PAUL: We'll go to the pictures. That's what we'll do. Take in a flick.

   (ANNIE, alone, listening for Oedipus.)

ANNIE: I put out my hand to the bear, he lays his heavy dry paw into it and we wander farther and farther into the woods as it gets darker and darker. I think at first that I'm leading him, but it turns out he's leading me. His step is sure, if weary. There's a light--yellow, just a pinprick bouncing between the branches. It gets brighter as we get closer. It's got to be coming from behind a lit window. I think, oh, he's taking me to his house, which I immediately realize is ridiculous, I mean, he's a *bear*, it's not like he's going to live in a *house*, right? But we are getting closer and closer to it, hand in hand. And you're right, it's just like you imagine it. Thatched roof, curl of smoke coming out of the chimney. It's got a softness to it, this house, a *rounded* thing, like a cat sleeping in a little patch of green grass. Nothing bad could be inside such a place. And we stand outside it, he and I, and it belongs to neither of us, such a place. We can't even imagine the kind of people who would live such a blessed life – certainly
   (MORE)

ANNIE (cont'd): no one we've ever known. The windows are steamed up with the warmth of their lives, whoever they are, and we can't see in. The glass reflects us back to ourselves. Our hollow eye sockets, the stupid expressions of woe and exile. And it's getting colder and colder. He can feel me shivering next to him and he puts his arms around me, the grey brown fur is coarse against my cheek. I know he thinks he's comforting me. And knowing that he thinks that, I am content.

(A door opens. PAUL is there, home from prison.)

ANNIE: But the journey is not over. Not yet. And we go on.

IZZY (to us): That was the closest he ever came to being caught, Pammie MacAfee, because that was the only time he went so far as to break into a girl's house. But that was all they could get him for. You can't put a man in jail for staring at a little girl, no matter how hard he's doing it. And the goings-on in the tree house? Maybe all they did up there was to have tea parties. That's all he said they did anyway. The only people who knew different were the little girls, who weren't so little anymore, most of them. All the Susies and Sallies and Edies sunk now into adulthood with married names and children of their own tugging their skirts in the grocery store. Except of course, there was Annie, watching from behind the cart as she wheeled it down the aisles. There were women of a certain age who would catch a glimpse of Paul as he stood perusing the canned goods, and they would flinch, almost imperceptibly. They needn't have worried. Even if he looked up at them, his eyes would just roll over their faces like a wave. He never remembered them. They had become invisible to him. It was their daughters he could see now. The little towhead girls burbling monologues, patting at their mothers' hips as they pointed longingly to whatever looked sweetest on the shelves. The girls would crane their necks as their mothers yanked them away, trying to wave back to the nice man with the gentle eyes. On the way home Annie and her brother don't speak as they wheel the wire cart down the street. And the home they're headed toward? It's a mansion, not to put too fine a point on it. An American palace. A ball room, a billiard table, twenty guest rooms, a dining table that once sat one hundred people, with delicate gilt chairs that took the weight of tycoons and duchesses, admirals and foreign royalty. To say that the place has been neglected, however, is to put it far too mildly. The slate roof has fallen into three of the five great attics and the sound of squirrels and other wildlife in the upper rooms can be quite distracting on a still day. Beds have become burrows for mice and the horsehair from the silk upholstery has been strewn through the halls in bird flight as the sparrows carry it for their nests in the rafters of the ballroom. Chandeliers, wrapped in muslin dust cloths years ago, look like enormous hornets' nests, bearded and ribbed with grey dust, streaked with grime. Ivy has sealed all the windows, closing the entire house in a dappled green aquarium light. I decide at last that it

(MORE)

IZZY (cont'd): is time. I've got to get her out of there. I search for tracks through the scat and dust on the parquet floors. Human tracks, as opposed to the skittering marks of the animals on their errands. I follow the ones I think are hers as they thread through the hallways until I reach the ballroom, an empty vastness, the air animated only by the occasional flight of birds to corners and high rafters. The floor is a sea of dust, down the center of which is the seam of her bare footprints leading to where she stands in the center, lost in thought.

    (ANNIE is barefoot.)

ANNIE: Hello, stranger.

IZZY: Hello.

ANNIE: To what do I owe the pleasure?

IZZY: Just stopping by the old hearth and home.

ANNIE: Home Sweet Home.

IZZY: I'm only surprised it's still standing. You must have mice running over your face all night.

ANNIE: It's not so bad.

IZZY: I didn't even look for Paul's burrow. Where is he holed up?

ANNIE: Where do you think?

    (IZZY thinks for a moment and it's obvious.)

IZZY: The nursery?

ANNIE: Got it in one.

IZZY: Isn't it teeming with wildlife? I thought the roof had caved in up there.

ANNIE: He likes them. He feeds them Kellogg's. He's up there like Francis of Assisi, covered with blue jays. He's a picture.

IZZY: Well, I hope they peck his face off.

ANNIE: They won't, they're crazy about him. He sings to them.

IZZY *(fascinated in spite of herself)*: What does he sing?

ANNIE: Pretty sappy stuff. From movie musicals mostly. He's quite a crooner.

IZZY: Shirley Temple numbers?

(*Bad little pause.*)

ANNIE: Did you say why you came?

IZZY: I thought it was time.

ANNIE: Time for what?

IZZY: Time to get you out of here.

ANNIE: You've made the decision, is that it?

IZZY: Yes.

ANNIE: You consult with Eddie about this?

IZZY: Of course I didn't. Why would I talk to Eddie about anything?

ANNIE: I thought you two were tight.

IZZY: We're barely on speaking terms.

ANNIE: So it was just you, all on your own-ee-o, decided enough was enough?

IZZY: It is, you know it is. You've done enough for him. If he wants to live in this palace of rats, that's his lookout, let the place cave in on the son of a bitch, good riddance, but not you.

ANNIE: This is my home.

IZZY: Of course it's not.

ANNIE: It is. I feel entirely at home here.

IZZY: So you wander the hallways, remembering the good times, is that it?

ANNIE: There were some good times.

IZZY: Were there?

ANNIE: Parties they threw? People dancing. Right here.

IZZY: We weren't allowed down.

ANNIE: No, but we'd sit at the top of the stairs and listen. You could imagine it. The musicians playing over there, the ladies lifting their arms and – *(she dances.)* It wasn't all terrible.

IZZY: You want to know one of my first memories? Father running after Mother, trying to stop her screaming. Him bunching her dress in his fist to pull her down. That's when I realize how old she is. She's so exhausted, I think, from running such a short distance. The way she was panting. But what made her think she'd ever get away from him? Then he's holding her down on the floor, his hand over her mouth. I don't know how long it lasted. How long he had to wait before she'd get up and go on with it all. Being his wife.

ANNIE: I saw him kiss her fingers.

IZZY: You did not.

ANNIE: They were standing in the garden. It was before a party. She'd just picked a white flower for his buttonhole and put it on him. She patted his chest. He put his hand over hers on his chest/ and then –

IZZY: You know that didn't happen. You saw it in a movie.

ANNIE: You're so hard on them. They couldn't help being what they were.

IZZY: Is that right? Is that what you say to Paul? "It's all right, Paul, I know you can't help being what you are?" That must be a comfort to him.

ANNIE: That's not what I say to him.

IZZIE: No? What do you say?

ANNIE: I just tell him, you know, that he has to try, as hard as he's ever tried to do anything ...

IZZY: Try?

ANNIE: Not to, you know, ever, ever ...

IZZY: What

ANNIE: Never again. I tell him, You just have to try as hard as you've ever tried to do anything not to ... *(IZZY won't help her.)* Not to touch them. The girls. Ever. Ever again.

> *(Long pause.)*

IZZY: Pathetic.

ANNIE: It's the best I can do.

IZZY: No, the best you can do would be to leave him.

ANNIE: He wouldn't be able to take care of himself.

IZZY: So what?

ANNIE: He might, if I don't watch him, he might ...

IZZY: Yes? So this time they might put the bastard away for good. Get him off the streets at last.

ANNIE: They'd kill him. In prison. They almost did as it was, even without –

IZZY: Would that be such a terrible thing? His death?

ANNIE: Yes.

IZZY: Why, Annie? Look at what he is. Why are you doing this?

ANNIE: He's my brother.

IZZY: He's my brother too. I wouldn't cross the street to spit in his face.

ANNIE: I owe him.

IZZY: What on earth do you owe him for?

ANNIE: You want to know *my* first memory? I'm looking up, I must have been in a crib, and he's just grinning at me. And he's got a peacock feather, it's

> *(MORE)*

ANNIE (cont'd): green and blue, you know, and he's running it over my legs and arms. It felt delicious. And every time I try to catch at it, he gets it away. I guess he was tickling me.

IZZY: It's the way you play with a cat.

ANNIE *(realizing it, somewhat taken aback)*: Yes.

IZZY: You were his little lynx cat.

ANNIE: Yes.

(*Long pause.*)

IZZY: I wish I'd known what he was when we were all kids together. I'd have stood up in my playpen and wrung his neck.

ANNIE: He deserves love.

IZZY: Of course he doesn't.

ANNIE: Everyone deserves love.

IZZY: That's the stupidest thing I've ever heard.

ANNIE: He *has* my love.

IZZY: You can't mean that.

ANNIE: I do. I love him.

IZZY *(appalled)*: This is sick. You've become sick with this. Him. Please, please, Annie, come away with me.

ANNIE: I can't.

IZZY: It's time. You know it is.

ANNIE: I can't. I can't leave him.

IZZY: Yes. You can. You have to.

ANNIE: What will happen to him?

IZZY: I don't know. I don't care about him. I care about you.

ANNIE: If you care about me, help me with him.

IZZY: I can't.

ANNIE: Well, then that's all we can say to each other.

IZZY: Please, Annie. *(She puts her hand out.)* You're done. It's finally finished. No one could ever have done more for him.

ANNIE: No. *(Pause.)* Not yet.

IZZY: When?

ANNIE: I have to figure it out. I'll figure it out. Then I'll come. I promise. *(IZZY leaves. ANNIE turns, she's heard something.)* Yes?

> *(She kneels, listening. EDDIE comes on, he's Paul's twin. He speaks directly to us.)*

EDDIE: No, I'm not him. I'm the other one. Eddie. Not that anyone's ever been all that crazy about *me* either. I'm quite a peach. Locking little sisters in closets and so forth, you heard about that. And that ain't the half of it. But at least I'm not him. That's pretty much all I've ever had going for me. That I'm not him. So you're thinking, what gives with this family? How come they're all nuts? And I'm the boy to tell you. You want to know what happened here? At first it's just a romance novel, one of the racy ones. The girl from the wrong class—Josie, the Irish scullery maid--hooks the heart of Lloyd, the millionaire's son. Pretty hackneyed stuff at first. He gets her pregnant, oh dear, but Daddy never finds out, 'cause Lloyd invents a dying mammy in the home place Josie's gotta go tend, so she's safely out of sight somewhere when she has the thing, then it's rushed off for adoption lickety-split. Josie comes back to work looking like death on a soda cracker, and anyone with two eyes in his head can figure out why, but no one, not even the folks below stairs, knows the whole sordid story. And you'd think that'd be the end of it, right? It's the sort of thing happens every day of the week, often in the best families, and no one's the wiser. But no, not with this pair. 'Cause, what do you know, he's nuts about her. He knows he can't keep her in the house anymore but he's got to keep her someplace. He fires her himself, makes a terrific show out of it, but almost ruins it by winking at her as he slams the door of the cab on her. Thing is, the cab takes her and her tiny trove to a nice little apartment several neighborhoods

(MORE)

EDDIE (cont'd): away, where she gets to stretch out for him on a good wide bed with soft sheets, while the pretty lace curtains are closed up tight. Splendid, right? But no. He knows how this is supposed to work: he's supposed to find some thin-lipped blue-blood to marry and then the pressure's off, everybody's happy, his parents, his wife, his mistress in the pleasant apartment. Nothing could be easier to pull off in fact, he's quite a catch. Every time he turns around, some eligible girl is dropping her fan at his feet in an opera box or bumping into him at the dances and apologizing prettily, but he can't stay interested. He spends the nights dancing forgettable girls around his daddy's ballroom and all the time he's thinking about the one who used to clean the floor, skirt hoisted up above her red knees. Pretty soon he's dropping his cigarette on the front steps and telling her address to the cabbie as they trot away. He looks back at the place, it's lit up like a ship, music pealing from the tall open windows. He doesn't care. He just wants her. Pretty soon his parents start looking at him funny when he tosses his coattails behind him to sit down at dinner. It's a silent trap of a house, this place, and he can't see his way out of it. He's on the verge of confessing everything and blowing his inheritance, the whole shebang, when the most amazing stroke of luck occurs. Scare headlines on the society pages: a sudden storm, a boating accident. The rest of the party survive it, but his parents drown together. He wears crepe for a year and then brings his bride home from a quiet wedding out of town. No one knows her. Well, that's not true. There is one old servant, the one Lloyd couldn't bear to fire when he took over his daddy's house, and the old man has to look the other way when she walks past because he doesn't trust his face not to betray him. It has been years now and she's changed, God knows, but he knows Madam for what she is. What she was. Thing is, she's no dummy. And she's a stunner, there's no dispute about that. Those who thought her crass when she first arrived come to find her charmingly direct as the years go by. Her husband can't believe his luck when he looks down through the candlesticks at her. He thought he'd just live off the pile his father left him, but she convinces him to keep the business going; she chivvies him into deal after deal, and she's never wrong. She eyes the competition over the turtle soup and then tells him in bed at night what she picked up while dancing with an ambassador or playing whist with some senator's wife. Then one night there's a young comer down at her end of the table. This is the kid who's been making quite a splash downtown. He comes from nowhere as far as anyone can figure out, did his bit in the trenches and then came home and started his little empire with a fistful of money. He's got no refinement whatsoever. Nobody's dear old granddad is safe from him, nor is granddad's pile of dusty dollars. He's a killer. And not bad to look at. They hit it off right away, and by the end of the evening, whenever he puts his mouth close to her ear to speak over the din of the china and chatter, she gets a shiver of lust running through her, lights her up like a Christmas tree. She's never felt like this. And the thing of it is that neither has he, and him being such a forthright

(MORE)

EDDIE (cont'd): fellow, he tells her right to her face that night, just as he's taking her out on the dance floor one too many times to be quite discreet. Well, it's a disaster, of course. But what can they do? She's lying so much to her husband that even he gets suspicious, the dear old goat. She's never home now, and every time she gets in late from the ladies' auxiliary, or wherever she said she was, her eyes are just a mite too bright. Lloyd's having the worst luck all of a sudden, the business starts going belly-up. Her tips aren't so foolproof anymore, and there's one company that's gunning for him now, he can't get out of their crosshairs. Every time he beefs about it to her, she goes quiet and looks flushed. She's got no advice for him, so the poor fool decides to trust his own instincts, which are not to be trusted. Then comes the morning when he realizes what's been done to him. The kid, that boy who ate right out of his silver spoons not so long ago, that punk as good as owns him. The whole thing's gone kaput. But that's not the end of his day. He gets home that night to find she's gone, the wife, left that very night with the kid himself. He could pursue them, they haven't been gone long. He plays out that awful scene in his head, the one that takes place in the lovebirds' swank cabin, where the champagne is on ice and the negligee is draped across the bed. He can see it all. But what he couldn't bear would be to look into her face and see what hasn't been there for him for years, he realizes it now, years he hasn't seen it ... there's only one thing to do. He doesn't have to think about it more than a few seconds. He goes down into the gunroom and cocks his best one and puts it into his mouth and pulls the trigger. When the widow remarries and almost immediately gets pregnant, you'd think that she'd be the happiest woman on earth, right? But she's acting funny, pacing the floor at night, talking to herself. People assume it's just the pregnancy, but when she gives birth to healthy twin boys, she's no better. Sure, they throw parties every now and then, lavish affairs that would pauper just about anyone else in their circle, but the guests show up as if at gunpoint and no one seems to have any fun. And she's not the dependable hostess she once was. She gets herself pie-eyed at her end of the table and starts talking a blue streak until she's suddenly sobbing into her napkin, or she can't stop laughing, which is almost worse. The house begins to fall apart, roof slate starts collecting in the unweeded garden. Rats start rummaging in the pantries. Nobody's paying much attention. The help gets harder to keep; word on the street is that the whole household gets fired every six months. Except one. The old geezer her first husband couldn't fire. She keeps him on board, no one knows why. All he does is glare at her. The two girls follow us twins and we're pretty much left to ourselves. When we pass her room in the hall, we can hear our mother sobbing or talking to herself. It becomes a rare event even to glimpse her in the halls. Shocking too – she looks like hell. We study the portrait in the hall, that sleek woman with the limpid eyes, and we see nothing of the bent shadow with a ducking head that our mother has become. Every week or so, dinner with nanny is interrupted when Father steps into the nursery. No one, including him,

(MORE)

EDDIE (cont'd): quite knows what to say, so he goes around the table, absently patting heads and smiling unconvincingly until he leaves and we can go on eating. He's just another stranger, just one more person who has nothing to do with us. So no one sees it coming when one morning the upstairs maid finds Mother has hanged herself. The cry goes up and Father is running down the hall in his nightshirt. Then there's complete silence. It goes on for a long time. Long enough, we find out later, for him to read her note. Then there's the sound. It's not really human, but it's definitely coming from an animal, and it's repeated, like a motor turning over and not catching. Paul and I run in there and see him at it. He's stabbing at his eyes with the pins of her brooches, the diamond ones he gave her back in the good old days. The ones she could never bear to keep in the safe and tossed like loose change from her pocket on her dressing table at night. The blood is spattering all over her bed, the carpet, and also her bare feet, which are swinging, pale and boney, right near his face. He didn't even cut her down. The girls are screaming and Paulie's just standing there with his mouth open. And now the servants are running in and trying to cope with it all. Which is when I see the note, sliding from the bed to the floor. I read it later, after he's taken off with Annie and the house is finally quiet except for the weeping below stairs. It's about what you'd expect. She knew, you see, from pretty early on. She even thinks, she says, she might have known it from the very beginning, though she can't stand to think about that. There was something familiar about him from the start, something she recognized. But she couldn't help herself. Flesh of her flesh, but she couldn't help herself. And over the years, the truth she kept swallowing back, that snake in her belly ... in the end, it just wouldn't stop its battering against her clenched teeth. It wanted out. So it drove her crazy, hanged her, then slithered out into the dying rooms of this dying place and took up residence for good. But here's what I think: There were a lot of snakes in this house and she could smell every one of them. Her husband wasn't the only one of her sons who worried her. After all the lying she'd done, she was a connoisseur of deceit. Could sense it anywhere. Oh, you know she only had to walk into that nursery and look at my brother to see what he wasn't saying shining like wet paint all over his face. Not to mention the little girl gnawing her fingers in the other corner of the room. But what could she do? She knew it was all her fault. The children are bound to pay when they're the spawn of such a marriage. *(He smiles.)* We're all monsters, see? Not just him, not just me. Every single one of us. That's what my sister can't seem to tell you about. We should none of us have ever seen the light of day. What can we expect from life? Love? Happiness? Fulfillment? *(He laughs.)* It can't go well for the likes of us.

> *(He leaves. ANNIE is tapping and listening, alone at the kitchen table. It feels like it did at the top of the play. IZZY comes in and speaks to us.)*

IZZY: Familiar? Yeah, here we are again. I just want to tell you where she is.

(MORE)

IZZY (cont'd): It's the old kitchen. This is where she spends most of her time. Making meals for two in a kitchen fitted out to feed a banquet hall. It hasn't seen a lit match for years, but you could roast a good-sized boar on a spit in the fireplace there, it's that big. There's a radio that's something of a conundrum – either that or a miracle, depending on your view of things. It shouldn't work. The electricity should be kaput in this place, right? But sometimes it does. Mostly it doesn't though. It's like the demented dowager in the corner everyone's given up on 'cause she hasn't spoken in years who suddenly tells you a plausible story about going boating with Thomas Edison. Disconcerting, if mildly entertaining. My brother's been out all night, so she's talking to my father while she waits for him. It's the usual set of questions, the ones she's asked us all, except my father's the only one who might be able to give her the real goods, at least on that last one. So far he hasn't.

ANNIE *(tapping)*: You've reached the end of the journey. What do you see? Describe it to me. Describe it to me like I'm standing next to you and I'm blind.

(Silence. They listen.)

IZZY: All the lines go dead. Happens every time.

(Silence. They listen. IZZY steps toward Annie and talks to her, ANNIE doesn't look up at her.)

IZZY: This is the part where you start to wonder, don't you, Annie? You start thinking, have I ever really heard anything? Anything at all? Or have I just been ruining my knuckles all these years, tapping messages to someone who never tapped back? Some dead man, who's, you know, *dead*. Was I making all that up? Just fooling myself? Hearing what I wanted to hear?

ANNIE: Shut up! I can't hear.

IZZY: No, you can't, can you? But really, honestly, did you ever?

ANNIE: Just because *you* can't,/doesn't –

IZZY: My question is: O.K., even if he exists, somehow, somewhere, dead, even if he's out there, down there somewhere, even if that's true – why would he want to talk to you? I'm very unclear on how this underworld of yours works. So he's just sitting around waiting for you to call him? You can just summon him and he'll come like a well-trained dog? Don't they have anything better to do, the dead? Isn't death, I don't know, *grander* than that? Why wouldn't he just forget you, forget all of this, move on to bigger things?

ANNIE *(controlled)*: I don't know how it works, all right? I wish I did, I spend my life trying to ... I just hear things. I can't argue with you about it because there's no logic to it. He speaks to me.

IZZY: How do you know it's him? Couldn't it be, I don't know, like listening in on a party line in some rural telephone exchange? Just voices in ether, wires crossed?

ANNIE: It's him.

IZZY: How do you know?

ANNIE: Because always, always, there is this sense of ... I don't want to tell you, you'll just ...

IZZY: What?

ANNIE: Love. A sense of that. His love for me. It's something I know.

IZZY: Uh-huh ...

ANNIE: I knew you wouldn't believe me.

IZZY: It's not a question of believing you, I'm just –

ANNIE: – he hasn't forgotten me.

IZZY: He's dead, Annie, it's not like /he –

ANNIE *(emphatic)*: He hasn't forgotten me. He's waiting for me.

> *(Pause.)*

IZZY *(to us)*: Yes, well, that's a conversation we didn't have that night. But I guess that's how it would have gone if we had. But I wasn't there. And this is what happened.

> *(IZZY leaves. Silence. Suddenly, PAUL enters. It should be a shock, loud, abrupt, surprising ANNIE into a yelp.)*

PAUL: Sheesh, Annie, scare me half to death, why don't you? What you doing up this late?

ANNIE: Just waiting for you.

PAUL: How come?

(*Pause.*)

ANNIE: You been in the tree house all this time?

(*Pause.*)

PAUL: Think I might want to move out there when it gets warm again.

ANNIE: Throw some tea parties?

(*Pause.*)

PAUL: I saw a girl yesterday. Thought I'd ask her maybe. She's got a little grey coat and a little grey hat with a bunny fur trim. Looks like bunny fur. I might ask if I can touch it.

ANNIE: Paul. Paulie. Do you know that if you touched that girl, even a little bit, you could go back to jail and never get out?

PAUL: I guess.

ANNIE: Do you, though? Do you really know that?

PAUL: Sure.

ANNIE: It's the truth, Paulie.

PAUL: I know that. I do.

ANNIE: Still you were going to ask/that girl –

PAUL: Just thinking about it. (*Pause.*) She might like it. She looked like she might like it.

ANNIE: Do you know it's wrong?

PAUL: That's what everyone says.

ANNIE: Do you think it is?

PAUL: What if she likes me?

ANNIE: It doesn't matter.

PAUL: It doesn't matter?

ANNIE: No. She's too little, that girl, to know what you're thinking about. You know that.

PAUL: Yes.

ANNIE: You've always known that.

PAUL: Yes.

ANNIE: Even with me.

>   *(Pause.)*

PAUL: But you liked it.

ANNIE: No.

PAUL: You did. You told me so.

>   *(ANNIE begins to cry.)*

ANNIE: I hated it.

PAUL: You said you loved me.

ANNIE: I did. And I hated it.

>   *(PAUL looks at her while she cries.)*

PAUL: Well, here's a fine how-di-do.

ANNIE: It's never going to stop, is it?

>   *(Pause.)*

PAUL: I know what you want me to say.

ANNIE: It's all right. You can tell me. It's never going to end, is it?

PAUL: First time I made a little girl cry, first time I made one bleed, I took her back to the playground and I gave her a popsicle and we sat together until she stopped crying. Then I told her to tell her mother she'd fallen down on something, fell down in a weird way, but that she was all right. She was fine, wasn't she? And she didn't have to talk about me, did she? Wouldn't say anything to anyone? I didn't leave until she said that was so. I came back here in the late afternoon and I got up on the roof. I made myself look all the way down, right to the bricks in the garden path, 'cause I knew that's where I was going to end up when I jumped. Seemed like the best thing to do. It was all so clear, suddenly. My whole life. I could see all the way to here, Annie. This kitchen tonight. And I didn't see the point of it. Seemed like the easiest thing in the world, just step off, that's all, like stepping down into a street. How hard could that be, right?

ANNIE: Why didn't you do it?

PAUL: Heard something.

ANNIE: What?

PAUL: Like a kitten mewing. It was right under my feet. Couldn't figure out what it was for the longest time.

ANNIE (realizing): Oh, no.

PAUL: Then I knew.

ANNIE: No, no.

PAUL: That was you in the attic closet. Right below me.

ANNIE: God Almighty.

PAUL: So I went down and opened up that door. Saw you in the dark there. Your little cat's eyes. Took you in my arms and carried you downstairs.

ANNIE: Oh no.

PAUL: And I never went back up on the roof again.

ANNIE: It was me.

PAUL: It was you, Kitty. You're what I came back down here for.

(Pause as they consider this.)

ANNIE: Have you ever been happy?

PAUL: Sure, Kitty. Plenty of times. Remember when we went swimming that time, that beach with the starfish?

ANNIE: I don't remember it, starfish.

PAUL: Sure you do. *(She shakes her head.)* You had a green tin shovel, brand new, for building sand castles, and a sun hat that was too big for you. It kept blowing off and I kept having to run down the beach to get it for you. And every time I took off after it, you'd laugh.

ANNIE: That was some other little girl.

PAUL: No, I remember.

ANNIE: One of your other little girls.

PAUL: It was you.

ANNIE: I can't imagine it.

PAUL: You with your little shovel on the beach?

ANNIE: Me laughing.

PAUL: You laughed all the time, mostly at me. You were happy.

ANNIE: I've never been happy, Paulie.

PAUL: You were happy with me. I know that for a fact.

ANNIE: You have no idea who I am, Paul, never did.

PAUL: I know you, little Lynx Cat, I look in your eyes and I know exactly who you are.

ANNIE: I don't know what you're seeing when you look at me.

PAUL: That little girl.

ANNIE: That girl's been dead a long time, Paul. Years and years. You killed her.

PAUL: Aw, Annie, you shouldn't be like that/with me –

ANNIE: – I shouldn't, Paul? You know what? If I had looked down from the roof and seen my life laid out before me like that, the whole damn thing, right up to this moment right now? You and me having this little chat in this kitchen here? I'd have backed up too. But I would have backed up so that I could get a good flying start. Would have gone off that roof like a kid jumping into a waterhole on a hot sunny day, wind-milling my arms and legs, whooping fit to beat the band. *(Pause.)* If I could have been given to see what you saw. If I could have been given to know what would happen to all of us.*(Pause.)* Do you see the point of it now? Your life?

PAUL: I guess I lost track of it somehow. The point. Or maybe there isn't one. Doesn't have to be.

ANNIE: I think there does, Paul. I think there has to be.

PAUL: Well then I guess I don't have one. My life, it doesn't have a point.

ANNIE: Well that's a sad, sad thing, isn't it? Mine neither.

PAUL: Well, of course *you've* got one. A point to your life.

ANNIE: What is that?

PAUL: You're the only thing ever made any sense to me.

> *(Long pause while they look at each other.)*

ANNIE: I went to see a pharmacist the other day. Went clear across the city, found a nice fellow who doesn't know me from Charley's aunt. I walked away with something I've been thinking about showing you for a few days. And the way we've been talking tonight, I'm thinking this just might be the right time. *(She takes out a vial.)* It wasn't hard to get, turns out. I just talked to him about this dog of mine, a "beloved" dog, a "big, beloved dog," "been in the family for a long time," and I didn't want to have to see it suffer anymore.

> *(She gives the vial to him.)*

PAUL *(thoughtfully holding the vial)*: You don't want to see it suffer.

ANNIE: He listened really hard, very sympathetic. Sweet face on the guy. He goes in the back room and makes this up. Says he doesn't normally hand out this kind of thing, but he had to do the same himself one time. Nearly broke his heart, he said, but he came up with this special, dog meant so much to him. His own recipe.

PAUL: What kind of dog, did he say?

ANNIE: Doberman. One of those police-type dogs. Name of Ricky.

PAUL: What was wrong with it?

ANNIE: Well, it seems he was a skittish creature. Man picked him up as a stray and he was in pretty bad shape. What happens is, the dog just falls head-over-heels in love with him and they had a fine old time for awhile there. Until some new neighbors move in next door, folks with a passel of kids. Somehow this gets on Ricky's nerves, he starts snarling at them, baring his teeth and so forth. It was like he was a whole different dog around these kids, that's what the man said. Brought out the absolute worst in him, those kids did. So one day the man's leaving the house for work and don't you know, one of those kids is walking by the house and Ricky barrels past him, out the door like a flash and he's attacking that kid and oh, what a mess.

PAUL: Was she all right?

ANNIE: No, she wasn't, Paul. She was never going to be all right again. So you know what this man felt he had to do? Much as he loved that dog, he knew that dog just couldn't go on living. Because it was just a matter of time before some little girl was going to walk by again and that dog, that dog just couldn't help it, he would go for her. So he came up with this. It's homemade.

PAUL: Homemade's best.

ANNIE: Said it's quick as a wink and it just puts you to sleep.

PAUL: Like a dog you love.

ANNIE: Right. Then it'll do its business.

PAUL: What was it like? For Ricky? Did the man say?

ANNIE: Said they had a nice evening together. And then he poured the stuff

(MORE)

ANNIE (cont'd): into a little bowl of something – plain custard, I think – mixed it up for him well and he licked it right up. Then, he says, the dog just turns three times in a circle, right there at his feet, curls up and commences to snoring.

PAUL: The dog snored?

ANNIE: For a while anyway, until he wasn't snoring anymore.

PAUL: 'Cause he was dead.

ANNIE: That's right. Custard in his belly and a little doggie smile on his lips.

PAUL: Little doggie dead smile.

ANNIE: It was a nice death Ricky had. Don't you think?

PAUL: For a dog.

ANNIE: For anyone, Paul. For anyone. To have someone care so much about you that they take that kind of trouble to make good and sure you don't suffer even a little bit when your time comes.

PAUL: And my time has come. That what you're saying?

ANNIE: Yes, Paul. That's what I'm saying.

    (Pause.)

PAUL: So I just drink this?

ANNIE: Just break the wax seal there, see it there? You twist it off and/then, just –

PAUL: – but I'm bigger than a dog, did you/say – ?

ANNIE: – he told me this could do the trick for a creature of up to two-hundred pounds.

PAUL: *Big* dog.

ANNIE: Uh-huh.

PAUL: *Big* "beloved" dog.

ANNIE: Uh-huh.

(He laughs a little. She joins him. Then silence. They look at each other.)

ANNIE: So I'm just going to, um, go to my room, go lie down, you know, for a while. Leave you alone, let you have the place to yourself.

(She starts to leave, doesn't know quite how to manage this. Pauses behind him, almost touches him. Doesn't.)

PAUL: Annie? *(She is standing behind him.)* Thank you.

ANNIE: You're welcome.

(She leaves. He senses that she's gone, but doesn't want to look back to check. He's staring at the vial, which he has set in front of him on the table. Quickly, he reaches out, takes it, twists the cap off and then places the opened vial back in front of him in the same place. He stares at it fixedly for a few moments. He starts whistling some tune {"Daisy"?} under his breath and he backs his chair carefully away, as if trying not to wake the vial. When he gets the chair out from under the table he stands up and backs away, still staring at it. Then he's still. Suddenly he turns his back on it and goes directly over to a corner of the room, where there's a radio. He turns it on. It's between stations, sitting in static, so he fiddles with it until some kind of song comes on. He might sing with it, dance a bit, quite pointedly not looking at the vial on the table. Finally he switches off the radio, then turns and looks at the vial. He goes back to the table and sits down again, as if with a terrifying dinner companion. He stares at the vial. Long pause. Lights change, a sense of hours passing. ANNIE enters silently and looks at him.)

PAUL: I couldn't do it.

ANNIE: So I see.

PAUL: I'm sorry.

ANNIE: It was just a thought.

PAUL: I'm so sorry.

ANNIE: I didn't think you would. You've never done anything I asked you to do, never *not* done anything I asked you not to do. Why should you start now?

(With sudden violence, PAUL leaps up and grabs the vial and tries to put it to his mouth, but he can't, he throws it and smashes it in the sink. They look at each other. He starts to cry.)

PAUL: Goddamn it, Annie, why couldn't you help me?

ANNIE: Help you?

PAUL: You know me. I can't. I can't.

ANNIE: I know. I know.

(PAUL sits back down in his chair, his back to her, weeping.)

PAUL: I'm sorry.

ANNIE: I know.

(She starts to move around the kitchen, getting milk out, syrup, a pot.)

PAUL: What you doing?

ANNIE: I'm making us some hot chocolate.

PAUL: Why?

ANNIE: You like it, don't you?

PAUL: Yeah, sure.

ANNIE: You're tired. You've been up all night.

PAUL: I am tired, it's true.

ANNIE: I'll make you cinnamon toast and hot chocolate, then you'll go up to the nursery, go to sleep, and then we'll see what happens.

PAUL: We'll see what happens.

ANNIE: We'll see what happens tomorrow. Today. Looks like it'll be a nice one.

PAUL: Boy, listen to those birds! What a racket, huh?

ANNIE: Guess they're pretty excited about the sun coming up.

PAUL: They always are.

> *(During all this, ANNIE has been calmly lighting the stove, pouring milk into a pot, mixing the chocolate into the milk, stirring. Now she gets out a loaf of bread and a large knife. She slices the bread.)*

PAUL: Doesn't matter if it's cold or sunny, it can be miserable out, pissing rain, snow, they don't care, they still sing.

ANNIE: I've noticed that.

PAUL: Don't suppose they know much about anything, they just think, "oh, life," right?

ANNIE: I guess they know enough then.

PAUL: Guess so. And the thing is, Annie, I've been thinking, you know –

> *(Without warning, she stabs PAUL in the back with the bread knife. He slumps forward, his forehead hitting the table, dead. She's frozen where she stands. Silence. Suddenly, the radio comes on, it's static, between stations. She stares at it, then down at PAUL, then at the radio. The static organizes itself somehow into something rhythmic. She stares at the radio. It's like Morse code. Slowly, tenderly, she moves to the table and begins tapping, her hand next to PAUL's head. A kind of a conversation ensues. Lights slowly down. IZZY alone.)*

IZZY: And that's how they found her. So it's not surprising, really, the way it all turned out. *(We hear ANNIE in the dark, her teeth chattering. But we can't see her.)* I did what I could. I did what she asked me to do.

> *(IZZY meets up with BRENNAN, outside the prison, where he met ANNIE.)*

BRENNAN: Can't say I see the resemblance.

IZZY: No, I haven't her courage.

BRENNAN: Is that what you call it?

IZZY: Well, what would you call it?

BRENNAN: Cussedness? Sure, she's mad too, isn't she?

IZZY: So why are you helping her? Couldn't you lose your job?

BRENNAN: I run the damn place, who's going to fire me? You?

IZZY: I don't know why she should trust you.

BRENNAN: Ach. We're old friends.

IZZY: Are you in love with her or something?

BRENNAN *(laughs)*: Wouldn't that just fix me? To fall in love with the likes of her. *(Serious.)* No, Miss. That type chills my blood. She doesn't understand but only the *idea* of things – that's all she can get ahold of – the *idea* of this, the *idea* of that – never the bloody living truth of the matter. Poisonous madness, that. I'll steer clear, thanks.

IZZY: So you hate her? That's why you're doing this?

BRENNAN: Hardly. I've gone to some considerable trouble for her, you should know, Miss. But then, this family of yours, you're a demanding lot, aren't you? You no less than the rest of them.

IZZY: I'm sorry. I just find this hard. She's my sister.

BRENNAN: Well, it's not up to you finally, is it?

IZZY: No.

> *(She takes out a vial, identical to the one from the previous scene, and hands it to him. He pockets it.)*

BRENNAN: She'll get it tonight. After lights out. *(They stare out at the water.)* Did she tell you, Miss? This is where she wants her ashes sprinkled?

IZZY: Here?

BRENNAN: Quite determined, she is. You know how she gets.

IZZY *(smiles)*: I do. *(Pause.)* Well, it's a pretty spot.

BRENNAN: That it is. Strangely enough. And she'll be among friends.

> *(He exits while IZZY goes to meet ANNIE, who enters wearing handcuffs, a prison uniform. Her teeth are chattering, she shakes uncontrollably.)*

ANNIE: Did you get it?

IZZY: Yes.

ANNIE: And you gave it/to – ?

IZZY: Yes.

ANNIE: Good. *(She gets perceptibly calmer.)* Good. *(IZZY cries.)*
Why are you crying?

IZZY: Because I'm angry. So goddamned angry with you. It didn't have to
happen this way, you could/have –

ANNIE: – that was not my perception. But we don't need to argue anymore.
That's one thing, isn't it? You'll be free of all my yammering.

IZZY: Yes, you win.

ANNIE: – Izzy, come on, stop it. I've been a terrible sister.

IZZY: Yes, you have been. But you're the only one I've got.

ANNIE: And that's our little tragedy, isn't it? We're all we've got. What a
family.

IZZY: What a family. And you're no better than any of us.

ANNIE: I never said I was.

IZZY: Didn't have to. Look at your grand finish: "downright heroic," someone
said, this pointless gesture. Which I guess I'm the only person who knows is
really just a fancy way to kill yourself.

ANNIE: Pretty elaborate.

IZZY: Isn't it? Such a lot of trouble when you could have just dusted off
grandpa's pistol and stuck it in your mouth; but then people might have figured
out your dirty little secret.

ANNIE: Which is what?

IZZY: You hate life. You always have, and I guess I shouldn't blame you for that, knowing what I know, but I do, Annie, I do. I mean, yes, it's a mess, life, start to finish. It's a bad night in the fun house, the whole damn thing. And death is not. It's clean, right? You're safe from the world, safe from yourself. What a relief. Oh, right, I know, what do I know? It's just, I've always been suspicious of this sweet nether world of yours where there is finally order and peace, just how very *nice* death is — In fact, it is only by being dead that one attains anything like *lovability* in your/scheme of things —

ANNIE: You've always missed the point, Izzy. Death isn't someplace *other*, the dead don't up and *leave*, where would they go? Where else is there? They're *here*. We're steeped in their voices. Just listen. Ah, God, it's here, they're all here, shining in the air like mist. Death is the element we live in, it's so obvious. Even the most commonplace things are speaking to us, always, and always about the dead, murmuring constantly, these walls are singing, the filaments in the lights are humming with it, you just have to listen. Everything is always telling us about the beauty of death, the beauty of the dead —

IZZY: — the dead aren't beautiful, Annie, all they are is dead. All they are is not here. That's all we know about them. That's all we can ever know about them. *Life* is the element we live in. Life is all we'll ever know of beauty. Why could you never see that? And if the dead can speak, they don't speak to us.

ANNIE: They do. All you have to do is listen.

IZZY: I've never, not once, heard anything.

ANNIE: You haven't listened hard enough. You've never wanted to hear badly enough, you've never really/believed —

IZZY: — will you…? *(Pause.)* Will you speak to me?

ANNIE: Yes. If you listen.

IZZY *(pause, as she tries to believe it, then —)*: No, Annie, I'll listen, but you'll be dead. And that will be that, and so I'll never hear you again. And every silence will remind me that you chose this. And not just once, over and over again, you had the choice and you chose death.

ANNIE: It chose me. It was never my decision, Izzy. Death has taught me everything I know. It has been my kindest companion, always. Where would I be without death? I would never have known love.

IZZY: I've loved you.

ANNIE: I know.

IZZY: I don't want you to go.

ANNIE: Well, I can't stay.

IZZY: I don't know how to think of you, dead.

ANNIE: Oh, but I can tell you. I finally know. Paul told me.

IZZY: Paul?

ANNIE: He told me that night.

IZZY: When?

ANNIE: After I killed him.

IZZY: What?

ANNIE: The answer to the last question. I asked him: "You've reached the end of a long journey. Tell me what you see."

IZZY: "Describe it to me like I'm standing next to you and I'm blind."

(PAUL, dead, raises his head from the table and speaks.)

PAUL: What do I see? I'm looking down with my dead eyes through the table, through the floor, down through the foundation of the house, then it's dirt, rocks, hardness, but that doesn't matter. I'm something impossibly heavy and bright and I'm dropped into something impossibly dark and there's no bottom to it. It goes on and on, the falling. I've been falling for lifetimes now, Annie, until this, what's happening now.

ANNIE: What's happening now?

PAUL: I'm back in that forest of yours.

ANNIE: The one with the bats?

PAUL: No, I'm past them now. It's just trees.

ANNIE: What time of day is it?

PAUL: It's dawn, just like it was up there. The birds waking up. Pretty dark, but the sun's on its way. And now, yes, it's a kind of a clearing. No, it's a stone, a big flat stone, smooth. I'm surrounded by the forest. The trees are thick around me, I can't see forward or back.

ANNIE: What do you do?

PAUL: I lie down on it, the stone, it's cool on my back. I look up.

ANNIE: What can you see?

PAUL: The sky, Annie. Only the sky.

> (Pause.)

IZZY: I want to believe him. You.

ANNIE: You don't have to. I know it's true.

PAUL: We're waiting, Annie, we're all here waiting for you.

> (ANNIE stands.)

ANNIE: It's time.

IZZY: Do you remember the teaspoon?

ANNIE: What?

IZZY: When we were little, the questions. You asked me what my body of water was and that's what I came up with: a teaspoon full of water. And when you asked me what I did with it, I/said –

ANNIE (remembering): – that's right. You gave it to me.

IZZY: Because I assumed you were with me--we were always together, why would an imaginary trip be any different? – and I figured it would be a long journey, so you might get thirsty. And that was the best I could do. That's what I had to give you.

ANNIE (she smiles): You did. You said that.

IZZY: Yes.

ANNIE: You did that. Remember that.

(*ANNIE leaves. Sound of waves, loud. IZZY stands on the cliff looking out.*)

IZZY: The funny thing is that if she asked me now, I'd be able to tell her, finally. This is it. Right here: Standing on this silent ground, looking out to sea. Listening and not hearing. But listening still. And always for her. This is where the journey ends.

(*Sound of waves.*)

END OF PLAY

Let's Have Fun
The Gospel of Sticky
An Introduction to the Sticky Plays
by David Marcus

The Postmodern world we inherited from our parents, who actually believed in things like "the actual," for example, is most beautifully depicted by Borges'[1] idea that the map has become the terrain. In morality, the dogmas, or rules, which had once been viewed as the sacred window into the preferences of the divine, have become the Moral. The Ten Commandments are no longer a road map to obeying the unquestioned will of G-d, but rather the object, the terrain, to be studied and compared to all other moral codes, in order that the overlaps might tell us something about the nature of an innate secular moral reality. Theater, indeed all storytelling, has always had an essential moral component; the earliest plays in English are pageant plays, while modern shows like *Doubt* or *Angels in America* serve as moral maps. They intend to point the way towards the tolerance and kindness that most well-educated, well-off people, feel are *a priori* truths, even without evidence.

Just as all maps have legends, drawings, curled-up corners and tears to let us know that we are looking at a simulation and not the real, theater has lights and sound effects and costumes and chairs in neat rows, to remind us that what we are seeing is not real, but rather a dream, which properly interpreted can ease our way through life, and tell us how to be. Sticky is not a map. We will not guide you, we don't care what you do when you leave. Sticky is, more than anything else, an attempt to be the terrain.

It is a simple event: a bar, filled with people, some of whom are there to see, some there to be seen. Nobody is told where to sit. For the first few minutes you're just in a bar, just getting a drink. Eventually I get up, with a drink and few bad jokes, to tell people about the first play. Generally, I am unprepared – borrowing a program from an audience member, yelling to Libby or to Ali in the booth, about whether I'm properly lit, moving tables around for the scene, appearing basically like a drunken mess. This clowning is not entirely unplanned, nor is it entirely planned, it is often said that the best place to hide something is in plain sight: "Guess what? We're just hanging out ... there is no one behind the curtain ... now that that's out of the way ..." And on to a play, not on a stage, just by the bar, or at one of the tables, a single light and people start talking. Don't feel trapped – like most things in life it's only ten minutes

[1] See Borges, Jorge Luis. *Collected Fictions*, Viking, 1998, 325

long, and afterwards we'll take a break, you can smoke, get another drink – please get another drink – that's how the space gets paid.

So on and so forth, and then it ends; no curtain calls, those absurd humiliating marches of shame that say, "Yeah, I'm up here, you're down there, thanks for the applause, not why I did it, but thanks." At Sticky, if you really want to let someone know you dug the work, have a drink with them, they're right there, and we only work with nice people, mostly. And that's the trick – being in a room with people – that's what theater is.

Theater is unique among the arts in its social dimension. One can watch a movie, look at a painting, listen to a song, read a novel or play a video game, all by oneself, in a room of one's own, even on an iPod of one's own. When you see a play, or go to the theater, it is implicit that you be in a room with people. This is not a minor distinction. Yet this social dimension, often taken advantage of by theater management or development folks, is mainly ignored by theater artists. Theater's social events, opening night parties, talkbacks, NPR evenings, and young philanthropist meet and greets, are separate from the artistic product. The play stands alone, as Art, that thing to be venerated by the gathering of people bettering themselves.

When we shift our focus from theater as object to theater as event, new horizons open for us. Instead of asking, "What will the audience take from this?" we ask, "What will the audience experience?" Theater is like sex. When properly executed you don't say, "That was really fascinating sex, it puts things in such an interesting perspective." You just say, "wow," and light a cigarette.

These ideas about theater have been in the ether for as long as I have been involved. Brad Rothbart – whose 1999 reading series, "Underground Voices"[2] at Theatre Double was an awakening for me – used to say, "Theater needs to be more like a rock show." Jim Simpson's recent production of *Offending the Audience*[3] at The Flea, showed that decades ago, writers were struggling with these ideas, and that by having sexy young actors look the audience dead in the eye and say, "this is not a play," the artifice was broken, expectations were nullified, and we were all just in a room together. Also the plays of Len Jenkin, in their mysterious other worldliness, always seem to acknowledge the audience. Afterwards you don't feel like you just saw something, you feel like you went someplace. Most recently my young friend J.C. Lee, in an important and impassioned blog[4], talked about how theaters need

---

[2] "Underground Voices" reading series, Brad Rothbart, Literary Manager, Theatre Double Repertory Company, Philadelphia, PA 1999.
[3] *Offending the Audience* by Peter Handke, produced January 2008 by The Flea Theater, Jim Simpson directing
[4] http://rantsravesandrethoughts.blogspot.com/2008/11/big-idea.html

to be community gathering places, social places, even – gasp – commercial places capable of sustaining themselves economically without the largess of government charity.

So far, for the most part, theater of this kind has been an outlier; three hundred-seat theaters, *New York Times* reviews and even Obies are still mainly dedicated to theater as Object, the play, the actor, the writer, the director. These are considered artistic products, measured not only against each other but also against the vast history of the stage. The actual physical experience of going to a play is familiar and locked in – it's like going to Mass, you know when to stand, when to sit, you know the responses. And make no mistake, theater uses its own physical rituals for the same purpose, as if to say to the audience, "behold, you are about to receive the word of..." I prefer Revelations 3-8: "Behold I have set before thee an open door."

The rituals of theater, its brittle fourth wall, its distinctions and hierarchies, have no place in Sticky. If an actor wants to write or direct, they do it, if a writer wants to act, they do it, or a director, and so on. Your friend has a play you really want to do? Super. You want to try a dance piece? Sounds like fun. Even audience members come up to Libby or Ali or me and say, I want to be involved and usually – especially if they are persistent – they become involved; but, honestly, they already were. Come to Sticky, get on the team, show us what you've got. Get drunk, get laid, make an ass of yourself, do all three ... you're the show, as much as I am, as much as the plays or the band or the bartenders are. A little bored by the play? We hope not, but that girl's cute, did she just look at you? Maybe she's bored, too. Here comes a break, go find out. We live together, you and I – all of us – we share a pointless speck of time with each other and we make our own fun. Let's have fun.

Blue Box Productions has produced nearly two hundred short plays in our Sticky series, of which twelve follow. Please do not think of these as a "best of," the very notion is absurd. Frankly, by the third or fourth play of any given evening of Sticky, very few people are in a condition to make such austere judgments, least of all its producers. These plays were chosen for reasons conscious and unconscious, sentimental and political, objective and subjective (which of course are the same thing depending on if it's you talking), but all of them, at some point, hit the mark. Other than being ten minutes long and set in a bar, these plays have very little in common, they are testaments to our slogan that "anything that can happen, can happen in a bar." Borges was right, the map has become the terrain, the signifier has been split with more force than the atom. There is no Ideal to appeal to, or to strive for. There is only us, let's have fun.

THE STICKY PLAYS

Blue Box Productions
www.blueboxproductions.net

THE STICKY PLAYS

Stacy Rock and Megan Messmer in Katherine Ryan's "The Kitchen Staff"

Serial Monogamy
by Arden Kass

* * *

Produced in Sticky: March 28, 2000: Bar Noir, (Philly), directed by Jeremy Chacon. With W. Shay Hammond and David Marcus; January 26, 2004: Belly Bar, directed by, Libby Emmons. With David Marcus and Stacy Rock; and October 2004: Big Sticky, The Flea Theater.

* * *

(A MAN sits at the bar dressed in a dark suit, perhaps with an ascot. He wears white gloves and sips from a drink. A newspaper lies open in front of him, which he scans and marks with a pen from time to time. NANCY observes him for a while, then stands next to him at the bar.)

NANCY *(to the bartender)*: Hey Toots, how ya doin' tonight? Gimme the usual. And one for my uncle here. *(To the MAN.)* What's your name?

VIDAL: Vidal. No, thank you. I'm fine.

NANCY: Vidal like Sassoon?

VIDAL: No, like Gore.

NANCY: Al Gore?

VIDAL: Gore Vidal.

NANCY: The writer?

VIDAL: No, the apostle.

(Silence. She mugs at the audience: "Get him.")

NANCY: Nice attitude, Vidal. Tough day at work?

(VIDAL says nothing. Does something to his paper.)

NANCY: You know, the thing is, a bar's a pretty sociable kind of place. Most people don't come to a bar to be left alone.

(VIDAL lights a cigarette with gloves on, smokes.)

VIDAL: I'm not alone.

NANCY: Oh, excuse me. *(Beat – she looks around him.)* So who are you here with? Harvey the White Rabbit? Just a joke. *(No response.)* Look, I'm not tryin' to harass you, I'm just makin' chit-chat. I'm actually waitin' for someone myself.

VIDAL: "With whom are you here."

NANCY: I just told ya, I'm waitin' for someone. What're you, deaf as well as mute? Just a joke.

(She elbows him.)

VIDAL: The grammatically correct way to phrase your question is, "For whom are you waiting?"

NANCY *(skeptically)*: Ohhhh, right. Gee, thanks, Vidal.

VIDAL: This is why Western society is disintegrating all around us. No regard for language. No regard for manners. No respect for – never mind. It's futile.

(He focuses on his newspaper. Finds something and stabs it.)

NANCY: No, Go on, go on. You were on a roll there. I knew we could find *something* to chat about.

VIDAL: Listen, Miss –

(He blackens something in the paper.)

NANCY: Nancy. Nancy Ann. If we get friendlier, I'll tell you the rest. Gotta be careful about stalkers. Serial killers. *(He reacts.)* Not that you – I mean, you don't look like what you see on TV, but you never know. Just a joke.

(He burns something out of his paper with his cigarette.)

VIDAL: Jack the Ripper was actually quite refined in appearance and manners. So you do have a point. The average American serial killer, however –

NANCY: Is a slob with greasy hair and a three-day beard. I know. I watch them on TV getting led into the courtroom all wrapped up in a chain, in those orange prison clothes. They all look like slobs.

VIDAL: I suppose if a slob, as you say, of that description were to sit down next to one in a bar, it is very unlikely that one would pursue an acquaintanceship with that person. In fact, one would most probably change one's seat.

NANCY: This one sure would.

VIDAL: Of course, there are as many types of serial killers as there are victims. Many of them blend into society quite successfully. Until you discover that their friendly neighborhood paper boy is chained in their basement.

NANCY: Yeah. The parts of him that are still attached to his body.

(He stabs out the cigarette.)

NANCY: Just a joke. Anyway. If a serial killer came in and sat down next to me, even if he wasn't wearing an orange jumpsuit and a leash, I'd definitely get an inkling. A sense.

VIDAL: Would you?

NANCY: It's like dating, right? You've been on a date?

VIDAL: I suppose so.

NANCY: Well, are you married?

VIDAL: No. Not at present – are you?

NANCY: No. What do you think I'm doin' sitting here with you? Waitin' for me husband to come back from the seas? Anyway. If you're not married, then you must be dating or – something. Maybe even – reading the personals?

VIDAL: The only reason I would read the personals is to correct the atrocious grammar of the "desperately seeking."

(He goes back to circling and blackening.)

NANCY: Well, call it whatever you want. But I'm sure you're doing something about it. Humans'll do just about anything to find companionship.

VIDAL: You've studied the subject?

(He marks ferociously.)

NANCY *(giving him a look)*: Yeah. Anyway, like I was saying, if you've been on a date, you know "the feeling."

VIDAL: The "feeling"?

NANCY: You know – I don't know what to call it. You walk into a room, you see the guy or in your case, whoever it is you're meeting, and you know. He's a decent guy or he's a creep. He's a cocky son of a bitch, he's a wimp – you know what I mean.

VIDAL: And you're convinced that serial killers share these characteristics with the rest of the world –

NANCY: They're humans, right? We're all human. Join me this time?

VIDAL: No thanks, I've reached my limit.

NANCY *(to the Bartender)*: Hey, Toots, another one. And don't forget the cherry. *(To VIDAL.)* It's just a thing I do. A "peculiarity." Reminds me of when I was a kid. Just – totally innocent, you know? I know it's goofy. Whiskey with a cherry. And it has to have a stem for good luck. But he indulges me. Right, Toots? One night he called me Hon, so now I call him Toots.

VIDAL: Then you're a "regular" here.

NANCY: Not exactly regular – no one's "regular," right?

VIDAL: But you come here often.

NANCY: Hey, I thought you'd never ask! No, only kidding. Just a joke. Nah, just once in a while. Two, three time a week.

VIDAL: But tonight, you're expecting someone.

NANCY: Yeah. Yeah, I guess. But, I don't know.

VIDAL: Don't know what?

NANCY: Well if he'll show up, first of all, or if I'll get "the feeling" –

VIDAL: Then it's someone you don't know very well.

NANCY: Not yet. Hey. If you don't have to answer questions, why do you get to ask them?

VIDAL: Good point. Withdrawn.

NANCY: So WHOM are you waiting for, Vidal?

VIDAL: "For whom are you waiting, Vidal?"

NANCY: What're you, an English teacher?

VIDAL: I have been.

NANCY: But not now.

VIDAL *(as he corrects, then stabs his paper, his rage mirroring his words)*: No. Not now. I suffered from an exquisite sensitivity to errors in English grammar. Certain infractions – dangling prepositions among them – there were "incidents."

NANCY *(nibbling her cherry)*: No shit. So, what *do* you do? When you're not correcting grammar in a bar? While waiting for someone whose identity you're protecting.

VIDAL: I'm currently self-employed.

NANCY: Oh yeah? And what do you employ yourself at?

VIDAL: At *what*.

NANCY: What do you do, Vidal –

VIDAL: At WHAT are you –

NANCY: You know, this is not exactly the way to charm your way into a woman's heart.

VIDAL: As I recall, you spoke to me first.

NANCY: Two points. Truce. God. *(She checks her watch.)* Three more minutes and that's it. People can be so rude, you know? Oh right, look who I'm asking – or should I say, to whom I am inquiring –

VIDAL: *Of.* OF whom I am inquiring.

NANCY: Thanks, professor. *(Standing.)* You know, this night is not working for me. I gave it a chance – God knows I'm always willing – but –

VIDAL *(almost holding her arm)*: No, don't – Miss – NANCY …

NANCY: What, don't tell me you were enjoying yourself? I've gotten more laughs outta one of my maraschinos here.

VIDAL: I do admit I have a difficult time getting to know people at first.

NANCY: Oh, *shy.* Well, why didn't you say somethin'? We all got our peculiarities. Square curves, round corners. Not everybody can be Regis Philbin.

VIDAL: Thank God.

NANCY: OK, Round Two. So, what do you do when you're not being self-employed as a serial killer grammar freak? Just a joke.

VIDAL *(ripping something out and crumpling it in the ashtray)*: I'm a consultant.

NANCY: Isn't everybody? To who? I mean, "whom." *(VIDAL ignites the scrap in the ashtray.)* You know what? I just got "The Feeling."

VIDAL: But –

NANCY: Nope. Gotta go. This is too weird, Vidal. I gotta go home. Right Now.

> *(She goes to pay her bill. He beats her to it.)*

NANCY: What was that for?

VIDAL: Truce.

NANCY: Thanks. Peace.

> *(She bends down to get her bag, turns to go, walks a few feet. Her cell phone rings. She answers.)*

NANCY: Yeah. Thanks for calling. Have a nice life. *(She hangs it up.)* Schmuck. I could tell from his ring.

VIDAL *(standing and moving to her)*: You've been jilted?

NANCY: Doesn't matter. I'm sure he wasn't Mr. Right anyway. Maybe Mr. Right Now. Just a joke. Later, Toots. *(She walks on, then stops.)* You know, I don't see *your* Ms. Right showin' up with bells on, either, Vidal.

VIDAL: No. She doesn't appear to be.

NANCY: So now you can just go back to enjoying your own delightful company. And your perfect grammar.

VIDAL: Yes.

NANCY: Well?

VIDAL: Were you expected anywhere else?

NANCY: No. Except by my cat. He spits up hairballs on my bed if I'm late.

VIDAL: Just a "gag"?

NANCY: Was that – a joke?

VIDAL: A feeble one.

NANCY: Can I ask you one more question?

VIDAL: *May* I – , Nancy. Sorry –

NANCY: Forget it.

　　　(She walks away. He scuttles after her.)

VIDAL: No. I apologize. The grammar. It's *my* peculiarity. Please. Ask me anything.

NANCY: OK, talking about peculiar. The gloves?

VIDAL: Gloves? Oh. I – the newsprint? The errors – in the paper – dialogue, headlines – advertising – I need to remove them. Destroy them. They stain my fingers –

NANCY: That's beyond peculiar, Vidal. That's bizarre.

VIDAL: Yes. But as you say, we all have our square curves.

NANCY: Yeah, but within limits.

VIDAL: Do you like films?

NANCY: Dig 'em to death.

VIDAL: Have you ever seen *In Cold Blood?*

NANCY: Yeah. Like ten times! It's my all-time favorite. Except maybe *Silence of the Lambs.* Or *Fatal Attraction.* No, *Psycho.* I had went to see the new one, but it was so lame.

VIDAL *(barely containing himself)*: HAD WENT? Ah, I have a copy of the original. And I have a home entertainment center in my basement – it's state of the art. Would you care to –

NANCY: Well, gee. I don't know. I mean, we just met in a bar. And you're pretty darn peculiar, Vidal. But – I guess you're a pretty decent guy, underneath it all. But irregardless. No. Well – OK. Yeah, I guess it's worth a shot.

VIDAL: Or a stab, as they say. Just a joke, Nancy Ann.

(He takes her by the arm, smiles creepily, and escorts her out.)

END OF PLAY

The Kitchen Staff: 9 Scenes
by Katherine Ryan

* * *

Produced in Sticky: March 29, 2004: Belly Bar, directed by David Marcus. With Robert Hancock, Matthew Korahais, Tim O'Brien, Stacy Rock and Ana Valle; October 2004: Big Sticky, The Flea Theater; November 9, 2007: Bowery Poetry Club; directed by Jon Kern. With John Fico, David Marcus, Megan Messmer, Dan O'Brien, and Stacy Rock.

* * *

7.

(The Firewood Bedroom. AMANDA and JENNIFER hands the lip gloss and puts on a gob of the lip gloss. JENNIFER kicks the lip gloss. AMANDA hands JENNIFER the lip gloss. JENNIFER puts on a gob of the lip gloss. JENNIFER hands AMANDA the lip gloss.)

JENNIFER: Who work down there?

AMANDA: Lately I know for certain.

(AMANDA puts on a gob of the lip gloss.)

JENNIFER: I am taking the free computer classes offered by the company.

(AMANDA hands Jennifer the lip gloss. JENNIFER puts on a gob of the lip gloss. JENNIFER hands AMANDA the lip gloss.)

JENNIFER: Who work down there?

AMANDA: Lately I know for certain.

(AMANDA puts on a gob of the lip gloss.)

JENNIFER: I am taking the free computer classes offered by the company.

(AMANDA hands JENNIFER the lip gloss. JENNIFER puts on a gob of the lip gloss. JENNIFER hands AMANDA the lip gloss.)

JENNIFER: Who work down there?

AMANDA: Lately I know for certain.

(AMANDA puts on a gob of the lip gloss.)

JENNIFER: Lately I am taking the offered. I am offered. Lately I am offered.

AMANDA: Who ...

JENNIFER: I listen to people talking.

(AMANDA hands JENNIFER the lip gloss. JENNIFER kicks the lip gloss.)

AMANDA: Lip gloss?

JENNIFER: I kick the lip gloss. I puts on a gob of the lip gloss.

AMANDA: I puts on a gob of the lip gloss. Who work down there? Who work down there?

JENNIFER: Lately I know for certain. Who work down there? Who work down there?

8.

(The room. The ACTUARY actually hanging on the wall. BULKY eating and drinking. SMALL hiding in shadow of square hole door, small, hesitate, faintly and slowly pouring.)

SMALL: THE ACTUARY!

BULKY: The Actuary hanging on the wall.

(The ACTUARY actually hanging on the wall.)

SMALL *(small):* Who work down there? *(Hesitate.)* Who work down there? *(Faintly.)* Who work down there? *(Slowly pouring.)* Who work down there?

BULKY
(Drinking beer. Eating salty peanuts.)

2.

(The darkest room. Dull pictures hanging on the wall. BULKY and SMALL eating and drinking and BULKY skin crawling.)

BULKY *(eating salty peanuts)*: Lately I know for certain. I feel more deeply. I do not forgive.

SMALL *(eating salty peanuts)*: It is. It is.

BULKY: Okay. I can hide. At a bar.
  (Drinking beer.)

SMALL: People say ... in the game. People say ... it's all so stupid. I am taking the free computer classes offered by the company.

BULKY: I listen to people talking.

SMALL: If that's what you think. People say ... facts. Information. I can't fucking summarize that. I am taking the free computer classes offered by the company.

BULKY *(eating salty peanuts)*: And beer.

SMALL: *(drinking beer)*: In a bedroom. In the game. People say ... I can't fucking summarize that. I am taking the free computer classes offered by the company.

BULKY *(drinking beer)*: The game. "Red one, please." A gob of the lip gloss. The other test. "Are you? They were on *my* team."

SMALL: That's not it. That's not it. *(Eating salty peanuts.)* I just don't want to condemn.

BULKY: I'm all for 'em.

SMALL: I don't wanna say those words.

BULKY: I'm all for 'em. *(Eating salty peanuts. Drinking beer.)* I'm all for 'em.

SMALL: I'm all for 'em. Sleeping with one of the tight-suited men. I am taking the free computer classes offered by the company.

BULKY *(skin crawling)*: I'm all for 'em.

4.

(The high peak and the shadow of the square hole dull room. The KITCHEN STAFF slowly moving, falling, faintly stupefying, crawling, and are pouring. The ACTUARY building clumsy sheetrock dividers slowly because cold and building clumsy sheetrock dividers.)

ACTUARY: I'm trying to grasp experiences I have. Lately I know for certain ... I know more facts. Or maybe it's just ... I can go there a lot these days. I don't ... if that's what you think. *(The ACTUARY building clumsy sheetrock dividers slowly because cold.)* "The fucking assholes. The fucking assholes who work down there." Laundry. Rain-puddled sheetrock. I live in a different place. In a bedroom.

(The KITCHEN STAFF slowly moving. The KITCHEN STAFF falling.)

ACTUARY: The kitchen staff. Falling. *(The ACTUARY building clumsy sheetrock dividers.)* A different place. ... It's okay. I did it. I did it. The highest peak. That's not what I thought it was about. Are you? The numbness is stupefying.

(The KITCHEN STAFF faintly stupefying.)

ACTUARY: I can go there a lot these days. I'm afraid of how vast.

(The KITCHEN STAFF crawling.)

ACTUARY: I'm trying to grasp experiences I have. Lately I know for certain... I know more facts. Or maybe it's just ... I can go there a lot these days. I don't ... if that's what you think.

(The KITCHEN STAFF are pouring.)

3.

(The high peak and the shadow of the square hole dull room. The KITCHEN STAFF slowly moving and hesitate. The ACTUARY axe down a tree for firewood, hesitate, building clumsy sheetrock dividers and acclimate.)

ACTUARY: It doesn't smell like anything. Axe down a tree for firewood.

(The ACTUARY axe down a tree for firewood.)

ACTUARY: Who work down there. Who work down there. *(The ACTUARY hesitate.)* Cold.

(The KITCHEN STAFF slowly moving.)

ACTUARY: That would be nice ... if you were dreaming. If I didn't have to say anything at all. Who work down there. Forgetting. Who work down there. Who work down there. *(The ACTUARY building clumsy sheetrock dividers. The ACTUARY hesitate.)* Who work down there. The kitchen staff. Thin wrists. The Kitchen Staff. Thin wrists. The Kitchen Staff.

> *(The KITCHEN STAFF hesitate. The KITCHEN STAFF slowly moving. The ACTUARY acclimate and building clumsy sheetrock dividers.)*

5.

(The dark room. The dull wall hanging on the wall. SMALL hiding in square hole door. BULKY and SMALL drinking and eating. BULKY skin crawling. SMALL hesitate.)

SMALL: I do not. I don't. I do not. I do not. I don't. You are not trapped. They are. *(Hesitate.)* If you are going to stay in there. For firewood. You see? Would that help? *(Hesitate.)* The joy has been taken out of those words when I say them. Would that help?

BULKY
> *(Eating salty peanuts.)*

SMALL: You spit that out.

BULKY: Amusing.

SMALL: Smoke, chat. In a bedroom. Smoke, chat. Sleeping with one of the tight-suited men. I am taking the free computer classes offered by the company.

BULKY: Drinking beer. Tonight.

SMALL: You said you were so close. Sleeping with one of the tight-suited men. They are. It breathes and it smells. Just becomes bigger with each new time I see. Clumsy in there. If you are going to stay there. *(Hesitate.)* THE ACTUARY.

BULKY: I see that you do. You can kill them. You can go and move around. In the meantime, you must build walls, sheetrock.

SMALL: The actuary. Actually, actual. The actuary.

BULKY: You can kill them. Who work down there. Who work down there. "The game ..." "I am taking the free computer classes offered by the company." *(Drinking beer. Skin crawling.)* EITHER YOU'RE MAKING SOMETHING OR YOU'RE FORGETTING THAT THING THAT YOU MADE THAT YOU NOW HATE.

SMALL: Drinking beer. Drinking beer. I am taking the ... if I didn't have to say the assholes.

BULKY: If I didn't have to say the assholes. If I didn't have to say the assholes. I do not forgive. If I didn't have to say the assholes.

6.

(The dark room. The Actuary hanging on the wall. BULKY and SMALL eating and drinking, hands the lip gloss and puts on a gob of the lip gloss. BULKY sad clown face.)

BULKY: I do not forgive. I do not forgive.
(Drinking beer.)

SMALL
(Eating salty peanuts.)

BULKY: Okay. I can hide. At a bar.
(Drinking beer.)

SMALL: People say ... in the game. People say ... destruction, slowly moving. Sleeping with hesitate. The joy. Over his shoulders.

BULKY: Not a noble death.

SMALL: Not a noble death.

BULKY: I feel more deeply.

SMALL: I feel more deeply.

BULKY: I feel more deeply.

SMALL: I feel more deeply.

BULKY: Not a noble death. I feel more deeply. I feel more deeply. I feel more deeply.

SMALL: I feel more deeply. I feel more deeply.

BULKY: I feel more deeply. Not a noble death. You can kill them. You can go and move around in that loosey goosey way that you do.

SMALL: I AM TAKING THE FREE. I AM TAKING THE OFFERED. I am deeply offered. I am taking that loosey goosey way that you do. I feel more taking.

BULKY
(Eating salty peanuts.)

SMALL: I live in a different place. I forgive. That's the thing.

BULKY: I do NOT FORGIVE!

SMALL: Preparing for service.

BULKY: I do NOT FORGIVE preparing for service behind the altar.

SMALL: Faint. The actuary.

BULKY: The actuary, the highest peak, speaking of ... consciously, for some time. I love. Like you. A gob of the lip gloss. I did it. I hands Jennifer the lip gloss. Amanda, we do this dance. They hug. Last time I didn't.

SMALL: That's not it. That's not what it's about. Speaking of.

BULKY: They were once my Amanda. Jennifer. If that's what you think.

SMALL: I'm afraid of how vast ...

BULKY
(Drinking beer.)

SMALL: ... Pouring. Or maybe it's just ...

BULKY: Amanda and Jennifer. Executive Assistants. Kickball For movies.

(BULKY hands SMALL the lip gloss. SMALL puts on a gob of the lip gloss. SMALL hands BULKY the lip gloss.)

BULKY: I feel so sad.
(Sad clown face.)

(BULKY hands BULKY the lip gloss. BULKY puts on a gob of the lip gloss. BULKY hands BULKY the lip gloss.)

SMALL
(Drinking beer.)

BULKY: Smoke, chat huddle. And then we do this dance. And then –

SMALL: In the game ... people say. In the game. So ... it's okay. You forgive.

BULKY: I do NOT FORGIVE.

SMALL: Now they are your words. Amanda, and Jennifer. We do this dance. If that's what you think. So ... it's okay. Thrilling or heart-quickening. In the game. People say ... they hug. It is. It is. I want to go ... I feel more deeply. Or maybe it's just ... like you. I love being in its family because I can hide. I can hide, people say ... okay ... at a bar. The game. The bedroom. In the game. In the ... love. Now they are your words.

BULKY: I listen to people talking.

SMALL: If that's what you think. People say ... facts.

BULKY *(eating salty peanuts)*: And beer.

9.
(The higher peak. The KITCHEN STAFF acclimate.)

1.
(The darker room. Duller pictures hanging on the wall. BULKY and SMALL eating, drinking, and hesitate.)

BULKY *(eating salty peanuts)*: Lately I know for certain. I feel more deeply. I do not forgive.

SMALL: It is. It is.
(Eating salty peanuts.)

BULKY: Okay. I can hide At a bar.
(Drinking beer.)

SMALL: It is. I can't fucking summarize that. People say ... facts. I can't fucking summarize that.

BULKY: I listen to people talking.
(Eating salty peanuts. Drinking beer.)

SMALL: People say ... facts. In a bedroom. *(Drinking beer.)* I can't fucking summarize that.

BULKY: I listen to people talking.

SMALL: I am taking the free –

BULKY: I can hide. At a bar. I listen to people talking.
(Drinking beer.)

SMALL: I can't fucking summarize that. I am taking the free computer classes offered by the company.

BULKY: In a bedroom. People say ... it's all so stupid. You can kill them.

SMALL: In the game. It's all so stupid. People say ... in the bedroom. I can't fucking summarize that. I am taking the free computer classes offered by the company.

BULKY *(drinking beer; eating salty peanuts)*: You can kill them. And beer.
(Drinking beer.)

SMALL: And beer. *(Eating salty peanuts.)* And drinking beer.

BULKY: The game. It's all so stupid ... futile. "Are you? They were on *my* team."

SMALL: The game. I am taking the free computer classes offered by the company.

BULKY: I listen to people talking.
(Eating salty peanuts.)

(Hesitate.)

SMALL: People say ... facts. In the bedroom. I can't fucking ... people say. The bedroom. It's all so stupid ... futile.

BULKY
(Drinking beer. Drinking beer. Drinking beer.)

SMALL: I am taking the free computer classes offered by the company.

BULKY: A gob of the lip gloss. A gob. People ... it's all so futile. A gob.

SMALL: I am taking the free computer classes offered by the company.

BULKY: I do not forgive.

SMALL: I can't fucking summarize that. I listen to people talking. *(Eating salty peanuts.)* I am taking the free. I am taking the offered. I am deeply offered.

BULKY: And beer. And it's all so futile, stupid, people say. You can kill them.

SMALL: Who work down there. Who work down there. Who work down there.

BULKY *(eating salty peanuts)*: You can kill them. Who work down there? Who work down there?

SMALL
　　(Drinking beer.)

BULKY: It's all so ... people say so.

SMALL: If I didn't have to say anything at all.

BULKY: If I didn't have to say anything at all. I do not forgive.

SMALL: I can hide, at a bar.

BULKY *(drinking beer)*: Who work down there. I'm all for 'em. I do not forgive.

　　(Eating salty peanuts.)

END OF PLAY

I Love Neil LaBute
by Gary Winter

* * *

Produced in Sticky: August 23, 2004: Belly Bar, directed by Ali Ayala. With Libby Emmons, Brett England, Matthew Korahais and David Marcus; October 2004: Big Sticky, The Flea Theater, directed by Ali Ayala. With Jim Boyle, Matthew Korahais, Ana Valle and Matt Wells.

CHARACTERS
Neil LaBute #1
Neil LaBute #2
Neil LaBute #3
Joseph Smith (female actor)

SETTING
A bar.

* * *

SCENE 1

(NEIL LABUTE #1 *sits at a bar table with a drink.* NEIL LABUTE #2 *enters with drink and sits.*)

NL #2: Hi Neil LaBute.

NL #1: Hi Neil LaBute.

NL #2: Hi Neil LaBute.

(NL #3 *walks in with a drink.*)

NL #3: Hi Neil LaBute.

NL #1: Hi Neil LaBute

NL #2: Hi Neil LaBute.

NL #1: Blackout.

(There is no blackout. NL 1,2,3 all just stare at their beer bottles.)

NL #3: Lights up.

(They all drink.)

NL #1: Okay. What do you want to do now?

NL #2: I don't know if I should write a play, a film or a poem.

NL #3: A poem. Hey! That's a swell idea.

(They all look serious for a moment. Then they all start cracking up laughing.)

NL #1: Hey – you're funny Neil LaBute.

NL #3: Hey thanks Neil LaBute.

NL #2: Hey let's make a film.

NL #1: We're out of money.

NL #3: Money? What're you fucking stupid? We just rob the bar and we'll have money. How do you think any film gets financed?

NL #1: I didn't know that.

NL #2: Just watch, asshole.

NL #1: Hey Bartender! Yeah you bitch! Empty the cash register and toss over a wad of cash or I'll come over there and shove this beer bottle up your armpits. Then we'll work on your other orifices.

(Nothing.)

NL #3: Please, Bitch.

(A roll of money comes flying over the bar and into their booth.)

NL#3: See. You gotta know how to talk to people, fuck face.

NL #2: So look, Neil LaBute. I want to make this film about three guys who are married. They hate their wives and pain-in-the-ass kids. They hate their jobs. Their bosses are assholes. Their co-workers are like shit-eating mole-rats. So these guys get together one night and get shit-faced. They sign a contract in blood on a napkin.

NL #1: They all agree to fuck each others' wives!

NL #3: And make each wife not tell anyone else!

NL #2: Then they agree to fuck each other's daughters!

NL #1: And the daughters can't tell anyone or the fathers stop supplying them with crack.

NL #3: And they won't pay for their high school graduation breast implants.

NL #2: And they'll cut off their boyfriend's balls on prom night!

NL #1: They should do that anyway!

NL#3: We are fucking geniuses.

(They drink and high five.)

NL #2: Blackout!

(They stare at their beer bottles.)

NL #1: Lights up.

NL #2: I'm not sure if this is a film or a play.

NL #3: Well, Neil LaBute, a fucking play is language-driven.

NL #2: And a film is visual-driven.

NL #1 *(snooty British accent)*: Is this a language-driven story or visual?

(They all contemplate this very, very seriously. Then they all look at each other and crack up.)

ALL: Ahhhhh! It's a fucking movie. We're fucking geniuses.

NL #3: Blackout.

(They stare at their beers.)

NL #1: Lights up.

(They all have legal pads in front of them.)

NL#2: Okay! Let's write a scene.

NL#1: We got three couples. John and Betty. Alice and Peter. Mark and Sarah.

NL #3: This is fucking amazing! We're not even sticking with our original idea.

NL #2: John is having a mid-life crisis, even though he's only 26. Peter and Alice throw a Bar-B-Q, where all the couples meet. John gets trashed, and Betty is embarrassed. They fight. John storms into Peter and Alice's bedroom, where he sulks about his miserable life. Then Sarah walks in. She tells John not to sulk, that Betty is an uptight asshole. John agrees and rapes Sarah. Sarah is pissed, but says, what the fuck. Turns out she too is having a midlife crisis. So they agree to meet every other night at a motel and fuck. John and Sarah seem rejuvenated.

(Pause. They think.)

NL #1: What next?

NL #3: Mark suspects Sarah is fucking John, but he's a wimp and doesn't say anything. But Peter has been arrested for molesting one of his 8-year old students, and Alice knows Sarah is screwing John.

NL#2: Alice shouldn't know. She's too stupid.

NL #3: Okay. Alice just decides to have an affair with Mark, but John finds out and cuts off Mark's balls.

NL #1: Why should John cut off Mark's balls when John is screwing Mark's wife?

(Silence.)

NL #3: Then Betty should cut off John's balls and fuck Peter.

NL #2: How can she fuck Peter if he's in jail?

NL #1: Yeah, and we already established that Peter only likes little girls.

NL #3: What if Peter got out of jail and got counseling?

NL #2: Betty has to remain sweet and naïve. That way everyone else can look like complete assholes.

NL #1: Way to go, Neil LaBute.

NL #3: Good thinking, Neil LaBute. That's why we're like a fucking modern-day Shakespeare.

NL#2: Thank you, I agree Neil LaBute. We have a window unto the human soul.

(*JOSEPH SMITH, founder of the Mormon Church, appears.*)

NL# 1: Who the fuck are you?

NL #2: Who the fuck are you?

NL #3: Who the fuck are you?

NL #2: The whorehouse is on Clinton Street.

NL#1: Hand jobs outside the Lincoln Tunnel, bitch!

JS: I am Joseph Smith, founder of the Church of Jesus Christ of the Latter Day Saints.

(*NL #1, #2, #3 think about this a second then all crack up laughing.*)

NL#3: Hey asshole. I'm a Mormon. I know what Joseph Smith looks like.

JS: What does he look like, Neil LaBute the Mormon?

NL#1: He's 6 feet 8 inches, is 200 years old and has a white beard.

JS: Is that so, Neil LaBute the Mormon?

NL #2: Yeah I'm Mormon I should know!!! Don't you read *Entertainment Weekly*? If you did you wouldn't be asking such stupid questions.

JS: Well I'm Joseph Smith you idiot.

NL#3: Prove it, asshole!

> (JOSEPH SMITH *waves her hands around. NEIL LABUTE #1,2,3 look on in awe.*)

NL #1: Whoa. That was incredible.

NL #2: I never seen anything like it. Deep shit.

NL #3: Only Joseph Smith, our beloved founder, could do that.

JS: Now Neil LaBute, are you going to stop embarrassing Mormons? I don't care if you make porn-slasher films with Mel Gibson, as long as you say you're an atheist.

NL#2: Oh, we couldn't do that.

JS: Why not?

NL #1: We'd lose all our credibility.

NL #3: By saying we're Mormon we can do whatever we want and people believe we're sincere.

NL #2: Without any religious affiliation we're fucked.

JS: I don't care! All you have to say about people is that they fuck their neighbor's husbands and wives. And that's it! That's all you have to say?

> (*Silence. All the NLs look at each other.*)

NL #1, 2 3: Yeah.

JS: Don't you think that's fucked up?

NL#1: No.

NL #2: It's real life.

NL #3: It has deep meaning. People screw each other. We're like, reporters of the human condition.

NL #2: Like, hey Joseph Smith, we just added child molestation.

NL #1: How about that?

JS: I'm excommunicating you from the Mormon Church, Neil LaBute.

NL #2: Why don't you join us, Joseph Smith?

NL#1: Wouldn't you like to be a screenwriter and playwright, Joseph Smith?

NL #3: Sure you would. People will think you're so cool.

(Pause. JOSEPH SMITH contemplates this.)

JS: Really?

(NLs nod.)

JS: Blackout!

(JS sits at the table. Takes out a white pad.)

JS: Lights up! So I think Betty is pretending all along to be sweet and naïve, but at the end of the film she ties Alice up and fucks her in the butt with a riding whip.

NL #1: Way to go Joseph Smith!

JS: Hey! I can write a movie!

NL #2: And you are exposing the underbelly of human nature!

NL#3: Just wait until you try and write a play!

(Blackout – this time, for real.)

END OF PLAY

Showing Skin
by Rehana Mirza

* * *

Produced in Sticky: March 1, 2005, Belly Bar, directed by Libby Emmons. With Jennifer Boggs and David Marcus; February 2006, Big Sticky, D-Lounge, directed by Jeremiah Clancy, choreographed by Vanessa Walters. With David Marcus and Taniya Sen.

* * *

(Two people are in an empty bar with a platform stage and chairs still on backs. Samir who goes by SAM; SHOBA who goes by Shoba. Fucking twentysomethings.)

SHOBA: There's some really bad shit that's going to go down here.

SAM: How do you know?

SHOBA: I can feel it.

SAM: I see.

SHOBA: Here. *(Hands him a razor blade.)* Cut me.

SAM: Why?

SHOBA: I want to kiss you.

(He slices her.)

SHOBA: I felt that.

SAM: Did you?

SHOBA: Yes.

SAM: You create bad shit.

SHOBA: I know.

SAM: All of your g-ddamn motherfucking feelings all the g-ddamn motherfucking time. Really it's just you manipulating the situation to your advantage.

(He slices her.)

SHOBA: That felt better.

SAM: Did it?

SHOBA: Yes.

SAM: I'm sorry.

SHOBA: Don't be.

SAM: I hated your set. During rehearsal last night. While you were rehearsing, I found myself hating it. I wanted to vomit on your sitar, anything to filter noise, even if it is just through chunks of chicken.

SHOBA: So you didn't like it?

SAM: No. Not at all.

SHOBA: What exactly about it?

SAM: I don't know. It's hard to describe. Your voice annoyed me. The notes hurt my ears.

SHOBA: Huh.

SAM: The general sound I guess.

SHOBA: I put my soul in that.

SAM: Humans don't have souls don't give me some cockamamie bullshit like that.

(He cuts her again. She screams and jumps back.)

SHOBA: Well what is it then?

SAM: Did that hurt?

SHOBA: No. I was just taken by surprise.

SAM: Oh. I just told you what it was. It was awful, fucking awful. Terrible, fucking terrible.

SHOBA: That was me up there.

SAM: I know, you were fucking G-d awful.

SHOBA: I thought I put everything I had ... I thought people would be able to see through me with one note.

SAM: I could see into the contents of my fucking stomach. See through my ass, you know what you find? Shit, fucking shit.

SHOBA: I'll let you fuck me there tonight. After the show.

SAM: No.

SHOBA: No?

SAM: Yeah. No. I still feel sick. You're not who I thought you were.

SHOBA: But I'm me. I was me.

SAM: Yeah but the talent, you know. I was fucking the talent and it felt good, I could come and you'd swallow it down and there'd be something I produced. Like a record album.

SHOBA: But with sperm.

SAM: Right.

SHOBA: Are you still gonna produce my album, baby?

SAM: I don't know. I was on the way out.

SHOBA: Now? You're leaving now? The show's going to start in a couple of hours. Please ... please.

SAM: If not now, when?

SHOBA: Never. Don't fucking leave me, don't you fucking dare.

SAM: Like that means anything to me.

SHOBA: I have killed you with my love seven times over a hundred and still you don't look twice. Spare me a second, will you please?

SAM: You never want just a second. You always want –

SHOBA: Just a second chance then?

SAM: You can't count for shit. It's what I used to love about you.

SHOBA: I know.

SAM: So you're letting me go?

SHOBA: Never.

SAM: Well I don't need your permission.

SHOBA: I know but please – don't I get one last phone call or something?

SAM: It's a last meal. The term. One last meal.

SHOBA: Yeah. That.

SAM: Maybe I'll let you suck me off or something.

SHOBA: No. That's not what I mean.

SAM: Well what then?

SHOBA: At the very least stay. Let me sing goodbye to you.

SAM: You're still bleeding.

(*He takes her arm, licks it gently, steps back.*)

SAM: I don't know if I could stand it.

SHOBA: You just have to stand through it.

SAM: Who else is playing tonight?

SHOBA: ka – fusion.

SAM: They're hot.

SHOBA: She's got a boyfriend.

SAM: Maybe I'll stay then.

SHOBA: Bastard. No. Don't stay.

SAM: Just for a couple hours.

SHOBA: I'm taking you off the list.

SAM: What?

SHOBA: I'm taking you off my guest list. Get ka-fusion to – or just pay the damn cover.

SAM: I ain't got any money.

SHOBA: I know. Don't I fucking know it. Get out of my life you loser. All this time I've been boiling your sperm in my belly. You fuckhead it ain't worth a dime, not even a warm belly at night.

SAM: You want this back then?

(He holds razor out.)

SHOBA: Yes.

SAM: You're gonna have to fight me for it then.

SHOBA: I'll fucking fight.

SAM: Yeah?

SHOBA: Don't think I won't fucking fight you.

SAM: So?

SHOBA: And I'm taking the cheap shots.

SAM: You can try.

> *(They circle each other slowly. They begin jabbing at one another. On the floor, wrestling, no one on top, no one winning until finally SHOBA lets out an unearthly sound, a note sustained and then shifting right into Raga scales until it ends in a scream of loss. He is pinned.)*

SHOBA: I'm alone, aren't I? You were never really with me ever?

SAM: I was fucking you.

SHOBA: Did you even see me?

SAM: Cover the face and fuck the body. I learned that in boarding school.

SHOBA: Your dark secret.

SAM: Yes.

SHOBA: Can't be gangsta with a boarding school uniform in your closet.

SAM: Hellz no.

SHOBA: I hate you.

SAM: I know. It's how it all started.

SHOBA: You're a fucking loser.

SAM: I never tried to sing though.

SHOBA: Fuck you. And yeah you did. In the shower once.

SAM: I got shampoo in my eye and screamed.

SHOBA: So that's why you bought Johnson&Johnson.

SAM: No more tears.

SHOBA: Yes. No.

SAM: I hate when you do that.

SHOBA: What?

SAM: Fucking say yes and no in the same breath.

SHOBA: It wasn't the same breath.

SAM: Yes it was.

SHOBA: It was two quick exhales.

SAM: So basically it's one breath.

SHOBA: Yes. No.

SAM: See? You can't do that shit. How the fuck am I supposed to know? Yes and no are like two very different things. It's like red and green at the stoplight.

SHOBA: My parents once interrogated me for three hours about if the light was red or green; they wouldn't take I don't know as an answer. They needed to rip into each other hard. They couldn't afford the ticket.

SAM: You've told me this.

SHOBA: I finally broke down and said –

SAM: Yellow. Is that supposed to be funny or some shit like that? Is it? Is it? Cuz if it is I'll fucking beat you.

SHOBA: Like in all the old plays and classic movies.

SAM: Yeah.

SHOBA: Take off your shirt.

SAM: It's too late for that.

SHOBA: You need to be in your wifebeater.

SAM: No.

SHOBA: Yes. In order to properly beat me.

SAM: You're not my wife.

SHOBA: I never asked to be.

SAM: Good.

SHOBA: Good.

SAM: But if I asked you'd say yes.

SHOBA: Hell no.

SAM: You would.

SHOBA: Didn't I just say no?

SAM: You're that type.

SHOBA: What type?

SAM: The type that would say yes if someone asked you to marry him.

SHOBA: Not just someone.

SAM: Me.

SHOBA: Yes. No.

SAM: Mother fucking hell – you will never change, will you?

SHOBA: I'm going to have to – the show starts in an hour.

SAM: Gonna skank it up?

SHOBA: If it's what I gotta do.

SAM: Gonna cover your off-notes with a crotch shot?

SHOBA: They can look but they can't touch.

    (He grabs her.)

SAM: But I can do whatever I want with you.

SHOBA: Yes. No.

(He collapses to the ground.)

SAM: You drive me insane.

SHOBA: I'm not doing any driving. I'm just along for the ride.

(She straddles him.)

SAM: I think I landed on the razor. It's cutting into my back like hell.

SHOBA: Good. That's what razors are meant to do.

SAM: It's not nice to stab a man in the back. Repeatedly.

SHOBA: But people do it.

SAM: Is that what we are? Just people?

SHOBA: Just people.

(She begins kissing him.)

SHOBA: And this is what people do.

(He breaks away.)

SAM: So you're keeping me on the list then, right?

SHOBA: Yeah. It's easier to keep it on than to take it off.

SAM: Good.

(They begin kissing again.)

SAM: And what time does ka-fusion come on again?

(She jumps up.)

SHOBA: G-ddamit.

SAM: What.

SHOBA: Just when I think, maybe ... maybe this time I'll come.

SAM: I'm just trying to plan my itinerary.

SHOBA: For the evening.

SAM: Yes.

SHOBA: For your late evening.

SAM: No.

SHOBA: Yes.

SAM: No. I said no. Quit trying to add a yes to it. You see how simple it is. Just no. Not yes no. Not no yes. Just no.

SHOBA: Her boyfriend's hot you know.

SAM: Yeah?

SHOBA: Hotter than you.

SAM: You'd think so.

SHOBA: What's that mean?

SAM: You have shit for taste.

SHOBA: I've tasted you.

SAM: I gave you a sampling. There's a difference.

SHOBA: Not fucking true.

SAM: Like hell it isn't.

SHOBA: I don't know what to say to that. Do you really think I'm terrible?

SAM: Your taste?

SHOBA: No. Me.

SAM: Yes. You can't help it though.

SHOBA: You used to think I was good.

SAM: I know. I used to think that and now I know you suck. But it's me, not you.

SHOBA: I knew it, I knew I shoulda bought the paint, the stuff that blocks sound.

SAM: Don't be stupid. I told you paint can't block sound.

SHOBA: It can. On the TV. The paint muffler.

SAM: Sounds like a fucking car part.

SHOBA: It would have protected me. From having you hate it. It hurts, it hurts because I didn't expect it to.

(She begins crying.)

SAM: Control yourself Shoba.

(She grabs razor from floor and slices herself repeatedly – wrists, legs, arms.)

SHOBA: The pain is mine, not yours.

(She goes to the bar, takes alcohol, pours it over her wounds. Lets out a shriek of pain, then joy, a beautiful note. Exhale. Relief.)

SAM: Waste of good liquor.

(He walks over to her. Begins licking the liquor off her skin slowly.)

SAM: How much time before the show starts?

SHOBA: Enough.

(They embrace.)

SHOBA: Oh G-d it still hurts.

(They sink down behind the bar together. Lights fade.)

END OF PLAY

piece by piece
by dennis moritz

* * *

Produced in Sticky: June 21, 2005, Belly Bar, directed by David Marcus. With Matthew Korahais and Eve Udesky; February 2006, Big Sticky, D-Lounge; April 27, 2007, Bowery Poetry Club, directed by dennis moritz.

* * *

(JENNIFER and JOE sit at an ordinary table. They have drinks. Does this mean a bar or a kitchen table. Is this a marriage or merely a friendship. The actors should not resolve this tension. But let it hang in the air. There should be interludes of music. Lights. Perhaps even people talking as though at a show. The characters look out at the audience as if seeing something or someone. But should not make eye contact with the audience. The characters can appear as though they are looking at a reverie or a day dream as they talk. Fast pace.)

JENNIFER: maybe you can believe them. i don't.

JOE: he wore hot pink as he did the walkway.
hot pink as he vamped down the catwalk.
over the top in hot pink. the entire outfit
visible see through a sheer top
peek a boo mini bottom a windy blouse.
he pushed his right hand on the side of his chin.
balled a loose fist under the right side of his jaw.
the face twisted up sidewise.
his face a mask twisted sidewise.
everything mannered and slow.
half speed. half speed. though the music was upbeat and loud.
slowly slowly he moved slowly
slowly in the upbeat fast sound.

JENNIFER: when they say things, do you look them in the eye.
when they insist, when they insist, what do you say.

JOE: i listen to the voice.

JENNIFER: i don't take anything at face value.

JOE: zoolander. tom cruise. will farrell or whoever.
will so and so and whatever.
now i like stripes and broadcloth shirts
i would vamp do the catwalk in upbeat moves.
my moves professional, corporate and clean.
no gender confusion. no gender confusion in the way i dress.
these are not a woman's pants or shirt.
get it. do you get it. sailor boy or sailor man
the gq the yachtsman lets say the yankee yachtsman ...
boaters. admiral cap. midnight blue.
boaters. admiral cap. midnight blue pants.

JENNIFER: i don't know any women who manage, any women who manage
to really figure it out. no one knows what to do ...

JOE: it's about being looked at. frozen out there and looked at.

JENNIFER: horrible. horrible. a horror story.

JOE: i want them to gasp cry hold their dicks no ...
let the room dim in sound and the light quiet down
to a physical rest
everyone breathing breathing in and out
breathing in and out as one ...
look. look at me.

JENNIFER: what if they tore you to pieces.

JOE: i want to live in their head for a flash.

JENNIFER: what if they pulled you apart piece by piece.

JOE: that's all right.

* * *

JENNIFER: i wouldn't do it forget it don't even think about it.

JOE: not to worry

JENNIFER: they could tear into me tear at me rip out my guts.

JOE: naw.

* * *

JENNIFER: when i'm walking out there, walking out there, walking out there in the world at large. i harden my face tense my muscles tense every muscle in my body. wear. wear. i wear clothes all over me. i am that women out there dressed in fluffy white clothes. all covered over. including my head. i am that woman whose face is covered up. i am the woman out there who walks around night and day. don't look into my eyes no way. i walk too fast for you to catch. not a chance. i walk ... fast.
i look normal enough even pretty even look ready to laugh. want to hear me laugh. want to. want to. what about it.

JOE: no.

JENNIFER: good.

JOE: i had enough.

JENNIFER: coming up coming right up.

> (*She lets out a loud violent scream then laughs. Lets out a wild violent scream. Then laughs.*)

JOE: gee. gee. jesus.

* * *

JENNIFER: i was never violated. never forced.

JOE: yes.

JENNIFER: never forced into anything.

JOE: if you say so.

JENNIFER: never forced into anything anytime.

JOE: if you say so ... if ... if ... if ...

* * *

JENNIFER: the world outside is a dream. the world inside also a dream. inside and outside a dream.

JOE: what about the republican national convention.

JENNIFER: inside and outside equally in balance. energy. energy. energy neither created or displaced. energy always out there and in here. inside our bodies. inside our bodies and mind. but invisible. a blank. a wonderful great invisible dream neither created or destroyed. invisible. can't taste. cannot feel it. has no odor cannot smell the invisible energy. all. all a dream.

JOE: what about the republican national convention.

* * *

JENNIFER: down south the old women talked about spirits.

JOE: well what of it.

JENNIFER: they talked about the spirits out there just as someone dozes off. half in a dream.

JOE: not a surprise.

JENNIFER: in a half dream when the sleeper or thinker is in a reverie in a half dream. the spirits proclaim themselves. push their attention on you.

JOE: talk to them. back and forth.

JENNIFER: what do you think what do you think happened.

* * *

JOE: we could have a baby. we could do it.

JENNIFER: why.

JOE: someone we would love.

JENNIFER: yes. yes.

JOE: we won't be around forever.

* * *

JENNIFER: i love riding horses. feel those huge perfect bodies under me.

JOE: never like it. always felt like i was about to fall a long way down.

JENNIFER: big tight muscles all over their bodies, hard and rhythmic.

JOE: it's a long way down from up there.

JENNIFER: alice walker talked about a girl who had an orgasm whenever she rode horses. she rode bare back. i do not. the girl had an orgasm lying on the ground over a small high spot on the ground. first time she had an orgasm she rubbed herself against a tree. have you ever thought about what it is what an orgasm actually is. the narrator said it was as if the girl made love to the world as a whole. all of nature at once.

* * *

JOE: for one minute. one second one instant. let me flash into all their minds at once. let me be a big flash they could not get away from. burned into their minds forever.

JENNIFER: you sound like a terrorist.

JOE: i'd die for it. burned up dead. flash. a smart cool and clean vamp down the runway.

* * *

JENNIFER: the old women down south. my mother's family, would talk about the spirits one saw out of the corner of an eye or when one slept half slept. half dreamed. the spirits alive out there in the visible invisible world.

JOE: scary stuff to tell a little girl.

JENNIFER: i was not scared. never scared. i knew if i stood up to them just said straight out leave, leave me alone, they would. but ... but ...

JOE: but what. you were probably so terrified you couldn't feel a damn thing.

JENNIFER: i wouldn't say leave. never.

JOE: huh.

JENNIFER: they're just people like ourselves. walking around like ourselves.

* * *

JOE: we could have a child.

JENNIFER: why.

JOE: love her. love her or love him.

JENNIFER: yes. i know.

JOE: even though i do not go that way. it would be simple.

JENNIFER: how.

JOE: i'd think of you as a man. make love to you as tho you were a man.

JENNIFER: what did you say.

* * *

JOE: don't you want to make it. goddam it. don't you want to be there out there in the world out there. don't you want to be in the world with respect. respected in the world at large. a mother. you could be a mother. the basic societal role. no one argues about how valid a mother is.

JENNIFER: you want a corporate job or a political ... a political elected office. *(She laughs and laughs.)* you want what a political appointment or an elected office. my god.

(She laughs and laughs.)

JOE: out there.

* * *

JENNIFER: often i have a dream. a real flat out dream. there are baby looking creatures. small soft big eyes. how could i not love them. i do love them. small soft creatures everywhere in my room. but as soon as i bend down to pick them up and cuddle, as soon as i bend down ... they flick out a long black forked tongue.

JOE: stop reading those books.

JENNIFER: i would love them except they are ugly and reptilian.

JOE: it's a movie a goddam movie a made up farce except instead of a laugh the audience gets scared.

JENNIFER: you arrange to have them rip out of your womb.

JOE: we could have a baby. i could wear my pressed blue cotton pants. a broadcloth shirt with vertical stripes. an admiral cap. boaters. i could speak like a yankee yachtsman. i could be clean and neat right down to my underwear. we could have a child. i would make love to you as though you were a man. it would be all right. it would all be all right. we'd fill out a perfect picture of family ... it would be ... it would be perfect. a perfect picture.

(Lights down.)

JENNIFER: fuck.

* * *

(JOE and JENNIFER looking at photographs.)

JOE: these are the pr pics. what do you think tell me. i want the look and concept right. pr photos need to project. i need to look iconic like an icon. me and the uber me. me and the concept of me. pictures are very powerful.

JENNIFER: no. not right.

JOE: repeatable and recognizable.

JENNIFER: what did you say.

JOE: the best pr images are repeatable and recognizable.

JENNIFER: no. no. go over the shots again.

JOE: andy warhol's 14 scenes from a car crash. saw the silk screen the other day. repeatable and recognizable. like andy warhol's picture sequence. 14 scenes from a car crash. picked up by the press.

JENNIFER: he's a genius.

JOE: bam.

JENNIFER: not sure about these.

JOE: family. these are pictures of just me. where's the family.

JENNIFER *(bangs table)*: damn.

> *(Lights down.)*

JOE: i mean it.

* * *

> *(JENNIFER looks in front of her and to the side as though following the motions of someone she sees.)*

JENNIFER: nice. very nice.

JOE: what.

JENNIFER: over the eye. yes. tilted off. rakish. call that a rakish ...

JOE: do you see something.

JENNIFER: the way the fabric falls ... pull it. pinch it at the waist. you're thin. the way you look so thin.

JOE: stop.

JENNIFER: rose and almond. rosy almond. i love tuberose ...

JOE: you're ...

JENNIFER: tuberose makes me feel giddy girlish.

JOE: nothing there.

JENNIFER: at a formal social occasion you'd make them drool.

JOE: nuts, daft.

JENNIFER *(to JOE)*: you want to have children.

JOE: what.

JENNIFER: family. a picture postcard family.

JOE: we could ...

JENNIFER *(to the apparition)*: play the music just like that. slow and lyrical.

JOE: and ... and ...

JENNIFER *(to JOE)*: she's wearing a wide brimmed hat that flops over her right eye. it has a ribbon that hangs down and sweeps her shoulder. her dress is pink, no rose. very soft and sheer. any breeze shifts the folds. as she moves the dress hangs and moves and breezes. the strong perfume is tuberose.

JOE: it's an apparition. an auditory and visual hallucination.

JENNIFER: she's a member of my family. she's an aunt back seven generations.

JOE: if we had a child ...

JENNIFER: she's rocking her daughter my sixth generation aunt. a pink fat baby. the rocking bassinet looks like a torture chamber. back and forth. back and forth. clink, clink, thud.

JOE: wait.

JENNIFER: it looks like a metal crib or a metal bassinet. steel. full of edges.

JOE: a crazy rural idea ...

JENNIFER: it feels like a broken womb. as tho my womb broke. a chip falling off.

JOE: that was her, them. maybe.

    (Lights down.)

* * *

    (Lights up.)

JENNIFER *(hits the desk)*: past highway 95 we will take a right. pass down rt 38E down rt 73S. on the left hand side there is a turn off marked byberry road. five miles down there's a house. victorian. late 1890. high dormers, peaked latticed windows, green clapboard walls. a tower pokes up to the side of the main roof. it is called the house of spiritual retreat. tina and i found the house back from the road not visible from the road behind trees behind a mound of something. we will walk into the house. inside there's a main stair with a sign saying highway to heaven. we will climb the stair in the late afternoon as the sun begins to set. it will be a clear day. the sun will redden a window visible from the top of the stair inside the tower. three stories up. four stories up. we will look out the window as the sun turns everything purple and red. it is spring. irises daisies lilies. the grass reddened as we look out. you will take me from behind. i will yell, howl. that's how we'll do it. when we'll do it. it'll be like making love to everything in the world. everything at once.

END OF PLAY

In Between
by Jesse Wann

* * *

Produced in Sticky: December 5, 2005, Mamma's Bar, directed by Ali Ayala. With Jeremiah Clancy and Elaine O'Brien; February 2006, Big Sticky, D-Lounge.

* * *

(TIM and DEBBIE sit on bar stools, martinis in front of both of them.)

TIM: I thought you understood.

DEBBIE: Understood what?

TIM: That I just wanted to have a beer and blow.

DEBBIE: What?

TIM: A beer and blow – and drink and dash.

DEBBIE: Oh, you mean one drink and then leave?

TIM: Yeah.

DEBBIE: Well ... you know, you seem a little nervous which I don't understand. It was a party for *your* friends.

TIM: Yeah, so?

DEBBIE: Since it was the first time I'd met them, it was weird that we left like that.

TIM: Like what?

DEBBIE: You know, after one quick drink. "Beer and blow" you call it. Seemed awfully abrupt.

TIM: I just didn't want to, you know have the small talk. It would have been endless.

DEBBIE: Meaning?

TIM: There were too many people to have any kind of interesting discussion. So you see it would have just been the same small talk over and over and over with all of those different people.

DEBBIE: Oh. But aren't they your friends, didn't you want to catch up with them?

TIM: I don't know, I guess not ...

DEBBIE: Okay ...

(They sip their drinks for a moment.)

DEBBIE: Did you not want to be seen with me?

TIM: What?

DEBBIE: You heard me.

TIM: What're you talking about? We *went* didn't we?

DEBBIE: Yeah but it was weird. Awkward. It was like you were embarrassed to be there.

TIM: I just don't need to be seen all the time, you know, be seen partying or party for the party's sake. I'll party if I have to, but you know, it's just not necessary all the time to party.

DEBBIE: But they were *your* friends. You said yourself that you never see them anymore.

TIM: I know, but, they are, they were friends from a different time. A crazier time. I'm a little older than you and we haven't been going out that long and so maybe you don't understand that you don't need to party all the time. Maybe you still need to party when there's a party, and that's cool, I understand that, but I just wasn't up for the party.

DEBBIE: Were there other girls you wanted to talk to at the party besides me?

TIM: What do you mean?

DEBBIE: Those girls we met, Vanessa and Claire looked at me with dagger eyes. Did you want to flirt with them but couldn't because I was there?

TIM: What? No, they're just ... I've known them a while, that's all.

DEBBIE: Have you slept with them?

TIM: I've just ... known them a while.

DEBBIE: But you seemed to be the most alive and excited during the time we talked with them. You had the biggest smile when we talked with them. Now, here with me, you just seem kind of disappointed.

TIM: That's not true, babe. I'm not disappointed. I'm, I'm really enjoying this – chat.

DEBBIE: But you didn't sleep with them?

TIM: At the same time?

         (She glares at him.)

TIM: I'm kidding. KIDDING. I've known them a long time ...

DEBBIE: So you said. Do you, sometimes, think that you could do better than me?

TIM: What?

DEBBIE: Well, you know. Better. Than me.

TIM: What makes you ask that?

DEBBIE: Well, because you're not as successful as you used to be?

TIM: What's *that* supposed to mean?

DEBBIE: Well, you know, because when you were still with Tiger Balm, you
                                                              (MORE)

DEBBIE (cont'd): were touring all over the world, reasonably famous, and having models hit on you left and right – you know.

TIM: Yeah, so?

DEBBIE: Well, were the girls you dated then better than me?

TIM: Better how?

DEBBIE: Nicer asses, legs, boobs, smiles. Sexier, more provocative. COMELIER?

TIM: I don't know.

DEBBIE: I think you do know. I'm not gonna pretend I'm as hot as they are – I have eyes too.

TIM: Well, who says I'm not successful now – that's not a very nice thing to say.

DEBBIE: Alright then – between successes.

TIM: I'm working on my own thing.

DEBBIE: I know you are.

TIM: Who says I can't have all of those things again?

DEBBIE: Is that what you want?

TIM: Isn't that what everyone wants?

DEBBIE: All of it?

TIM: Yeah, I guess –

DEBBIE: 'Cause when we first met you complained about that time with the band. I think the word you used was NIGHTMARE. Is that what YOU really want?

TIM: I guess. Sure, I want that. *(Short beat.)* Actually, I don't know what I want.

DEBBIE: Do you want me?

TIM: I *have* you.

DEBBIE: But do you still *want* me? Are you motivated toward me?

TIM: I'm here *with* you.

DEBBIE: If you could be anywhere in the world, would it be here?

TIM: I don't know. It can be anywhere?

DEBBIE: Would I be with you?

TIM: You *are* with me.

DEBBIE: But would I be with you in your fantasy? What about Vanessa and Claire from the party?

TIM: Look, I've just known them awhile, and I hadn't seen them in a while is all, it was nice to see them, that's why I was smiling.

DEBBIE: But you aren't smiling now?

TIM: You can't smile all the time, it's unnatural.

DEBBIE: Did they remind you of your days with Tiger Balm?

TIM: Well sure – they were around a lot.

DEBBIE: Do they remind you of your past success?

TIM: Yeah, I suppose. It was a heady time.

DEBBIE: So it wasn't *always* a "nightmare" it seems. Tiger Balm was good for the Tigers. If they remind you of the "heady time" what do I remind you of?

TIM: Can't we just ... why don't we go home and watch a movie. Did you pick up those sleeping pills?

DEBBIE: Are you going to fall asleep before you lay a hand on me?

TIM: What?

DEBBIE: Are we going to make love?

TIM: Yeah, okay, sure.

DEBBIE: I don't know if I want to.

TIM: Then why'd you ask?

DEBBIE: I don't know.

TIM: Why're you asking all these questions? I'm sorry I'm not as successful as I was – maybe I will be again, is that the point?

DEBBIE: That's not the point.

TIM: What is the point?

DEBBIE: That doesn't bother me, your success, or lack thereof.

TIM: It doesn't, then why –

DEBBIE: It bothers *you*.

TIM: Me?

DEBBIE: Yes, you. Everything, in comparison, is a disappointment – even the parts you hated. That's why me being at the party was weird – because I was not a part of that time. You were mixing two different versions of you.

TIM: It's just an in-between.

DEBBIE: Not for me.

TIM: What do you mean – you're *with* me aren't you?

DEBBIE: But you're not with me. You see, I'm not between anything, I'm here right now.

TIM: Well, of course –

DEBBIE: I'm not – *waiting for something else.*

TIM: That's not –

DEBBIE: I'm not *consumed with these comparisons.*

TIM: You're not? Maybe you just don't have anything to compare it to.

DEBBIE: I have ex-boyfriends. People I've slept with. People I've had crushes on.

TIM: Well do you want to call them?

DEBBIE: Who?

TIM: All those guys – do you want to have them meet us here?

DEBBIE: Why?

TIM: We could have, like, a big orgy of memories or feelings or something. Make a *party* of it.

DEBBIE: I don't *care* about the *party*.

TIM: You don't? You really seem to.

DEBBIE: I am not an in-between.

TIM: Of course not.

DEBBIE: I don't care about your past success.

TIM: You don't?

DEBBIE: Who says you're not more successful now than you were then. Tiger Balm's second album was CRAP.

TIM: What?

DEBBIE: DOGSHIT. UNLISTENABLE.

TIM: Oh.

DEBBIE: You see?

TIM: Yeah, you know, I always thought that too. You know, I fought to go back into the studio, but the rest of the guys were fucking coked out of their minds, chasing after every
girl, and –

DEBBIE: It was a NIGHTMARE?

TIM: Yeah.

DEBBIE: So, did you sleep with Vanessa or Claire?

TIM: Well ... yeah.

DEBBIE: Both of them?

TIM: Y-Yeeah ...

DEBBIE: Do you want to sleep with them still?

TIM: Um, no.

DEBBIE: Even though they have nice asses?

TIM: Well –

DEBBIE: And perky and nipply breasts that form fit their vintage t-shirts?

TIM: No.

DEBBIE: Even though they're prettier than me?

TIM: You're much nicer.

DEBBIE: Nicer?

TIM: Hot and heavier.

DEBBIE: Heavier?

TIM: In a good way. Heavier in the best sense of the word.

DEBBIE: And smarter?

TIM: Oh definitely.

DEBBIE *(leaning in, seductive)*: And different.

TIM: Definitely different –

DEBBIE: Different can be good.

TIM: Different is good.

DEBBIE *(taking his hand)*: Don't you want to do it different.

TIM: Yeah. I do. I do want to Do It Different.

DEBBIE: Do it different.

TIM: Yeah.

DEBBIE: Yeah.

TIM: Do it.

DEBBIE: Different.

(They toast. They kiss.)

END OF PLAY

Dirtfag
by Michael Domitrovich

* * *

Produced in Sticky: April 28, 2006, Galapagos Art Space, directed by Ali Ayala. With Damon Boggess, David Marcus and Ana Valle.

* * *

(Summertime. A bar in Brooklyn. ANYA enters. She is fiercely beautiful and a little haggard.)

ANYA: I am going to the bathroom. *(She squats.)* I am pissing. Pushing extra hard. Hoping. And pushing.

(She shakes her body violently, pressing against the walls of a bathroom stall.)

ANYA: A bathroom stall. A cubicle. Seems small. But not if you think. That something much bigger can be somewhere much smaller. And girls everywhere just like me can make the bigger thing come right the fuck out.

(She hits herself in the stomach. She is not sad, but determined. ANYA exits. SEAN sits on a stool. He has been drinking. He's Irish. Pale. Like a six-foot tall leprechaun with a violent sexual appetite. Every glance devours. TEDDY walks in. He is smaller, darker, and somewhat put together. He is looking for SEAN. Sees him. Goes to him.)

TEDDY: Pennsylvania station is positively overflowing. *(SEAN nods.)* But everybody's leaving. I'm the only one coming back. Say hello Sean.

SEAN: Wudup.

TEDDY: What're you doing?

(SEAN examines his beer.)

SEAN: Drinking.

TEDDY: You called me.

SEAN: Yup.

TEDDY: You told me to me to get back on the train right away. Because it was important.

SEAN: It is important.

TEDDY: So important you can't even look at me?

SEAN *(sighs)*: I'm thinking.

TEDDY: Sean.

SEAN: You want a drink?

TEDDY: Yes.

SEAN *(ordering)*: Beer.

TEDDY: No. Vodka. Raspberry Stoli. With Sprite. Or 7-Up.

SEAN *(not impressed)*: Raspberry vodka?

TEDDY: Sean. Darling. I have been to Penn Station twice already on this most horrible of holiday weekends. I am being poisoned by the sweat of upwardly mobile douchebags and I refuse to drink beer just because you ordered it. I am hot. I hate beer. And I'd rather be in Cherry Grove.

(SEAN looks at TEDDY. Turns on the charm.)

SEAN: Raspberry vodka then. It's good to see you Teddy.

TEDDY: Thank you.

SEAN: No. Thank you. For coming back.

TEDDY: I'm going to get into some shit with my boss.

SEAN: Don't they have another pizza boy?

TEDDY: There's always another pizza boy. But I'm me. I have regulars.

SEAN: I bet.

TEDDY: My milkshake brings all the boys to the Grove.

SEAN: For pizza.

TEDDY: For attitude.

SEAN: Attitude?

TEDDY: I will be sorely missed.

SEAN: You can be back by tomorrow.

TEDDY: If I turn around now.

SEAN: I'm just saying ...

TEDDY: You have got to be kidding me with this.

SEAN: If you have to be back for work ...

TEDDY: I do. In the morning.

SEAN: I understand ...

TEDDY: But I already did. When I was about to get on the last ferry and you told me to come back because it was important.

SEAN: Right. Sorry.

TEDDY: But it sounded serious.

SEAN: You wouldn't believe the day I had. Total craziness.

TEDDY: After we finished drinking at nine in the morning.

SEAN: It got nuts.

TEDDY: After we made out in Anya's room.

SEAN: She's here. In the bathroom.

TEDDY: After I sucked your dick and you took a shower.

SEAN: Yeah. After.

TEDDY: After I rode to Penn Station with you. On the pegs of your BMX bike which truly should belong to a fifteen year old.

SEAN: After I gave you the rest of my dexies.

TEDDY: So I could sober up before seeing my parents.

SEAN: After that.

TEDDY: After I grabbed your bike chain and pulled you close. After I kissed you in front of the escalators on 34th street.

SEAN: After you said goodbye.

TEDDY: Because I couldn't face Fire Island. Couldn't feel superior, casual, aloof. Couldn't become an object of desire in less than three hours. Unless I got at least a little close. To you.

SEAN: After that.

TEDDY: What happened after that?

SEAN: My bike was gone.

TEDDY: Your BMX?

SEAN: Cuz I still had the chain on.

TEDDY: The one I pulled. Around your chest.

SEAN: Cuz I was still kinda buzzed.

TEDDY: Cuz you gave me the rest of your dexies that you coulda used yourself.

SEAN: Yeah. I went back and my bike was gone.

TEDDY: You always lock it up.

SEAN: I was saying goodbye.

TEDDY: And you were drunk.

SEAN: And saying goodbye. I had a really good time with you. *(TEDDY looks at him carefully, silent.)* You're a good guy.

TEDDY: So are you.

SEAN: Not me.

TEDDY: You are. A good guy.

SEAN: Nah. Just some feckin pale ass Beantown dirtfag.

(*He burps. Big ole belch. Huge.*)

TEDDY: What'd you do about your bike?

SEAN: Walked.

TEDDY: You couldn't do anything else?

SEAN: No bike. Had to walk. Nice though. Heated.

TEDDY: Yes the streets are heated.

SEAN: Drank sodas.

TEDDY: It's July.

SEAN: I smoked a cigarette with the dude in the skirt when I got to Washington Square. I figured who's gonna steal my bike and not eventually get through the park. So I waited.

TEDDY: With a guy in a skirt?

SEAN: The one that stands in the middle of the fountain. Or on the corner by NYU. With the umbrella.

TEDDY: That's good Sean.

SEAN: He's a good guy.

TEDDY: Him too?

SEAN *(laughs)*:   Nah. I mean I killed time. Smoked a cigarette. Good guy to chill with. And then to leave.

TEDDY: I gotcha.

SEAN *(charming, sincere)*: I don't think you do.

TEDDY: I think so.

SEAN: I didn't mean it like that.

TEDDY: So good. What did you mean it like?

SEAN: I want to do something for you.

TEDDY: For me?

SEAN: Cuz I need something.

TEDDY: Yes. You need something. You always need something and you know I'm just the boy to give it to you.

　　　　(SEAN leans in.)

SEAN: But I want to give you something first.

TEDDY: What?

SEAN: Tell me why you came back.

TEDDY: Before you ask me for a favor?

SEAN *(laughs, leans back)*:   Tell me why. And I'll tell you if I agree.

TEDDY: I do all sorts of things when you're involved. Things that would be easier un-done.

SEAN: Tell me what I do that's enough to make you turn around from the ferry to Fire Island just cuz I said so.

TEDDY: You're my friend.

SEAN: Yeah. *(Laughs. Cocky.)* More.

TEDDY: More?

SEAN: Tell me more.

TEDDY: Oh Sean. If you only knew what I thought. When you do what you do.

SEAN: I want to know.

TEDDY: I think of when you made me take the bus up to Boston, and I wandered the fuck around Somerville looking for your basement apartment and there was no way to find you cuz your phone wasn't on, so I walked the streets and didn't see you till I walked all the way to Harvard Square and you were standing outside the Greenhouse Coffee Shop eating a slice of triple layer carrot cake with cream cheese frosting to wash down the three hits of ecstasy you'd just taken. You cried when you saw me. You hugged me and wouldn't let go. You told me you'd been waiting for me all week. And then you walked me to your bike and let me ride your pegs for the first time. And then we got drunk on 40's and took our shirts off and made out in the basement of your mother's house. You blew your nose on my shirt cuz you thought it was yours. But then you picked the one that was actually yours up off the floor and let me wear it. And that ... that was when you said you could see me being ... with ... you. If it were just ... if just one thing was different. You looked up at me and you said you were really crazy for someone. And you looked like a crazy person so I knew it was true. And then you said sorry but I would have to stay the night upstairs. In the guest room of your mother's house. In your t-shirt. So your new punk-rock-homo-pal could sleep a couple hours and fuck you up the ass which is new for you and hard for you, but you trust this guy and you feel something major for him and could I not be mad at you cuz if this made any more sense maybe you could figure out a way to make it not go like this and you know you invited me up and it's kinda shit to make me sleep in your mom's guest room but this is so new and different and crazy. And you know what I thought?

SEAN: That kid moved to North Carolina.

TEDDY: I thought you should do what felt right. I thought hearts are for following not for taming. I thought it was gonna hurt so bad the only way I could get through the night would be to smell your shirt and choke on beer and sweaty cigarettes until the fumes brought something that hurt a little less. I thought if my heart is broken, shattered by a drunken Beantown dirtfag, I could not be any more miserable or alive. But all I said was no problem. Wake me up at ten. Or whenever he's gone. And we'll have breakfast.

SEAN: He's gone. Moved. He didn't like Boston.

(ANYA enters.)

ANYA: What'd he say?

SEAN: Haven't asked him.

ANYA: We need money.

TEDDY: Excuse me?

ANYA: Not a lot.

TEDDY: My money?

SEAN: Anya.

TEDDY: What for?

ANYA: You didn't tell him?

TEDDY: What is it for?

SEAN: Anya needs it. For ...

ANYA: Not a lot.

SEAN: I'm paying half.

ANYA: But I'm still short.

TEDDY: How much?

ANYA: Six hundred.

TEDDY: Dollars?

SEAN: I wouldn't ask if it wasn't important.

TEDDY: I don't have six hundred dollars to give.

SEAN: I wouldn't ask if it wasn't important.

TEDDY: Why are you paying half?

SEAN: I'm responsible.

ANYA: For half. At least.

TEDDY: You're responsible?

SEAN: Partly.

ANYA: At least half.

TEDDY: This shouldn't surprise me. It doesn't. But then it does.

SEAN: I wouldn't ask if ...

TEDDY: You wouldn't ask if you didn't know I'd give it to you.

SEAN: It would mean so much to me.

    (Beat.)

TEDDY: Why do I love it when you make me feel this way?

SEAN: I will make it up to you.

TEDDY: Do you promise?

ANYA: I promise. He will. So will I.

    (TEDDY looks to ANYA. Back to SEAN.)

TEDDY: I'm writing a check.

ANYA: Make it out to cash.

TEDDY: Six hundred dollars?

SEAN: Thanks Teddy.

TEDDY: I can't afford this.

SEAN: I'll make it up to you.

ANYA: There's a check cashing place on Seventh Avenue.

(TEDDY has written the check. He tears it out and gives it to SEAN.)

TEDDY: How do you plan on making this up to me? Cuz I know you're not going to pay me back.

SEAN: I will. I promise.

(SEAN kisses TEDDY.)

ANYA: Go. Now. Cash it.

SEAN: Now?

ANYA: Then come back.

SEAN: OK. Don't leave.

(SEAN leaves.)

TEDDY: He won't pay me back.

ANYA: He won't have to.

TEDDY: How did this happen? When did you screw?

ANYA: It's not an issue.

TEDDY: Do you have a doctor?

ANYA: I don't need one.

TEDDY: For the procedure?

ANYA: It's taken care of.

TEDDY: I don't understand.

ANYA: I don't need a procedure.

TEDDY: You've had one?

ANYA: No.

TEDDY: Then why the money? Six hundred dollars? Twelve?

ANYA: I've bled enough. Or I will bleed. Have been bleeding.

TEDDY: Are you crazy?

ANYA: And now I'm leaving. And he'll be yours.

TEDDY: Leaving where?

ANYA: You should thank me.

TEDDY: But I gave you my money.

ANYA: He would have followed that boy. All the way to North Carolina. They wanted to become organic farmers. He would have stopped drinking. Cleaned up. And slowly but surely every drop of Sean as we know him would have leaked out into the fields and our little man would be gone.

TEDDY: But is it true? Did you two ... ?

ANYA: I did what I had to. And now I'm moving to Montreal. Where dollars are worth more than here. Don't tell Sean.

TEDDY: He'll want to know.

ANYA: He needs to be let down. Needs to wonder. He's not so mysterious when he isn't in pain. Trust me. I've known him a long time.

TEDDY: Do you need anything else from me?

ANYA: I have a job at a club.

TEDDY: I want to help you.

ANYA: I'll find more work from there.

TEDDY: Do you really need to leave?

ANYA: Don't be such a pussy. This is your chance to get him. But he must be trapped. With no way out. He's got to be a prisoner.

TEDDY: I'm not like that.

ANYA: But if you were. And I think you are. You would be so perfect.

TEDDY: He is perfect for me.

ANYA: Then you'd be stuck together. And I'll be free. In Montreal.

<u>END OF PLAY</u>

The Question
by Adam Szymkowicz

* * *

Produced in Sticky: March 30, 2007, Bowery Poetry Club, directed by David Marcus. With Cara Francis and David Marcus.

CHARACTERS
Gina
Stu

SETTING
Someplace unromantic. A dirty apartment, a fast food joint, a dentist's office. Something like that.

TIME
Now.

* * *

(GINA is thinking. STU stares at her.)

STU: So?

GINA: It's unfair of you to bring this up. It's unfair here and now. Everyone's suffering and I can't even have any sympathy for them although I have felt from time to time, these windows of feeling for people not like me far away. But even those windows are gone now and I march in and out of our world like a zombie on a track and then you come in with your thoughts and proposals.

STU: It's been four years, Gina.

GINA: I feel everyday I want to cut my hands off or photocopy myself to death. Get caught in the fax machine, the paper shredder. Or the electric

(MORE)

GINA (cont'd): stapler. It's easier to talk to the phone callers or my well-coiffed and varied bosses if I swallow antidepressants in expectation of a full day of people throwing stacks of papers at me.

STU: But –

GINA: Five years ago I was chasing down suitors like they were wild beasts. And I caught most of them. Most of them I caught. Men, women, men and women. And I fucked regularly, some might say constantly. Sometimes on lunch or cigarette breaks. Always or often with some regret.

STU: Gina –

GINA: And the gallons of coffee I drank. Between lines of coke. And tabs of acid. Shrooms. Lots of pot. And the mystery pills my roommate brought home and hid between her toes. I was hung over or strung out all the time. I was always so tired. All the time tired. But that was before my life with you.

STU: I know, but –

GINA: And you ... you have bad breath all the time. You never wash the dishes and when you do, they come out with hair on them and you leave the dirty sponge in the sink. Sometimes you get drunk and you say the most horrible things to my friends, to your friends, to strangers. You temp all day. You are two hundred and twenty thousand dollars in debt from a questionable education. You're always on the internet.

STU: What's wrong with the internet?

GINA: You hate yourself seventy to eighty percent of the time. The other twenty to thirty percent of the time you hate me. Recently you piled all your laundry into a sort of a nest where you now sleep instead of in the bed with me.

STU: I have a bad back.

GINA: You don't wash. Your face is scratchy when you do touch me, which you rarely do. You never say *I love you* anymore. And you wear those goddamn pants every fucking day. Except when you come home and walk around in those ratty-ass boxer shorts you probably took from your dad's hamper last time we visited your folks.

STU: They're mine.

GINA: And it's not just one or two of these things. It's a collection of these tiny infractions and flaws and gaps in what there is and what there could be – not that I know or could tell you exactly what could be because everything seems pretty bleak and nothing seems possible in any way. I guess I'm trying to say I think I'm not happy right now.

STU: OK. *(Pause.)* But what does that mean? Do you want to get married or what?

    (Pause.)

GINA: I don't know. Let me think about it.

STU: OK. Cool.

    (GINA thinks. STU stares at her.)

END OF PLAY

Eve Udesky, Stephanie Silver & Dan O'Brien
in Libby Emmons' "The Worm Turns at the Fort Peck Hotel"

The Worm Turns at the Fort Peck Hotel
by Libby Emmons

* * *

Produced in Sticky: November 16, 2007, Bowery Poetry Club, directed by David Marcus. With Dan O'Brien, Stephanie Silver and Eve Udesky.

* * *

(CALLIE and JOE in the closed bar of the Fort Peck Hotel, Fort Peck, Montana. They are drunk. CALLIE in a bridesmaid dress, JOE in a short-sleeve button-down and tie. His tie is loosened, her heels are abandoned on the floor. CALLIE, JOE and SAMARA are all from the same high school class.

(AT RISE: CALLIE and JOE are laughing, calling good night to wedding friends.)

JOE: See you at breakfast!

CALLIE: Ten a.m. bloodies!

(CALLIE puts her legs up on JOE's lap, they get comfortable.)

CALLIE: Oh Joe, our own little Stevie.

JOE: I know, she looked amazing.

CALLIE: Sure, if you're into that sort of thing.

JOE: Virginal white?

CALLIE: I don't know how virginal it was.

JOE *(laughing, flirting)*: I do.

CALLIE *(laughing)*: That's right, you do.

JOE: God, she was wild.

CALLIE: I know, an' New York's not much of a place to settle down in to hear her tell it.

JOE: I bet she even shocks New York, sometimes.

CALLIE: She can get away with that stuff, but if it were me, New York would shock right back an' I'd be runnin' home West with my tail between my legs.

JOE: You're too hard on yourself, why are you like that?

CALLIE: I'm just honest, that's all.

JOE: Your version of honest.

CALLIE: What else is there? *(Reaching forward.)* Oh my itty-bitty toes just got crushed in these things.

JOE: They're worth it though.

CALLIE: Yeah? You think so? I got 'em at Payless.

JOE: Lemme see those toes.

>   *(She holds out her foot, he rubs her toes.)*

CALLIE *(enjoying it)*: I was always a little jealous of you guys y'know.

JOE: Of me and Stevie? Naw.

CALLIE: It was a real blow for me when you picked her instead of me.

JOE: I didn't even know your were interested.

CALLIE: Really?

JOE: You really think I woulda picked anyone over you?

CALLIE: You mean it?

JOE: You were a hot little number back then Callie, of you, Stevie an' Sammy you were the only one made it into my dreams every night.

CALLIE *(laughing)*: Oh stop.

> *(SAMARA, aka Sammy, runs in. CALLIE bolts upright. SAMARA has a camera.)*

SAMARA *(excited, freaked out)*: Oh my god you guys, I totally saw it, it was like floating right in front of me, in the mirror, with like these google eyes, just staring at me.

CALLIE: Google eyes?

JOE: You sure they weren't yers? 'Cause yers look a little googley.

> *(CALLIE and JOE laugh.)*

SAMARA: Yeah Joe, I'm sure, I even took pi'tures.

CALLIE: Of the google eyes.

> *(CALLIE and JOE share a look, laugh.)*

SAMARA *(frustrated)*: Yeah, look.

> *(She hands over the camera.)*

CALLIE *(looking through the images)*: These're all black.

SAMARA: No Callie, I swear.

JOE: These're all black Sammy.

SAMARA: Well what'd ya want me to do, I couldn't use the flash and it was dark in there.

JOE *(antagonizing her)*: Why couldn't you use the flash?

SAMARA: Oh my god, you guys totally don't believe me, Callie, listen. When have I ever made up anything that wasn't true?

CALLIE *(joking for JOE's benefit)*: You mean somethin' that wasn't true that I found out about?

SAMARA: Callie, I'm really serious, okay? This really happened, and that's not all.

JOE *(surprised by a photo)*: Oh my god!

SAMARA *(reaching for the camera)*: Gimme that!

CALLIE: Let me see.

> *(JOE keeps it away from SAMARA so CALLIE can see. CALLIE laughs, shocked by it.)*

SAMARA *(grabbing it back)*: Stop looking at that!

CALLIE: That girl is hot!

JOE: Is she your girlfriend?

SAMARA: I don't have a girlfriend, I don't do that anymore, listen, you guys, there are ghosts in this fucking hotel, jus' like the guy said, I swear, an' they came at me in my room, first as a set a fuckin' google eyes in the mirror, an then I backed up 'cause I was freakin' out an' the sink started spinnin' around.

CALLIE: The sink?

JOE *(joking with CALLIE)*: Didn't you know? This hotel has special spinnin' sinks.

> *(CALLIE laughs, SAMARA ignores him.)*

SAMARA *(spinning her fingers)*: In circles Callie, I swear.

CALLIE: Why would your sink start spinnin' around?

SAMARA: Because there's a fuckin' ghost in this hotel, jus' like the guy said, I swear to god. It was like –

> *(She makes hand gestures and sound effects of the sink spinning around fast.)*

JOE: Sammy, are you okay?

SAMARA: Seriously, like picture me, right?

JOE and CALLIE: Right.

SAMARA: An' everything's normal and THEN PICTURE ME WITH MY ASS IN THE AIR!

CALLIE: Samara!

JOE *(laughing)*: I can picture that.

SAMARA: For real Callie, I'm not makin' it up, there were orbs!

(She looks frantically through the photos on the camera.)
SAMARA: I swear on one a these there were orbs.

JOE: Hmmm. So you can jus' talk yourself outta somethin' like that?

SAMARA: Like what?

JOE: Like bein' a lesbo?

SAMARA: I'm not a lesbo anymore Joe, why d'ya think I moved home?

JOE: You moved home to stop bein' a lesbo?

CALLIE: I heard it was meth.

SAMARA: Who'd you hear that from?

CALLIE: Stevie's mom.

SAMARA: She's just jealous.

CALLIE: Of you or the meth?

SAMARA: Maybe she's just a bitch.

JOE *(taunting, school yard)*: Maybe you are.

SAMARA *(last-ditch attempt)*: Look, Callie, I know we never been too closer r whatever, but for real this really happened an' I like really need you to believe me right now 'cause Stevie won't even listen to me 'cause she's fucking married r whatever an there're ghosts in this fucking hotel I swear to fucking god.

JOE *(rising)*: Well, I think I might take a little walk around town, for old time's sake.

CALLIE *(picking up her shoes)*: I think I better be getting off to bed.

(CALLIE and JOE head off in the same direction.)

SAMARA *(to CALLIE, pointing the other way)*: Your bedroom's that way.

CALLIE: Well, y'know, maybe I'd like a little walk before turning in. You mind if I join you Joe?

JOE: Not at all Callie, it'd be my pleasure.

SAMARA *(suspicious)*: So that's how it is.

CALLIE: What's how it is?

SAMARA *(taking her time, lounging)*: I had a nice time talkin' with yer wife tonight Joe.

JOE: Did ya?

SAMARA: Sure did. She said y'all breed dogs down there in Texas.

JOE: That we do.

SAMARA: Says your favorite bitch got a litter a puppies on the way.

JOE: Any day now, that's right.

SAMARA: They must be cute when they first come out, all slimy an' blind, with only enough instinct to find their mama's teat an' suck on it.

JOE: It is quite a site to behold.

CALLIE *(to SAMARA)*: The only reason Stevie even invited you to this wedding is because she felt bad for you, you retarded little dwarf. *(SAMARA gasps.)* If she'd a had it someplace else, like in New York r wherever the hell Patrick's family is from she wouldn'ta invited you at all.

SAMARA: That's not true, she's my oldest friend in the world.

CALLIE: Oldest don't mean best, does it.

SAMARA: Oldest is better than best.

CALLIE: Then why isn't it called best? We all know how your poor mother had to drag you out of L.A., the meth, the lesbian pornos.

JOE *(pleasantly surprised)*: You've been in pornos?

SAMARA: So what? *(To CALLIE.)* You play like you're always Miss Perfect all the time, but what do you really do out there in Boise?

CALLIE: I'm not ashamed of the blue apron, I'm not ashamed at all. I work for a living, I don't fuck people for money.

SAMARA: So you were jus' gonna do Joe here for free?

CALLIE *(trying to save face)*: Joe? I wasn't trying to fuck Joe, we were just catching up on old times.

JOE *(trying to make peace)*: C'mon guys, let's not revert back to high school, we've all grown a lot since then. I mean, here we are at Stevie's wedding. I for one never thought she'd get hitched, an' that's comin' from a guy who went out with her all senior year.

SAMARA: Oh c'mon Joe, she only went out with you 'cause Marty went off to college an' she knew you had the hots for her from sixth grade.

JOE: Only 'cause she was the first girl I ever saw naked, I mean, besides my mom. Wait, that didn't sound right.

CALLIE: You saw her naked?

SAMARA: In Becky Morrison's garage in the dark. *(To CALLIE.)* They played Seven Minutes in Heaven an' Joe was afraid to take off his clothes so it was jus' Stevie standin' there in her socks an nothin' else until the time was up.

JOE: Not for the whole time, she put 'em on after a minute or two.

SAMARA: He asked her out after that but she said no way. *(To JOE.)* She said you were a pussy.

JOE *(defensive)*: I thought "heaven" was making out, not getting naked.

SAMARA: What's the difference?

JOE: What do you mean what's the difference? I wasn't gonna attack a skinny naked girl in the dark.

CALLIE: So you jus' – looked at her?

SAMARA *(smug)*: Looks like oldest counts for a little more than best.

JOE: It was dark.

CALLIE *(to SAMARA)*: If I'd a known her then I woulda known about it.

JOE: Plus she probably forgot about it.

SAMARA: We g-chatted about it a few weeks before the wedding, 'cause she said Joe's coming to the wedding with his wife an I said it's been a real long time since I saw Joe! An' she said no matter what she couldn't get that pi'ture of you standin' there in the garage, all dressed while she was naked, outta her mind. She said even while you were goin' out, all senior year, every time you guys did it she'd think a that an laugh an' laugh. An' I said what'd you tell him about why you were laughin' an' she said she'd say she was ticklish.

CALLIE: She is ticklish, you didn't know that?

SAMARA *(uncomfortable)*: No, I mean, I knew that.

JOE: Plus when you get high and screw, ya laugh.

> *(SAMARA freezes, hearing a sound. CALLIE and JOE follow suit, and they all look around quietly.)*

SAMARA: Did you hear that?

CALLIE *(maybe believing in ghosts)*: It sounded like a baby crying.

JOE *(having none of it)*: There's babies stayin' in the hotel, you two probably woke one up.

SAMARA: The guy before said that sometimes? Late at night? When the whole hotel is fast asleep, you can sometimes hear the sound of a baby crying in the lobby.

CALLIE: No!

SAMARA: Yes!

JOE: That's stupid.

SAMARA: You're stupid Joe. Standin' there in all yer clothes while a girl stands there naked waitin for Seven Minute in Heaven.

CALLIE *(laughing)*: I can't believe she went out with you after that.

JOE: Jesus, this is just like high school. You girls givin' me shit an' me standin' here taken' it. I don't need this. I'm a very successful breeder, my wife an I do amazing business. *(Tipping his imaginary hat.)* Good night to you ladies. See you at the next wedding.

CALLIE *(faux coy)*: Not one little kiss Joe?

JOE *(pointing a mean finger at her)*: Fuck you. *(To SAMARA.)* I hated you in high school.

(He storms off.)

CALLIE: Wow, he's really mad.

SAMARA *(finding it in the camera)*: Ha! Look, I found it – orbs, I told you, orbs!

CALLIE *(looking at it)*: Oh my god what is that!

SAMARA: Orbs. Orbs of the ghost. C'mon, the guy said before there's a chair on the third floor that no matter which way you face it, it always turns again an' faces the North window.

CALLIE: Why North?

SAMARA: I don't know, maybe the ghost's Canadian. Let's check it out.

CALLIE: Should we get Stevie?

SAMARA: Fuck her man, she made her choice.

CALLIE *(running off after her)*: Hey, you ever been to Boise?

END OF PLAY

David Marcus & Penny Bittone in Michael Niederman's "American Hosanna"

American Hosanna
by Michael Niederman

* * *

With Apologies to Alan Ginsberg

Produced in Sticky: June 13, 2008, Bowery Poetry Club, directed by Ali Ayala. With Penny Bittone and David Marcus.

* * *

(Barely Controlled Chaos.
Like Jazz.
At bar are ALAN and NEAL, two dreamers. It's far too late in the evening. But no one is going home yet.)

ALAN: Bars are for self discovery. You sit for as long as they let you, stare at your reflection, and reflect.

NEAL: And? What have we learned?

ALAN: I've determined that I've wasted my life.

NEAL: Oh, hush. Your life is fine.

ALAN: Where is it? I can't find it. It's all a blur. I've drunk away my youth, my twenties –

NEAL *(wistful)*: – Good times –

ALAN: – my righteous fury, my sense of entitlement, my good looks –

NEAL: Hey. Hey! You are an attractive man and any woman would be honored to have sex on you. In multiple positions and then she'd lie to you afterwards about how good it was!

ALAN: Aw, you're just trying to cheer me up.

NEAL: Fine. You got no looks to waste 'cause you, my depressive and melancholy friend, ain't never been pretty. Happy?

ALAN: Depressive and melancholy mean the same thing.

NEAL: No. You, sir, are Melancholy because you never stop bitching. You are Depressive because you cause me to be Melancholy too and bitch like you.

(*Beat. Sip.*)

ALAN: It all sucks!

(*NEAL's head goes* thunk *on the bar.*)

NEAL: It's gonna one of those nights again, isn't it?

ALAN: Everything sucks! My life!

NEAL (*Pentecostal*): Yes! Your life sucks!

ALAN: My job!

NEAL: Sweet Jeebus does your job suck!

ALAN: My girlfriend.

NEAL: The woman you love doesn't suck nearly enough. I feel your pain.

ALAN: Is it me? Do I suck? That must be true. I suck and I'm going to keep on sucking because suck is all I've ever known.

NEAL (*a rare moment of seriousness*): Well, yeah. We all suck. Everything sucks. Don't tell me this surprises you. The world is going to hell in a suck basket. The country is being driven off a cliff by madmen and voting for some charming sucker and jiver ain't gonna change that none. Hey – you really want to get depressed? Chew on this: we are the last generation that's ever going to know comfort. Think about that. The oil's going to dry up in fifty years and this, what this is, relaxing in a bar with cold beer and electric lights and tunes on the radio – all that's going to go bye-bye. We'll be out in the forest fighting for food along with the other animals. Just like God and Ted Nugent intended.

ALAN: No one's ever going to love me again!

NEAL: Are you serious! I'm talking about the end of the world and The Nuge and all you can think of is –

ALAN: I'm gaining weight and I'm poor and I think there's a mole on my neck that's only getting bigger.

NEAL: Christ! Could you – please, I'm having a good time – could you stop it and – here – *(Motions to the BARTENDER.)* Barkeep! Two more! *(To ALAN.)* Drink the Pain Away! If that's what this night is going to be, what with you crying into your beer and me propping you up with my unnatural good moods – that's fine, sure, whatever dude, that's what I get when I hang out with you – but can we at least be drunk when it happens so I feel like I've accomplished something?

ALAN: If I could black out then it'd be different. There'd be a goal. Let's drink until we go blind. But no. Consciousness is my curse! I SEE EVERYTHING!

NEAL *(to the BARTENDER)*: Remember those two more? Double it.

(*The BARTENDER will eventually put down four beers.*)

ALAN: You know, sometimes I wish I could just do something about it.

NEAL: *Do* something? Do *something?*

ALAN: If I fixed myself. Fixed the inner soul.

NEAL: As opposed to the outer soul?

ALAN: Healed myself so I could go forward and do good things.

NEAL: Depressive Heal Thyself!

ALAN: Go back to school. Get that degree that leads to a better job which challenges me creatively, and helps me to give back to the community and ...

NEAL: Higher education is for suckers. All that stuff? It takes years. Years we could be drinking.

ALAN: I could do it.

NEAL: Go back to school?

ALAN: Get that degree.

NEAL: Be all that you could theoretically be.

ALAN: This kind of self improvement –

NEAL: Self actualization –

ALAN: Self realization –

NEAL: Embracement of the purest self that is you, yes go on –

ALAN: I want it so much. And immediately! Like now!

(*ALAN snaps his fingers.*)

NEAL: Like that?

(*NEAL also snaps his fingers.*)

ALAN: I've been taught, from the television and the internets, that it's all just a click away, down the store, pay on layaway, but that's not true. I've got to work for what I want and even then it's highly unlikely that the morning will come and the sun will shine and the plants and flowers will grow and women will smile at me and lift their skirts and look to ME for inspiration and praise my hidden genius and challenge me to do great works and we'll be happy together and everything will be all right from now on. No! No, that's not going to happen. It will just be disappointment; a disappointment that will rain down like God pissing on my dreams.

(*NEAL applauds like a seal.*)

NEAL: God pissing on your dreams. Classic.

ALAN: You're a cock.

NEAL: Just because ninety percent of my body is cock ...

ALAN (*fake mocking laugh*): Hur hur hurh.

NEAL (*mocking ALAN's mocking laugh*): Hurh hurh hurh. (*To the BARTENDER.*) Two more please.

ALAN: We haven't even gotten to those yet –

NEAL: Two more please. Grand total of ... *(Counts.)* Aw, fuck, make it ten on the bar.

ALAN: You know what I want?

NEAL: Not if you're going to tell me.

ALAN: I want a magic button.

NEAL: There's a magic button now? Why was I not informed about the magic button? TELL ME ABOUT THIS MAGIC BUTTON!

ALAN: You know, that magic pink button that makes everything better when you press it.

NEAL *(whisper)*: I think that's called the clitoris. And you don't press it, you just rub it, gently.

ALAN: Whatever.

NEAL: No, not whatever, trust me, is very important.

ALAN: You press it – or rub it – and POOF!

NEAL: Poof?

ALAN: Poof. And all our dreams come true. For I am a modern man and am not conditioned to wait for a god damned thing.

NEAL: God Bless America.

ALAN: Could it be so easy?

NEAL: I say yes. Let's get that fucking button and tear it a new asshole!

ALAN: Right! No! Shit!

NEAL: What?

ALAN: There's no such thing as a magic button. I checked.

NEAL: MOTHERFUCKER! Are you sure?

ALAN: We don't have the technology.

NEAL: Damn you, facts and accepted logic.

ALAN: There's nothing we can do.

NEAL *(the lightbulb of inspiration)*: Yes there is. Sweet Hosanna there is. Two more, barkeep! Keep 'em coming.

> *(Two beers.)*

ALAN: You're planning something and it makes me a'scared.

NEAL: You should be a'scared. You're on the precipice of something great and you don't know it! Forget that job of yours which sucks so hard. Forget that weight gathering around your gut which serves as a constant reminder of too many nights like this. Forget that girl who never appreciated you and wasn't that good in bed to begin with!

ALAN: Wait how do you know she wasn't – ?

NEAL: If all this real life is bringing you down into a funk then I say fuck reality and dive head first into ... into ...

ALAN: Unreality?

NEAL: UNREALITY!

ALAN: But ... but that's impossible!

NEAL: Listen to me. Do you really want to turn things around?

ALAN: Of course I do.

NEAL: Then listen. What I'm about to propose might just be the thing to break this funk and make everything good again. It will turn your life around and make you into someone better. Taller. Charismatic with the ladies.

ALAN: I'm listening ...

NEAL: I propose that you and I – we quit our jobs –

ALAN: So far so good ...

NEAL: Buy a car ...

ALAN: ... Yeah?

NEAL: And then we go on a road trip and seek out the Real America.

(Beat. ALAN takes this in.)

ALAN: Oh. My. God. That might be the greatest idea in the history of great ideas.

NEAL: We leave tomorrow. Buy a car – no, fuck that, steal a car, hit the streets and hot wire a great white shark –

ALAN: You don't know how –

NEAL: Fuck what I know. Cars are part of the American spirit and these are American hands and they know how to hot wire because they were born with the DNA of diesel and carburetors in their knuckles. We will hot wire it and – Zoom Out!

ALAN: Zoom Out!

NEAL: Zoom Out across the George Washington Bridge to points unknown.

ALAN: New Jersey?

NEAL: Well, yes, at first, because I don't know how to pump my own gas! But we keep on going. We go through Jersey and Pennsyltucky because we both want something more. We want excitement and exhaust fumes and to chase that sun down the godforsaken American Highway. We'll drive.

ALAN: Not that far I can only take a few days off of work –

NEAL: You're not listening! Screw New York and everything that you know. These giant buildings haunt our dreams and will collapse in disrepair! It's unnatural! Living where you can't see the sun! Lets get the fuck out of Dodge! Flee to the great plains. Nebraska! Dakota! Sequoia! Where life grows OUT! Not Up, the way it does here in Jew York City

ALAN: Fuck you. I'm a Jew –

NEAL: Not anymore you're not. Jews don't live in America. In America we'll
(MORE)

NEAL (cont'd): learn how to be men again. We'll be farmers. Oil workers. COWBOYS. Our hands will be dirty and callused and we will go to bed proud. Our muscles will be wiry and strong like an underfed tragic Steinbeck hero. We'll take new names. Real strong American names. Bud. Tex. With these new personas we will swap stories while riding in the back of a pickup truck with migrant workers. The next day as the sun rises over the Texas desert you and I will bless the oil fields with our morning coffee and Skoal. Sunday mornings we will find a simple church in a simple town and pray to a New Testament God. Nearer my God to Thee. That night we'll meet a plump, blonde loving woman who stays home and bakes pie and by God we'll make a bride out of her. We'll be happy and content until the wind takes us again. Finally we will become what we were all along. The native. The First person. We'll smoke a pipe and succumb to alcoholism and dance around a fire as our spirit turns into a bird and then we fuck that bird in its cloaca as we fly up above this great land of ours. America is our home and we haven't been home in years. Let's drink to America, my friend! We'll be living there soon enough!

(They start pouring the beers down their throats. Most of it ends up dribbling down their shirts and heads. By the end of the chug they're not even trying to drink any more.)

NEAL: America! I'm with you in Rockland!

ALAN: America! I want to dance down Bourbon street and talk about how sad it makes me feel!

NEAL: America! My father worked with you until the mill shut down!

ALAN: America! I want to sip sweet tea and apologize for slavery!

NEAL: America! I want to sleep out under the stars and dream of a time when it all was simpler then.

ALAN: Everything used to be better! Everything used to be better!

NEAL: We'll make it better again! Holy. Holy. Holy Americana!

ALAN: Holy America we will find you!

NEAL: From the belly of the snake to the thrust of the buffalo as it fucks its way across the tundra, America we'll finally be together.

ALAN: I want to be a Cowboy!

NEAL: America we'll find you if it's the last thing we do. You can't hide behind myths and television anymore.

ALAN: Hey America! It's Howdy Doody Time!

NEAL: America I want you to have my baby! Together we'll repopulate the planet and they'll be no more war or hatred because America you and I will teach our children to love!

ALAN: America be my virgin bride!

NEAL: America I want to fuck you up the ass!

ALAN: America you're so fucking tight!

NEAL: America I'm gonna come all over your butterfly tattoo!

ALAN: American Tramp Stamp!

NEAL: America as I mix my jism in with your lower back ink, I'll look at the back of your head and I'll know that this is what Uncle Sam wanted for me all along!

ALAN: America I'm meant for greatness!

NEAL: America stop holding me back!

ALAN: America I'm coming to get you.

NEAL: For we have seen the greatest minds of our generation destroyed by madness, starving hysterical crazy from the idea of what once was but never truly were and for fuck's sake I'm going to find that again!

ALAN: AMERICA I KNOW WHERE YOU LIVE!

(They finish drinking/bathing in any beer they have left. Rest. Beat.)

NEAL: Two more.

END OF PLAY

Louis Vega & Anne Fidler in Brad Saville's "Yermo Blues"

Yermo Blues
by Brad Saville

* * *

Produced in Sticky: September 19, 2008, Bowery Poetry Club, directed by Brad Saville. With Anne Fidler and Louis Vega.

* * *

(*BOBBY – wearing a straw cowboy hat, dressed shabbily in cowboy boots, bluejeans and a bleach-stained t-shirt – stands on a chair, broom in hand, focused, looking at the floor, ready to strike at something while MELINDA – wearing a summer-dress, hair up – stands behind the bar, grilling hotdogs on a George Foreman grill, sipping a PBR.*)

MELINDA: Will you take that fucking hat off?

BOBBY: WILL YOU SHUT UP, GIRL! ... I, I saw him just now! He was stickin' his head out! Few more inches, and I would've had him!

MELINDA: How you know it's a "him"?

BOBBY: I don't. It's sort of the gender-less "him," you know ...

MELINDA: In my house we always called mice "her." Now, rats those are different, they're definitely "him." But, mice were always "her."

BOBBY: Well, him or her don't matter. (*Looking sadistically at mouse wall.*) Way I see it: lose your gender when you meet your maker.

MELINDA: That's the dumbest thing I ever heard, gender's a part of your soul.

BOBBY: Melinda, will you please shut the fuck up! Now, please baby. I'm at my wits-end here, and I gotta focus here.

MELINDA: I'll shut up when you take that hat off.

BOBBY: That's not happening.

MELINDA: It ain't sunny in here!

BOBBY: What'd you know?

MELINDA: I know it ain't sunny in here, and ... well, that hat's sole purpose is to keep the sun outta your face.

BOBBY: Yeah, so? ...

MELINDA: So, if you ain't wearin' it for practical reasons then you're wearin' it for fashion purposes, and, if that's the case, then you're wearin' it for other people, and the only person here, only person that's seeing you, that's other than you, is telling you that you look like a damned fool with that hat on.

BOBBY: I like it, and that's all that matters.

MELINDA: It vexes me.

BOBBY: That's your problem, not mine.

MELINDA: I don't do things that purposely annoy you.

BOBBY: That's not true.

MELINDA: Then, what –

BOBBY: You wear too much make-up.

MELINDA: No, I don't.

BOBBY: You're prettier without it, prettiest when you wake up first thing in the morning, I always say.

MELINDA: I like wearin' make-up.

BOBBY: I know you do, baby ... your relationship with your make-up is the same as mine with this hat.

MELINDA: But I been wearing make-up for fifteen years ... you only just

(MORE)

MELINDA (cont'd): bought that hat a week ago. Haven't taken it off for a minute unless you're sleeping –

BOBBY *(smirking)*: Or fuckin'... *(Walking over to MELINDA.)* If you remember correctly, I wanted to take it off last night, but you told me to leave it on ... *(Slapping MELINDA's ass playfully.)* Said you wanted to make it with a cowboy. You screamed it all breathy in my ear ... now, I couldn't refuse that ...

MELINDA: Take it off!

BOBBY: No one's in here. I just don't understand why you're getting so worked-up. I mean ... shit baby, as you said, no one's seein' me but you; no one's conscious of this hat, no one for several square miles.

MELINDA *(turning hot dogs)*: Well, I'm glad you just mentioned that.

BOBBY: Mentioned what?

MELINDA: The fact that there's no one here.

BOBBY: No one here?

MELINDA: No one around!

BOBBY: We're closed, baby.

MELINDA: No shit, I ... what I'm trying to say is that this ain't exactly a high traffic area, commercially speaking that is ...

BOBBY: But, we're not open.

MELINDA: Not even a fucking passerby.

BOBBY *(comforting her)*: But how are the passersby supposed to even know we're open if we don't –

MELINDA: Passerbys! Fucking passerbys!

BOBBY: People walking by –

MELINDA: In the middle of the fucking desert! In fucking Yermo?

BOBBY: You know just as well as I that there's a highway you can't deny:
(MORE)

BOBBY (cont'd): fifteen's the main-vein, heading straight to Vegas, people comin' from L.A., Bakersfield, Fresno ... we'll get 'em all.

MELINDA: At fifty-five miles per hour, with nuthin' to stop 'em but a traffic light!

BOBBY: We're lucky we got that.

MELINDA: Yeah, but what are you gonna do when the light's green?

BOBBY: That's what the sign's for –

MELINDA: Here we go again with the sign ...

BOBBY: It's significant, and it's not even lit up yet.

MELINDA: And when will it be lit up?

BOBBY: When I fix it –

MELINDA: And when are you gonna fix it?

BOBBY: It's at the top of my list ... *(Looking over to the mouse wall.)* As soon as I kill this mouse.

MELINDA: If you can kill that mouse, then you know what?... you can keep the dogs off the meat truck.

BOBBY *(smiling at MELINDA, curling his lips)*: I've been known to keep a few dogs off a few meat trucks ... *(Approaching MELINDA seductively.)* Also been known to lasso me an angel outta the sky ... now, if I can land me a sweet, soft woman like you, I think I possess the necessary faculties to kill this fuckin' mouse ... don't you think so?

MELINDA: I guess.

BOBBY: Ah, c'mon ... you "guess so" or you "know so"?

MELINDA *(smiling at Bobby)*: I know so.

BOBBY: Now, that's more like it.

   (MELINDA and BOBBY kiss and then embrace.)

MELINDA: Baby?

BOBBY: What is it, sweetie?

MELINDA: You really think you can fix that sign?

BOBBY: I can fix anything.

(*MELINDA gives him a look.*)

BOBBY: What? ... You don't believe me?

MELINDA: I'll believe it when I see it.

BOBBY: Well, you better believe it, Miss Melinda: once that sign lights up, all ten thousand magnificent watts, you won't have any choice but to believe it when you see it. Hell, folks all the way to Barstow won't have any choice but to believe it when they see it ... and customers, those travelers ... shit, those thirsty sons-of -bitches won't have any choice but to pull over when they see it. You wait and see – that sign'll lure 'em in to wet their whistles like a siren's song. Then they'll down that first cold one, then another ... pretty soon, those Vegas-bound bastards'll end up spendin' all their gamblin' money on cold beers and lap-dances from the prettiest dancer in all the great state of Nevada.

MELINDA: I said I wasn't doin' no lap-dances.

BOBBY: I know, I'm sorry. I forgot.

MELINDA: Unless you want me to make you jealous ... is that what you want? (*Approaching BOBBY seductively.*) You want me to make you jealous? (*Rubbing up against him.*) Get you all revved-up, watchin' me dry-hump some bearded trucker, my hot pussy rubbing against his hard cock, only thing keeping my honesty intact is a layer of mildew-ridden denim ...

BOBBY *(trying to ignore her)*: You're distractin' me, talkin' to me like that ...

MELINDA *(backing away, smiling)*: Well, excuse me: Lord forbid I should "distract" you –

BOBBY: Distracting me from my task at hand!

MELINDA *(making a kid's voice)*: Killin' a lil' old mouse.

BOBBY: That's right.

MELINDA: And, what would you do if you saw me givin' some big-dicked trucker a lap dance while he's shovin' singles in my panties –

BOBBY: I'd beat 'em to a bloody pulp –

MELINDA: Just like in Reno?

BOBBY: Yep ...

MELINDA: Fuck 'em up six ways from Sunday? Break his skull, put him in the hospital?

BOBBY: That's right ... *(Examining MELINDA.)* You don't like those memories, do you? I can tell ...

MELINDA: It's still fresh.

BOBBY: Don't like thinking about it?

MELINDA: Not so much.

BOBBY: You think I overreacted?

MELINDA: I think it was the sweetest thing anyone's ever done for me.

BOBBY: I'm glad you see it that way, cause the thought of another man even touchin' you just plain disgusts me.

MELINDA: Disgusts me too.

BOBBY: Really?

MELINDA: Yes, I don't want anyone else.

BOBBY: Me neither, baby.

> *(They kiss. BOBBY goes back to the wall where the mouse is supposed to be while MELINDA turns the hot dogs. BOBBY takes a mousetrap out of his pocket and sets it carefully by the wall. As soon as he sets it down, the trap goes off.)*

BOBBY: SON OF A BITCH!

> *(MELINDA watches as BOBBY proceeds to throw a fit, stomping the shit out of*

the mousetrap. He then looks at MELINDA, breathing heavy. MELINDA looks down at the cooking hotdog and then at BOBBY.)

MELINDA: Your hot dog's ready ...

BOBBY *(out of breath)*: Thank you, baby ... *(Giving mousetrap one last kick.)* Smells good.

> *(MELINDA puts a dog on the bun and hands it to BOBBY, who squirts mustard on it and begins scarfing down the dog. MELINDA puts ketchup on her dog, brings the hotdog close to her mouth, and then sets it down in disgust.)*

MELINDA: I'm sick of hotdogs, Bobby.

BOBBY: Hang in there: not much longer, Sweetness. Gotta tighten our belts for now, but, once we get this place up and running, it'll be fine wine and ... what's your favorite food again?

MELINDA: Shrimps.

BOBBY: Shrimps, huh? *(Pinching her cheeks.)* My li'l Bebe is a shrimp eater?

MELINDA: Uh-huh.

BOBBY: And how do you like your shrimps cooked?

MELINDA: I like 'em grilled.

BOBBY: There you go ... don't worry: pretty soon, I'll get you fine wine and grilled shrimps everyday, if you like.

MELINDA: You really mean that?

BOBBY: Shit-right: you're my queen now, and I'm gonna treat you thus.

> *(BOBBY freezes, and, as slowly and nonchalant as possible, he sets his hotdog down and picks up the broom. He then turns around and swats at the floor.)*

BOBBY: God damn it! I almost had 'em! You see him?

MELINDA: I didn't see nuthin'...

BOBBY: Well, I almost had him.

MELINDA: Her –

BOBBY: Him, her: whatever.

MELINDA: Why don't you just bait and poison it?

BOBBY: So what? ... we can smell this varmint decomposing in our wall for the next two weeks? C'mon now, girl: people don't wanna smell death whilst they suck back suds and look at titties ...

MELINDA: No, you're right.

BOBBY *(observing MELINDA, looking concerned)*: What's wrong?

MELINDA: Nuthin ...

BOBBY: Why aren't you eating?

MELINDA: Ain't hungry –

BOBBY: Bullshit, I can hear your stomach growlin' from here!

MELINDA: I told you: I'm sick of hot dogs. They smell like heaven cookin', but when push comes to shove ...

BOBBY: You'll eat it if you get hungry enough.

MELINDA: Maybe ... *(Taking lottery tickets out of her pocket.)* You got a quarter?

BOBBY: What'ch you need a quarter for?

MELINDA: I got some scratch-offs –

BOBBY: Scratch-offs? When did you pick up Lotto tickets?

MELINDA: When we stopped at that gas station in Baker.

BOBBY: I didn't see you buy 'em.

MELINDA: You were peein' ...

BOBBY: Shit, girl ... how many you got there?

MELINDA: Twenty.

BOBBY: Now, you're a smart girl ... what's gonna make a smart girl like you go and waste twenty dollars on something so foolish?

MELINDA: I enjoy it! ... besides, 'bout as foolish as that hat you're wearin'!

BOBBY: First of all, this hat was on the clearance rack for five dollars; second of all, I still have it; and third of all, as you can obviously see, it's still in good working-order. *(Taking a quarter out his pocket.)* Here: catch. *(Tossing quarter at MELINDA and she catches it.)* However, when you're done with those scratch-offs, only thing you'll have left is twenty pieces of cardboard, pile of grey dust, and that quarter I just gave you.

MELINDA: Your attitude's shit —

BOBBY: Practical, girl: we need to tighten our belts a bit: most small businesses fail as because of lack of start-up capital.

MELINDA: You know what?

BOBBY: What?

MELINDA: If I win anything, I'm not gonna share it with you.

BOBBY: Fine with me: I told you from the get-go when we hooked-up that you didn't have to do anything you didn't want to.

MELINDA: And I haven't.

BOBBY: But you came anyway.

MELINDA: I had to.

BOBBY: No you didn't.

MELINDA: 'Cause you asked me, then ...

BOBBY: You barely knew me.

MELINDA: I knew you when I met you.

BOBBY: You knew me? *(Laughing.)* All you knew 'bout me was that I was a

(MORE)

BOBBY (cont'd): broke dude, wearing a straw hat, who had inherited some sawdust bar in Yermo from a dead uncle. That, the expression on my face, and the look in my eyes: that's all you knew when we met.

MELINDA: I knew you were sweet on me ... I could tell that.

BOBBY: Every dude in that shit-hole strip joint was sweet on you.

MELINDA: But you were different.

BOBBY: How so?

MELINDA: The way you said things.

BOBBY: And how'd I say things?

MELINDA: Honest, pure ...

BOBBY: That still don't explain why you'd uproot and take off with me.

MELINDA: I believe in you.

BOBBY: That's nice to hear.

MELINDA: It's even nicer to say.

BOBBY: I ain't gonna let you down.

MELINDA: I know.

BOBBY: And how do you know?

MELINDA: Because you're golden: I can tell.

BOBBY: I swear to God! – you're the prettiest thing I've ever seen ... a Desert Tulip, you are! And you grill up one hell of a frankfurter!

MELINDA (*giggling humbly*): It ain't that hard.

BOBBY: No, but you got that touch with that grill ... slightly charred on the outside, juice poppin' on the inside ... yes, sir ... damned good dog, and fuckin' fine lady ...

(BOBBY, *seeing something out of the corner of his eye, quickly grabs the broom, turns around in one swoop, and strikes the floor with the broom. Maniacal smile comes to his face as he slowly raises the broom.)*

BOBBY: Whooooooweeee! *(Looking at MELINDA proudly.* I got him, baby. I got him!

MELINDA *(taking a bite of her hot dog)*: I knew you would, baby.

(Blackout.)

END OF PLAY

Bowery Poetry Club

501(C)ME
A Play on Moral Hazard
by David Marcus

* * *

Produced in Sticky: February 27, 2009, Bowery Poetry Club, directed by Jeremy Basescu. With Annie Scott, Barry Roth and David Marcus.

* * *

(AT RISE in a hipster bar, JACK arrives to meet JANICE and PETE.)

JACK: I'm so glad you guys could make it tonight, I have been wanting to talk to you about this for a while.

PETE: Our pleasure.

JANICE: And this place is so cute.

JACK: Isn't it? So, you know, we've known each other for a while now, and I was hoping that you two would consider being on my Board of Directors.

JANICE: Really? That's great!

PETE: What ... um, what Board of Directors?

JANICE: I've never been on a Board of Directors before.

JACK: Well, my grandparents moved to Arizona, so there are two spots open and you guys just seem perfect.

PETE: What ... um, what Board of Directors?

JANICE: Should I get cards made? Maybe that's too much ...

JACK: You could, it's not a bad idea ...

PETE: Jack, what Board of Directors, I mean when did you get a company?

JACK: I didn't.

PETE: Then what the hell are you talking about?

JACK: My Board of Directors, I've gone non-profit.

JANICE: Good for you!

JACK: Thanks.

PETE: What do you mean you've gone non profit?

JACK: I mean, I now have individual not-for-profit tax status, it's the 501(C)ME program that the Obama administration pushed through, it's a chance for individuals to really explore their place and meaning in society without the pressures of the marketplace to turn them into, you know, cookie cutter commercial bullshit and stuff.

JANICE: Obama is so great.

JACK: So, so great, its just unreal.

PETE: OK so wait, um, how does this work? I mean so like what? You don't pay taxes now?

JACK: It's better than that, anyone who gives me money or goods or services gets a tax deduction, you buy me a drink, or pay for a taxi, and bang, you can take it out of your taxes.

PETE: But why would anyone give you money?

JACK: Well, it depends on the particular granting organizations and individuals, but basically donors realize how vital I really am to our society, and that there must be a place for me, especially in the current political and economic conditions, I mean every great civilization has ... think about it like this, without significant support we could lose me, or see me basically washed out by the commercial markets, unable to create my unique and experimental existence.

JANICE: I think its a marvelous idea, just imagine, all that money we spent in Iraq, it could have been going to Jack, helping him to realizing his individuality.

PETE: Right ...

JANICE: So as Board Members, what would our responsibilities be?

JACK: General oversight of me, um, looking at budgets, you know, helping to decide what projects I should focus on.

PETE: What are you focusing on right now?

JACK: Well, currently I'm reading all the works of Evelyn Waugh, but in chronological order going backwards, which I'm pretty sure no one has ever done.

PETE: That's ... um, interesting ...

JACK: NYFA gave me forty grand for it.

JANICE: Sweet.

JACK: So also you guys would be useful bringing in new donors and, well obviously you'd be expected as Board members to make some small donation as well.

JANICE: Of course.

PETE: Of course.

JACK: It's a really exciting time now, my Gala is coming up and you know how fundraisers, they just take over, setting up the silent auction, putting together gift bags.

JANICE: I know, I know, it's like how do you even deal with your actual work.

PETE: And, what's your actual work again?

JACK: Being me.

JANICE: Honestly Peter, sometimes you're so dense.

PETE: Sorry.

JACK: And of course the Board has oversight over my development staff ...

PETE: Your development staff?

JACK: Of course. See that's how it works, this isn't just about me, I mean the ultimate goal of course is to support and promote me, but the economic footprint is huge, there's my development staff, my publicist, my web designer, it generates jobs you know ...

JANICE: It's just so wonderful, how you're giving so much to society, without you none of those people would have jobs, that's what I think people don't realize about not-for-profits, everyone makes money. Obama is so awesome.

PETE: I ... I don't know how I feel about this, I mean if you're so vital to society and everything, and I'm not saying you're not, I'm just talking here, but if you're so vital shouldn't the market sustain your existence, I mean wouldn't there be demand for you?

JANICE: Peter, what's wrong with you? Why are you being so rude?

JACK: No, it's OK, it's OK, I understand where you're coming from, Pete, but you have to understand that the market puts limits on us. The people created by commercial society are so formulaic and predictable, how are the really innovative and exciting ways of existing going to advance if we don't support them?

JANICE: Hear, hear, the important thing isn't how many people actually get to experience Jack, or even how many people want to experience him, the important thing is that by supporting Jack, we help his style of living diffuse into the culture.

JACK: That's very well put.

JANICE: The people don't know what's good for them, maybe if the education system was better, but for now, those with the resources have to do their part, think of the Medicis.

JACK: They've been doing this in Europe for decades, and you wonder why we lag behind.

JANICE: It must be great to be European, you know, having a sexy accent and being so smart and disdainful. I feel so ashamed around Europeans, you know?

JACK: We all do, but change has arrived. It won't be easy, but we can catch up.

PETE: I still don't get it, I'm sorry.

JACK: Hey I gotta make a quick call, the *New Yorker* is doing a thing on me. I'll be right back, you two talk. I'll get us drinks, this place makes amazing Pomtinis.

JANICE: This is so great for him, I mean it's so great that people are finally starting to realize how great he is.

PETE: Yeah, I guess so, I don't know, this still seems really strange. I mean, I want Jack to do well, but I'm not sure this is really helping him. I mean, let's face it, he can't support himself, don't you think he'd be better off if he was somehow, you know, sustaining himself economically?

JANICE: That is so Twentieth Century, when are you going to wake up? Things have changed, remember back in '06, we were looking at that duplex on Perry Street, and you didn't want an adjustable mortgage?

PETE: Yeah, I mean in three years we would have been paying seven thousand a month.

JANICE: No, you see, we wouldn't be, god you just don't get it, we would have gotten relief, that's what the government is for, they would have locked in our rates at two per cent now and I wouldn't have to be embarrassed to have my friends over.

PETE: We have a great place, we have two bedrooms, and we can afford it, without anyone's help, god does that mean nothing to you?

JANICE: It doesn't mean as much as the jacuzzi in the bathroom, you know you learned nothing, our entire culture just went through the greatest change that mankind has ever experienced in the history of the world and you act like it's still 1997.

PETE: I really liked 1997.

JANICE: I mean, you're so frustrating, why did you even vote for Obama?

PETE: Well, maybe I didn't vote for Obama.

(There is silence. The entire bar is looking at PETE and he is nervous now.)

PETE: Hey ... um, hey I'm really sorry, I, uh, I shouldn't have said that, it's been a long week, a long few weeks, actually. I'm not trying to be a downer, I

(MORE)

PETE (cont'd): swear, I ... I realize I probably should have voted for Obama, I mean he won, right? Don't get me wrong, I hated W, I hated him, it's just, god, I just, you know I believe in responsibility, like actually paying for things, I mean it's a Moral Hazard, but I can change, I know I can change.

JACK: Hey, is everything OK?

JANICE: It's OK, it's nothing ... it's just, never mind.

PETE: Yeah it's nothing, look we, we'd really love to be on your Board.

JANICE: Yes, we would.

JACK: Look that's great, and Janice, I would really love to have you on the Board, but look Pete, I, I'm not sure this is really for you, I mean I don't think you're going to provide the supportive atmosphere that I need in the room. And as much as it's important to me to reach out to people I disagree with and include them in the process, well, it's really not very important after all. Don't be sad though, have a Pomtini, and just think, you're involved still, every time you pay income taxes, a little of that will go to me, to make the world a better place through the advancement of Jack.

PETE: Can I still come to the Gala?

JACK: Of course.

END OF PLAY

Unbottling Post 9/11 America
An Introduction to *Sleeper*
by Mac Rogers

I ran across a term recently in a Stephen King novel about the owner of a construction company, forced into retirement by an accident, who decided to put more energy into his lifelong doodling habit and suddenly discovered that he was a passionate artist, churning out one wonderful painting after another in an astonishingly short time. He shows his work to a curator, who marvels not only at the quality of his output, but at the quantity of work he generated over so short a period. The artist was, the curator said, "unbottling" – releasing pent-up artistic energy after suppressing it for so long.

"Unbottling." I was taken with the term, so I Googled it, and I couldn't find a mention that seemed to match the curator's definition, so I concluded that King had invented the term for the novel. Still, made-up or not, the term refers to a very real phenomenon, and serves as well as any other for describing the artistic life of David Ian Lee in 2007 and 2008.

I know; I was there for all of it. I am a long-running volunteer at manhattantheatresource, one of downtown Manhattan's vital centers of new playwriting, one that makes a point of setting aside "Playground" nights every week for plays in development, and it was on one of these Playground evenings in Spring 2007 that I happened to see David's one man play, *The Latchkey Pool*.

Well, "happened to see" is disingenuous. I had an agenda.

I'm also a playwright, and I was desperately trying to cast a role in my own upcoming piece – the role of a playwright, as it happened! A fiercely intelligent, politically engaged playwright who believes in the power of properly deployed words to change the society around him for the better. It was proving to be a particularly difficult role to cast. Even tremendously gifted actors cannot always express intelligence as a forceful and compelling trait in their performances. But I bumped into David the day at the theater when he was prepping *Latchkey*, remembered his razor-sharp performance in a production of *Arcadia* I had seen the year before, and decided to scout him a little.

So it was the case that when I saw *The Latchkey Pool*, I had no interest in it as a piece of playwriting. I was treating it as an unofficial audition monologue. I stress this to make the point that, going in, I was very much not in a mental place to get caught up in the story of a brilliant but reckless journalist whose life is falling apart faster than he can put it back together. But that's what happened.

Like most of David's plays that I would see over the next year, *Latchkey* was deeply concerned with the politics of post-9/11 America's engagement with the rest of the world, but (also like David's forthcoming plays) he refused to allow it to become agitprop. He had something to explore, not something to declare. I called it a "one man play" rather than a "one man show" because *Latchkey* was no vanity piece designed to showcase David's talent to agents and producers (though he did play the reporter, superbly). It told a story, a story about a skillful and well-intentioned reporter whose dedication to his craft atrophied into a kind of obsession, one that endangered everyone around him. It was a play. It existed beyond David's performance of it, and it exists now. Someone else could perform it somewhere else, and if they do, I'd like to see it.

It was kind of a win-win situation in the end. David was perfect for the character in my play and wanted to do it, and I discovered a marvelous new playwriting voice. What I didn't know was that David had not, in fact, been writing for some years, and was only returning, with a vengeance, to the craft after a long absence where he focused on acting. David was unbottling, and with *Latchkey*, he had poured the first shot.

Everyone who knows David jokes about his tirelessness, manifested in late-night text messages and a punishing, near-continuous acting schedule. For me, the enduring image of David's relentless work ethic is one where he sits on the sofa on the manhattantheatresource landing, twenty minutes before he's due on stage in my play (where he would play a large, difficult role that required him to remain on stage for nearly three hours), huddled with his sometime writing partner and friend L. Jay Meyer working on their co-written play *Liberty & Joe DiMaggio*, which opened in September 2007, just over three months after *Latchkey* closed.

David made a point of performing *Liberty & Joe DiMaggio* (alongside L. Jay) over September 10th and 11th of that year because with this follow-up to *Latchkey*, he was taking on 9/11 as an event more directly. *Liberty & Joe DiMaggio* focused on a couple (played by L. Jay and David) who live in Lower Manhattan who are trying to find a way to carry on with their lives in the wake of this colossal shattering of every form of security – personal and political – they have ever known. One man becomes a miserable, terrified shut-in, while the other becomes a voracious political junkie who hides himself in a newly realized jingoistic belligerence.

It shouldn't have been so surprising that *Liberty & Joe DiMaggio* eventually revealed itself to be about one mind in anguished confrontation with itself. David and L. Jay, while crafting a good-faith portrayal of a very lost and human character, were also depicting a profoundly American quality of going to terrible extremes of morbid fear and pugnacious rage to avoid the vital grieving process anyone must undergo before they'll have any proper idea of how to carry on. While *Liberty & Joe DiMaggio* was certainly a collaborative effort between two playwrights, it was strongly distinguished by all the earmarks of David's style and enduring obsessions (fast, literate dialogue, a love of American geography, up-to-the-minute political engagement).

Which brings us to the play you're about to read in a minute or two.

Considering that David would be the writer, co-star, and principal driving force behind the production of *Sleeper* that would run at manhattantheatresource over two weeks in July 2008 (a little over a year after the debut of *The Latchkey Pool*), he could be forgiven for cooling his heels on the writing for a few months until his life quieted down a bit. That's certainly what I would have done. But David doesn't really do "quieted down," so in the run-up to the first read-through, in between furious bouts of last-minute casting, he somehow made the time to write *The Dog Show*, an intricately constructed revenge tragedy built around two college friends with vicious grudges spanning many years who vie with each other across class lines – and with the wife of one, a failed actress whose sexuality has been commodified throughout her professional life, caught between them.

David very kindly asked me to participate in a few early developmental readings of *The Dog Show* (playing the sort of nebbish-with-a-secret in which I specialize!), so I was able to examine this script a bit more closely than many of his. While not explicitly political, *The Dog Show* continued his tradition of telling what appeared to be a small-scale story revolving around fully realized characters that also served as a metaphorical examination of the modern American character. *The Dog Show* specifically interrogated power structures, and the ways in which the strong work their deceptions upon the weak. David seems to be taking his cue from this astonishing quote from an unnamed Bush administration aide to the *New York Times* in 2004:

> "We're an empire now, and when we act, we create our own reality. And while you're studying that reality -- judiciously, as you will -- we'll act again, creating other new realities, which you can study too, and that's how things will sort out. We're history's actors . . . and you, all of you, will be left to just study what we do."

By examining this political corruption through the metaphorical lens of corporate and personal vendettas, David once again deepened his examination of the United States in the 21st-century, and the people who thrive – and those who sink – in this environment.

If *Sleeper* is David's crowning achievement in this ongoing artistic exploration, I doubt it will remain so for long. *Sleeper* follows the struggles of an activist named Teri to forge an America worthy of the apparent loss of her humanitarian worker husband Bobby (played by David at manhattantheatresource) to a kidnapping along the Afghanistan-Pakistan border, a struggle that brings her face-to-face with Rachel, an enormously popular and charismatic right-wing pundit.

Sleeper draws from and builds upon the revelations of the other plays from his unbottling period. Like *The Latchkey Pool*, it depicts intelligent, passionate liberals who are crippled in their important work when they are unable to attend to their personal lives in the wake of tragedy. As in *Liberty & Joe DiMaggio*, the play explores the pitfalls of trying to skip ahead to some half-baked action or pose before one has completed a grieving process. And like *The Dog Show*, *Sleeper* takes a piercing look at how hard it is to be a nuanced thinker in a world where brazen viciousness is just so much more attractive and empowering.

To these themes, *Sleeper* adds a (at times difficult to read and watch) depiction of the utter deterioration of the political dialogue in modern, 24-hour multimedia America. The long confrontation between Teri and Rachel in the second act is punishing but necessary viewing for any liberal who wants to understand why progressive ideas foundered so badly in the years after 9/11. Teri, who is less prepared to be single-minded and vicious, is easy prey for a wolverine like Rachel. Meanwhile, Bobby and his captor Mahid have their own struggle to connect across barriers of language, culture, and history.

You're about to read *Sleeper*, so I don't want to give away too much. But bear in mind as you read that this story is the product of a remarkable eighteen-month burst of creativity, an unbottling of personal and political investigations of stunning vitality and relevance. David created this play in the midst of a crucible of activity, both immediately around him and around the contemporary world he follows so closely and with such a mingled sense of terror and hope.

Perhaps David won't continue unbottling at such a furious rate (and for his own physical and mental health, I hope he does not), but I have very good reason to expect that the bottle's still pretty close to full. I'm honored to have had a seat at the bar while he's pouring, and I'm not going anywhere.

SLEEPER
by David Ian Lee

SLEEPER

Francis Del Duca
Fifi Oscard Agency, Inc.
110 W. 40th St., Ste. 1601
New York, NY 10018
212.764.1100

Sleeper was originally presented by Small Pond Entertainment on July 20, 2008 at manhattantheatresource in New York City. Nat Cassidy directed the following cast:

KADIR KHALID YOUSEF..Micah Chartrand
MAHID YOUSEF...David Dartley
TOM/NIXON/ENSEMBLE..Jason Griffith
A PAGE/ENSEMBLE...Emily Hagburg
BOBBY GUFFIN..David Ian Lee
TERI'S FATHER/CHUCK/ENSEMBLE..L. Jay Meyer
TERI GUFFIN..Karen Sternberg
AL/MAN AT TH HOSPITAL/ENSEMBLE..........................Craig Lee Thomas
RACHEL ANDERSON..Kristen Vaughan

The Stage Manager was Sandy Yaklin, the Assistant Stage Manager was Alexis Thomason, the lighting was by Ben Sulzbach, the sound by Neal Freeman, the dramaturg was Dav Yendler, photography & graphic design by Sidnei Beal of III/Infinite Xposure Inc.

For my cast: With love and wonder ... always.

Characters & Casting

Rachel Anderson (40 to 45)
Teri Guffin (30 to 35)
Bobby Guffin (33)
Mahid Yousef (30)
Kadir Khalid Yousef (25)
An Actor (African-American, 30s)
       The Board-Op
       Tom
       The Caller (Leroy)
       Richard Nixon
       The First FBI Agent
       Womiq
An Actor (45 to 50)
       Teri's Father
       Benjamin Franklin
       Chuck
       The Operator
An Actor (30s)
       The Man at the Hospital
       Al
       The Television Host
       The Second FBI Agent
       Maroof
       The Home Nurse (Peter)
A Page (Female, early 20s)

Time & Place

PART ONE
March of 2003
In various cities and locations

PART TWO
April of 2003
In an undisclosed location
&
Five years later
A living room in Phoenix, Arizona

A Note on the Text

The dialogue in *Sleeper* contains a fair amount of Urdu, a little French, and just enough Russian and Arabic to either impress or irritate your friends at the pub. It is intended that most audience members feel alienated and confused (even potentially overwhelmed) by these passages. In this spirit, English translations are not included in the main body of the text, but rather in an appendix.

A Note on Staging

The design and staging of Part One may embrace the theatrical, with little concern for disguising the limitations of the theatrical space; it is suggested that Part One be staged in front of black curtains and with only the barest of props and set pieces, ideally using no more than a few simple boxes, forms, and chairs. Costumes should allow members of the ensemble to transform easily from character to character.

For Part Two, the abandoned room should be realized more fully – though the design elements may remain suggestive – and supported by practical costumes and props; Part Two should be firmly grounded in the literal world.

An interesting staging convention was employed – by sheer necessity – for the maiden production at Manhattan Theatre Source: The company remained on-stage during Part One, making costume changes in full view of the audience. This convention was dropped for Part Two, helping to reinforce a sense of desolation and unease.

That said, I encourage those producing the play to explore their own ingenious, inventive, and entertaining solutions to the challenges unique to Parts One and Two. I only caution that the title not drive the tempo; this play should move fast, with incredible urgency driving one scene into the next, one moment into the next, like a mad engine headed for the ravine.

Thanks. Have fun.

– David

* * *

Part One : Becoming

"By suffering comes wisdom."
                              - Aeschylus

"I know, I know for sure
That life is beautiful around the world.
I know, I know it's you
You say hello, and then I say I do."
                              - Anthony Kiedis, "Around the
                              World"

"Nothing is written."
                              - T.E. Lawrence, *Lawrence of Arabia*

SLEEPER

PART ONE

(Black curtains border the theatrical space. Empty, save for perhaps a few objects that are or will become beds, tables, chairs, etc. ... In the pre-show: Wind ... Lights up as TERI hurries into the space, followed by her FATHER. She points.)

TERI: *The Promontory Point.*

FATHER: Built in 1953 for the Chicago and Eastern Illinois railroad. And this one?

TERI: *The Desert Valley.* She was President McKinley's train car when he traveled in the south.

FATHER: Built in the 1800's for Southern Railway.

TERI: And in 1964, as she passed through Phoenix, Arizona, Mom stood there, you knelt there, and she said yes.

FATHER: Right there *(beat)*. You know your mother loved you.

TERI: Of course; she just had a different way of showing it. And this one?

FATHER *(arms around her)*: Ah, Teri, you used to love this game.

TERI: You loved this game, Daddy, I just loved riding on your shoulders.

FATHER: Do you remember what you wanted to be when you grew up?

TERI: A mommy ...

FATHER: No. A mommydentistballerinastronautrainconductor.

TERI: I hated ballet.

FATHER: We still have all your toe shoes. Both pair.

TERI: I'm sorry I quit everything.

FATHER: You never quit being my daughter.

TERI: Oooo. My insulin level spiked with that one.

>(*Hugs her father.*)

FATHER: I love your hugs.

TERI: That's 'cause I give 'em right (*beat*). I feel like I should cry but I can't. There's a flood, but it's being held back. It won't come. Funny, huh? I really wish I could talk to you.

FATHER: Aren't you?

TERI: I'm dreaming, Daddy.

FATHER: Are you?

>(*Enter NIXON, eating from a bag of kitty litter. He is followed by a man dressed as a HOME NURSE, carrying a large package sent via air mail. An attractive YOUNG MAN, Middle Eastern, films them with a video camera.*)

TERI: Oh, God, I hope so ... I won't remember this.

FATHER (*with a shrug*): Neither will I.

TERI: Dreams are like ...

FATHER: Trains?

TERI: Meteors. Meteors that fall out of the sky. They're just little fragments that burn out fast. To leave an impression they have to be huge. And destructive (*she turns to the three men*). Enough. Go.

>(*The HOME NURSE and NIXON exit, but the YOUNG MAN remains. He turns his camera on TERI, who shivers at his presence.*)

TERI: I can feel something else ... a war is coming, but not the one we expect.

FATHER (*pointing*): And this one?

TERI: I don't know this one. She's ... funny- looking.

FATHER: That's because she's British. Built in 1829 to compete in a time trial, she was damaged on the way to the rails and spent five days being taken apart and put back together. On the sixth day she raced. And lost.

TERI: And her name is *Perseverance*.

FATHER: You're on the edge of something, Teri. When you break through you're going to be a force of nature.

TERI: What if I can't?

(Her FATHER retreats as the YOUNG MAN pulls closer.)

FATHER: What if you stepped into what you could do, not what you can't do?

TERI: Daddy, don't go. No. No!

(An abrupt lighting shift. TERI is awake, she is alone. She touches the other side of her bed, already knowing it to be empty. LIGHTS up on the other side of the stage. RACHEL at a radio broadcaster's desk, wearing headphones. She does not sit, but stands, moving with and around her microphone. TERI remains lit. She lays in bed for a long time, finally shuffling about to find a box of videocassettes. She gets back into bed and sorts though the tapes like a collector.)

RACHEL: I wanna know why on weekends you never see kids traveling, but you *do* see women with dogs! I landed at Tampa International this morning, and everywhere I look are these skinny white girls with tippy-wippy little teacup dogs in their purses and the word "Juicy" on their sweat-suited butts. Enough! If you wanna fly on a plane, fly on a plane; if you wanna wear your jammies and carry Tinkerbell around, have a marsupial pouch surgically implanted and stay home!

(RACHEL's BOARD-OP appears, speaking into a broadcaster's microphone.)

BOARD-OP: Line three is ready to go nuclear, you've got four and seven open.

(RACHEL gives him a thumbs-up, continues on. A PAGE brings RACHEL coffee, papers, and news items. RACHEL sifts through them while speaking.)

RACHEL: Anyway ... I support late-term abortion if the term in question is Senator Crowe of Georgia's current Eighth 8th. A seventy-two72-year-old

(MORE)

RACHEL (cont'd): coward who walks like a fetus, Crowe gave yet another Senate floor speech yesterday in which he "wept for his country's demands of obedience and threats of recrimination in places of reason." *Whatever.* The Democrats have only one position: lying down. Such cowards; I haven't seen anybody spend this much time on their knees since my wedding night.

(*startled looks from her BOARD-OP and PAGE.*)

It was a Catholic Mass, what?

BOARD-OP (*headset*): Line three wants to talk to the station manager.

(*RACHEL does a little dance, middle fingers in the air.*)

RACHEL: Hillary's got that unblinking look of terrified appeasement; I swear, she has a face full of Botox like Lewinsky had a face full of Bill. On the Senator's webpage, it says her favorite movie is *The Wizard of Oz.* That makes sense: the story of a girl and her friends without hearts, brains, or courage; they don't know where they're going, but they've got *fabulous* shoes.

BOARD-OP (*headset*): We're full up, Rachel. And, the operator is on line seven?

RACHEL (*off-mike*): Christ-on-ice, give him the inside line. (*Back on.*) But the worst is Georgia's Senator Crowe. Remember a month after 9/11, when a Palestinian guy with a name like a song out of *The Lion King* got on a plane and faced Mecca when the stewardess asked if he'd prefer chicken or fish? Crowe whined that the airline didn't have a "right to discriminate." And now, he thinks we're being unfair to Saddam? To *Saddam?* Lemmie tell ya, discrimination is not always a bad thing. The ability to discriminate is what keeps us alive. It's a gift from God, and anyone who tells you to ignore that instinctual survival mechanism is not looking out for you. Folks, if we go to war with Iraq, watch out for Senator Crowe. He's bordering on treason, and if that means I have to take him out behind the Senate and do him *Old Yeller*-style ...

BOARD-OP (*headset*): Line three —

RACHEL (*pushes a button*): Line three, you're on.

(*A caller, portrayed by the actor who plays AL, appears on the periphery of the stage.*)

LINE THREE: Yeah, I don't unders —

RACHEL (*pushes a button*): Oh no, we just lost line three. Meanwhile, there's a

(*MORE*)

RACHEL (cont'd): line open. We've got the whole damn state, so if it's in Florida it's just 669-WTLK. Your calls, and some big news of my own after the break ... I'm Rachel Anderson and this is *American Agenda*.

(RACHEL pushes a button. Energetic synthesized music to take her to commercial. The lights on RACHEL fade. Meanwhile, TERI speaking into a telephone:)

TERI: So, why do they call it Bengal Spice? Is it because it's made with real Bengals ...? I'm finishing the tea I bought for Valentine's Day. You're either asleep or in the air, but when you wake up or you get to the hotel, know I love you and am thinking about you. *(Checks the time.)* Six o'clock in the morning. I had a bad dream. And it just, reminded me...you know, I think my brain is still wired for an Answering Machine Age, because I just keep talking, thinking you're gonna pick up. But, you're not. So. Sweet dreams. I left something for you in your bag; watch it. I love you. Talk soon.

(TERI hesitates. Hangs up. Holds the phone in one hand, in the other her remote control. Points the control, pushes a button. Lights out. Lights up on RACHEL's husband, CHUCK, reclined on a sofa. RACHEL enters with sunglasses and luggage. Drops the luggage. During the following she will cross in and out of the room as she strips off her stockings, settles home, and mixes a drink.)

RACHEL: The flight. From Hell. The in-flight televisions were broken – they were all stuck on C-Span *TWO*! – so I had to endure the Unholy Trinity:

CHUCK *(overlap)*: Uh-oh.

RACHEL *(continuous)*: John "Molasses" Conyers. The lovechild of Daffy Duck and Truman Capote, Barney Fucking Frank. And ... the dishonorable gentleman from Georgia, Harry Crowe!

CHUCK: Give Senator Crowe enough rope, he'll hang himself.

RACHEL: Chuck, I'm on a crusade and that jackass is my Saladin. Where in the Hell is the Bombay Sapphire, Mommy needs a drink!

CHUCK: We're out.

RACHEL: Balls!

CHUCK: Brandy went over to a friend's house.

RACHEL *(suggestive)*: Ooo, a night without the fruit of my womb?

CHUCK: When I was sixteen I didn't spend as much time out as she does.

RACHEL: Buns, when you were sixteen you didn't have a newly bald vagina.

CHUCK: She pierced her navel.

RACHEL: Like a damn aborigine. We have to stop her before she puts a cup holder in her lip and a Slinky around her neck.

(RACHEL curls around her husband and pulls on her drink.)

CHUCK: Welcome home, Noodle.

RACHEL: Thank you for allowing me the center ring.

CHUCK: I just like to hear you work.

RACHEL: Hear me work, you say? Well, that's something we should talk about!

CHUCK: How'd it go in New York?

RACHEL: Not so fast, Buns. You: The lawn looks fantastic!

CHUCK: I had that Jose do it, my damn back —

RACHEL: I'd suggest amputation, but you'd make for an awkward dance partner.

CHUCK: I ain't the man you met in college, Rachel.

RACHEL: We live in a fallen world, Chuck. It's all goin' to the dust.

CHUCK: If it's still hurting come Easter I'm gonna tell the doc to just fuse the damn vertebrae and be done with it.

RACHEL: Do we get one of those wheelchair parking stickers?

CHUCK: Are we gonna need one if we have to move to New York?

RACHEL: You didn't listen to the show this morning! *(Exiting to refresh her drink)*. I announced it in the last hour.

(Lights up on another part of the stage. BOBBY with a MAN in a business suit, seated at a table, various folders and briefs open before them. They speak while working ...)

MAN: In the interest of full disclosure, Bobby, I should tell you I met on behalf of the hospital board with the guys from Blue Cross, Blue Shield and Cigna last week. *(BOBBY chuckles)*. Are you gonna tell me they're selling an inferior product?

BOBBY: No, my only concern is to help make your job of helping people easier for you and more affordable for them.

MAN: You're the most expensive consultant we've ever hired.

BOBBY: I prefer the term "advisory liaison."

RACHEL *(entering)*: I met with the suits. And in two weeks *American Agenda* is picking up a dozen new markets including four million bean eaters in Boston –

CHUCK *(overlap, figuring it out)*: Wait, Boston ...?

RACHEL *(continuous)*: Eight million corrupt windbags in Chicago and –

CHUCK *(overlap, supportive)*: No, no – !

RACHEL: Fifteen million sinful listeners eating Chinese takeout in shoebox apartments; yes, ladies and gentlemen, they're putting me on in New York City!

CHUCK *(overlap)*: No! No, oh oh oh, Noodle! That's fantastic!

(With a little difficulty CHUCK rises and embraces his wife.)

MAN: The board was very impressed with your proposal.

CHUCK: I am so proud of you!

MAN: This hospital has seen a precipitous rise in expenditures over the last five years –

BOBBY: Then let's turn this thing around before you're looking at a continued net loss for the next five years.

RACHEL: They're moving me out of East Coast drive time –

MAN: I like the sound of that.

RACHEL: I'm hot ten to twelve Eastern Standard. I'm never seeing another sunrise ever again: we can stay in bed and try to break the rest of your back, you filthy –

> (*They kiss.*)

MAN: I blame the Goddamn Boomers.

BOBBY: The whole industry is seeing more cases reliant on Medicare.

MAN: That cardio craze from the Eightie80s gave us a generation of people with great hearts but their joints are shot all to hell.

BOBBY: And with the new advancements in silver nanotechnology you're gonna be replacing a lot more hips and knees.

MAN: Do we have to?

CHUCK: So we don't have to move?

BOBBY: Yes, you have to.

RACHEL: No, we don't have to move.

MAN: Why?

RACHEL: I told them I've got a home in Tampa and a daughter I don't wanna pick up and a husband just this side of traction –

CHUCK (*overlap*): Hey!

RACHEL (*continuous, pushing CHUCK back to the sofa, straddling him*): And they said Dame Anderson, we grovel at your Peabody Award Winning feet.

CHUCK: Thank God, we don't have to move to New York.

BOBBY: Are you serious?

RACHEL: This is the Golden Ticket, Mr. Man. I wanna publish, I publish.

> (MORE)

RACHEL (cont'd): You wanna be the spokesman for a line of barbeque grills or camping equipment, all I ask is that you wear a big sweater someone could conceivably have knitted for you.

MAN *(light)*: Don't look at me like that.

CHUCK: Jesus wept. It's a new world.

RACHEL: Not as new as you are old, Buns.

> *(Lights out on RACHEL and CHUCK.)*

MAN: Yes, I'm serious. Why can't we cut the Boomers? They're a huge expenditure.

BOBBY *(light; this is easy)*: Look, I can't help you exclude people, I can only help refine what you accept as insurance and what procedures you perform. But, let's just say you want to cut out hips and knees: That means old people, that means wealthy people, and that, my friend, means Jews. And you are now a hospital in the greater Los Angeles area that has pissed off the Jewish community, and: Look, there go your prize Surgeons Steinberg and Goldman across the street to do end-to-end anastomosises for Our Lady of Holy I-Told-You-So. Or, you can listen to me and just send Aetna to Community.

MAN: You know, my mom's Jewish.

BOBBY: Really? Did *she* jog?

MAN *(a little laugh)*: You're good, Bobby.

BOBBY: That's why I'm the most expensive consultant you've ever hired.

> *(The men begin packing up.)*

MAN: We meet again next week? *(A nod from BOBBY.)* Flying home to Phoenix?

BOBBY: No. Next I'm in Detroit then D.C. then Louisville, then I'm back with you.

MAN: You spend more time in the air than you do on the ground. When you get back to L.A. let me know if we can do anything for you.

(BOBBY's mobile phone rings. He answers and holds it with his shoulder as he signs paperwork. TERI appears in a separate light, on the telephone, a strawberry in hand.)

BOBBY: Hello?

TERI: We need a phone date. I have crepes and champagne.

BOBBY: I'm a little busy.

TERI: Wanna guess what I'm doing with a strawberry right now?

MAN: Bobby, if you need a moment ...

(BOBBY shakes his head.)

TERI: Here's a hint: the activity I'm involved in would be much more fun as a team sport rather than a solo effort.

(BOBBY has set his phone down to make the signing of papers easier; the MAN points, saying, "Here…and here.")

TERI: This little strawberry on my tummy, running it up along my neck, over my – Ooo…! I have some cream here, too. Oh, so good, I wish you were here to eat strawberries with me.

(BOBBY finishes signing paperwork, picks up the phone. He and TERI listen in silence for a moment, unsure if the other has hung up.)

TERI: Bobby?

BOBBY: Yeah?

MAN: Bobby ...

BOBBY: Look, I'm in a meeting, Hon, I'll call you from the hotel.

TERI: Okay, when – ?

(But he has hung up, and the lights go out on TERI.)

MAN: Ah, the demands of family. I'm taking the boys to Disneyland this weekend.

BOBBY: I worked there in high school. I ran the PeopleMover. We called it the PeopleMaker, because kids got into those dark hallways, and ...

MAN *(overlap, a knowing laugh)*: Yeah ...

BOBBY *(continuous)*: Of course, we also called it the PeopleRemover because it once dragged a kid a tenth of a mile. They hosed what was left of him off the track.

   (Beat.)

MAN: You're grim, Bobby.

BOBBY: Yeah ... so, hey, have fun with the kids!

MAN: You too. I mean – *(Little laugh.)* You know what I mean. I didn't know you were from California.

BOBBY: I did my MD at UCLA.

MAN: We've got so many ... Undocumented Migrants. The ERs are jammed up worse then the freeways. We treated a girl this morning for sub-acute Coccidioidomycosis –

BOBBY: Valley fever?

MAN: She probably picked it up while she and her parents were running from the Minute Men in the desert south of San Diego. She could go to the community hospital ten minutes up the 405, but instead she's in here every two or three weeks.

BOBBY: How old's the girl?

MAN: I don't know, girl-aged. Every two or three weeks. And that cost gets absorbed by our patients. I mean, we have to do something, we can't afford to help *everybody*.

BOBBY *(the plan)*: Well, now you're doing something.

MAN *(shaking hands)*: I'll see you in a week, Bobby. And get some rest on the plane, you look like hell.

BOBBY: Heh ... do you still prescribe?

MAN: No. But we are in a hospital. Back in my office, I think I've got some Ambien or Lunesta –

BOBBY: No, non-benzodiazepines don't work.

MAN: There's a Sav-On by the overpass, do you want a script for a Flurazepam substitute –

BOBBY: No, I've started to reject those.

MAN: What do you need, Bobby?

BOBBY: Phenobarbital.

> *(Lights out. Elsewhere, TERI, on the telephone. It rings several times. Then, in crosscut, we see her FATHER answer the phone.)*

FATHER: Hello?

TERI: Happy birthday, Daddy.

FATHER: Thank you!

TERI: It's Teri.

FATHER *(near continuous)*: Well, I'm having a very happy birthday.

TERI: I'll be by tonight –

FATHER: Oh, it's been a very lovely day. I got this train set made of wood. I wish you could see the train set this pretty lady gave me.

TERI: Mom's not there, Daddy.

FATHER: How is Al doing? He's such a talented young man. He's going to build something remarkable one day. Maybe he could build something in New York.

TERI: I'm not dating Al. I'm married to Bobby. Bobby. He's a doctor ... kind of.

FATHER: Oh. How's Katie? You should be ashamed, I miss her.

> *(A small pause.)*

TERI: It's good to hear your voice.

FATHER: Teri ... did you know I was your father?

> *(Lights out on TERI, full up on BOBBY. An airport bar, perhaps the sound of a plane taking off. BOBBY sits, nursing a bourbon, his carry-on at his side. Enter TOM, who catches sight of BOBBY.)*

TOM: Big Bad Bobby Guffin!

BOBBY: Tom, hey!

TOM: How are you, old buddy?

BOBBY: Old.

TOM *(to an unseen BARTENDER)*: Maker's Mark, two more?

BOBBY: You in town for the HMO conference?

TOM: Nah, not really. I was recruiting over at the Jewish Hospital.

BOBBY: Recruiting ...? Funny, you don't look Jewish.

TOM: Do I look like Sammy Fuckin' Davis, Jr.? No, I'm talking to their Hand Transplant Center.

BOBBY: Best in the country.

TOM: They're working with the University of Louisville and a French team out of Amiens for the go-ahead on face transplantation. Incredible stuff. They're just waiting on approval and a handsome donor. *(BOBBY snorts.)* And you? How's – ?

BOBBY: Teri and I moved to Arizona last year to be closer to her father, after, uh –

TOM: Yeah. I heard, I'm sorry –

BOBBY *(overlap)*: Yeah, it's –

TOM: Yeah, I ... *(Awkward silence.)* Arizona ...?

BOBBY: Yeah. But I'm headed through L.A. on the way home. I was just here for a few days, pushing.

> (The BARTENDER, *portrayed by the actress playing the* PAGE, *puts down two bourbons. The men raise their glasses.*)

BOBBY: Hey, cheers.

TOM: *Molodyets.*

BOBBY: What's that?

TOM: *Molodyets.* It's Russian.

BOBBY: Ah. I seem to remember tutoring you in French.

TOM: Well, this I picked up on the road. *(A small, unreadable chuckle. They drink.)* What the hell are you pushing in Louisville for?

BOBBY: Same as always: consulting, cost reduction.

TOM: Kindred and Humana have the insurance turf pretty well staked.

BOBBY: I'm starting a gang war. What about you?

TOM: I'm building roads.

BOBBY: You lay asphalt in a Valentino?

TOM: No, I wear Canali when I work the steam roller.

> (Hands BOBBY *a business card.*)

BOBBY *(reads)*: Builders Beyond Borders.

TOM: We're an NGO. Technically, we're not affiliated with the United States, with the Coalition, with anybody. We're supported by individual, generous donors. Philanthropists and off-shore money cats looking to make the world a better place to take a deduction.

BOBBY: U.S. money?

TOM: Some, but mostly French, Israel, the Japs. It keeps us in mittens.

BOBBY: Not the kind of thing we covered in anatomy.

(Pushes the business card back.)

TOM: World needs roads, Bobby. Wanna get AIDS vaccines to Botswana? Water across the Sahara? From Rome to Pompeii to San Francisco, the road is the sign of life, the birth canal for civilization. It's the vagina of city planning, Bobby.

BOBBY: That's an interesting push.

TOM: The K-to-K Road in Afghanistan. The Russians came in, started it. And no one can get it done. For decades. It's like that tunnel under Boston, except without drunken Irish people everywhere.

BOBBY: You're saving the world? You, the guy who got First Years at UCLA to tie bows around their cadavers' penises ... ?

TOM: I'm on the P.J. Road: Peshawar to Jalalabad, through to Kabul. We're linking Afghanistan to Pakistan. Peshawar has four major hospitals, including nuclear medicine. Afghanistan? Total mess. There are almost a dozen health facilities between Kabul and Jalalabad, all military, all bogged down with red tape tighter than Britney Spears' poontang. I mean, it's baby steps, but: once we have that road ... *(Beat. BOBBY flags the BARTENDER.)* We're helping people. It's hospital administration on a global scale, Bobby. Before they dig or blast or bust out road flares it's approval, planning, negotiations –

BOBBY: You're in Afghanistan?

TOM: Occasionally. And you thought the commute on I-10 was a blowjob with teeth.

BOBBY: Sounds dangerous.

TOM: Statistically, you're more likely to get hit by a drunk driver than you are to get hurt working with us.

(The BARTENDER refills their drinks and exchanges a flirtatious glance with TOM.)

BOBBY: That's because, statistically, I drive a car everyday. In Phoenix. Not Afghanistan.

TOM *(dark humor)*: Actually, you have better protection west of the Durand Line because you're in enemy territory. East of the line, you're in Pakistan, and as allies go that's a lot more dangerous. But: sometimes you have to show people the way. And when that's not working, you have to give them a road.

BOBBY: Wow. I'm really impressed. *(Toast, drink.)* You know, I'm not just consulting, did I mention I won the Nobel Prize?

TOM: Really? That pay good money?

BOBBY: Oh, yeah.

TOM: You are trying to fix a broken system one hospital at a time. And that is great, noble, and wholly impossible.

> *(They smile. Old friends.)*

TOM: It's so good to see you, my friend. *(Downs his drink, tosses some money on the bar.)* Gotta roll, I'm headed home. I haven't had takeout pizza in weeks.

BOBBY: Hey, did you go to the Slugger museum while you were in town?

TOM: Yeah!

BOBBY: Get one of those cool little souvenir bats?

TOM: Yeah!

BOBBY: They're not gonna let you take it on the plane.

TOM: Always the good news with you, Bobby. *(Pushes his business card back across the bar to BOBBY.)* I'm stateside through the end of the month. If you're ever in New York we should play racquetball. I'll tear your open ass apart.

BOBBY: You're more man, Tom.

TOM: And prettier, too. Not everyone can get away with a lavender shirt. Say hi to Teri.

> *(TOM exits as the lights shift to RACHEL and the HOST of a cable news show.)*

RACHEL: The only country of even remote significance saying "boo" is France, and they're immediately suspect as Chirac still trades cookies for Saddam's chocolate milk.

HOST: Russia and China have raised concerns –

RACHEL: Russia's a colossal waste of space and the last time China got anything right my daughter was in diapers and Richard Nixon had a guest pass at the Beijing YMCA. The fact is Saddam supports terrorists with training and sanctuary and his thirty pieces of *dinar*, so do we really want to wait for the day when he can support them with the nuke he's been trying to build since '89?

HOST: Atlanta, Georgia: you're on with Rachel Anderson.

(*A caller – LEROY – appears on the periphery of the stage.*)

LEROY: Yeah, I just, I just don't know what to believe, with the media –

HOST: We're not telling you what to think, we're just telling you how it is.

LEROY: Y'all sound so ready for war and –

RACHEL: Sane people never want war. But what you have in Iraq is an insane man with two bedbug kids holding sane people captive. Iraqis don't want to see Saddam attack America any more than we do.

HOST: Are you suggesting we attack Iraq because Iraqis *don't* want to attack the U.S.?

RACHEL: Darlin', I'd never suggest anything as idiotic as what just came out of the hole on top of your neck.

LEROY: I just, I saw our Senator Crowe on the television and he said that, you know, we're a righteous people, and this'll hurt how people think about our country, that we're doing this, sellin' something, and they don't want it.

RACHEL: Caller, what's your name?

LEROY: Uh, Leroy.

RACHEL: Leroy, if we don't save these people and save them right now, save them from the *burqas* and the beheadings and an abortive version of faith enforced by a scimitar's tip, if we don't do that it'll be our greatest moral failing
(*MORE*)

RACHEL (cont'd): since slavery. If we do nothing and say, "This is the life they've chosen, it's what they want, it's good enough for *them*," we cease to be righteous. What's the difference between that and having once denied some of our citizens the right to vote? Or serve in a desegregated military? And all because something lesser was "good enough" for them? This is about doing what is right. And the people who seek to do wrong? The dictators and the mullahs and the slave owners that wish to halt the call of Democracy? They can be killed or converted, but they cannot be allowed to lash another child to the whipping post. We're not selling freedom, Leroy. You don't have to sell something people were given by God. It would be immoral to not act now.

HOST: Rachel, thank you so much for coming on the program.

RACHEL: My pleasure.

HOST Rachel Anderson, listen to her show. Right back with more of your calls, and later: William Kristol. Don't go away.

(*A SHOW RUNNER, portrayed by the actor playing the PAGE, appears.*)

SHOW RUNNER: And we're out.

(*RACHEL removes her body micke, readies herself to leave.*)

HOST: Now I know how Ed Sullivan felt after "I Wanna Hold Your Hand." Are you sticking around New York? I'm sure you can take a few meetings this afternoon you couldn't have stolen this morning.

RACHEL: Nah, I'm a big tease. Buns and I are on a flight to London in a few hours and I promised not to leave him alone on this island any longer than I had to.

HOST: London?

RACHEL: I'm receiving an Ailes Award. It's not pointy, is it? I'd hate to have to check it on the return flight.

HOST: You didn't take the bait on Senator Crowe. Giving up the ghost, or are you still gunning for him?

(*RACHEL grins, winks, and makes a shooting gesture with her finger. Then, genuine:*)

RACHEL: I'm this close ... see you soon.

HOST: I'm sure you will.

> (RACHEL is gone. Lights out. BOBBY and TERI on separate sides of the stage. BOBBY in his hotel, dressing, TERI in Phoenix. They speak via telephone.)

TERI: How was D.C.?

BOBBY: White.

TERI: What? The marble, the snow, the people ...?

BOBBY: All the cities start to look alike after awhile. I'm back in L.A. and it's just Long Island with neon.

TERI: The news said there's gonna be a big protest march in D.C.

BOBBY: I didn't notice.

TERI: I might go.

BOBBY: Why do you want to do that?

TERI: I don't know. Because I don't really understand what's going on.

BOBBY: That's a fantastic reason to march, make sure someone gets you on camera saying that.

TERI: That's not what I meant ... I'm taking an Urban Rebounding class after spinning.

BOBBY: Huh?

TERI: Urban Rebounding. It's a lot of trampolines and bouncing off of blocks, steps —

BOBBY: You're taking a jumping class.

TERI: This is like when you referred to my Pilates as yoga with rubber bands.

BOBBY: You're going jumping after you go biking.

TERI: Put like that it's not sophisticated and sexy. I look good! Seriously, call Tussauds' it's time to take measurements ... you know what I was thinking about today? That trip we took in college. We just flew to Paris and took the train to Frankfurt and Brussels and Amsterdam. Remember Amsterdam?

BOBBY: Hazily.

TERI: Why don't we do that again?

BOBBY: Do what?

TERI: Travel.

BOBBY: All I do is travel.

TERI: No, all you do is work. Why don't we throw our things in a suitcase and just take an adventure?

BOBBY: Because all I do is work. *(Beat.)* I saw Tom the other day.

TERI: Oh? How is he?

BOBBY: Important.

TERI: "No human thing is of serious importance." You know who said that ...?

    (BOBBY grunts noncommittally. Beat.)

TERI: We didn't get to do The Grown-Up before you left.

BOBBY: I know. *(Beat.)* If you want to go on an adventure, you want to take a trip, you should go to Europe –

TERI: I want to go with you, I haven't been since college.

BOBBY: They don't move the countries around.

TERI: I'm not worried about getting lost, Bobby. I don't need a tour guide, I'm not looking for a Sherpa –

BOBBY: We didn't ... before I left because you stayed up all night watching those tapes.

TERI: I stay up because you don't come to bed.

BOBBY: Because you stay up watching –

(Silence. Both are frustrated with the conversation.)

TERI: Bobby, when you get home, can we mmm ... have some fun?

BOBBY *(overlap)*: Uh –

TERI *(continuous)*: I mean, fool around a little bit?

BOBBY: ... Yeah ...

TERI: Did you call my father, it was his birthday –

BOBBY: No, shit, I completely forgot. I'm sorry –

TERI: It's okay. He didn't notice ... birthdays, holidays: they've always been a mixed bag in that house. Good years, I can remember looking for presents hidden under the swamp cooler in the den. Bad years ... well, bad years.

BOBBY: I'm sorry. *(Beat. Now dressed.)* I need to hop in the shower/I've got to get –

TERI: No, it's okay, don't worry. When are you coming home?

BOBBY: Monday.

TERI: I love you.

BOBBY: You, too ... I'm always proud of you, Teri. I am.

> *(TERI hangs up, the lights go out on her. BOBBY hangs up, tosses the phone onto the hotel bed. From his carry-on bag he pulls a videocassette tape with a red case. He holds the cassette in one hand, in the other his remote control. Points the control, pushes a button. Lights out. Sounds of the London tube; a recorded voice says, "Mind the gap, please." Lights up on a good looking YOUNG MAN, Middle Eastern, sitting with his backpack on the seat beside him. CHUCK stands, reading an international edition of* Time *that features RACHEL under the headline AMERICA'S VOICE? CHUCK holds his back, grimaces. The YOUNG MAN moves his backpack, and motions toward the empty seat.)*

CHUCK *(sits)*: Thanks. Not used to being on my feet so long.

YOUNG MAN *(not impolite, but not looking for a conversation. British accent)*: It is alright.

CHUCK: Easier to read sitting down, too. *(A curious glance at the kid, then indicating his magazine.)* What do you think of her?

YOUNG MAN: Very American.

CHUCK *(thinking it a compliment)*: Yeah. I'm buying every copy I can for the folks at home. Where you from?

YOUNG MAN: Excuse me?

CHUCK: Where's home for you?

YOUNG MAN: London.

CHUCK: Oh.

YOUNG MAN: I have a home in the winter.

CHUCK: Oh. I have a home in Tampa. *(Beat.)* "Mind the gap," that's funny, isn't it? We were in New York before we came over, their subway's not like this. It should be, "Mind the gap between your ears," that city. Like Sodom and Gomorrahamorah, "Set forth for an example suffering the vengeance of eternal fire." Nothing's an accident, what happened to that Dog Shit City.

YOUNG MAN: I have only been once.

CHUCK *(back to his magazine, sotto voce.)*: Dog Shit City ...

> *(Lights fade ... elsewhere: TERI approaches a man (AL) seated on a park bench, reading a news paper. She sits next to him. They wear parkas, heavy winter coats. Snow.)*

TERI: Is this the local paper? I'm new in town.

AL: Yeah, that's the one. And if you're a liberal dyke you'll love it and if you're a conservative you'll see it's just a pack of lies.

TERI: Well, I'm just gonna be over here, practicing my cunnilingus while aborting a Future Farmer of America.

AL: That's a lot of mouth on you, lady.

TERI: You know nothing of my mouth.

AL: It's good to see you, Teri.

TERI: You too, Al.

(*A hug, a friendly kiss.*)

AL: How long are you in town?

TERI: The weekend. Bobby's here for a convention. We're at The Plaza.

AL: Do you often ride in his carry-on?

TERI: My hollow leg is great for smuggling shampoo on the plane.

AL: You're Homeland Security's Public Enemy Number One.

(*They grimace at their respective bad jokes.*)

TERI: Too soon?

AL: Nah. We're a hip town. I mean, we still have security checks at the Bank Center and the Milwaukee Art Museum –

TERI: Because when the terrorists next strike it'll be Waukesha County.

AL: Don't mock.

TERI: They hate us for our gouda.

AL: I think they don't want us competing with the poppy fields. When cheese is digested it breaks down into an opiate, you know. That's true.

TERI: Explains the people dressed in green and gold with blocks of cheddar balanced on their heads like Bedouins ... why do we say, "When the terrorists next strike?" Why is that a foregone conclusion?

AL: Why are you here, Teri?

TERI: I needed a break.

AL: Milwaukee in March?

TERI: I live in Phoenix, Al. I wore a tank top on New Year's. *(Pause.)* Wow. The museum really is something.

AL: What does it look like to you?

TERI: Hmm?

AL: It's something I ask, when people first see it. Seeing it in a picture is one thing, but up close ...

TERI: A giant paper crane. Spun sugar.

AL: Huh. The wings are over two-hundred feel tall. They're called the *brise solier*. When the weather gets bad those wings close over the museum.

TERI: This isn't bad?

AL: It can always get worse.

TERI: It can.

AL *(back to the museum)*: The architect's a nice guy. Buys rounds of Cristal like its Mardi Gras.

TERI: You know the architect?

AL: Well, we met at the opening and then I touched base when I was on spec in Zurich. He didn't remember me but he remembered my bid for the Dubai Tower.

TERI: It looks so delicate. Like the breeze would snap it into pieces.

AL: He's doing a bridge in Israel next. There's talk that he'll design the new transit hub at the World Trade Center.

TERI: I don't get why you're here and not New York or Paris or ... somewhere great. You've done really well, Al.

AL: I've done really well, Teri. I can be wherever I want. And: it's the cheese.

TERI: My father asked about you the other day. He asked about you. He can't remember me, he can't remember his wife, but he remembers you.

AL: I'm memorable.

TERI: It was his birthday. He thinks Mom bought him a train set. *(Beat.)* I feel like I'm losing my mind. Like the world is slipping from me, faster and faster, and I have nothing to hold onto. And I want someone to blame. Something real I can hit with my fists until they bleed.

AL: How is Bob? I mean, not right now: at this convention.

TERI: I live with a ghost. There's something residual about him in those rooms, but never him. When I wake up I can tell if he's home because I feel the weight of him. His sadness, pulling me towards ... something. I'm drowning, Al.

AL: No. You're just someone who's at her best when she's a little bit hungry and a little bit angry. But...you can't fight all the time.

TERI: I don't fight. I'm too tired to fight anymore.

AL: You used to. When we were in school, you'd leave it all out on the field. I wondered, if you got what you wanted – family, kids – what would become of the firestorm that's you. You're not a Donna Reed baking cookies kind of girl, Teri. But, you got Bobby, and ... I just build things. Kinda futile, really. Everything I build, it's coming down someday.

TERI: We lose everything. Every relationship we have, they all end, either in break-up or death – Jesus, I sound like him.

AL: Maybe the purpose of life is to learn to accept loss

TERI: Then I guess I'm not very good at life ... God. Those giant wings. It's not a paper crane. It's a skeleton.

AL: You know, conventioneers don't usually stay at the Plaza. That's odd, that they put you up there.

TERI: They didn't.

AL: But here you are.

TERI: Here I am.

(A shared look. History and expectation pass between them.)

AL: You should have gotten a room at the Pfister. Great rococo ceilings. You should see them.

(Lights slowly fade. Meanwhile, lights up on BOBBY, seated at a table, various folders and briefs before him. The actor playing AL crosses the stage, removes his parka, and becomes the MAN in a business suit.)

BOBBY: Well, this is a little afield of what we put together for you. With the revenue our plan saves this hospital by, by determining insurance qualifiers for this location and those ... suited for another, there is ample funding to not alter the status of your ER.

MAN: The board is very happy with your plan. We've used it as a model, I've gone over it myself, but you failed to take into account one big insurance qualifier: having insurance. The board wants an Urgent Care Facility that tends exclusively to our patients.

BOBBY: But –

MAN *(continuous)*: Our insured patients. And Priority One non-insured; we'll still do GSW's, heart attacks, celebrity overdoses.

BOBBY: The goal of our service is to help patients by reducing hospital costs.

MAN: By reducing hospital costs by reducing the number of people qualified for care. And this does that. Significantly. We've gotta cut expenditures. Do you know how much a single aspirin costs us?

BOBBY: It's not an option.

MAN: I'm sorry?

BOBBY: This girl you told me about last time ... ?

MAN: What girl?

BOBBY: This girl with the Valley Fever.

MAN *(begins thumbing through a stack of files)*: Oh, yeah, sure –

BOBBY: Her family comes to your hospital because they trust you. *(Beat.)* I'm trying to help. That is what you hired us to do, right? And I'm trying to tell you that this is not a viable option. It's going to disrupt care for a number of patients, to say nothing of the ethics involved –

MAN *(overlap)*: I don't want to be engaged on ethics, Bobby, and neither do you.

BOBBY *(continuous)*: – and then you're gonna have a monsoon of bad public opinion –

MAN: Bad public opinion? From whom? Our patients, who will see the quality of their care increase and their wait times diminish and their costs reduced? I doubt they'll take to the picket lines. This is California –

BOBBY: I did my MD – I met my wife at UCLA.

MAN: I'm sorry Bobby, but it's this or no dice. You do have competitors, and I'm sure we can find at least one with the foresight to include this option.

(BOBBY is silent, stunned. The MAN retrieves a large stack of folders.)

MAN: I'm sorry, that was ... needlessly aggressive. Look, I wanna show you something. *(Begins to set out case files.)* This is yesterday: Mendoza. Garcia. Garcia. Gonzalez. Perez. Santos. Santos. Villanueva. And – *(counts)* – one, two, three, four, five Martinez. Plus, these. *(Another dozen or so folders.)* No surname given. No address given. And we'll see another two dozen of these today. These expenses get passed on to our insured patients, whom, under your plan, there are going to be fewer of anyway. That's fewer patients to assume the burden. *(Beat.)* Look, these are not GSWs or kids who've fallen off their skateboards. These are disabilities and chronics and ongoing conditions who abuse our current ER policy of blind eyes and open doors. *(Pulls a file.)* Here's your girl. Santos, Christina Marie. Nine years old. Father, unknown. Mother only gave her last name, Santos. Address, none. There's a phone number, but a hundred bucks and a bag of freeway oranges says it's a disposable cell Mom got at Stater Brothers.

BOBBY: Don't show me that.

MAN: Her viral exposure became sub-acute because instead of getting admitted somewhere and having this resolved with vigorous antifungal medication, they bounce in, they bounce out, like this is a Motel 6.

BOBBY: Then you should have admitted her.

MAN: She doesn't have insurance, Bobby! She doesn't have a father, her mother doesn't have a name, and the only record of her existence is there, right there, in blue ink. They could go to Community –

BOBBY: Her mother's terrified that if she goes to Community they'll report to I.N.S. –

MAN: Or maybe our hospital is closer to home and gas is gonna top two bucks a gallon this year. But they keep choosing to come here.

BOBBY: She's nine, I'm not sure how ardently she argued for that choice.

MAN *(overlap)*: Don't get glib with me, Bobby. You are tight-roping over a breech of contract. And I don't think you or your company wants that.

> *(Beat.)*

BOBBY: Okay, so ... we can include a precedent clause that allows any current patients to see their treatment finalized.

MAN: Finalized? These are ongoing. And, I'm sorry, we can no longer be a venue that provides a free service to the detriment of our real patients, the people who pay for and have a right to this hospital.

BOBBY: That's not fair.

MAN: It may not be fair, but it is still their right. The Emergency Room is not an alternative form of health insurance, it's an Emergency Room!

BOBBY: These existent cases are people who came from a third world country with a first world façade. They've –

MAN: These cases aren't existent. Not in the eyes of the board. And if you can't help –

BOBBY: I can't help –

MAN: IF YOU WON'T MAKE them non-existent ... Bobby ... come on, don't do this. You're stressed out, you're tired.

BOBBY: No, my eyes just look like they're open because they are.

MAN: We solve the ER or no dice.

BOBBY: You're closing the ER.

MAN: We solve the ER or no dice.

(They sit for a moment. The MAN begins to collect the folders.)

BOBBY: Wait. Stop. Just, just wait a second here. Now…in addition to the Urgent Care Facility, you maintain bare-bones Emergency services: reduced hours, tending to Priority Ones. And with a little juggling of the insurance charter you may be able to qualify for some, for a degree, of state funding –

MAN: This is a private hospital –

BOBBY: A degree, a degree. For the cost offset –

MAN: It still wouldn't cover your girl.

BOBBY: And with the offset funds you keep the people that need help.

(Beat. Lights up on another part of the stage, revealing the OPERATOR, wearing a brimmed hat pulled low.)

MAN: Bobby, it's noble, it really is. But Community is just ten minutes up the freeway, I've driven it myself, and my car doesn't have flashing lights and a siren. We hired you to do this.

BOBBY (beat; acquiescence with a sigh …): Yeah.

MAN: So you can build in these changes?

BOBBY: Yeah.

(Lights on BOBBY and the MAN fade, they disappear. Meanwhile, RACHEL enters and approaches the OPERATOR.)

OPERATOR: Operator?

RACHEL: I need a connection.

(They meet. He hands RACHEL a folder, which she opens.)

OPERATOR: Klan rally in Georgia in '42.

RACHEL: Oh, that's so yummy. Senator Crowe's sheets are almost as white as he is.

OPERATOR: I got it legal.

RACHEL: Oh, good puppy, time for biscuit.

> (RACHEL puts an envelope in the OPERATOR's outstretched hand.)

OPERATOR: Anything else? I can get you two of the parents of the Flight 11 highjackers ready to go on record.

RACHEL: Mommies and daddies with terrorist progeny don't play in the dinner hour. Find me a chick with huge tracks of land who gave Mohamed Atta a lap dance on September 10th, I'm sure she'll be photogenic.

> (RACHEL and the OPERATOR exit in opposite directions. Lights change. BOBBY on one side of the stage, TOM on the other, wiping sleep from his eyes. They speak via telephone.)

BOBBY: Is it safe?

TOM: Hmm?

BOBBY: Is it safe?

TOM: Marathon Man, why you callin' me at this hour? Ready to play some ball?

> (Lights up elsewhere. CHUCK sits, anxious. Pensive. RACHEL bursts into the room, tosses aside her carry-on.)

RACHEL: Did! You! See! It! Holy mother of baby Moses in a basket, did you see it?!

CHUCK: They've been playing clips all afternoon.

BOBBY: Is it safe?

RACHEL: But did you see it, did you see it?

CHUCK: They've been playing clips –

> (RACHEL's cell rings.)

BOBBY: You asked for my push, here's the push:

RACHEL *(on the phone)*: Rachel Anderson ...

BOBBY: Today I helped a hospital in Los Angeles push a nine-year-old girl with no health insurance and a potentially fatal fungal disease out the door and into the uncertain street for the purpose of lowering the cost of Aspirin. So again, I ask you —

RACHEL: Okay, and what's O'Reilly make on his front end ... ?

BOBBY: Is it safe?

> *(RACHEL blows a raspberry into the phone, hangs up. Lights out on BOBBY and TOM.)*

CHUCK: You've been getting a lot of calls. *(RACHEL's phone rings again.)* Your phone's ringing.

RACHEL *(checks the number, disregards)*: Every time a phone rings an angel reminds me how good it felt to buttfuck a senior United States Senator. The photos have gone viral. The one, of Crowe lighting a twenty-foot cross on fire: every network is using it.

CHUCK *(overlap)*: I saw —

RACHEL *(continuous)*: Unless Senator Crowe went as a ghost in a dunce cap for Halloween, those white linens are gonna be tough to spin. And this man voted against the Iraq Resolution? Well, sorry; you cannot cry tolerance for the leader of a terrorist state when as Exalted Cyclops you used to canoodle with a Grand Wizard of your own.

CHUCK *(overlap)*: I know.

RACHEL *(continuous)*: If anything, Crowe should support the invasion for the nostalgia he'll experience when we hang Saddam!

CHUCK: You've been getting phone calls here all day.

RACHEL: How'd they get the home number?

CHUCK: Calls from New York.

RACHEL *(stops for a moment, knows what this is)*: Yeah. We should talk about that –

CHUCK: You said we didn't have to move to New York.

RACHEL: That was the old statement, this is the new statement.

CHUCK: I don't want to move the family to that city.

RACHEL: The family? Buns, it's gonna be just you and me soon.

CHUCK: Brandy wants to go to the University of Florida.

RACHEL: Brandy wants to go to the University of Florida this week because her dad was a Gator and her *ardour du jour* is a Beta Theta Pi pledge named Truck. If you'd played at Notre Dame maybe she'd wanna nail a Fighting Irish.

CHUCK: I don't want her so far.

RACHEL: Jesus, I was across the street from Radio City Music Hall three hours ago. We can keep the house, you don't have to –

CHUCK: I don't want you so far.

RACHEL: Well dammnit, Chuck, what the hell other options do you see? Am I supposed to just stop, just be content with the sixty percent I've got when I know I could have a hundred and ten?

CHUCK: I prayed about this.

RACHEL: And? Are we playing Rock 'em Sock 'em Requests for Divine Intervention?

CHUCK: We're a team, Rachel, but I'm trying to hold onto something.

RACHEL: You're trying to hold onto a life, that, I'm sorry, ended twenty years ago with a bad sliding tackle and two splintered lumbar. And here in the Land of the Wistful Misty Eyed we've raised a beautiful girl and we've built a wonderful home and we've accomplished everything we can. But now it's time to take the next step, Buns. *(RACHEL's cell phone rings. She checks the number.)* I have to take this. I'm sorry. *(Answers phone.)* Yup ... no, I just walked in the ... oh.

(Lights up on BOBBY and TOM, finishing their telephone conversation.)

BOBBY: Can we talk in a few hours?

TOM: *I* still sleep, Bobby, what'll you be doing?

BOBBY: I dunno.

RACHEL: Oh, God.

BOBBY: My flight's soon. The hotel has a VCR.

RACHEL: Yeah, yes.

TOM: It's 2003, Bobby. Time to experience the exciting world of DVD.

BOBBY: I like what I understand.

RACHEL: I understand ... thank you.

> *(BOBBY, TOM, and RACHEL hang up their phones. Lights out on TOM. BOBBY stands, contemplative.)*

RACHEL: Senator Crowe held a press conference. He's resigned. The network wants me back in New York to discuss hosting.

CHUCK: Sitting in for O'Reilly or Hannity – ?

RACHEL: My own show. *(Beat.)* Do you understand? A senator resigned today. A senator who stood in front of Saddam and cried sovereignty. Who didn't care if two men pervert our most sacred covenant with God. Who opposed Rehnquist, Scalia, Thomas, who fought like hell to get Ginsbuerg and O'Conner on the bench. He resigned today. And Buns, we did that. We *are* a team. We are more powerful than the electorate. This is what I was born for, what I've been chosen for. This is the most important thing I will ever do. I have prayed, and hard. But this is the cost, and God ain't a cheap date, Baby. If this is the call then into the fire we go.

> *(BOBBY dials his phone.)*

CHUCK: You've wanted this. Noodle, I just wanted to watch you.

RACHEL: And you can. Every night.

(Elsewhere, lights up on the MAN from the hospital.)

MAN: Hello?

BOBBY: Hi, it's Bobby Guffin.

MAN: Bobby?

BOBBY: I've got another idea for your insurance charter.

MAN: What –

BOBBY: Yeah. Hey, listen: why don't you go fuck yourself?

(BOBBY hangs up. The lights go out on the MAN and on BOBBY.)

CHUCK: I prayed about this, and ...

RACHEL *(staying with him)*: Buns ...

CHUCK: It's not very fair.

RACHEL: Of course not. God's not fair. He's just.

CHUCK *(Beat. Acquiescence with a sigh)*: Yeah.

(RACHEL kisses CHUCK, holds him.)

RACHEL: You are the reason I breathe. *(Speed dials, speaks into her phone.)* I need a connection. And it needs to be big.

(Lights out. In low light, to one side of the stage, TERI curled up, asleep on the sofa. BOBBY enters, coming home. He touches his wife's hair gently. She wakes.)

TERI: Hey ...

(They kiss.)

BOBBY: Teri –

TERI: Shhhh.

(TERI pulls BOBBY to her, crawling atop him, kissing him. Meanwhile, on the opposite side of the stage, FRANKLIN and NIXON enter. They watch with

mild interest. RACHEL enters. Looks at FRANKLIN. Looks at NIXON. Looks at the couple.)

RACHEL: Nice ...

FRANKLIN: No. They're having some trouble finding their way.

NIXON: Put some fur around the way, won't have any trouble.

RACHEL: That's disgusting.

NIXON: You dreamt it.

FRANKLIN *(extends his hand)*: Benjamin Franklin.

RACHEL: The kite's a handy tip.

FRANKLIN: I invented modern democracy and the flexible catheter.

RACHEL: Shame that's not on the hundred dollar bill. *(Turns to NIXON.)* And ... ? *(NIXON groans, performs his classic two fingered salute.)* But ... you're brownish.

NIXON: Irony?

FRANKLIN: Theatrical convention.

RACHEL: I dream in affirmative action.

FRANKLIN: Oh! A war is coming, but not the one you expect.

RACHEL: Yeah, I've heard.

NIXON: You don't understand. When somebody in show business participates in the political arena, he or she is doing something that is a personal pain in my ass.

RACHEL: I'm sorry?

NIXON: You're a showgirl with a microphone.

RACHEL: Dick, go find Checkers.

NIXON: You're better off kickin' those gams in a chorus line than running your yap on the boob tube about the politics of men.

RACHEL: I'm sorry, but suck my dick, Dick. They should've socked it to you in '72: you left us buried up to our necks in dog shit and shame and it *took* someone in show business with a ballerina for a son to dig the Republicans out.

FRANKLIN: Oh! I was an avid proponent of Republicanism.

RACHEL: See? Now you're talkin': a real Republican who can represent all that's good about our party.

FRANKLIN: A strong Federal government, the patriotism in being taxed one's fair share, and, for God's sake, relief for the Negroes, particularly those we've unfairly held in bondage!

RACHEL: Yeah ...

NIXON: You sound like a goddamned hippie.

FRANKLIN: When I was the ambassador to France –

RACHEL: Uh-oh ...

FRANKLIN *(continuous)*: Jacques-Donatien Le Ray de Chaumont and I shared many wonderful conversations about our *nouvelle* country –

RACHEL: I'd like to retract my previous statement.

NIXON: You're not recording this, are you?

FRANKLIN: Of course, we disagreed on the fallacy of religion. Needless to busy myself with that, I say, especially now that I've had the opportunity of knowing the truth with less trouble.

RACHEL: I'm dreaming this against my will. You're an undigested bit of beef.

FRANKLIN: Ugh. That's why I was a vegetarian.

RACHEL: I'm having a neo-conservative nightmare!

> (*NIXON and FRANKLIN step closer to RACHEL, suddenly more aggressive, more intense. We catch a sliver of RACHEL previously unseen: she is deeply afraid.*)

NIXON: "As South Vietnamese forces become stronger, the rate of American withdrawal can become greater."

FRANKLIN: "As they stand up, we'll stand down."

NIXON: "I have not, and do not intend, to announce the timetable for our program."

FRANKLIN: Your dream has no exit strategy.

NIXON *(seizes RACHEL violently)*: There is a war coming.

> *(NIXON, FRANKLIN and RACHEL disappear as the focus returns to BOBBY and TERI. TERI has become more aggressive, attempting to make love to her husband. They tumble to the floor, hungry, desperate.)*

TERI *(sotto voce, urging)*: Come on ...

> *(BOBBY stops. He shudders, shakes his head.)*

BOBBY: I'm sorry.

> *(TERI moves away. Both are half-dressed and uncomfortable.)*

TERI: Are you seeing someone?

BOBBY: No ... are you? Seeing someone? *(TERI, hurt, stares at BOBBY)* I'm sorry ... I'm sorry I can't be your lover right now, Teri. Not like this.

TERI: You're not my lover, Bobby, you're my husband.

BOBBY: I love you, but you –

TERI: You know what "but" means? "Please ignore everything I just said." *(Beat.)* You say we'll talk, we'll talk, but we don't talk. Even now, we're not talking. You're not here, you're not home, we can't talk. You're always somewhere –

BOBBY: I'm working.

TERI: You hate your work.

BOBBY: Everyone hates their work, that doesn't mean I can just quit doing what I do.

TERI: Yes, it does —

BOBBY: You have no idea what it's like out there.

TERI: I'm not stupid.

BOBBY: I have never said that.

TERI: Just because I don't have a two hundred thousand dollar set of letters after my name, that doesn't make me stupid.

BOBBY: No one has ever called you stupid, Teri, but you have never seen anything through. You don't know —

TERI: I've what?

BOBBY: You drop out of college, you don't have a job —

TERI: I'm seeing *you* through — !

> (*Lights out on BOBBY and TERI, lights up on TOM. He stands, speaking on the telephone, facing front. A return to the conversation with BOBBY earlier.*)

TOM: Ever heard of Operation Mongoose? Back in January, our guys found a bunch of Talibaddies hiding on the Durand Line between Afghanistan and Pakistan. We killed almost twenty of them, destroyed their supplies, captured their base, and ate all their ice cream. Heh. American press is good, they show you where the rockets are launched from, but Al Jazeera shows you where they land. We've got these fuckers on the run, Bobby. The war's over. Slash and burn, Afghanistan is last year, now it's Iraq, maybe Iran or Syria. Shit, we could plant a flag on top of the Vatican if John Bolton had the go. So ... Bobby, we build roads.

> (*Lights back up on BOBBY and TERI. TOM remains lit.*)

BOBBY: You don't understand this —

TERI: You expect me to?

TOM: It's not like you'd be some journalist knocking on doors in Karachi, looking up the worst men in the world.

BOBBY: You've never been political.

TERI: I care about politics, I watch/the news, I read the –

BOBBY: Where it really matters, helping people – there's nothing grey about this road, it's black and white.

TOM: It's hospital administration on a global scale.

TERI: And so you have to go to *Afghanistan*?

TOM: For every three weeks in the States, you'll spend one week there.

TERI: This is insane!

BOBBY: There is nothing for me in this, this perpetual bleak and grey.

TOM: You'll help people who really need help.

BOBBY: There is nothing for me here.

TOM: That is what we're not talking about, right?

BOBBY: I need something.

TOM: You?

TERI: *I'm* here.

TOM: You'll have whatever you need.

TERI: Bobby, you are blind.

TOM: You'll have money, total support.

TERI: I flew to Milwaukee. I've been gone for two days.

TOM: You'll fly in an independently owned and operated, heavily modified French-made C-160. You'll be freezing by night, you'll wear SPF Crisco by day. You'll travel light, never alone. You'll have escorts. You'll have translators, guys we get from the local provinces so they have the right dialect.

BOBBY: Did you sleep with Al?

TERI: You're the one who told me to take a trip.

TOM: Hey, if you can't change the people around you, change the people around you, right?

BOBBY *(sotto voce)*: Did you sleep with him?

TERI: And Europe seemed ... far.

BOBBY: It's okay if you did.

> *(Wham.)*

TERI: Why would you say that ... ? It's not okay. I didn't ask if you were having an affair so you could tell me it's okay for me to. I asked because I want to make love to my husband but his dick won't work and I can see in his eyes that there's someone else in this room.

BOBBY: Of course there is. *(TERI understands, is about to speak. BOBBY shakes his head.)* We don't say her name.

> *(TERI shudders.)*

TERI: Not fair. That's not fair.

TOM: "Receive the Builder of the World with reverence," wrote St. Augustine, and, lo, that reverence was meant for you, Baby. You are a child of Prometheus. You help to undo every atrocity committed in that part of the world over five thousand years of recorded history, and you do so with a road four lanes wide, two in either direction, 147 miles long, tunneling through mountains made by God. You'll leave your mark on this world, Bobby. And they'll see it from space.

TERI: Not fair ...

> *(TERI sits on the edge of the bed, not facing her husband.)*

BOBBY: Teri... it's late, can we talk about this later? Can we talk in a few hours?

TOM: *I* still sleep, Bobby, what'll you be doing?

(TOM hangs up the phone, the lights fade on him and he vanishes. Almost imperceptibly, the sound of wind ... quiet, but growing in intensity ...)

TERI: No, I didn't sleep with Al.

BOBBY: This isn't happening because of Al, or, or –

TERI: Or Katie, her name's Katie!

BOBBY *(overlap)*: Or anything else! We were getting here eventually.

TERI: Wait ... what do you mean? What is this "this" that's happening? *(BOBBY doesn't answer. We are aware of the wind now.)* Don't you dare say nothing. Don't you dare sit there and say nothing ... I will not lose you. I will kill everyone left in the world before I lose you. I don't know how, but I'm seeing you through, to the end of ends ... Bobby, you want to change lives, don't go wandering in the desert, start here with your own family.

BOBBY: We don't have a family anymore.

(Blackout, harsh and abrupt. The sound of wind is unbearable. A moment ... the wind tapers ... lights up on BOBBY, on his mobile telephone. His tie is loosened, perhaps he holds his jacket over his shoulder. His carry-on is by his side.)

BOBBY: Hey. I'm at the airport in Kabul. I was in Jalalabad this morning, at the site. These people; it's just sand and crumbling buildings and ... we're doing good here, Baby ... the project leaders are having dinner tonight with someone representing Karzai. Or maybe it's Karzai himself, I don't know, my translator, he's ... huh. He knows all the lyrics to *Imagine* and *I Am the Walrus,* but we're struggling a bit on the non-John Lennon related material.. ... anyway, I'll call you when I get back to the hotel. Tomorrow we're being escorted into the Pashtun region, along the border. I get to have one foot in Pakistan and the other in Afghanistan. You'd get a kick out of that ... I don't know where you are, but ... uh ... I lo – I'll, uh, call you tonight. I love you, Teri.

(BOBBY hangs up and walks out of the scene. The wind is gone. The lights shift to two FBI AGENTS. They face front, speaking out.)

FIRST AGENT: Teri, they'd have sent pictures to the *Wall Street Journal* if they wanted to make a point.

SECOND AGENT: Or to Al Jazeera if they wanted support.

FIRST AGENT: But they didn't go to the media. And that's a good thing. It means they want to handle this quickly and privately.

SECOND AGENT: It means they want to play ball.

FIRST AGENT: It means they don't want to hurt him, Teri. They want their money and they want their demands.

SECOND AGENT: So we wait.

> *(Another part of the stage. The OPERATOR, wearing a brimmed hat pulled low, appears as RACHEL enters.)*

OPERATOR: Operator?

RACHEL: I need a connection.

> *(They meet. He hands RACHEL a folder, which she opens. We do not see the contents, but we see in RACHEL hypnotic revulsion. Dread.)*

OPERATOR: The other networks are gonna have that by the end of the day.

RACHEL: No one else has this? *(She closes the folder.)* Tell me you got it legally. Not how, just –

OPERATOR: Yes.

> *(RACHEL reaches into her pocket, puts an envelope in the MAN's outstretched hand. They exit.)*

FIRST AGENT : Teri, where have you been?

SECOND AGENT: The NGO is ready to wire the money.

FIRST AGENT: We have you on a flight to Paris, then Prince Sultan Air Base. We figured you'd wanna see him soon as possible.

> *(Lights shift up on RACHEL, another part of the stage. She faces front.)*

RACHEL: On tonight's *American Agenda*, a horrific breaking story you won't hear anywhere else –

FIRST AGENT: Oh, Jesus Christ ...

RACHEL: What you're about to see is disgusting, so if you have kids, here's your chance, get them away from the television.

FIRST AGENT: What have you done, Teri?

SECOND AGENT: We were doing everything right!

RACHEL: These photographs are of Bobby Guffin, an American working on a humanitarian building effort in Afghanistan, believed to have been abducted by terrorists working with Al Qaeda.

SECOND AGENT: *We were doing EVERYTHING RIGHT!*

RACHEL: This is a nasty problem. If he's alive and held in Afghanistan, then they'd better let him go or the 82nd Airborne needs to carpet bomb Kabul until the Afghans think they've been prison-raped by a freight train. But if he's held in Pakistan ... well, Pakistan is our ally and our friend. And we don't invade our friends, especially not our friends with nuclear weapons. And if Bobby Guffin's dead ... well, we've seen what happens when the sleeping giant of Democracy is roused. So this is an appeal to the monsters that have America's son: let Bobby go. This is just me, Rachel, talking. Here on *American Agenda.*

> *(Energetic music plays to take RACHEL to commercial, the same theme as her radio show, only fuller, more bombastic. It quickly fades, as TERI appears and the rest of the company vanishes. She faces front, looking at something.)*

TERI: You'll never guess where I am, Bobby ... I waited for you. Nine days. The FBI offered me a direct flight home from the base in Saudi Arabia. But ... I'm taking the scenic route. I'm in Amsterdam. I'm standing in the same spot where, eight years ago, you asked me to marry you. Not where I said yes, but the first time. When I said I wasn't ready, that things were complicated with Al, that you didn't want to marry me, it was just the hash talking. I didn't know I was already pregnant. You stood there, I stood here ... I waited for you. I'm in the Van Gogh Museum. Second floor. Facing *The Potato Eaters.* So bleak and grey, but so lovely and alive. And the quote that was written on the wall, beside the painting ...? It's gone. But if I close my eyes, I can see it. If I close my eyes ... *(She does. A shudder. The flood, just held back.)* I can feel you, Bobby. *(She opens her eyes.)* "The time has come for me to do that which I cannot do in order that I may learn to be able to do it."

> *(TERI leaves the stage. Suddenly, from all around, yelling ... screaming ... a language that is not English. KADIR rises from the audience and rushes the stage. He destroys the theatrical set pieces, hurling them to the sides. He rips down the black curtains, revealing an abandoned room ... graffiti painted on the*

wall ... bullet holes ... a dirty mattress ... BOBBY is dragged in by WOMIQ and MAROOF, their faces obscured by black headscarves . BOBBY's shoes are missing, his jacket and tie gone, his remaining clothes bloody and torn. His wrists are bound with electrical tape, a bag is over his head. The two men hold him down as KADIR uses a knife to strip off his clothes. He is beaten, the bag left on his head, his wrists left bound. Photographs are taken. BOBBY, nude and bloodied, is filmed with a video camera. The bag is removed. BOBBY vomits blood. A gun is held to his head. More photographs.

(The lights go out.)

END OF PART ONE

* * *

PART TWO: EXODUS / ENGUILDED

"Some months later I smell of woodsmoke and snowfall,
In the months when I can't stop thinking of you ..."
- Lauren Beth Ferebee

"The drums stop ...
This is the kind of silence that frightens white men."
- Robbie Robertson, "Making a
Noise"

"Get away from her, you bitch!"
- Lt. Ellen Ripley, *Aliens*

PART TWO

(An abandoned room ... graffiti painted on the walls ... bullet holes ... a dirty mattress ... In the intermission: Pakistani folk music. The music resolves, and we are left with persistent wind, which takes us to darkness ...

(Lights up. TERI and BOBBY in bed. He is nuzzled up against her, sleeping. She eats strawberries from a bowl perched atop her very pregnant belly. They are swaddled in white sheets. It is a beautiful morning.)

TERI *(nudging BOBBY)*: Wakey-wakey. *(Nothing.)* Wakey-wakey.

BOBBY: Nnnghh.

(TERI wedges a half-eaten strawberry on the tip of BOBBY's nose. His eyes do not open.)

BOBBY: What is on my face?

TERI: Guess and I'll let you stay asleep.

BOBBY: Wait. I think there's a catch here. *(TERI eats the strawberry off the tip of BOBBY's nose.)* Oooo!

TERI: Wakey ... come on, we want you to play with us.

BOBBY: We do, huh? *(His eyes open. TERI feeds him a strawberry.)* Tasty. *(A quick kiss from TERI.)* Tasty.

TERI *(playful)*: Yeah, I know what you like. Ooo! *(Runs a berry over her neck, eats it.)* Mmm. "Doubtless God could have made a better berry, but doubtless God never did."

BOBBY: Who's that?

TERI: William Butler.

BOBBY *(shifts, speaks to TERI's pregnant belly)*: Are you going to grow up to be a great big nerd like your mom?

TERI: Yup. She's gonna be brilliant. And fearless, like her dad. *(BOBBY nuzzles into TERI's embrace.)* Without you this was a house, it wasn't a home.

BOBBY: Home ... I still can't say that without it feeling good.

TERI: Oh, Baby ... we're not here yet.

BOBBY: Hmm?

TERI: "We do not rejoice in victories, we rejoice when strawberries bloom in Israel."

(On this last, blood begins to fill TERI's mouth, dribbling absently over her chin.)

BOBBY: Who's that? Huh – ? Jesus, Teri, look at your mouth!

TERI: You know nothing of my mouth ... oh, Bobby, you are blind. Wake up.

BOBBY: Teri, I –

(TERI stands, wrenches the sheets off of BOBBY. He wears dirty sweats. His wrists are bound with electrical tape.)

TERI: WAKE UP!

(A sudden lighting shift. Bleak and grey. TERI is gone, BOBBY is awake. He breathes raggedly, painfully. Elsewhere: MAHID and KADIR enter, high energy. We recognize MAHID as the YOUNG MAN from the London Tube.
NOTE: The actors playing MAHID and KADIR should attempt no accents for this scene; the convention is that the two men "speak" in Urdu and we "hear" them in English.)

MAHID: Madness! This is Madness! What could have possessed you?! Not only to have done this –

KADIR *(overlap)*: I had no choice – !

MAHID *(continuous)*: THIS! – but to have involved me!

KADIR: Maroof drove him here, Womiq sent the pictures, and we were fine, we were fine! But he would not stop screaming. Nothing we did, nothing Womiq said to him, he would not stop screaming!

MAHID: Did you hurt him?

KADIR: Mahid, please –

MAHID: Did you hurt him!?

KADIR: That was never our intention. *(MAHID slams his fists against the wall.)* Womiq got scared and left. Without Womiq, we had no way to communicate with his people, with his wife, with *him*! And when Maroof left this morning, I did not know what to do, Mahid.

MAHID: Why didn't you tell me?

KADIR: I'm telling you now.

MAHID: Before I got into the car, before we left Islamabad?

KADIR: You would not have come. *(MAHID nods furiously.)* I did not know what to do!

MAHID: If you spoke English, you could talk to him –

KADIR *(overlap)*: Please, do not lecture me.

MAHID *(continuous)*: You would not need me.

KADIR: I am not Pakistani, I do not need to speak like a Pakistani – !

MAHID *(overlap)*: You spent ten years in Islamabad; how, in ten years –

KADIR *(continuous)*: Ten years or ten thousand years, I know who I am and I will not learn an infidel's tongue! Why does he not speak my language? Who is he, to come here to work, and he does not know – he does not even try! – to speak my language? And I should speak his? *(MAHID paces.)* Are you cold?

MAHID: I am fine.

KADIR: You should not have worn that jacket.

MAHID: It is the only one I brought from London, I am sorry if you do not approve.

KADIR: It is very Western.

MAHID: Kadir? Are you threatening me?

KADIR: Of course not. I mean I cannot believe it is very warm. Please. *(Beat. KADIR tries to hug MAHID, who flinches.)* I do not know when I last saw you.

MAHID: Najiba's wedding.

KADIR: So long? How have you been? *(Nothing.)*
You look healthy. *(Disbelief from MAHID.)* I am trying to talk to you, Mahid.

MAHID: Najiba's husband died. Her baby died. Najiba is sick. They may have found my father's remains, but I must somehow explain how he managed to pay union dues for ten years without a social security card. Oh, and I now cook with grape seed oil rather than cold pressed olives. How are you?

KADIR: Your father was a martyr.

MAHID: I must believe that —

KADIR: He was.

MAHID: Or believe he was a coward who turned his back on all of us.

KADIR: Mahid —

MAHID: Damn it, Kadir, how could you be so stupid! *(Beat.)* Who is he?

KADIR: He represents men building a road through the mountains of Safed Koh.

MAHID: He is helping to build through *Al-Safed Koh?*

KADIR: And not just a road. Tunnels.

MAHID: They have spoken of that road for years. Bhutto and Tarar endorsed it, Musharraf and Karzai —

KADIR: I did not! I did not.

MAHID: They will come for you, Kadir.

KADIR: Not until he is gone and this is over.

MAHID: You have lost Maroof, you have lost Womiq; this *is* over!

KADIR: How is Najiba?

MAHID: Weak. She could not make the *Hajj* again this year.

KADIR: There is no effort or power except with Allah's will.

MAHID: I want to take her to London, Kadir. I cannot keep coming back here every time she needs to see a doctor.

KADIR: This is not a doctor's matter. Let her speak to the Imam.

MAHID: Najiba is my sister, she could be helped!

KADIR: Her husband waits for her in Paradise. I love her more than I miss her, but I know, too, what is permissible and what is not. And so do you. *(Beat.)* Did you *Hajj*? *(Nothing.)* Did you?

MAHID: Yes. A shame I did not see you somewhere between *Al-Safa* and *Al-Marwah*.

KADIR: You would not have.

MAHID: That was sarcasm.

KADIR: I know; another Western keepsake best left at home. You would not have seen me because I have not performed the *Hajj* in years.

MAHID: Do not worry; my opinion of you has not changed.

KADIR: I have not been able to *Hajj* because of my work.

MAHID: All work and no play make Kadir a dull boy.

KADIR: This is not a joke –

MAHID *(overlap)*: You say that *after* bringing me here?

KADIR *(continuous)*: Maybe you have forgotten. Maybe your long nights in the West have left you infected and that is why you turn your back, why you abandon that which is yours –

MAHID: Kadir ... do you know what you sound like, speaking of ownership and borders and rightful inheritance? You sound like the Israeli occupiers.

KADIR *(overlap, seizing MAHID)*: Blasphemy!

MAHID *(continuous)*: I am not saying I agree or wish to justify that thinking –

KADIR *(overlap)*: Because you cannot!

MAHID *(continuous)*: But that is what the world will hear.

KADIR *(releases MAHID)*: I am not beholden to the world, I am beholden to Allah. None has the right to be worshipped but Allah; there is no partner unto Him.

MAHID: The American is not a soldier –

KADIR: They are all soldiers.

MAHID: He is a guest in this country –

KADIR: The Soviets came as guests and stayed for a decade, leaving landmines and death. The Americans went to the Two Holy Places and spread an infestation of soldiers, tanks, and planes. Guests? Guests do not bring detonators and trucks, guests *leave*. An occupier sets his tent upon the rock and claims it only for the passage of the night, but guests leave when they are no longer welcome. I want him to leave, and leave with his road. Right or wrong, I defend my country, Mahid. So that it still belongs to me. They have taken the land from us before, so many times. If we cannot push them into the sea, if we allow them to have pushed us across the mountains, what then? No. I push back. I push until it is writ across both skies, "This is mine!" I will not abandon my home again. And I will not be made to flee. *(Pause. KADIR touches MAHID affectionately.)* Do you want anything to eat?

MAHID: No.

KADIR: The American had chocolates in his bag. They are good. *(A look from MAHID.)* What? They were melting.

MAHID *(a sarcastic snort)*: You are stealing candy.

KADIR: Mahid, three days ago I stole a man. Let us approach the situation with the gravity it deserves.

MAHID: I was on the bus the other day. We rode past Trafalgar Square. There were people with signs. Protesting.

KADIR: Now, that is undignified.

MAHID: Do you think the Americans will find Saddam?

KADIR: The Soviets were difficult to repel because perseverance is in their blood. Americans see nothing through. Not when it turns brutal. *(Beat.)* You should be careful, riding the buses.

MAHID: This can only end poorly, Kadir. What have you involved me in? They could listen to your telephone calls, they could be watching us with satellites now —

KADIR: Mahid, in these mountains a man can disappear. The Americans could not find an eagle on their heads. And the French? They are not even trying! They are ready to give us the money and be done, Mahid!

MAHID: If they find us —

KADIR: If they find us, what then? An invasion? They cannot. Karzai is a puppet, and Musharraf is Bush's well-dressed dog. We are safe, Mahid, so long as we abide the plan.

MAHID: Maroof and Womiq leaving, was that part of your plan?

KADIR: I did not say it was *my* plan. And: there are contingencies. For everything. But if you wish to leave, you can. You can walk away and never hear of this again.

MAHID: You would have me leave on foot?

KADIR: Mahid. I will drive you. You can pretend you never saw this place.

MAHID: No. I cannot. And in another ten years: What will you want then?

KADIR: In ten years, who is to say either of us will still be capable of want? Mahid ... you say this will end poorly. But it does not need to. Please, stay. Either stay and help to prove me wrong or else to see this end the best way possible: They send their money, they receive their man, and they leave with all that they brought with them.

MAHID: Kadir ... you champion a great, impossible cause.

KADIR: If the only causes championed were possible, where would we find great men? *(MAHID weighs the situation.)* His name is Rob —

MAHID: Stop! I do not want to know more than I already do.

KADIR: If you cannot do something good for me, please do not do me any bad.

(Pause.)

MAHID: What do you need?

KADIR: Two things. Talk to his organization; their office is in Paris. They have set up the trade, everything is ready. You need only translate.

MAHID: You should have had a translator on board before you launched your ship.

KADIR: I had a translator, one who said he spoke Pashto and French and "Good New York English." And now I am alone.

MAHID: What is the second thing?

KADIR: He needs to eat. He has not eaten since he got here.

MAHID: He is quiet now? (KADIR nods.) You are not alone. Let us go see him. Then call who you need to call.

(They gather food, water, a flashlight.)

KADIR: It will be colder down with the American. Are you certain you do not want something else?

MAHID: I am fine.

KADIR: You had snow in London?

MAHID: Yes. It came later this year.

KADIR: It is coming later every year.

(A lighting shift: darkness, cut by the beam of a flashlight, carried by KADIR. He is followed by MAHID, carrying a bowl of food. They approach BOBBY.)

KADIR: Usko kuch khaana parey gay. Agar kayega nahin, to beemaar ho jaayega. Agar beemaar huwa, to hum mushkil mein aajayangay.

MAHID: Mushkilain tumhare samne hai, tumhe nazar nahin aa rahin? Uski haalat dekho!

(The flashlight beam shines on BOBBY's face.)

MAHID: *Arre yaar* ... hello, can you, can you understand me?

KADIR: *Usko boolo ke khana khaye!*

(MAHID takes the flashlight from KADIR.)

MAHID: *Batti kholo.*

KADIR: *Usko khana pare gay!*

MAHID: *Khayega, khayega* – it is going to be okay – *Kadir, wo tum se dara huwa hai. Tum ja ke batti kholo –*

KADIR: *Tum rahogay uske saath?*

MAHID: Haan, haan, mein rahoonga.

KADIR *(embraces MAHID):* *Shukriya, Mahid!*

MAHID: *Tum* please light on *karo,* Kadir!

KADIR: *Karta hoon. (As he hurries out.) Uspe nazar rakhna!*

MAHID: The lights will be on in a moment ... just a moment ...

(Lights come up. BOBBY and MAHID stare at one another.)

MAHID: Here. Eat. *(MAHID sets the food in front of BOBBY.)* You need to eat. *(No response.)* Lentils and rice. See? *(BOBBY reaches for the bowl, moving slowly, with some pain.)* Eat slowly or you will get sick. *(BOBBY stares at the food, at MAHID.)* You have drinking water? *(BOBBY nods.)* If you need to go to the toilet, tell me.

(MAHID takes in the room. He is uncomfortable, but reveals nothing.)

BOBBY: You're British?

(MAHID hesitates. He keeps his distance.)

MAHID: The men who have taken you represent a Pashtun tribe. You will be treated with humanity while you are their guest. Eat. *(BOBBY does not.)* The

(MORE)

MAHID (cont'd): Safed Koh Road does not recognize the sovereignty of the *Ilaak-e-Ghair* Federally Administered Tribal Area. Progress must stop immediately, and a tribute made by your NGO.

BOBBY *(almost sotto voce)*: Safed Koh? We call it the P.J. ...

(MAHID uncaps a jug of water and sets it near BOBBY.)

MAHID: Drink slowly.

(MAHID stands over BOBBY. A threat or a friend? Eventually BOBBY takes the jug and gulps. He spits and chokes.)

MAHID: Your throat is swollen. Drink slowly.

BOBBY: I know. *(Drinks.)* Thank you. My name is –

MAHID: I am here to see that you eat and that you do not hurt yourself.

(Consideration of this last stops BOBBY.)

BOBBY: And if I don't eat?

MAHID: You will eat.

BOBBY: Where am I ... ? Am I still in Afghanistan? Please, just ... tell me: what side of the Durand Line am I on? *(Nothing.)* Does my wife know I am alive? *(MAHID grimaces at having learned a personal detail.)* Does my wife know –

MAHID: Do not ask me questions for which I have no answers.

BOBBY: I need to talk to my wife.

MAHID: You need to eat and be still.

BOBBY: I can barely move.

MAHID: That is good.

BOBBY *(pushes the bowl away. MAHID stands still, unreadable)*: I'm not hungry ... how do I know it's not poisoned ... ? I'm very scared ... look at what they've done to me! I – I need a hospital, I have at least two fractured ribs. If, if they puncture my spleen or my kidneys, I could die ... come on, I've seen the men on the other side of that door ... please, I'm in a lot of pain. Please –

(MAHID moves suddenly. He eats a handful of food. He eats another, then pushes the bowl into BOBBY's hands. MAHID stares at BOBBY. BOBBY slowly begins to eat. The lights shift. A PAGE wearing a headset, walkie-talkie, and stopwatch pushes or carries on a comfortable, antique-looking chair. TERI follows. The PAGE seats her and adjusts her body microphone. MAHID and BOBBY remain lit. BOBBY eats, MAHID watches him. If the staging will allow, perhaps playing spaces are shared, the two realities existing congruently. During this:)

PAGE: You're on a seven- second dump/delay. Say anything obscene or inappropriate, we're not gonna bleep you. We'll hold –

TERI *(small laugh)*: Inappropriate?

PAGE: We'll hold for seven seconds, and Rachel will start up once we re-link the feed. After that –

TERI: I'm sorry, could you be careful? That chair belonged to Bobby's grandmother.

PAGE: After that, it's thirty seconds before we can dump again, so watch what you say.

RACHEL *(enters)*: I think she means watch what you say to me – not the most gracious way to thank you for your hospitality. *(Shaking hands.)* Hello, Teri. Thank you for welcoming us into your home.

TERI: I expected more people.

RACHEL: Nah, when we go remote it's a small crew. Takes us back to the good ol' days.

TERI: Yeah, those.

RACHEL: So ... any Old English you wanna get out of your system? I can take a shot before we get in the ring.

TERI: I don't need a freebie, Rachel, that's fine.

RACHEL: I mean: Is there anything personal you'd like to say?

TERI: You think I've anything to say that's not?

PAGE: Thirty seconds!

RACHEL: Good girl. If it's business it better be personal. *(RACHEL sits in a chair opposite TERI. The PAGE adjusts her micke, offers her notes.)* No Code Pink t-shirts, no declarations on banners. Whatever bug up your butt wants to talk, the words gotta come out of your mouth.

PAGE: Twenty seconds!

TERI: Whatever I want to say?

RACHEL: Just keep the FCC off my sack and we'll have a nice ride.

TERI: Why this interview? Why now?

PAGE: We're hot in ten.

TERI: Your producer told me –

RACHEL *(smiles)*: Let's have some fun.

PAGE: In your ear, Rachel.

RACHEL *(adjusting an ear piece)*: I gotcha! Jesus, you're tense; I can hear your thighs squeak!

> *(We hear RACHEL's theme music, quiet and filtered. The PAGE stands to the side, raises her right hand, and with her fingers counts down from five. Points to RACHEL.)*

RACHEL: On tonight's *American Agenda* ... darling of the liberal media and a thorn in the Conservative side: You wanted Teri Guffin on this program and we said sooner or later we'd hunt her down. So we're live tonight from Phoenix, Arizona, where Teri has finally agreed to come on *The Agenda.* Thank you for welcoming us into your home, Teri.

TERI: Of course, Rachel.

RACHEL: Now, you had a few conditions if you were to come on *The Agenda,* and we've met those. We're live. You get the whole hour. And you're gonna get to ask me a few questions as well. Other than that, it's all out there, it's all on the table. So.

TERI: I'd like to begin by asking why you just lied to your viewers –

RACHEL: I didn't lie.

TERI: You implied I've been avoiding your show, and you know that's not –

RACHEL: Well, for years I've wanted you on *The Agenda*.

TERI: I've been blacklisted –

RACHEL: Not true.

TERI: Your producer called me out of the blue this week and said you absolutely had to have me on the air –

RACHEL *(overlap, calm certainty)*: Not true ... nope ... no ...

TERI *(continuous)*: That it was timely and couldn't afford to wait, and what I want to know is –

RACHEL *(overlap)*: Not what happened.

TERI: Why, in the five years since my husband disappeared, when I reached out to your program was I continually mocked and shouted down?

RACHEL: We've got the hour, there's no need for us to talk over each other. Now, I can't tell you exactly how our producers book guests. I don't know, I don't get it. But I do know I've wanted to talk to you, not only because your story is of such personal interest to me –

TERI *(overlap)*: Oh, yeah.

RACHEL *(continuous)*: But because – having been the person to break Bobby's story and inadvertently push you into the spotlight – I feel it's my obligation to call you on some of your behavior.

TERI: My behavior?

RACHEL: I don't think you should be allowed a free pass, Teri. Look, what happened to Bobby was a tragedy –

TERI: No one knows what happened to Bobby.

RACHEL: True, but I'm sure we can agree the specifics probably didn't make
(MORE)

RACHEL (cont'd): for a lovely afternoon at the beach. And no one is questioning that. No one is questioning that you've been through hell. But I don't think that means you or your actions are above scrutiny. In the five years since your husband's disappearance, you've become a prominent fringe political operative and the self-appointed scourge of the current administration. And I care about Bobby – and his legacy, we're gonna talk about that – but no one holds your feet to the fire and I don't see how your suffering should entitle you to speak without being held accountable.

TERI: Well! Then! First off: no, my suffering does not entitle me to a redress of grievances; for that I've got the First Amendment to the United States Constitution as part of the Bill of Rights, a document I've heard you quote often on this show. Second, as there has never been a full investigation, nor any evidence to suggest what happened to Bobby once he crossed the Pakistani border, I find it presumptuous to use so eulogistic a word as "legacy." And third: you've still not answered my question, Rachel, which is: why this interview, why this interview *now*, when for the last five years you have ignored my attempts to contact you, belittled my work on behalf of my husband, and only now -- during sweeps week, in an election year! -- have you sought me out. All of which I find fairly beguiling and discourteous, when it was *you* who capitalized on Bobby's disappearance in the spring of 2003 to launch this insipid television program in the first place.

   (Pause.)

RACHEL: We're cable. We don't do sweeps. I'm sure it's safe to say the President is not in your Top Eight on MySpace, yes?

TERI: If the President had been honest about the state of affairs in post-war Afghanistan, my husband would be sitting with me today.

RACHEL: If Bobby hadn't gone to post-war Afghanistan he could be doing anything anywhere today, though it's unlikely you'd be the famed leader of a radicalized liberal cult.

TERI: We are a protest movement.

RACHEL: Mm-hmm! You've protested the war in Iraq, the war in Afghanistan, the RNC, the '04 election, the '06 midterms, propositions on ballots in Arizona, California, New Mexico, Texas; you protested *The Passion of the Christ* and the opening of a Wal-Mart in Guam. This is your "work" on behalf of Bobby?

TERI: I attack people in power who create conditions for harm.

RACHEL: How many folks are on the payroll of your little guerrilla operation, Teri?

TERI: None. I have one or two volunteer assistants.

RACHEL: Including your dad?

TERI *(not sure where this is going)*: No.

RACHEL: He administers The Katie Guffin Fund, yes?

TERI: He –

RACHEL: What's that about?

TERI: My daughter Katie passed away in 2001. Dad started a scholarship fund in her name. Every year we give five hundred dollars to an incoming ASU freshman.

RACHEL: And Dad still does that?

TERI: He ran the website, briefly, until his condition worsened. Now he just opens mail if it comes to the house or sometimes endorses checks.

RACHEL: My husband does that. Opens the mail, whether it's for him or not.

TERI: Yeah?

RACHEL: Yeah, drives me crazy. You accept checks?

TERI: If you wanna make a donation, Rachel, there's an address on the webpage.

RACHEL: We've heard a story about your father, back when you were yea high and times were lean: Mom bought a train set for Christmas, just a little something special –

TERI *(overlap)*: Oh, God ...

RACHEL *(continuous)*: And Dad got upset, started yelling, "We can't afford this, how stupid can you be?" And then he smashed the train set against the wall in the den. You were eleven. Do you remember that?

TERI: Who told you that?

RACHEL: We have good sources, Teri. So: Dad's always been a little irrational? Had a bit of a temper?

TERI: Everyone knows my father's very sick, you don't have to –

RACHEL: I haven't mentioned your father's illness because it's tragic and unfortunate, but if he's collecting cash in the name of a Guffin, any Guffin, he's up for grabs.

TERI: My father has nothing to do with my work challenging a President who has lied, who has –

RACHEL: Lied?

TERI: Either he's a liar or he's incompetent at discerning truth from fiction.

RACHEL *(overlap)*: Wow.

TERI *(continuous)*: He's made rash, ill-informed/decisions with devastating results –

RACHEL: Well, that doesn't sound like anyone we know, huh?

TERI: *(continuous)*: Decisions that deserved contemplation beyond the President's prayers and gut instinct – his *uninformed* gut instinct!

RACHEL: Oh, and now you're insulting people who pray?

TERI *(overlap)*: Of course not.

RACHEL *(continuous)*: I mean, I pray.

TERI: Me, too –

RACHEL: I pray a lot!

TERI: But when the car is broken you take it to Pep Boys, not to church.

RACHEL: And when your daughter is sick, you take her to a hospital, I get your metaphor. But, as usual, you're saying a lot of incendiary stuff – I know I'm insulted – and you're not backing it up and none of it is true.

TERI: None of –

RACHEL (*casual*): None of it, none of it.

TERI: You're gonna dismiss –

RACHEL: None of it. I reject your premise. I see in George Bush a man willing to do whatever it takes to fulfill his duty to keep us safe.

TERI: The President doesn't take an oath to keep us safe. He takes an oath to defend and protect the Constitution –

RACHEL: I meant his duty as a man. See, I value human life more than some moldy parchment. Shouldn't you?

TERI: What?

RACHEL: Value lives: Such as Bobby's! If I gotta choose between life, liberty and the pursuit of happiness, or the best two out of three and getting the bad guys who took him, I'll pony up.

TERI: I...I –

RACHEL: I wanna win! Doncha wanna win?

TERI: It's – it's not so simple –

RACHEL: I mean, I read about the bad things being done by bad people to good people – like Bobby – and I get furious. Furious! I get furious.

TERI: What? I, I – uh –

RACHEL: Listen to me, I'm more furious than you are.

TERI (*explodes: genuine, though it's standard stump speech*):
This country should be furious! We've lost seven-tenths of the Bill of Rights, *habeas corpus*, *stare decisis*, rational fu – (*Almost curses, catches herself*) – thought, and the general moral belief that we shouldn't use the same tactics of persuasion as the Corleones!

RACHEL (*overlap*): Mind your naughty bits.

TERI (*continuous*): This country has been lulled into apathy and malaise, when it should be furious!

RACHEL: Yeah, but, see: I'm furious for Bobby, and you're pouting 'cause there's no protest movement.

TERI: I'm f – *(Another near F-Bomb.)* I'm furious, I'm – yes, there is a, a protest movement, but, but –

RACHEL: Maybe the reason there isn't one is because the Left can't get their stuff together.

TERI: I think –

RACHEL: And your music *sucks!* That's why this doesn't look like 1969. Where's your John Lennon?

TERI: Well, we had the Dixie Chicks.

RACHEL: Oh, please, no one cares; the Chicks are never gonna be bigger than Jesus, the closest they can hope for comes once a month and that's only because they're retaining water. *(Shock from TERI.)* See, here's what's wrong with the Radical Secular Left-Wing Agenda: you have no agenda, there's no cohesive vision!

TERI: That's absurd.

RACHEL: You were arrested in 2006 at a science museum in –

TERI: At a "science" museum in northern Kentucky where they have robot dinosaurs in the Garden of Eden.

RACHEL: Yep. And you were arrested in 2006 for masturbating an audio-animatronic of Eve?

TERI: Not true.

RACHEL: Well, I may be fudging the verb, maybe you were fellating Methuselah.

TERI *(overlap)*: No!

RACHEL *(continuous; she laughs)*: I mean, what were you doing?

TERI: The charges were dropped –

RACHEL *(laughing)*: Were the PETA freaks upset the T-Rex didn't get grass-fed, free-range meals, what?

TERI: This isn't funny.

RACHEL: Yeah, you are.

TERI: I want to have a serious discussion about policy and change –

RACHEL: And give a passing nod to your husband who can't.

TERI: Who can't what?

RACHEL: Nod. Because he's not here. But you're right, I said you'd have your chance to say what you wanted to say. So?

(TERI reorients herself, a little dazed from RACHEL's onslaught of rhetoric.)

TERI: We're eating ourselves alive.

RACHEL: Is this a Monsanto riff?

TERI: We're eating –

RACHEL *(overlap)*: I mean, this is the soapbox you wanna pitch from?

TERI *(continuous, sacrificing clarity for volume)*: We are a country devouring itself –

RACHEL: Did you know: a mouse will eat its own tail if it gets hungry enough? *(TERI is silent: stunned, losing, and knows it.)* You can take a shot at Disney if you wanna roll with the implied metaphor. I'm just tryin' to help you out here. *(TERI opens her mouth. Nothing comes out.)* Teri, this is why no one listens to your team. No one listens to the Dixie Chicks, no one goes to see Michael Moore's crummy movies. Your compatriots have piled up like evacuees on a Saigon helicopter pad. And Teri, you are scattered all over the place! Is this just what comes of a gal who switched from art history to political science to women's poetry before dropping out of UCLA with an M.R.S. degree?

TERI *(overlap)*: How dare –

RACHEL *(continuous)*: I mean, come on: the President's bad, Americans are bad, fake dinosaurs are bad! Everyone's bad except for the people who gave Bobby his last haircut and took a little too much off the top.

TERI: You fucking bitch.

RACHEL: Dump it.

PAGE: Five seconds.

(They wait ...)

RACHEL *(genuine tenderness)*: You're doin' good, Hon.

(The PAGE points to RACHEL.)

RACHEL: So, you held an —

TERI: You are a fucking bitch.

(Whoops. The PAGE gasps, looks to RACHEL.)

RACHEL: And you are awfully defensive. That language —

TERI: You'd be defensive, too, if we were talking about Brandy.

RACHEL: My daughter's neither relevant nor on the table

TERI: From the photos on the internet I doubt there's a table she hasn't been on.

RACHEL: We're not talking about my daughter.

TERI: No, we're not. We're not talking about her Facebook page supporting Barack Obama. Or the matching tattoos she and her guitarist boyfriend got to celebrate her C- in Freshman Economics.

RACHEL *(overlap)*: Shut up! Cut her mike.

TERI *(continuous)*: We're not talking about her dormitory at the University of Florida —

RACHEL *(overlap)*: Cut it! Drop us, drop us!

TERI *(continuous)*: Or that her telephone number is 352.392.2161.

RACHEL *(overlap)*: Are we out?!

PAGE: We're out!

(*RACHEL bolts to her feet. Walks away.*)

TERI: We have good sources, too.

(*TERI sits still, satisfied. RACHEL sees her as if for the first time.*)

RACHEL: That was a hell of a stunt, Teri. Don't worry, when we come back from commercial, I'm not going to ask for an apology. We'll move along.

PAGE: You wanna come right back?

RACHEL: You bet the face your mother rode in on I do. How much time?

PAGE: We ran the McCain spot, we're back in thirty or we can toss to the news desk –

RACHEL: Oh, no. I'm in this beast.

(*RACHEL sits. Looks at TERI. Silence.*)

PAGE: Fifteen seconds.

RACHEL: Did Bobby have good dental, Teri? Those are pretty white teeth.

PAGE: In your ear, Rachel.

RACHEL: Mm-hmm.

(*The PAGE stands to the side, raises her right hand, and with her fingers counts down from five. Points to RACHEL.*)

RACHEL: Thanks for stickin' with us; we've got Teri Guffin here on *The Agenda* –

TERI: You go too far, Rachel.

RACHEL: People may think so.

TERI: My husband was not –

RACHEL: People may think I'm cruel or unfair, but I'm willing to do whatever
(*MORE*)

RACHEL (cont'd): it takes to get the truth out of you. *(Pause.)* Do you think Bobby's still alive? *(Nothing.)* 'Cause I don't see you devoting time and energy and money – Bobby's money – to finding him. Instead, you march around insulting our troops, camp outside Crawford toying with treason, and generally look ... well, like an emotionally unbalanced widow.

TERI: You insinuate, and you insinuate, and ... *(This is hard.)* My husband was not, was not beheaded. I would just ... I would feel it, I would know it, if he was. *(Back in control.)* I am an intelligent woman.

RACHEL: All the more reason I find your behavior questionable. *(Beat; genuine.)* What were you saying before the break? It was obviously important to you. Something ... uh ... dietary?

TERI: We're eating ourselves alive.

RACHEL: Yes, that.

TERI: We're devouring ourselves. We've jettisoned responsibility and common sense; we turn on the television and stuff garbage into our heads –

RACHEL *(overlap, understanding)*: Hmm.

TERI *(continuous)*: And until we get our priorities straight, Bobby's dream of a world where the sick and the hurt are treated with humanity and dignity ... it'll stay a dream. We can't sustain this. You can't sustain something that's broken. You have to stop and fix it.

> *(With a crash, all light goes out. In the darkness, we hear KADIR reciting the Maghrib, his afternoon prayer. Lights reveal KADIR and his prayer mat. Elsewhere, lights reveal BOBBY and MAHID. Time has passed. TERI and RACHEL are gone. KADIR's prayer turns sotto voce. BOBBY strains briefly against his bonds. MAHID checks his watch, frustrated.)*

BOBBY: I was in a Kinko's once. It's a store where –

MAHID: I know what a Kinko's is.

BOBBY: I was in a Kinko's once, making photocopies late at night and they got a bomb threat. The SWAT team showed up and we all had to evacuate, but first the manager made us pay for our copies. I wasn't allowed to leave because of three dollars ... I used to say, "I know exactly what my life is worth, it's worth three dollars in photocopies."

(KADIR finishes his prayer. His light fades. MAHID looks at his watch. Mutters.)

BOBBY: What is it? What are you waiting for – ?

MAHID: You only speak English? You only speak English?

BOBBY: No, I ... I don't only speak English. I also –

MAHID: Is that so? *Mein jo bol raha hoon wo tum samaj rahe ho? – Inta fahimnee hella? Tee seechas ponimaiyesh menya, Amerikanskaya suka? – Yahaan koi* McDonalds *ya* Starbucks *tumhe nahin milega. Tum jaante nahin ho ke tum kitne khushkismat ho.* *(MAHID shakes his head)* American ... !

> *(KADIR enters the space, hurriedly. He carries a cheap mobile phone and a notepad.)*

KADIR: Mahid! *Wo paise bhejnay ke liye tayyaar ho gaye hain. Yeh lo, sab kuch is pe likha hua hai. Baat karo un se. (Hands MAHID the notepad as he dials the phone. Listens. Hands it to MAHID.) Phone utthao.*

MAHID: *Kis se baat ho rahi hai?*

KADIR: *Pata nahin, koi* accountant *hai.*

MAHID: Paris *mein?*

KADIR: *Haan,* Paris *mein.*

> *(KADIR exits.)*

MAHID: Brilliant ... *(Into the telephone.) Allô? (Refers to notepad throughout for information scripted by KADIR.) Je vous appelle au sujet de* Robert Guffin ... Bobby, okay... *(Noticeable discomfort at having learned BOBBY's name.) Il va bien, il va bien, mais il est prêt à rentrer. Etes-vous prêt à transférer la somme ... ? Bon...le numero du compte est zéro zéro zéro, tiret sept, tiret dix-neuf, tiret quarante, tiret neuf, tiret zéro trois neuf, quatre-vingts. Bien reçu?*

> *(During the above, KADIR enters with BOBBY's carry-on. He unceremoniously dumps the contents on the floor and throws the carry-on aside. KADIR seizes BOBBY by the face.)*

KADIR *(overlap, to BOBBY): Ey, sewer ki owlaad. Tuj mein se bhoo aa rahi hai. Kapde badal ke jaa na.*

(KADIR grabs at BOBBY's broken ribs. BOBBY howls. MAHID pulls KADIR away, all the while speaking on the phone.)

MAHID *(continuous : D'accord…Desolé, desolé ... oui, oui ... (A look to BOBBY; their eyes meet.) Non, desolé, je ne peux pas faire ça. Au revoir. (Hangs up, pushes KADIR.)* Yeh kya karrahe ho?

KADIR: *Kyun, kya hua?*

MAHID: *Woh phir chillaega.*

KADIR: *Bhaley chillaega?*

(MAHID hands KADIR the phone and the notepad. During the following, KADIR pops open the phone and removes the SIM chip.)

KADIR: *Tumhari maghrib ki namaaz chhootgayee. Ya phir tumne idhar padhlee, uske mowjoodgi mein.*

(KADIR gesticulates toward BOBBY.)

MAHID: *Woh* phone *ka sub patay maloom karlengay.*

(KADIR crushes the used SIM chip under his heel.)

KADIR: *Tum fuzool mein ghabraate ho,* Mahid. *Wop kapde baad mein badal lega. (About to exit, KADIR reaches into the waistline of his pants. Removes a   revolver, stuffs it into MAHID's hands.) Yeh lo.*

MAHID *(overlap): Yeh kya kar rahe go? Hargiz nahin!*

KADIR *(continuous): Aagar kuch huwa to chup karane mein kaam aayega!*

(KADIR is gone. MAHID stands for a moment, uneasily holding the revolver. BOBBY, having seen the above exchange, begins to shake, wracked with growing panic. Then:)

BOBBY: *Je parle français. Je pense que le français est une langue incroyablement belle.*

MAHID: *Tu parles français?*

BOBBY: My conjugation's okay but my accent has always been pretty weak.

(MORE)

BOBBY (cont'd): Didn't stop me from tutoring my roommate in college, though ... you said my name. *(Nothing.)* What did the man on the phone ask for? When you said, "Sorry, I can't do that"? *(A look from MAHID, who then moves to repack the contents of the carry-on.)* If there's anything in there that you want you can have it. Nothing too exciting, just clothes and a shaving kit. A tape from my wife. And some chocolates from Charles de Gaulle.

MAHID *(repacking)*: Soon you can change your clothes.

> *(MAHID packs the carry-on. BOBBY struggles weakly against his bonds.)*

BOBBY: Thank you for the food. The bread was good ... "a meal without bread is an incomplete meal." Isn't that what you say? ... my side hurts. But, you were right, breathing shallow helps. Thank you ... so, now you know my name. But you haven't told me yours.

> *(Pause. MAHID stands; still packing, he absently holds the cassette in the red case.)*

MAHID: You haven't asked.

BOBBY: Right. Well, what's your name? *(No response.)* I mean, I am your guest, right? *(No response.)* Where am I?

MAHID: I am not your friend, Bobby. *(Finishes packing.)* I am glad you are going home and it is best you are safe and well, but do not imagine that I think differently from the men who brought you here.

BOBBY: You sound different.

MAHID: The only difference is that I see more to be lost than gained in threatening you.

BOBBY: In threatening me? Or in hurting me? Is there a difference? *(Nothing.)* Are you just the interpreter, or are you the muscle that stays quiet? *(A snort.)* Or are you the guy who makes the meatballs? Are you fucking Clemenza? *(Laughs, nearly manic.)* No, of course you don't know who that is.

MAHID: "Leave the gun, take the cannoli." *(BOBBY is stunned.)* But, I like *Dr. Zhivago*: "I hate everything you say, but not enough to kill you for it." *(MAHID eyes BOBBY.)* When the Soviets came, if you had money, you went to Iran or Pakistan. Only the poor stayed. And the poor fought the war. Sound familiar?

BOBBY: You opposed the Soviets?

MAHID: I was seven when the Soviets came. My father was an architect – a brilliant man! – and in the middle of the night he, my sister, my uncle, his two sons – my cousins – we fled the homes he had built in Kabul, scurrying into the mountains as rats when the lamps are out ... we stayed in a place not unlike this. What choice did you give us?

BOBBY: Me?

MAHID: Yes, you. You funded the *Mujahideen*.

BOBBY: I was just a kid –

MAHID: *I* was just a kid. You accept no culpability because you have no sense of perspective. You didn't find yourself a refugee in Islamabad, five men in one room, taking turns in one bed. We learned Urdu. And English. And I watched my cousins go back across the mountains to fight – to fight your enemy with your guns! Guns you continued to send across the border, like poison, like cancer –

BOBBY: Kinda like the opium you send our way now? I mean, if we're gonna talk culpability ...

MAHID: You are very clever, so explain to me, please: why? Why did you arm the *Mujahideen*? Hmm? And please, do not bother to speak of "liberation." Do not bother with words even you do not believe in.

BOBBY: Oil?

MAHID: No. For once, no.

BOBBY: I don't know.

MAHID: Guess.

BOBBY: Better the devil you know than the devil you don't.

MAHID: You think us devils?

BOBBY: No, no ...

MAHID: You are lying. But whether or not you think us devils, you know us

(MORE)

MAHID (cont'd): now, don't you? *(Stares at BOBBY.)* America wanted *Mujahideen* to lure the Soviets into quicksand and quagmire. The Great Game all over again! But why? Why? I was a boy, and this I could not understand: Until I watched for the first time *The Bridge on the River Kwai*. How I loved this story of Western prisoners of war who built a bridge: Not because they were forced to, no, but just to show their captors they *could*. Such hubris! *(Beat.)* Where did you go to school?

BOBBY: I did my MD at UCLA.

MAHID: And your childhood?

BOBBY: L.A.

MAHID: See? No sense of perspective. *(Pause.)* I studied at the School of Languages, Linguistics, and Film at Queen Mary and Westfield College, University of London. I have double degrees. I speak six languages. I have homes in England and Pakistan. And all of this because my father did not want to see me wander back across the Durand Line and be consumed by the fire that took his brother's sons. The fire that later consumed his brother. Consumed everyone he knew. And then one day my father sent a note to my home in London: "Care for your sister. I am to leave and may not return from where I am going. May Allah guide you to the best in this life and the next!" *Allah tumhein dunya aur akhirat dono naseeb farmay!* And then? Nothing more. My father vanished the year I left school and my sister married. I heard whispers that my father was ... was going to do something I was not born to imagine, something I could never do. Something about the Russian spoken in our streets. Something about the Hindus who built *their* roads and mocked us and butchered Kashmir while America smiled – after you *failed us* in keeping whole our land! But then I heard something new: Whispers that he was lost. That he had forgotten. That he sought the proximity of his devils by distancing himself from the religion of Allah. But this I knew could not be. For years I heard nothing, but I knew: I knew my father was waiting, like a scorpion under the rock. Silent. Until the day you counted your three thousand3,000 dead and gave them names. And on the telly I saw my father. They called him a janitor! An immigrant! A "good Muslim"! The American Dream! And this is a lie. No one can make me believe my father, who built his business and built our home – and, when the sand changed, built them again – that this man spent his last years giddily cleaning the floors of devils. No. You cannot tell me that. And now his name is on a wall and decorates plaques and will be read every year. Honey ground into the dirt of your three thousand3,000 dead. I suffer more for what has been done in his name than for the loss of his life. He is called "hero," by you, and his end is meant to justify THIS! And now the invaders walk my streets and they speak English. *(Pause.)* What is your favorite movie ...? Hmm?

BOBBY: *Star Wars.*

MAHID: Uhh! The two worst things to come out of America are the democracy of George Bush and the cinema of George Lucas.

BOBBY *(wan smile)*: Ah, George ...

MAHID: He should be ashamed of his fairytales for children. The opportunity handed him has been derailed by an infantile, naïve worldview full of magic and strange spirits. So pathetic, this story of a little boy so afraid of his great and terrible father! *(Beat.)* And then there is George Lucas.

>   *(They laugh. A shared moment.)*

BOBBY: You know: I want to help.

MAHID: Oh?

BOBBY: I'm here because I want to help.

MAHID: How – ?

BOBBY: This road will help people get to hospitals, help them get care –

MAHID: Wanton suffering is never the will of Allah ... do you know I have a sister?

BOBBY: You said, before.

MAHID: Your road is a lie. It will not bring us to hospitals, but it will one day bring your tanks and your men.

>   *(Elsewhere, TERI enters, takes her seat. She looks worn.)*

BOBBY: What is your sister's name?

MAHID *(suddenly uncomfortable with their familiarity, MAHID moves away)*: Why? I don't understand you, *American.* You are going home, and I am eager to be done with you. You may choose to name and rename the places of the earth that have no lines, but in the end it is of little consequence. I speak six languages. Do you know why?

BOBBY: What six languages?

MAHID: Do you know why?

BOBBY: What six languages?

MAHID: Farsi. Urdu. Arabic. French. Russian. *English*. And why? Because: time is long.

> *(A pause. Something troubles BOBBY. Elsewhere, RACHEL enters.)*

RACHEL *(on the telephone)*: Hello, Buns. Are you watching ... ? You're TiVo-ing it ... what? ... no, Greenwich Avenue doesn't run East-West ... or North-South ... I don't know, it's slanty! Buns, the gays ain't straight, why would the infrastructure be ... ? Ah. Good luck. *(Hangs up.)*

MAHID: There is a saying: Americans have all the watches, but we have all the time.

RACHEL: How you doin', Kid?

MAHID: You're shaking.

RACHEL: You look warm.

BOBBY: I'm cold.

TERI: It's these lights.

RACHEL: Here. *(Reaches into her purse, pulls out two small pads.)* I still keep a few of these on hand, just in case. For your pits.

TERI *(hesitates, then takes the pads)*: Thanks.

> *(RACHEL sits, looking over notes. Meanwhile, MAHID has helped to put a blanket over BOBBY's torso.)*

TERI: Who's Buns?

RACHEL *(small laugh)*: My beloved husband of twenty-two years has gotten himself lost in the West Village, looking for what he believed was a Civil War memorial called the Stonewall Bar. I don't know what's more disconcerting: that Chuck may wind up drunk on Peach Schnapps at Marie's Crisis or that he thought he'd find a monument to Rebel sympathizers in a town with a major league team called the Yankees.

TERI: The first time Dad and I visited New York he took me to the New York Public Library.

BOBBY: I want to go home.

TERI: We stood on the steps.

BOBBY: I want to go home.

TERI: He pointed at the two stone lions and said, "What's his name? And that one?"

RACHEL: Patience and Fortitude.

MAHID: You're going home.

RACHEL: The names of the lions.

BOBBY: Americans have a sense of perspective. It's just ... we're scared because we haven't had to make any tough decisions in a long time.

TERI: Yeah.

MAHID: No. No, a long time ago Americans decided not to make any decisions at all.

TERI: Rachel, earlier: it got personal.

RACHEL: If it's business, it better be personal. I call my husband Buns because in college Chuck played tight end.

TERI: I am sorry I said Brandy's –

(*RACHEL puts up her hand, stops her.*)

RACHEL: My daughter is off the table. Your daughter is off the table, or at least she has been since they finished the autopsy and rouged up her little cheeks, so – mother-to-mother – let's just get that squared away. I'm not about to dredge up Katie, I would never do that to you, so please pay me the same courtesy. And if your heart and head are so thick you can't understand that then take heed, because not for two fuck-all seconds will I allow you to come on this

(MORE)

RACHEL (cont'd): program and play me at the expense of my child. Do not try to handle me. Mention Brandy again, and you will unleash a fury not seen since God walked on two feet.

> *(The lights on TERI and RACHEL shift abruptly: we flash forward, catching them mid-interview.)*

RACHEL: Who is Guantánamo Bay Detainee Number 238?

TERI: Womiq Shah Durrani. He and another man –

RACHEL: Current whereabouts unknown.

TERI: – yes – posed as guides and took Bobby from Kabul International to a small house outside of Peshawar.

> *(KADIR bursts into BOBBY's room. He roughly pulls a bag over BOBBY's head.)*

RACHEL: Where your husband was held by Kadir Khalid Yousef, current whereabouts also unknown.

KADIR: *Mahid! Jaldi aao!*

MAHID *(overlap)*: *Kya hua?*

KADIR *(continuous)*: *Iddher aao!*

> *(KADIR and MAHID exit. The lights on BOBBY fade low but remain present.)*

TERI: Yes.

RACHEL: Womiq admits to beating Bobby, to helping strip and photograph him – those horrible photos we all remember – then he got scared and bailed on his friends a few hours later. Right?

TERI: That's his testimony.

RACHEL: From GitmoITMO, where Womiq's mail has been forwarded the last three years. The Pakistani Police and the FBI found no sign of Bobby when they searched the house in the Fall of 2005. So that testimony is the last clue to Bobby's whereabouts, right?

TERI: Right.

RACHEL: Just making sure: that's the last of Bobby's moments anyone can confirm.

TERI: Yes. That and the call to the Paris office.

RACHEL: Somebody rang Bobby's NGO with a Swiss bank account number.

TERI: Yeah.

RACHEL: Yeah, the day you went public; that's worth remembering. Had Bobby shown a previous interest in building roads for hostile third world countries?

TERI: Bobby saw an opportunity to improve health care for people who need it. That was what lit him on fire, okay?

RACHEL: How was your marriage at the time of his disappearance?

    (Pause.)

TERI: I'm not going to answer that.

RACHEL: Why'd you go to the media, Teri? Why'd you come to us?

TERI: I didn't go to you, I went to Olbermann and Blitzer and Bill Moyers.

RACHEL: I got over it. Why didn't you just sit quiet like the FBI asked? Do you take any blame for Bobby's homecoming having gone belly-up?

TERI: It had been three days. We hadn't heard anything in three –

RACHEL: You couldn't just sit still?

TERI: Could you?

RACHEL: If I'd been instructed by people smarter than me, you bet your ass. So I find your criticism of this administration a bit unpalatable; it was *you* who broke formation, Teri. It was you who sought out the cameras. *(Pause.)* Has that made you at all reticent to come forward with new information?

TERI: I know I need you.

RACHEL: Need us? *(Tiny pause.)* Teri, was your husband beheaded by Kadir Khalid Yousef?

TERI: My husband was not beheaded.

RACHEL: 'cause your gut instinct says so, your so *well-informed* gut instinct? Was he beheaded by Kadir Khalid Yousef? *(Nothing.)* When I was a little girl I helped my granddad paint the garage: pearly white, red trim. And I accidentally dipped the tip of a red brush into the white paint. Granddad threw the whole jug out, because just a drop taints the white. Makes it impure. That's kinda how the truth works, Teri. Catch a person fudging and they're tainted. So, last chance: was your husband executed by Kadir Khalid Yousef or any member of his team?

TERI: I have hope. And you can't kill that.

RACHEL: Yes. I can.

(Lights up on KADIR, facing front.)

KADIR: Mahid, listen!

RACHEL: Are you familiar with Guantánamo Bay Detainee Number 421?

KADIR: He contacted me.

RACHEL: Otherwise known as Mohammed Sheik Samir?

KADIR: I am bringing him here. Now.

RACHEL: Or as the Ten of Diamonds, for those with the home game?

KADIR: I am bringing Mohammed Sheik Samir here.

RACHEL: His GitmoITMO testimony was classified until 12:01 this morning. So it's understandable that you'd draw a blank on hearing his name.

KADIR: This is not madness.

RACHEL: But I cannot say the same for him.

KADIR: This is the art of inevitability.

RACHEL: No, when they had Samir under the faucet and *your* name came up, the room got chattier than a schoolgirl's first sleepover.

KADIR: This is Allah's will served cold.

RACHEL: Because Samir designed the playbook Kadir Khalid Yousef was operating from when he grabbed your husband.

KADIR: This is a private land!

RACHEL: Mohammed Sheik Samir handed out owner manuals to any angry young man with a tan who wanted a part of the franchise:

KADIR: And that road? It still would not help your sister.

RACHEL: Track the target, get the target, get the cash, send the target home. Unless —

KADIR: Mohammed Samir?

RACHEL: And this is where you come in, Teri —

KADIR: He has bought the American.

RACHEL: Unless another, untraceable buyer hears about the target and offers something more.

KADIR: He may do with him as he pleases.

TERI: I don't ... I don't understand.

KADIR: I will put the knife high in the American's neck, behind the ear. I will do this myself.

RACHEL: They were playing catch-and-release.

KADIR: You will hold him down.

RACHEL: Bobby was almost off the hook.

KADIR: It will be fast, Cousin.

RACHEL: But when Mohammed Sheik Samir saw you on the evening news, with your pictures of Bobby, your very small story got a whole lot bigger.

KADIR: If you do not wish to help, you may run.

RACHEL: I may have capitalized on your husband's disappearance, but —

KADIR: Know this:

RACHEL: You sold him out.

KADIR: Mahid, no matter what you wear, we will recognize you ... look at you, wearing that jacket. You stink like one of them.

RACHEL: On September 19th, 2005, under intense invasive questioning, Mohammed Sheik Samir confessed to having purchased Bobby Guffin from Kadir Khalid Yousef for the purpose of execution by beheading.

KADIR: Thirty minutes. We will be back here in thirty minutes. Help us then or disappear, Cousin.

TERI: No ...

RACHEL: And that's the last anyone heard of Bobby. *(Lights out on KADIR.)* Except for you. Because you received a package from Pakistan sometime in the last five years. And among the contents of that package was a videotape.

TERI: What?

RACHEL: What's on that videotape, Teri?

TERI: Who told you this?

RACHEL: You're done asking questions.

TERI: I don't know about any videotape.

RACHEL: What's on the tape?

TERI: I don't know about any videotape.

RACHEL: Remember that white paint, Teri —

TERI: I don't know about any videotape!

RACHEL: You should. Your father signed for the package. *(TERI makes a sound: part-gasp, part-moan.)* Maybe he's not so irrational. Maybe it runs in the family ... so: which is it, Teri? Are you a liar? Or are you just incompetent?

TERI: I will not dignify your cruelty with an answer.

RACHEL: My cruelty gets the job done.

TERI: You can do whatever you want to me, you can humiliate me –

RACHEL *(overlap)*: You don't need my help.

TERI *(continuous)*: You can bloody my name –

RACHEL *(overlap, sing-song)*: I'm a little martyr, short and stout ...

TERI *(continuous)*: But don't do this to Bobby. This this this – *wild story!* Don't do this. I don't think –

RACHEL: Well, number one, I don't really care what you think! For five years you've been bitching and moaning about your civil liberties and your library records and the violated rights of people who, it turns out, lopped off Bobby's head and submitted it to Sundance. You've been doing that – hurting America – all the while whimpering about poor, forgotten Bobby and never really fighting *for him.* You don't want Bobby found. You don't want his story to end for fear of your fading star. Only now? There's a tape. And you've got it.

> *(TERI shakes, seemingly on the verge of meltdown. She cries. Then suddenly: An odd smile and a broad laugh. Relief.)*

TERI: Oh God ... oh God ... ! *(She laughs, takes a few deep breaths, wipes her eyes – and when her gaze finds RACHEL we see a definitive transformation. Resolve. Steel. A warrior.)* "The tree of liberty must be refreshed from time to time with the blood of patriots and tyrants." You know who said that?

RACHEL: What's on the –

TERI: Do you know who said that?

RACHEL: No, Teri.

TERI: Thomas Jefferson.

RACHEL: Fine, but after he said that he didn't strap C-4 and a box of drywall screws to his chest and walk into the Continental Congress, did he?

TERI: If I've lost Bobby, that is no excuse for what I've seen happen to my country.

RACHEL: Do you hate America more than you miss your husband?

TERI: America is a great idea worth defending but what the hell good is that defense if we sacrifice the idea in its own name?

RACHEL: Gotta sacrifice something. I mean, we can't kill *everybody!*

TERI: These have been the worst seven years ever –

RACHEL *(overlap)*: Ever? Worse than the Holocaust or the Great War –

TERI *(continuous)*: THE WORST. EVER. Except for you. Except for you! All of this suffering has been a blessing to you.

RACHEL: If you think I wouldn't trade my relative success for just one of the three thousand3,000-plus souls stolen from us, you're –

TERI: Which soul?

RACHEL: Hmm?

TERI: Which one? I know the one I want back. Do not tell me I have not sacrificed.

RACHEL: *Then don't tell me that the fact you've lost a husband means I can't question you!* You don't get to be someone I can't respond to, you don't get to jerk me around; I get the same scattershot ideas-all-akimbo hodge-podge bull-crap answers out of you that I get from your protest movement.

TERI: I'm not scattered, Rachel, I just see the big picture. Bobby's fight belongs to me. Lethal air and toxic water, that's part of it. Oil that costs a hundred dollars a barrel, that's part of it. A government that embraces superstition over science: baby, you know that's part of it. And if you don't think a war of choice fought on two fronts effects the practical affordability of health care, I suggest you drop by Walter Reedade and inquire as to the cost of an aspirin.

RACHEL: I support –

TERI: And, yes, in failing Pakistan we failed Bobby. We bare culpability, Rachel! My husband was cast to wolves, but we turned the wolves feral.

RACHEL: Do you have evidence, videotaped or otherwise, to suggest that your husband, Bobby Guffin, is *dead*, Teri?

TERI: You think I'd ever tell you? Bobby doesn't belong to you, he's mine. He's *mine*.

RACHEL: You gave him to us, Teri.

> *(Elsewhere, MAHID enters. The lights remain low. MAHID crosses to BOBBY and removes his hood. They move slowly, slightly suspended. They do not speak, but there is the sense of communication passing between them.)*

RACHEL: This has been the top-rated cable news program for 195 weeks straight. We've got two Peabodies and a Polk. And it's because I fight for the truth: ugly, unwanted Truth that must be wrenched and clawed into the world. The year before Bobby went AWOL the most watched shows on television were sitcoms about single mothers and Godless Manhattanites. And now? *The Agenda* ranks in the top three programs among those same viewers. You may think me monstrous, loathe my froth and fume, call me a grotesquery of womanhood, but such is my harsh gentility. For this is The War and I come bearing a sword. We live in a Nine/Eleven world.

TERI: Well. When do we start living in a Nine/Twelve world? It's been seven years, when do we get to Wednesday?

> *(Silence. RACHEL's eyes belay blood thirst. The PAGE points to RACHEL. Points again.)*

PAGE *(into headset)*: Rachel –

RACHEL: You have a lovely home, Teri. Sure you don't wanna fire up the VCR? *(Silence.)* No? Nothing? *(Silence.)* Any last thoughts? *(Silence.)* Hillary Clinton: is she as sleazy as everyone seems to think? *(Silence. To camera.)* Teri Guffin, Everybody! We're back in the studio tomorrow with Republican Prophet Mike Huckabee, on *The Agenda* and no doubt more forthcoming than – ! *(Points to TERI.)* We'll see you here, on *American Agenda*.

> *(Lights dip on RACHEL and TERI. Full lights up on BOBBY and MAHID.)*

MAHID: They will hold you down. It will be fast. You will not scream ... no help will come for you, Bobby: you are in Pakistan.

RACHEL: Tell Ivan I want the van packed in twenty.

PAGE *(removing Teri's mickie; kind)*: Thank you, Teri.

BOBBY: Why?

TERI: What else did Mohammed Sheik Samir say?

MAHID: I don't know.

PAGE: I don't know.

RACHEL *(to her PAGE)*: Don't talk to her, Sugarbutt.

MAHID:
You occupy. You invade. You never understand. Or maybe ...

TERI: What else did Mohammed Sheik Samir say?

MAHID: Maybe a high-profile Israeli is just a good find.

BOBBY: I'm not Israeli. I'm not from Israel.

MAHID: Oh, my friend: you are.

PAGE: He said the house was empty.

BOBBY: Please ...

TERI: What?

BOBBY: Help me.

RACHEL: When Samir got to the house outside Peshawar Bobby wasn't there.

BOBBY: Help me.

RACHEL: He says. don't get your hopes up.

MAHID: I cannot.

RACHEL: Those mountains find White Men.

TERI: I won't quit, Rachel.

MAHID: I cannot.

TERI: If I cannot have Bobby then I want the world back.

RACHEL *(comes in close to TERI; private)*: Samir was full of shit and so are you. I'm not wrong: there's a tape. Even when I'm wrong I'm not wrong. *(Exiting.)* Move it, Sugarbutt. I wanna be at Sky Harbor before the snowbirds clog up the freeways.

> *(RACHEL is gone. The PAGE clears the two chairs.)*

MAHID: It will be fast, Bobby.

TERI: What's your name?

MAHID: Only moments.

PAGE: Katie.

TERI: Thank you, Katie.

> *(The PAGE exits.)*

MAHID: They may offer you a sedative. So that you will not fight, to make for a better video. You should take it. You will feel less. It may not hurt at all.

> *(Lights have faded on TERI and her portion of the playing space. Perhaps she moves closer to BOBBY and MAHID. It may almost appear as though she is watching ...)*

BOBBY: When my daughter was four, we took her to Disneyland for the first time. Teri and I wanted her to be old enough to get it, you know? And one day we just packed our bags, put her in the backseat with Bill the Penguin, and drove out to Anaheim; I have pictures of her, dressed like a princess. And about halfway through the day, she got really sleepy. And then she couldn't breathe. She had this fever ... we took her to Anaheim Medical Center. They gave her antibiotics and discharged her but before we went back to the Park her doctor told us that her heartbeat sounded kinda funny. So, when we got home: a few more tests and checkups and another night in the hospital ... and they found

> *(MORE)*

BOBBY (cont'd): this hole, this tiny little hole in the wall of her heart. Not a problem: yet. But. So, the night before her surgery, she slept in bed between me and Teri. She asked if it would hurt, if she would feel anything, and I said, "No, honey, you're gonna be asleep. You're gonna be asleep and you're gonna dream about Bill the Penguin and Mommy and Grandpa and when you wake up, your good little heart is gonna be all better." And she said, "I'm not scared." And the next morning, we rolled into the O.R. with Teri holding her left hand and me holding her right. And she said, "It's okay, I'm not scared." The surgeon said she was a champ: they had her down, patched the atrial septum, and closed up in under eight hours. Teri and I took turns staying awake by her bed, so someone would be there when she woke up ...

TERI: I can feel you.

BOBBY: When she woke up, she was screaming. Fingers like claws. She fought so hard against the restraints she broke her wrist ... when a patient goes under general anesthesia, they're administered a neuromuscular paralytic, to keep them from moving, and then the actual anesthetic to knock them out and kill the pain. One in fifteen-thousand patients experiences significant resilience to anesthetic intrusion. But the paralytic remains in place. They can't speak, they can't move. It's called "unintended intra-operative awareness." My four year old felt them spread her ribs apart. She felt the tap of the surgeon's finger on her heart to bring the rhythm back. She said they left dark air inside of her. She screamed and screamed, "I could feel it, Daddy. I could feel everything."

MAHID: What is your daughter's name?

BOBBY: Katie.

TERI: I can feel you, Bobby.

BOBBY: There's a website all about her. In follow-up she experienced a tissue embolism and she died. *(Pause.)* I don't want the sedative. I don't want your help. I want ...

TERI: My love ...

BOBBY: ... strawberries.

> *(TERI takes a breath. Lets go. She exits. MAHID rummages through BOBBY's luggage.)*

MAHID: How often do you shave? *(He removes a shaving kit. From the kit, removes*
(MORE)

MAHID (cont'd): *a small pair of scissors.)* Here. Your wrists. *(He cuts the tape around BOBBY's wrists. During:)* The man on the phone wanted to speak with you. That is what I was sorry for. I had to say no because ... *(Nothing.)* Wanton suffering is never the will of Allah. *(He tosses down the scissors, walks away from BOBBY, keeping his back to him)* Outside of this room there are mountains. A man can disappear and never be found.

> *(An uncertain moment. MAHID stands with one hand absently placed on the handle of BOBBY's carry-on, looking perhaps like a man about to take a long trip. Then MAHID pulls the revolver. He shoots BOBBY, who falls back onto the mattress. All light in the theater goes out. Almost imperceptibly, the sound of wind ... Elsewhere, TERI, on the telephone. It rings several times. Then, in crosscut, we see her FATHER answer the phone.)*

FATHER: Hello?

TERI: Daddy, it's Teri.

FATHER *(overlap)*: Of course, hello.

TERI *(continuous)*: Is Peter there? I need to talk to Peter.

FATHER: Okay. *(Speaks offstage.)* This lady wants to speak with you.

> *(Enter PETER, a home nurse. He takes the phone.)*

PETER: Hello?

TERI: Peter, this is —

PETER *(overlap)*: Teri? Hi, what —

TERI *(continuous)*: Peter, listen. Listen to me. Are there any packages there for me?

PETER: No.

TERI: Nothing?

PETER: Is this about the interview? We watched tonight, I couldn't believe ... Teri?

> *(TERI, wrought. Then an idea:)*

TERI: There's a space under the swamp cooler. In the den. Check there please?

PETER: Uh. Okay.

> *(PETER leaves. TERI and her FATHER wait. Elsewhere, lights up on TOM, facing front.)*

TOM: After much negotiation and administrative effort, I'm pleased to announce Builders Beyond Borders will break ground next month on a sophisticated and modern high-speed causeway linking the Afghan cities of Jalalabad and Kabul with the Pakistani city of Peshawar. Thanks to a generous donation from the Solomon Foundation we will employ nearly one hundred locally contracted workers in the construction of the Benazir Bhutto Pass, so named in celebration of Afghanistan and Pakistan's shared heritage and hope for Democratic progress.

> *(Lights out on TOM. PETER returns, carrying a large package sent via air mail. Elsewhere, lights up on MAHID. He stands with BOBBY's carry-on.)*

PETER: Yeah, there's a package here. It's ... uh ... it's addressed to Katie.

TERI: Where's it from?

FATHER: That's for Katie.

PETER: It's Air Mail. There's no return address.

MAHID: Bobby *jahaan jaa raha hai, shayad waapas nahin aaye.*

TERI: Look at the date stamp.

PETER: There's ... uh ... a couple of stamps. A steam engine.

MAHID: *Allah tumhein dunya aur akhirat dono naseeb farmay!*

PETER: It, uh, it looks like Kings Cross.

TERI: Kings Cross?

FATHER: Steam engine ...

> *(Teri's FATHER gestures for the phone.)*

PETER: Yeah, in London. Kings Cross Station.

MAHID: May Allah guide you to the best ...

TERI: It was shipped from the U.K.?

FATHER: *Perseverance.*

PETER: Yeah.

MAHID: In this life, and the next.

(Teri's FATHER takes the phone.)

FATHER: Teri: it's *Perseverance.*

(Lights out. Lights up on RACHEL. Coming home; stripping off her stockings, tossing off her bag. There is a package on a table, smaller than we saw with PETER. The package has been opened. The actors portraying MAHID, PETER, TOM, and Teri's FATHER have moved to the sides of the stage. They watch.)

RACHEL: Buns? Where y'at? Come on, Buns, we're ordering Rosa Mexicana tonight. *(He is not to be found.)* Chuck?

(RACHEL sees the opened package and its contents: a letter. A red videocassette case. RACHEL reads the letter. As she does, TERI steps into a separate light and speaks, facing front. The actor portraying KADIR joins the ensemble.)

TERI: Dear Rachel: You were right. Mostly. My father did sign for a package. Four years ago. I opened it yesterday. Inside was a videotape. The State Department confiscated the original videocassette, but I'm sending the enclosed copy to you. You should know I've also sent copies to Blitzer, Olbermann, and Bill Moyers. Good luck, Rachel. Regards: Teri Guffin.

(TERI steps out of the light and takes a place with the ensemble. RACHEL picks up the red videocassette case. Empty. Her eyes travel front, beyond the fourth wall, to her television and VCR. She holds the red cassette case in one hand, in the other her remote control. Points the control, pushes a button. Sits. During this, the actors portraying BOBBY and the PAGE have taken places with the ensemble. Along with TERI, they provide the video's narration, their dialogue casually loose and overlapping:)

BOBBY: Turn this way and smile.

TERI: Smile for Daddy.

BOBBY: And what are you?

KATIE: A princess.

TERI: Oh, you are?

BOBBY: Oh, yeah?

TERI: Like Cinderella?

KATIE: No, like *that* one.

TERI: Which one is that one?

BOBBY: Are you like the Little Mermaid?

KATIE: No, I don't have fins.

TERI: Ohhh.

BOBBY: Oh, I thought you had fins, I'm so sorry!

KATIE: No, I have feet. I'm like that one!

TERI: Which one is that one?

BOBBY: Are you ...

KATIE: I'm Sleeping Beauty.

TERI: Oh, because of your blonde hair.

BOBBY: I see now.

KATIE: I need a kiss.

BOBBY: From Bill the Penguin?

KATIE: No, I need a kiss from my prince!

TERI: Oh, well where's your prince? Where do princes live?

KATIE: In a castle.

TERI: Oh, we should look in the castle then.

KATIE: In that one.

BOBBY: Do you wanna take your picture with the prince?

KATIE: Yes!

BOBBY: Or are you afraid?

KATIE: I'm not afraid. And then, and then I want to see –

TERI: What, what do you wanna see?

KATIE: Everything!

>(*RACHEL pushes a button on the remote. Silence. We become aware that RACHEL has been sobbing, near soundlessly. RACHEL points the control, pushes a button.*)

>(*The lights go out.*)

END OF PLAY

Appendix: Translations & Transliterations

Urdu translations by Saad Padela

KADIR: **He has to eat. If he does not eat he is going to get sick and then we will have a real problem.**
> *Usko kuch khaana parey-ga. Agar khayega nahin, to beemaar ho jaayega. Agar beemaar huwa, to hum mushkil mei aajayangay*
> (He will have to eat something. If he does not eat, he will get sick. If he gets sick,then we will have trouble.)

MAHID: **You have a real problem, look at him!**
> *Mushkilain tumhare samne hai, tumhe nazar nahin aa rahin? Uski haalat dekho!*
> (Your troubles are right before you, can you not see them? Look at his condition!)

(The flashlight beam shines on BOBBY's face.)

MAHID: **Oh, no** ... hello, can you, can you understand me?

KADIR: **Tell him to eat!**
> *Usko boolo ke khana khay!*
> (Tell him to eat the food!)

(MAHID takes the flashlight from KADIR.)

MAHID: **Turn on the lights.**
> *Batti kholo.*
> (Open the light.)

KADIR: **He needs to eat.**
> *Usko khana pare ga!*
> (He'd better eat!)

MAHID: **He will.** – It is going to be okay. **Kadir, he is terrified of you. Please. Go, turn on the lights –**
> *Khayega, khayega. – It is going to be okay. – Kadir, wo tum se dara huwa hai. Tum ja ke batti kholo –*
> (He will eat. Kadir, he is afraid of you. You go turn on the lights.)

KADIR: **You will stay with him?**
> *Tum rahogay uske saath?*
> (You will stay with him?)

MAHID: **Yes, yes I will.**
    Haan, haan, mein rahoonga.
    (Yes, yes. I will stay.)

KADIR *(embracing MAHID)*: **Thank you. Thank you, Mahid.**

MAHID: **Just ... turn on the lights, Kadir.**
    Tum please light on *karo*, Kadir.
    [I decided to keep the old translation for this ... in his frustration, he's
    neglecting to use the proper Urdu words for "please" and "light."]

KADIR: **Thank you.** *(As he hurries out.)* **Watch him!**
    Kartaa hoon, kartaa hoon. Uspe nazar rakhna!
    (I am doing it, I am doing it. Keep an eye on him!)

* * *

BOBBY: I'm not going to try to run, could you just ... ? *(Shows his wrists. No
response.)* I don't only speak English. I ... I also –

MAHID: **Do you understand what I am saying to you now?** – *Inta
fahimnee hella?* – *Tee seechas ponimaiyesh menya, Amerikanskaya suka?* – **There are
no McDonalds here, my friend. No Starbucks. You don't know how
lucky you are.**
    *Mein jo bol raha hoon wo tum samaj rahe ho? -- Inta fahimnee hella? -- Tee
    seechas ponimaiyesh menya, Amerikanskaya suka? -- Yahaan koi McDonalds
    ya Starbucks tumhe nahin milega. Tum jaante nahin ho ke tum kitne
    khushkismat ho*
    (Are you understanding what I am saying to you? You will not find any
    McDonalds or Starbucks here. You don't know how lucky you are.)

    *(KADIR enters the space, hurriedly. He carries a cheap mobile phone and a
    notepad.)*

KADIR: **Mahid! It is time to talk to his organization. They are ready to
wire the money. Everything you need is written here.** *(Hands MAHID the
notepad as he dials the phone. Listens. Hands it to MAHID)* **It is ringing.**
    Mahid! *Wo paise bhejnay ke liye tayyaar hain. Yeh lo, sab kuch is pe likha huwa
    hai. Baat karo un se.*
        *(hands MAHID the notepad as he dials the phone. Listens. Hands it
        to MAHID)*
    Yeh lo baat karo.

(Mahid! They have agreed to wire the money. Here, everything you need is written on this. Here, talk to them.)

MAHID: **Who am I talking to?**
Kis se baat ho rahi hai?

KADIR: **I do not know, an accountant.**
Pata nahin, koi accountant hai.
(I don't know, it's some accountant.)

MAHID: **In Paris?**
Paris *mein?*

KADIR: **In Paris.**
Haan, Paris *mein.*
(Yes, in Paris.)

(KADIR exits ... KADIR enters with BOBBY's carry-on. He unceremoniously throws it in the corner.)

KADIR *(overlap, to Bobby)*: **You should change before you go ... you stink ... piece of filth ...**
Ey, sewer ki owlaad. Tuj mein se boo aa rahi hai. Kapre badal ke jaa-na.
(Hey you, offspring of a pig! You smell. Change your clothes before you go.)
[calling someone the offspring of a pig is about as bad as you can get.]

∗ ∗ ∗

MAHID: **What is the matter with you?**
Yeh kya karrahe ho?
(What's this you're doing?)

KADIR: **What did I do?**
Kyun, kya huwa?
(Why, what happened?)

MAHID: **He will scream again.**
Woh phir chillaega.

KADIR: **So what?**
Bhaley chillaega.
(Who cares?)

(*MAHID hands KADIR the phone and the notepad. During the following, KADIR pops open the phone and removes the SIM chip.*)

KADIR: **You missed the *Maghrib*. Unless you did it in here, with that.**
  (*KADIR gesticulates toward BOBBY*)
  Tumhari maghrib ki namaaz chhootgayee. Ya phir tumne idhar padhlee, uske mowjoodgi mein.
  (*KADIR gesticulates toward BOBBY*)
  (Your Maghrib prayer was missed. Or maybe you prayed in here, in his presence.)

MAHID: **They will find out who owns that phone.**
  Woh phone ka sub patay maloom karlengay.
  (They will find out everything about that phone.)

(*KADIR crushes the used SIM chip under his heel.*)

KADIR: **You worry too much, Mahid ... he can change his clothes after the call.**
Tum fuzool mein ghabraate ho, Mahid. Woh kapde baad mein badal lega.
  (*About to exit, KADIR reaches into the waistline of his pants. Removes a revolver, stuffs it into MAHID's hands*)
Take this.
  Yeh lo.

MAHID (*overlap*): **What are you doing? No!**
  Yeh kya kar rahe go? Hargiz nahin!
  (What's this you're doing? Absolutely not!)

KADIR (*continuous*): **Just in case. To make him be quiet. Please.**
  Aagar kuch huwa to chup karane mein kaam aayga.
  (If anything happens, it will help you to keep him quiet.)
  [You can always add an English "please" to an Urdu sentence. There is no universal phrase for "please" in Urdu...it's different according to the context. And most people say "please" anyway.]

* * *

Care for your sister. I am to leave and may not return from where I am going. May Allah guide you to the best in this life and the next!
  Najiba ka khayal rakhna. Mein jahaan jaa rah hoon, shayad waapas nahin aaoonga. Allah tumhein dunya aur akhirat dono naseeb farmay!

(Take care of Najiba. I may not return from where I am going. May Allah grant you good fortune in both this life and the next!)

* * *

KADIR: **Mahid! Quick, come with me.**
Mahid! *Jaldi aao!*

MAHID *(overlap)*: **What's happening?**
Kya hua?

KADIR *(continuous)*: **Come, quick!**
Iddher Jaldi se aao!

* * *

Bobby may not return from where he is going. May Allah guide you to the best in this life and the next.
Bobby *jahaan jaa raha hai, shayad waapas nahin aaye. Allah tumhein dunya aur akhirat dono naseeb farmay!*
(Bobby may not return from where he is going. May Allah grant you good fortune in both this life and the next.)

* * *

French translations by Andrea Lindblad (& Candice Holdorf)

MAHID: Brilliant ... *(Into the telephone.)* **Hello.** *(Refers to notepad throughout for information provided by KADIR.)* **I am calling regarding Robert Guffin ... Bobby, okay ... he is fine, he is fine, but he is ready to go home. Are you ready to wire the capital ...? Good ... the account number is zero zero zero. Dash seven. Dash nineteen, dash, forty. Dash nine, dash zero three nine eighty. Confirm ... ?**

MAHID: Brilliant ... *(Into the telephone.)* Allô? *(Refers to notepad throughout for information scripted by KADIR.)* Je vous appelle au sujet de Robert Guffin ... Bobby, okay ... *(Noticeable discomfort at having learned BOBBY's name.)* Il va bien, il va bien, mais il est prêt à rentrer. Etes-vous prêt à transférer la somme ... ? Bon ... le numero du compte est zéro zéro zéro, tiret sept, tiret dix-neuf, tiret quarante, tiret neuf, tiret zéro trois neuf, quatre-vingts. Bien reçu?

* * *

MAHID *(continuous)*: **Okay ... uh ... yes, yes ... I'm sorry, I can't do that. Goodbye.** *(Hangs up, pushes KADIR.)* **What is the matter with you?**

MAHID *(continuous)*: *D'accord ... desolé, desolé ...oui, oui... (A look to BOBBY; their eyes meet.) Non, desolé, je ne peux pas faire ça. Au revoir. (Hangs up, pushes KADIR.) Yeh kya karrahe ho?*

* * *

BOBBY: **I speak French.**
> *Je parle français.*

MAHID: **You speak French?**
> *Tu parles français?*

BOBBY: **Yes. I hink French is an incredibly beautiful language.**
> *Oui. Je pense que le français est une langue incroyablement belle OR est une belle langue incroyablement.*

* * *

Russian translation by Jonathon Kels Phillips

You now understand me, American bitch?
> *Tee seechas ponimaiyesh menya, Amerikanskaya suka?*

* * *

Arabic translation by Sameer Sheikh

Can you understand me now?
> *Inta fahimnee hella?*

Contributors

CYNTHIA CROOT (Essays) – is a theater and radio director, humanitarian activist and writer living and working in New York City, the Pacific Northwest and other locales farther flung. Current projects include creating a radio documentary on the international sex trafficking industry, producing *The Millay Sisters* (about the poet Edna St. Vincent Millay), and forging an international theater collaboration between students in the US and Middle East – principally Damascus, Amman and Tehran. She is 2007/2009 NEA/TCG Career Development Fellow and Associate Professor at Whitman College, WA. www.cynthiacroot.com.

MICHAEL DOMITROVICH (Plays) – off-Broadway productions include *Artfuckers*, *Real World Experience*, (both directed by Eduardo Machado) and *On Island* (directed by Mary Kate Burke). His plays *Dirtfag*, *Caregivers*, *Goatgod*, *Nucularfamily* and *Godbrothers* were presented in BlueBox Productions' "Sticky" at Galapagos, the Bowery Poetry Club and La Mama Etc. (all directed by Ali Ayala). He is co-author of *Tastes Like Cuba: An Exile's Hunger for Home*, (published October 2007, Gotham Press) and was a guest columnist in *Paper Magazine*'s "Beautiful People" issue in April, 2008. He has a BFA in Cinema Studies from NYU Tisch School of the Arts.

LIBBY EMMONS (Plays) – is a playwright. Producing Director: Blue Box Productions. Curator: Sticky series. Short plays, NYC: Desipina, Crown Point, Working Man's Clothes, LaMaMa Etc., Polybe + Seats, and other; Acorn Pictures, LA; InterACT, Thieves Theatre, Theatre Double, Philly; SacActors, Sacramento; Subversive Theatre Co., Buffalo; Sticky U.K., Sheffield, UK; RAT Conference, Rosario, Argentina. Full-lengths include *The Sustainable Future* (Blue Box), *Decomposition in Blue and White* (Philly), *Dirty and Leo in Tokyo* and *Eyes of the Prophet*, her thesis and winner of the John Golden Award. Collaborator: *MacBeth Project*, RAT Conference; *The Charlotte Salomon Project* and *A Sea Change*, Polybe + Seats. BA: Sarah Lawrence College, MFA: Columbia University. Recipient: Liberace Fellowship, Miller Scholarship, others. Commissioned: Williamstown Theater Festival, Act 1 Company, 2006. Nominated: Dramatists' Guild's Wasserstein Prize, 2007. www.blueboxproductions.net.

ARDEN KASS (Plays) – is an award-winning playwright and independent producer of her own theater pieces in Philadelphia, PA. She has been writing plays and text-based interdisciplinary works since the early 1990's. Her plays have been produced by Multi-Stages, InterAct and Brat Theatres, Theatre Exile and of course, Blue Box. A member of the BMI Music Theatre Workshop in New York (as a librettist), Arden has also written feature film scripts, poetry, children's stories, published essays and cultural/arts features and performed her monologues on WXPN Radio. In 2005, she wrote and co-directed 3 one-hour documentaries on rock stars for A & E TV. Her new play APPETITE will be showcased in a national new play workshop in July 2009. Once hailed by a local critic as a "vastly-underrated Philadelphia playwright", Arden hopes to achieve world domination in her class, eventually becoming a universally-underrated playwright. Contact: ardenkass@earthlink.net; 215.779.0610.

DAVID IAN LEE (Plays) – is an actor and playwright. He appeared in the New York debut of Ronan Noone's award-winning *The Lepers* of Baile Baiste, created the role of Caligula in Nat Cassidy's *The Reckoning of Kit & Little Boots*, and originated the role of Karel Capek in Mac Rogers' celebrated *Universal Robots*. Regionally, he has performed with Actors Theatre of Louisville, Utah Shakespeare, Sedona Shakespeare, Tennessee Rep, Milwaukee Rep, First Stage Milwaukee, Arizona Repertory Theatre, Arizona Theatre Company, and L.A.'s Haugh Performing Arts Center. His other plays include *The Dog Show*, *Liberty & Joe DiMaggio* (with L. Jay Meyer), *Pinecone*, *The Latchkey Pool*, *A Preserving Suite*, and the upcoming *Long Sought, More Perfect*. A graduate of the William Esper Studio, David received his BFA in Acting & Directing from the University of Arizona and has studied with the Upright Citizen Brigade and the London Academy of Music and Dramatic Art.

DAVID MARCUS (Plays) – is a New York-based actor and the Artistic Director of Blue Box Productions. His acting credits include *Margo Veil, An Entertainment* at the Flea Theater; *Artfuckers*, Theater for the New City; *Summer Shorts*, 59E59; and *The Sustainable Future*, BBP. He also co-starred in Brad Saville's film, *Williamsburg*. As Artistic Director of BBP he has overseen the Sticky series along with Libby Emmons, Ali Ayala, Matthew Korahais and David Scholnick. He has also served as Stage Manager for several shows on Ellis Island, and served a brief and unremarkable term as President of the Bat Theater Company at the Flea Theater. www.blueboxproductions.net.

ELLEN MCLAUGHLIN (Plays) – her plays include *Days and Nights Within, A Narrow Bed, Infinity's House, Iphigenia and Other Daughters, Tongue of a Bird, Helen, The Trojan Women, The Persians* and *Oedipus*. Producing theaters include The National Actors' Theater, The Public Theater, New York Theater Workshop, Classic Stage Company, the Actors' Theatre of Louisville, the Intiman in Seattle, the Mark Taper Forum in LA, Oregon Shakespeare Festival, the Almeida in London and the Guthrie Theater. She is the recipient of grants from the Fund for New American Plays and the National Endowment for the Arts. She is the winner of The Great American Play Contest, the Susan Smith Blackburn Prize and the Writer's Award from the Lila Wallace-Reader's Digest Fund.

REHANA MIRZA (Plays) – is a filmmaker, playwright, and Artistic Director of Desipina & Company. Her plays have been produced by Blue Box, 2G, Asian American Theatre Company, Ma-Yi Theatre Writer's Lab and have been published by the Alexander Street Press. Her short film, *Modern Day Arranged*

Marriage, won the NBC ShortCuts Festival Audience Award and was acquired by LOGO. She recently completed her first feature length film, *Hiding Divya*, (www.hidingdivya.com), starring Madhur Jaffrey, Pooja Kumar, and Deep Katdare. BFA: Dramatic Writing, NYU's Tisch School of the Arts; MFA: Playwriting, Columbia University. www.desipina.org.

DENNIS MORITZ (Plays) – has written over thirty theater pieces that have received professional productions. Venues include the Public Theater (New Works Project), BACA Downtown, the Nuyorican Poets Cafe, St. Marks Poetry Project, HERE, Painted Bride, Freedom Theater and Theatre Double. His play, *Just the Boys* was published in *Action: the Nuyorican Poets Theater Festival*. His book, *Something to Hold On To (Nine Theater Pieces)* was published by United Artists Books. Currently he studies and creates new work at Temple University. Dennis is sticky for Sticky.

MICHAEL NIEDERMAN (Plays) – is a playwright and screenwriter whose work has been performed at the Soho Think Tank, The Workshop Theater, American Theater of Actors, The Player's Theater, Second Stage, Gene Frankel, The Lion Theater and the Bowery Poetry Club. His films have screened all over the world, and have been honored at such film festivals as the Los Angeles International Film Festival, Sundance, and the Museum of the Moving Image. Michael is a member of the National Association of Latino Independent Producers, a contributor to the Actor's Studio playwrights/directors lab, and a founding member of Crosstown Playwrights. www.ignitedstates.com.

ERICA PARISE (Cover Photography) – is moving swiftly around the set - her goal is to be unnoticed as to not interfere with the flow of the crew. Choosing creative angles and framing is a key priority for her to find the perfect shots and of course the poster. Erica is a New York-based still photographer specializing in production stills for film, TV and theater. Her work has been published in the *New York Times*, *Time Out* magazine as well as various online publications. View her portfolio online at www.cinestillsnyc.com.

LANE PIANTA (Essays) – a Texan by birth and interdisciplinarian by choice, Lane (performer, director, playwright, songwriter) received his BFA in Theatre Studies from UT Austin in 1997. He also holds an MFA in Theatre from Towson University where his original work *Songscapes* explored the cross-application of song structure with composition in physical score. Thanks to Ben for his time and especially to his wife Mariana for her incredible support, understanding and love.

MAC ROGERS (Plays) – is a playwright and performer who lives in Brooklyn with his fiancé, Sandy. *Playscripts* published his play, *The Second String*. His play,

Universal Robots was anthologized in the New York Theatre Experience's *Plays and Playwrights 2008* anthology, and *Hail Satan* won a FringeNYC 2007 Outstanding Playwriting Award. Along with Sean and Jordana Williams, Mac wrote *Fleet Week: The Musical*, winner of a FringeNYC 2005 Outstanding Musical Award. Mac's other plays produced in New York include *Dirty Juanita*, *The Sky Over Nineveh*, and *The Lucretia Jones Mysteries*. As an actor, Mac was nominated for a New York Innovative Theater Award for his performance in Nosedive Productions' *The Adventures of Nervous Boy*.

KATHERINE RYAN (Plays) – in New York, Katherine's plays (some under the name Kate E. Ryan) have been produced or developed by 13P, Clubbed Thumb, the Flea, the Ontological, Soho Rep, Target Margin, and The Vineyard. Katherine is a member of the playwrights collaborative, 13P, is Co-Chair of Soho Rep's Writer-Director Lab and is former Co-Curator of the performance series, "Little Theatre" at Tonic. MFA from Brooklyn College. Thanks to Mac Wellman for the mid-Sept. 2001 assignment that inspired this broken play. www.katherineryan.org.

BRAD SAVILLE (Plays) – is a novelist, playwright, and filmmaker. His novel, *Grotesque* was published when he was twenty-three. His award-winning feature, *Williamsburg*, became a darling of the film festival circuit and is now on Special Edition DVD. His plays, *Jism*, *Mint Julep*, *Gregor*, *Crazy*, *The Brothers Slaughter*, *Two Rooms in Davis*, *Monkey Trick*, and *Yermo Blues* have been produced on stages throughout NYC. Brad currently runs his production company, Cadillac Films, and serves as Managing Director of Eastwind Theatre Company. cadillacfilms.com.

BEN SPATZ (Essays) – has over fifteen years of experience as a performer, director, and leader of theatrical research. He has been leading the Urban Research Theater project since 2004, first in Poland and then in NYC. Ben offers workshops in song-based physical performance in NYC and internationally. He is a doctoral student at the CUNY Graduate Center and a teaching fellow at Brooklyn College. For more information, please visit www.urbanresearchtheater.com.

ADAM SZYMKOWICZ (Plays) – studied playwriting in graduate programs at Columbia and Juilliard. Plays include *Deflowering Waldo*, *Open Minds*, *Anne*, *The Art Machine*, *Pretty Theft*, *Food for Fish*, *Hearts Like Fists*, *Herbie*, *Incendiary*, *Old Fashioned Cold Fusion*, *Bee Eater*, *Temporary Everything*, *Susan Gets Some Play*, *The Fat Cat Killers* and *Nerve*. Szymkowicz is a two-time Lecomte du Nouy Prize winner, a member of the Dramatists Guild, MCC Playwright's Coalition and Ars Nova Play Group. His plays have been published by Dramatists Play Service, in the

New York Theater Review and in various Smith and Kraus collections. www.adamszymkowicz.com.

JUSTIN TRACY (Essays) – Writer, director, and social actionist, Justin is currently researching aggression in male primates and is fascinated by the interconnection of myth and history. The Radical Theater movement's interplay with modern values strikes him like a dew-rusted gauntlet. He lives in Brooklyn.

JESSE WANN (Plays) – has had a variety of plays produced at Sticky over the years and is delighted to be included in the *NYTR*. He lives in Brooklyn, and has just completed his first novel, *Kingdom Of One*.

GARY WINTER (Plays) – Gary's plays have been produced or heard at The Flea, The Long Wharf, HERE, Cherry Lane Alternative, GEVA, Curious Theater, Playwrights Horizons, E.S.T., South Coast Rep, defunktheatre, Audacity Theatre Lab, PS 122, Brick, Little Theater and Sticky. Support from MacDowell and Yaddo, Rita and Burton Goldberg Award, John Golden Award, Dramatists Guild and Lark Fellowships, and a Spielberg Righteous Persons Fellow to study Eastern European Jewry in Krakow, Poland. Literary Manager at the Flea 1998-2008. Reviews theater for the *Brooklyn Rail*. Gary is a member of OBIE-winning 13P. MFA:NYU. www.garyjwinter.com.

Last Word

7 Avenue A   *Manhattan*

www.ingramcontent.com/pod-product-compliance
Lightning Source LLC
Chambersburg PA
CBHW031150020726
47499CB00002B/310